LOVE

TO

WATER

MY

SOUL

DREAMCATCHER COLLECTION
  A Sweetness to the Soul (winner of the Wrangler Award for
    Outstanding Western Novel of 1995)
  Love to Water My Soul
  A Gathering of Finches
  Mystic Sweet Communion

KINSHIP AND COURAGE SERIES
  All Together in One Place
  No Eye Can See
  What Once We Loved

TENDER TIES HISTORICAL SERIES
  A Name of Her Own

NONFICTION
  Homestead
  A Simple Gift of Comfort (formerly *A Burden Shared*)

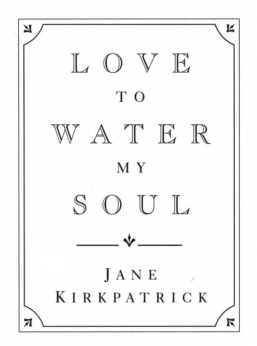

LOVE
TO
WATER
MY
SOUL

JANE
KIRKPATRICK

Multnomah® Publishers *Sisters, Oregon*

LOVE TO WATER MY SOUL
published by Multnomah Publishers, Inc.

© 1996 by Jane Kirkpatrick

International Standard Book Number: 0-88070-938-3

Edited by Rodney L. Morris

Cover design by David Carlson

Printed in the United States of America

For information:
MULTNOMAH PUBLISHERS, INC.
POST OFFICE BOX 1720
SISTERS, OREGON 97759

Library of congress cataloging-in-publication data
Kirkpatrick, Jane, 1946-
    Love to water my soul/Jane Kirkpatrick.
        p.cm. ISBN 0-88070-938-3 (alk. paper)
    1. Indians of North America--Oregon--Fiction. 2. Paiute Indians--Fiction. I. Title
PS3561.I712L6   1996   96-21135
813'.54--dc20   CIP

04 05 — 10   9

This book is dedicated to

Pearl Ida Bauer Rutschow

and

Zelma Waurega Anderson Kirkpatrick

Strong and faithful women

and my first and second mothers.

ACKNOWLEDGMENTS

The words in this work of fiction are mine alone, but whatever depth and delight they convey is the result of many minds and hands.

As with *A Sweetness to the Soul*, I am again indebted to the Warm Springs, Wasco, and Paiute people who have shared themselves and their stories with me. I especially thank Wilson Wewa, director of the Culture and Heritage Department of the Confederated Tribes of Warm Springs, for elder stories about the times in Harney County and life at early Seekseequa; linguist Henry Millstein and the Paiute language class and teachers Pat Miller and Shirley Tufti; Dr. Terry Tafoya, Taos Pueblo and Warm Springs tribal member, for the story of the old shards mixed with new clay giving strength; elders Bernice Mitchell, Olney Patt, and Margaret Charley for stories of Sherar's Bridge; and numerous others who have indirectly added to this work: Winona Frank, Leah Henry, Vivian Wewa, Lucinda Green, Normandie Phelps, Pauline Allen, Sylvia McCabe Selam, Gladys Squiemphen, Bobby and Becky Bruno, Nola Queahpama, Faye Waheneka, Sue Matters, Elaine Clements, Versa Smith, Nancy Seyler, Nancy Yubeta and others who I hope will forgive me for not including all their names. I thank Bo and Mary Macnab of Sherman County, Oregon, for loaning me an original court report of the 1931 testimony taken from elders in a land claim between the "Warm Springs Tribe of Indians of Oregon and The United States," and the people of the Sherman County Historical Society, and especially the von Borstel family. I thank GIA Publications, Inc., of Chicago, Illinois, for permission to quote lines of their published song "If You Believe and I Believe," copyright 1991 by WGRG The Iona Community (Scotland).

My efforts are supported by previous works such as *The First Oregonians* published by the Oregon Council for the Humanities, and especially Minerva T. Soucie's writings about the *Wada'Tika* Burns Paiute Tribe, and Henry Millstein's article about the Confederated Tribes of Warm Springs; Patricia Stowell's *Faces of a Reservation,* published by the Oregon Historical Society; Eugene Hunn's work, with James Selam and family, called *Nchi'i-Wana: Mid-Columbia Indians and Their Land,* which is not only a treasured gift but was my first awareness of the 1872 earthquake and an unusual prophet from the past; and O. Larsell's 1945 article printed in the December *Oregon Historical Quarterly* titled "History of Care of Insane in the State of Oregon." Thanks belong to the people of the Harney County Historical Society, their museum, and their book *Harney County: An Historical Inventory* by Roy Jackson and Jennifer Lee; to Margaret M. Wheat's *Survival Arts of the Primitive Paiutes,* published by the University of Nevada Press and the Frenchglen community in Southeastern Oregon who carry this fine book in the shadow of Steen's Mountain. Thanks to Gae Whitney Canfield for *Sarah Winnemucca* and to Keith A. Murray for *The Modocs and Their War,* both books published by the University of Oklahoma Press; to the Museum at Warm Springs for access to their research library; and to Sarah Winnemucca Hopkins and her autobiography published in 1883 by G. P. Putnam, *Life Among the Piutes.* I am grateful to Catherine S. Fowler for her book *In the Shadow of Fox Peak: An Ethnography of the Cattail-Eater Northern Paiute People of Stillwater Marsh* and to Judith Hunnel Budd whose loan of this research and whose constant support and encouragement are blessings beyond measure; to her daughter Christine Kelly whose Reno bookstore cheerfully accessed a variety of materials on my behalf; and to Canyon City residents George and Nancy Zahl and the people at the Grant County Historical Society who led me to newspaper accounts of Indians in the 1880s. I thank them and many other friends for their research and interest in my work.

I am also very grateful to the people of Oregon and throughout the nation who have set aside 185,000 acres that include the Malheur, Harney, and Mud Lakes, ponds and alkali flats, desert and rimrocks as part of the Malheur National Wildlife Refuge in the lands once roamed by Wadaduka people. I am especially grateful for the staff's stewardship of grasses and waters, animals and waterfowl, for adjoining ranches that are managed with wildlife habitat in mind, and for the U.S. Department of the Interior Fish and Wildlife Service's museum, whose preservation and explanations allowed me to step inside the past with greater authenticity. The encouragement I receive at the Warm Springs Early

Childhood Education Center where I work and at the Moro Community Presbyterian Church where we worship is deeply valued. I am grateful to Alice Archer and Carol Tedder for early manuscript copyediting and agents Joyce Hart and Terry Porter for their belief in me. Rod Morris's encouragement and editing are gifts I treasure. I am grateful to the Questar family for valuing quality and believing in this series. And finally, I acknowledge Jerry, my best friend and husband, who lovingly supports my efforts and who, without complaint, endures a houseful of dogs and dirty dishes so I can spend my days in the 1800s. Thank you all.

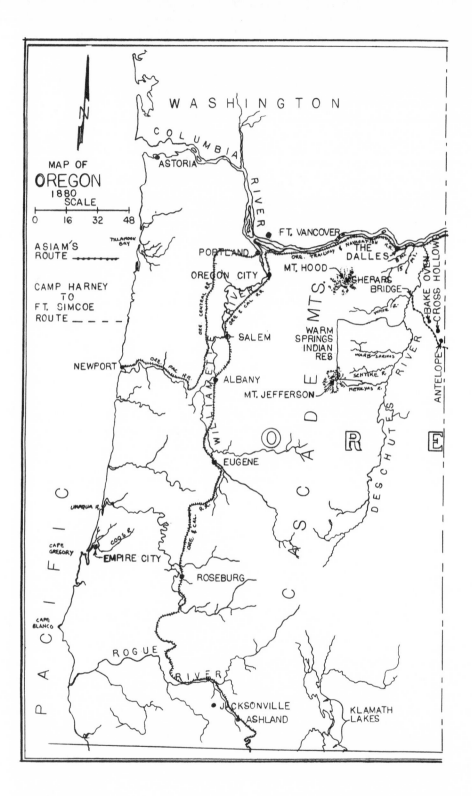

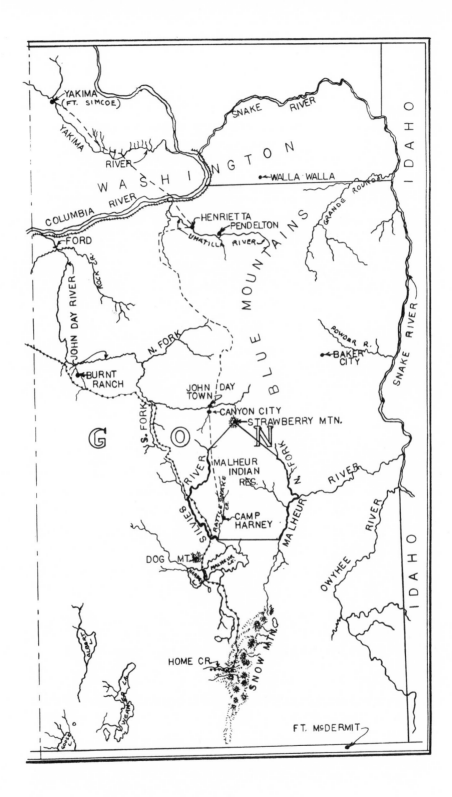

*"But whosoever drinketh of the water that
I shall give him shall never thirst."*

JOHN 4:14

*"I will not leave you comfortless:
I will come to you."*

JOHN 14:18

*"Shaped like a whirlwind and woven with twists of willows, tules,
and tradition, the burden basket fit on a woman's back.
A tumpline across her forehead held the basket steady.
She carried only essentials inside, what was needed
for huckleberry picking or gathering greasewood or seeds.
Few things fit in the narrow bottom; most essentials
were visible near the top. Those who walked beside her could see
if her shoulders bent with the bulk of her burdens or could tell,
even without words, if her head ached from the weight.
Assistance could be offered. And so two could walk together
toward their destination, helping bear each other's burdens."*

DESCRIPTION OF A PAIUTE BURDEN BASKET

PROLOGUE

LIKE A DOUBLE-EDGED OBSIDIAN KNIFE, my life was sliced two ways, and carried with it strength for the task and a keen edge to find my way.

I even carved and shaped my name, deciding Alice M did fit me. But it is Thocmetone that I cherish. It means "Shell Flower" and I received it my third year with the Wadaduka people. It was in 1870 or so. I once wore Asiam, the word the Modocs called me, thought they heard me call myself that name when they first found me wandering and dust-shrouded on the Oregon desert, separated from those most familiar. I added others through the years, but Thocmetone pleased me most for it was given as a gift and as a sign that I was loved.

It is such love that makes things grow, even yellow shell flowers that bob and weave in the desert spring. It is such love that guides and strengthens for a journey. And it is the memory of such love that waters my soul, fills me up enough to let me nourish others.

This is a memory told many times, though for years kept only to myself, tied into a chain of leather knots. When I found what quenched my thirst, I took the necklace off. But I remembered, and tell the story now so you will be encouraged and find through it the way to fill your longings, too.

THE FIRST KNOT

M A R K I N G

THE WAGON MOVED AWAY FROM ME in a swirl of dust, the clank of hames and harness, creaking of wooden wheels, shouts through the mid-day Oregon heat. To this day, when I view the back of a woman's bonnet I see the canvas opening of a wagon disappearing into Oregon Territory, leaving me behind.

Even now, years later, little memories flutter across my mind, often when I least expect them. The smell of hot canvas and broken sage arrives on a day I fill our chuckwagon, preparing for spring branding; a gold chain with crossed bars glittering against a throat of white appears with a flash of sunlight on the ripples of a river. The smell of cabbage from the asylum's kitchen once brought the memory of my mother's kraut-covered apron. Even the fleeting brush of a blanket against my cheek at night reminds me of a military uniform that must have been my father's. These images come with the speed of a hummingbird's wing and then flit away, leaving only an empty ache in the wake of their passing.

I must have been in the last wagon.

Like the faint impression a face leaves in a pillow, I remember things as though they are not really there. I imagine more. Like waking to the scent of sagebrush pushing against sunbaked cloth, the noise of bird calls, leather flapping against the oxen's hides, a dog barking at a rabbit, people coughing through the wagon dust in the distance, my face and arms a sleepy mass of tied-quilt crinkles. It must have been that way.

My mother would have held the reins, driven the team, thin calico stretched across her bony back. She had auburn hair, I think, streaked with lighter shades. It would have peeked out of the O at the back of her dirty blond bonnet.

My father would have ridden somewhere ahead with the train, along with a brother—there must have been a brother—whose face, like my parents, is now foreign.

We were making our way to Oregon and the ocean and a new beginning. I did not know what a beginning was then, but the hope of a new one must have been my father's dream, one that made him load our beds and blankets into wagons and join with others looking for their new beginnings, too.

And then they were gone.

Who knows why. Did a bird catch my eye while I walked beside the wagon's wheels? Did I follow it? Was I reaching for something, a dip of water from the barrel? Or maybe just standing at the back, watching junipers and sage pass by, and then fell out? Maybe I slept and walked in my dreams. I paw through my faint memories like a dog seeking last season's buried bones. I wonder how and why it happened, why I was left alone there in the dust. Nothing rises from my digging. I know only that I sat in dirt the wheels left behind, frightened and alone.

I have seen a spider in the sweet grape arbor suspended from a single strand just before it reached its destination, seen it almost complete its journey, working hard. Perhaps it celebrated in satisfaction, its goal so close. And then I have watched a breeze whisk it away, force it to start again, and been reminded that what we long for can so easily be discarded by some new challenge to our souls, unless we hang on tight to what we wish for.

It was like that for me the day I watched the wagons leave. A sharp spear of pain stabbed me. Pain as piercing as a missing friend, as overwhelming as a lost chance. A pain so quick it stole my breath; so deep, the ache laid heavy on my chest and spread like stains of blood through water.

I must have called to them, shouted, "Mama! Papa! Wait!" I could not stop them, did not stop them. They continued on. In times since I have felt that same heavy fear awash with disappointment.

The wagons rattled through the dust, kept to the ruts as though nothing new had happened, nothing was amiss within their world.

Would I have watched the dust grow ever smaller, tried to follow them on my bare feet? Was I hurt, bruised or injured by a fall? Must not have been injured, I think now, or those who found me would have let me be. But still, the picture of myself as one who simply sat and waited, tears staining my faded dress, does not fit well on these narrow, older shoulders. Neither does the image that I played in powdery dust simply holding hope.

I like to think that I reached out and did not wait to seal my fate. I like to think that I ran after them, my cries lost to the wagon sounds and distance.

But who knows? Some things are forever left to chewing without the satisfaction of a swallow.

The wagon O disappeared in the distance like a dream before dawn. I belonged there, behind that opening. But no longer.

The sunset would have turned a faded pink, the color of my pinafore. Bumps formed on my pale skin and I shivered, must have. Through pinched and swollen eyes, I imagine my father in his gray uniform finding me, looking down at his wayward child, and in his booming voice commanding, "As you were," as I have memories he once did.

My brother and I would answer, "As I am," hands clasped behind our backs, legs firm and wide apart, eyes an arrow straight ahead.

"At ease," he'd say and smile, the memory floating to me on the faint aroma of tobacco.

It is a ritual I recalled often in the days when I first dreamed of finding them if they could not find me, a ritual with strange detail, a memory lost and made again within my longing.

"As I am," I'd murmur to fall asleep, no one else to sing a lullaby. "As I am" is how I wished to be.

Did I have plans? Yes. I would use my strong, long legs for someone with few years, my contrary ways, to find a way to answer to them once again that I was present, "as I am."

"They search for you, na?" Lukwsh said years later, her voice always ending in a question.

I imagined that they searched, frantic, like a mother separated from her calf in the Silvies stream in spring, running along the shoreline, bellowing to it as water swirls and twists it, bouncing helpless against the shore, spit back into the current and away.

"White people with big eyes and hair on faces always rush, like water,"

Lukwsh told me, her hands pressing *wada* seeds into riced flour cakes. "Maybe wagons move too far before they see you gone. No time for rushing back to find you. *Tibos* always race like rivers through rocks, like at Tlhxni," she said. "Maybe their headmen advised them not to return to find a small child."

I could not imagine what might keep my father from searching. He would have spent days riding, calling, his shoulders brushing through the blooming sage, his throat parched from the desert air. His hands would have ached with bending greasewood back to look beneath, his throat dry and sore from calling out my name, some name, belonging to his lost child. He would have offered money, maybe even land, to those who had news that I still lived and had not been lost to snakes or Indians or hungry coyotes.

My mother surely would have searched, too, gathered desert dirt beneath her nails hoping to discover some small sign that I still lived. Even my brother might have put aside his interests to look for tracks, if they had let him.

"So you became a gift to Lukwsh," the woman told me, speaking of herself. Lukwsh, with her kind and toothy smile. Lukwsh, who was a calfless mother before me. But that is a later story, a later knot.

The Modocs found me first and so I was not sitting in the sand for my parents to whisk into their arms if they came looking, *when* they came looking.

Traveling at distances behind wagon trains that intruded across their lands, the Modocs sometimes killed while raiding. Applegate and Wright had warned the wagons of the Modocs danger, said not to camp at Bloody Point. Our "new beginning" wagons must have listened. I remember no Indians while in the presence of my parents. And I saw no remnants, later, of things that seemed familiar brought back in Modocs' hands.

Watching carefully when they returned from raids became a familiar way for me. It is a behavior still I claim, this watching, looking, hoping I will recognize a wooden box or piece of faded cloth discarded along a dusty trail. Even now, while sifting through the treasures of a traveling peddler's cart, I look for something he has traded that once belonged to those I loved. It is a foolish task but one that gives me hopeful pleasure.

The Modocs sought abandoned treasures, too, like cattle, oxen, pieces of leather, a discarded pot or pan, vacant wagons. On good days, they might find a valued horse or iron wheels they made into bullets; a lost soul on other forages, someone they could take revenge on for their losses, make a slave of or trade with tribes spending time in The Dalles or south in the wild city of Yreka. These things I learned of later.

That day, the Modocs found only me: a small white girl with no people and no bonnet, an abandoned white child with braided hair streaked like the color of wet sand stuck to the tears on her face.

I have a faint memory of them, those large men with grease on their bellies. They rode horses. One reached and pulled me up then dropped me like a rock behind him.

Did I scream and kick and hit at him? Did I pound his back, tell him to leave me be? Did I cry?

When I try to bring the memories back, I feel the ache of wanting so to stay, and I wonder if that longing is a part of who I am, that I cling to what is past even when no hope lives there, even when the sunset carried cooling with it and scorpions and snakes. I just wanted what had been, like wishing for the love of someone who has left.

Why they paid attention to me is a mystery. I was nothing more than a fluff of cattail resting in the dirt, so light a wind could have blown me far away. But something made them ride my way. Something made them stop to pick me up instead of killing me or leaving me behind. And something made the Modocs let me keep a thin gold chain tucked beneath my dress when they took me to my new beginning.

This white child is not raised but does grow up.

Each year becomes a good year when there is enough to eat and I find myself still able to breathe cool desert air, watch large white birds lift over lava beds and marshy lakes, have room in a covered place to sleep. Each year is a good year when I hear news of *tibo*, a white person, and wonder if they wear a locket that bears my likeness or have a gold chain not unlike the one I hide inside my treasure basket, a gold chain that once had a crossed bar and must have been my mother's.

For three, maybe four summers, I lived with the Modocs as I did when they first dropped me dirty and tired before a wickiup of willow covered with tule mats. I did not know that someday I would reach in reedy water for the strips of bulrushes and split the tule leaves myself for a wickiup I shared.

Someone with a wide face must have tossed me a piece of roasted meat that first night and pointed to a mat where dogs lay sleeping in the corner. I see myself grab the deer meat before the dogs could reach it, huddle to the ground and chew, my eyes staring into dogs', challenging. The skinny-tailed dogs sniffed around me, gave up low growls, and when I left the bone, they must have fought for it but without effort. The dogs' ribs did not show. They were valued beings I could learn from as I worked for those who fed me and moved like a stray dog from lodge to lodge to make my way.

The Modoc village carries with it memories of mats warmed by dogs' bodies and of making the best of fitful sleep.

I dreamed of wagons and warm faces. I must have. Often someone shouted in the night in words I did not understand. Their anger woke the dogs and startled me awake, made me aware of the emptiness of my stomach that precious food had failed to fill. I turned my face into a dog's fur to muffle gasping breaths and shaking shoulders that marked my nights and many waking moments.

The mirror reflects the image of a grown woman years later. A widow's peak looks back at me. Fitting for the *kooma yagapu,* one who "weeps for a husband," that I am. I wear face powder and rouge. But years and the inventions of men have not faded the *nabawici* that marks my face.

I do not remember when the Modocs held me down to make it, but I recall others who had it done. Old women with needles and hot ash made the marks along the jawline or on a child's chin. Drawn with the black of an old fire and a sharp bone, it told all that a child was lost and did not belong.

When I first saw my markings in the reflection of a still lake beneath a snow-capped mountain, I felt my eyes pool with hot tears, bringing to the surface a hunger and depth of disappointment that covered me like a skin. I determined then that the black lines were meant to mark my journey, and they made me choose again to do what must be done: stay alive but not forget that I would leave.

Many Modocs died in raids, some at the hands of men in uniforms with long guns led by other Indians dressed in buckskins and feathers. Children were kept out of the way, but I did my best to let myself be seen, hoping they had come to rescue me.

"Asiam! Down!"

Long Braids grabbed me, a child with six or seven summers. The Modoc woman scowled as she dragged me like a squirmy marmot resisting a bear. A dry desert wind blew my hair back from my hot face.

"Stay!" she hissed and pushed me. My knees scraped on sharp lava rocks. Her breath came short from the effort of dragging me while watching over her shoulder, bending low. She forced me beyond the soldier's Springfield musket's range.

For a moment my heart felt light with her orders. Someone worried about me, wanted me saved, and pressed me inside the caves to keep me from harm.

"Ayah! You with no ears! This way!"

She insulted my listening, but I did not mind. She planned to save me.

She pulled at my hair as we disappeared into the lava caves, our moccasins leaving no tracks on the rocky ground. She brushed at spiders, and my eyes adjusted to the darkness of the caves. Long Braids would fight for space with snakes who slithered into small rock holes, but for now she worried about keeping me out of sight. A warmth filled me.

But like a prairie hen enjoying bugs, I didn't recognize the hawk's shadow overhead.

"Watch her!" Long Braids told the others huddled in the cave. "Keep her from sight. She makes the soldiers fight harder. Down!"

She pushed me to my knees then left to help her man reload. So. The soldiers fought stronger when they risked their lives for white women or a lost child.

My eyes adjusted to reveal a Modoc woman too old to fight, waiting out this war. The pops and blasts of guns sounded like hard rain on water, the smell of powder drifted heavy, back into the caves. I could remain sheltered or make another way.

While Modoc men such as Lives in Pain or Jack shot their traded guns and arrows across the desert toward the muskets, I made my choice. I crept along the cave wall, scooted like an otter on my side before the old woman could barely set her eyes to see. I slipped around the nubby lava edge and found another channel, smaller but with light promised at the end. The presence of the walls close to my shoulder and the darkness made my breathing hard. I fought the heavy feeling pushing up against my throat. I imagined high places of sky over me instead of the close curve of lava over my head.

As fast as fear and hope would let me, I eased closer to the sunshine, and when the late afternoon sun brushed my face, I felt relief. My eyes searched the colors of the uniforms the Modocs aimed at.

I tried to think of how to signal the soldiers. But they were nothing more than dark seeds against a blue sky. Not one face had features; not one man stood close enough to hear a child's voice.

I imagined one face wearing kind eyes, like my father's eyes, or teasing eyes like those of my brother's, perhaps a soldier now, sent to rescue me or offer ransom, as though they trusted I still lived.

Hands over my ears blocked the sounds, but I refused to bury my face. My head scraped against the sharp nubby rocks, but still I stared while people who had fed me shouted orders, grunted, and moaned in pain. Without warning, Long Braids grabbed my hair and pulled me down. "Do you wish to kill us?" she hissed.

My mind wore a mixture of wishes: that the soldiers would know my father and could take me to him—without harming those who marked me but still fed me as they could.

She held me down with the weight of her body. Silence followed. She released me and moved away as though I held no value.

Acrid smoke drifted across the still battlefield, and dead lay scattered on the dirt beyond the lava caves. No soldier's dead; their bodies had already been taken away.

Slowly, like marmots after a hawk has passed, people's heads eased out from the lava openings to see what remained. Several caves away, I watched Long Braids scold at someone I could not see but knew it was her man. She wrapped his wounds and paid no attention to me, a child staring after the distant dust of departing soldiers.

I remained where I was, a still-lost child left behind.

Who could guess what caused that fight, why the soldiers came when they did? In later years, I knew of many skirmishes with soldiers and other bands, some brought on by the Modocs' raids. They did not always act in self-defense. I heard them talk of rushing at wagons that sliced across their lands or how they planned to resist the raids of Paiute people, roaming bands with fewer hides to trade who the Modocs said stole wagons and horses then sold them as though they were their own. "We lost good people to those Paiutes," I heard Keintpoos say. "We trade food sometimes for the ammunition they have. The soldiers think we burned their wagons for it, not just traded. Those Paiutes," he'd say in disgust and shake his head.

So I believed there would be more contact with the soldiers if I just waited, more chances I could leave. At least this was what a small white child came to believe by watching, listening, planning how to find her way.

When I was old enough to help make tule lodges, I noticed children and women who were not Modocs or Shastas or Klamaths joined the Modocs. They looked cloud-skinned like me. One became a "together with wife" of a Modoc warrior, and I spoke almost forgotten English with her, discovered she had no wish to leave, chose to stay, had found what she was seeking.

"It's best to make the most of where you are, dearie," she told me as she twisted willow into a basket, her knuckles large and looking in pain. "Can't complain when you have a place to lay your head and a good man bringing in game fer ya. More'n I had before with my own people," she says. "Kentuckians, they were, and they never once touched me with the hand of kindness I've known here." She smiled, the space between her teeth making her look younger than her many wrinkles.

Sometimes the fairer-skinned Indians were traded, marched before warrior horses to The Dalles on Nch'i Wana, the big river called the Columbia. The braves returned with blanket wealth draped across the backs of better horses.

Other captives died of hoping to go home, refusing food, waiting to be rescued. Some were burned while tied to leafless trees, though this was only whispered of, given as a threat to me by children. I had never seen it.

"Leave us!" a round-faced girl said once, then grabbed at small stones spread in the circle before her. They were playing the stone game called jacks. Her words were said to a puny girl, Rose, the daughter of a sickly woman who fought with whiskey when she had it. Rose had done nothing I could see to interfere, wanted only to belong, like me.

"What stinks of wet dog?" said another girl.

She sniffed her nose to the air while three other dark-eyed girls giggled at Rose's unwashed smell. Rose lowered her eyes but stayed. I guessed what she was feeling, for I had felt it too.

The first girl wrinkled her nose again, told Rose to move, and pushed her until she fell. The sniffing girl continued with her game as though she'd just stepped on an ant. She threw a larger pebble upward and tried to pick up four or five smaller ones kept inside a circle of hemp rope. She hoped to get them all before the larger rock hit the ground.

But my small white hand reached beneath hers and caught the rock instead.

"Ooh. Spring Water is mad, now," said one of the girls kneeling at the circle.

"Put it down," she snapped, her attention now on me. She looked uncertain of my intentions. No wise *tibo* ever interfered.

"This is not for you to play. Give it to me!"

I resisted and fueled her rage.

"You will be strung by your fingers! Burned from that tree!" She nodded her head to a charred juniper standing alone. "I will see to it!" She stomped her foot. "Give it," she demanded, her eyes narrow like a snake's.

The river stone felt smooth with a faint slick of oil from a child's fingers that often held fish. Rose picked herself up, but her eyes showed more alarm now than when she'd been shoved, and I wondered if my interference had really been for her.

"You'll burn!" Spring Water screamed.

I pretended I did not hear her threat, though my heart pounded and my thoughts told me to find another way to make a friend.

Spring Water began stomping around the girls kneeling at the circle. She kicked at Rose. Anger clenched her jaws.

"You better run, *tibo*," the girl closest to me whispered. "Rose is not worth it."

I might have gone off. I had no hope of turning this to something good. But her words fired me. So instead of dropping the stone at Spring Water's feet or scooting away to avoid her arm raised to strike me, I surprised her and myself by moving toward the danger, rather than away. In one quick step, I stood to meet the surprise in her eyes, then dove past and flipped the stone into Rose's surprised hands.

"Your turn," I said and walked away, imagining the surprise I left behind, pleased that they would see me as one who would not back down.

My feet walked wide past the charred juniper. I heard Spring Water shouting at me that I would still likely burn, but when I looked, I saw my efforts had been worth it: Rose had been allowed to keep the stone and make one try at the jacks. I would have liked to take a turn myself, but my heart told me it would never be.

The juniper stood black against the desert. It could have been a lightning strike that darkened the thick bark and marked it to the roots rather than a burning.

Don't think of it, I told myself.

I remembered captives who died from longing. They caused my heart to ache in understanding and made me wonder if I chose wrongly to stay here, gathering greasewood, making fires, picking huckleberries in season, watching from a distance the pleasure of stone-playing girls, accepting kicks and pokes and threats, just to stay alive.

But I chose it: to watch and learn and have the strength to search. You are alive to choose, I told myself. The thought kept me warm on nights when snow dusted the dogs' backs and my own and drove me toward the future like an arrow.

Once or twice I spied children with their *nabawici* who were hugged and called by name, rescued by a *moo'a*, grandmother from another tribe, or parent—a child recognized at a gathering as one who was lost who had been found. Outside the circle of belonging, I touched my marking with my dirty fingertips, watched the reunions bathed in warmth, and wished for someone who might search for me, know me by my name, and take me home.

Sometimes I dreamed of tall people in strange-looking skirts and shirts who wrapped me in their arms, the rough of their clothes brushing against me, the sweetness of their breath fresh against my face. But in the mornings, when the sun rose over the high Oregon desert and cast cool rays against mountain snows, I would feel the breath of a dog and the scratchiness of a dried tule mat against my skin and know anew the ache of loneliness.

Then I chose to have the markings on my face and all I could remember of my past urge me on, remind me of the journey I had chosen: to find my people and my place.

WADADUKA

"BUILD THE FIRE UP, STUPID GIRL! Your poor fire-tending tells people a lazy man lives here."

The voice of Lives in Pain, once a Modoc warrior, came as though pushed through deep mud instead of being carried by a warm wind blowing at the opening of his lodge. In recent weeks, his words were often woven with demand. I tried to leave before he whined, but failed.

"Oh, little Asiam. You can have some fish with me, after you get it. Get greasewood, too." His arm reached out to stop me as I slipped by to the outside of his lodge. I wiggled from his grasp. He stepped closer.

"Maybe I should move you on?" His fingers reached for my shoulder, found it, pressed hard enough to make me catch my breath. "Maybe to someone who will work you more. Am I so unkind?" he asked, stroking my arm as though I were a pet. Two hairs hung from his pocked chin, and he pulled at them with fingers soft as dough. I jerked, tried to step backward.

"The fire will die unless I tend it," I said. He held me a moment then let me go, a marked child making her escape.

In my four or five seasons with the Modocs, I learned their words for seeds and fish and forgot many of my own. But I spoke little to this man or any other. Lives in Pain had no patience with his helpers. He jabbed with large kicks or prodded with a stick if one moved too slowly.

I scurried to the basket kept in the cool dark of his tule lodge shaped like a mound of mud. A dog I sometimes made my bed with followed me in, yawned and stretched, his tongue panting while he waited for scraps.

"Move, Pinenut," I told the dog, who eased closer to the fish basket, tripping me as he pushed his dark body beside me. His big head hung low, staring like he'd found a prairie chicken among the tules. His chest showed healed scars, evidence of his fights. His tail wagged at the smell of fish, and wetness hung from his mouth like strands of melted honey and dribbled onto the hunk of dried fish I set aside for Lives in Pain.

"He won't like that soggy piece," I whispered but smiled inside at the trick the dog played on a man I could not afford to challenge.

I lowered my eyes as expected when I handed the food to the man who commanded me, then stepped backward to get fresh greasewood for his fire.

"So quick!" he cooed at me in his thick voice, as he ripped at the dried fish with his front teeth. He gave the softer piece of fish a look of interest, pressing it between his fingers. He grunted as he felt the wetness, then to my satisfaction, he shrugged and popped it in his mouth.

"Come back," he said, his words muffled with food as I moved beyond his reach. "You want a piece of this?"

"Later," I said, shaking my head.

His eyes followed me as he chewed. "No need to run away," he said.

"The greasewood is farther," I told him, pointing to areas beyond the cluster of wickiups. "I must hurry so your lodge will not be marked as lazy by a cold fire. I can eat soggy fish when I get back."

I found greasewood and some juniper branches and dragged them back slowly so by the time I returned to Lives in Pain's fire, he sat as I hoped. His head nodded back in sleep, his mouth hung open like a dark cave. Unchewed salmon stuck on a back tooth, more dribbled from his fingers.

I laid the branch on the embers of his fire with careful quietness, breathed on it, felt the smoke water my eyes. The dog gently pulled what remained of the cooked salmon from Lives in Pain's fingers, and we slipped away.

We disappeared into the shadows of the sagebrush to sit. The dog pranced toward me like a spirited horse, his strong legs stepping one in front of the other. He lowered his head for a scratch. I pulled a crumb or two of salmon from his whiskers and popped them into my mouth before he cleaned his face against my chest.

"We planned it well, Pinenut," I said scratching the dog's ears. "You got some salmon, too." The dog yawned. "We're far from his calls or kicks tonight," I told him.

I tried not to think that we also sat far from a warm wickiup, far from the laughter of children at play or the pleasure of precious food given with kindness.

Lives in Pain's lodge was not my usual place—I had none. I moved from wickiup to wickiup as told, a new mat to wake to every morning if someone needed help. Mostly my hands worked for old ones or those ill who coughed out orders. They said to call them *Moo'a*. But a true *moo'a* would invite her grandchildren in to share the deer meat or antelope while she talked of tender things. A child's real *moo'a* would plan a naming or help to teach her grandchild basket work.

These were not the things that I belonged to. At those gatherings of people, aunties, uncles, cousins, all, I watched from a distance, did not hear the gentle chatter of their voices that put the *onga'a* to sleep in their cradle boards. My mind learned early to push down the feeling that forced its way out through the water pooling in my eyes.

I could not stay to watch such scenes.

Instead, I shook my head, took a deep breath, and looked for things to do. Fix a basket for a *moo'a*. Corner a young woodchuck, a marmot sitting on a warm rock, catch it and call it my own. Pull ticks from the scruffy fur of a dog. Watch who came and went. These I could do, though they did not take away the loneliness of watching others in their pleasures, did not relieve the longing in my chest that burned like unquenched thirst.

Watching and deciding kept me on the path I chose, learning all I could, becoming strong and separate so someday, I could leave.

I noticed that warriors with wealth like Keintpoos, who *tibos* called Captain Jack, had many horses and they rode them to the gathering places and trade sites, while most others walked. They brought back puffed-up chests and news of change and showered colored trinkets on their wives and children. I dug some from the dust, abandoned. Their words caused much arguing in the lodges with the chosen headmen. Some medicine men laughed at them and said they brought back tall tales mixed with too much whiskey. Others said they threatened the safety of the Modocs with their disobedient leaving and could cause bad things to happen to all Modocs by a few stepping over the usual way things were done.

Young men of warrior age journeyed to trading places, too, but stayed for a season or more, picking up *tibo* words and ways. Some even worked in their wooden houses, learned English there or on the ranches in Northern California. I heard them speak of strange things like "china plates" and "ivory combs" in ways that seemed familiar. Their actions, too, brought strong words from elders. Some believed they wrapped the people's end in their new blankets bought with *tibo*'s money. But I watched some elders raise new rifles in gratitude for the far-seeing ways needed to keep the Modocs strong.

Once I thought of traveling with the younger men when they left for California or the ranches, going without their knowing. I would take a separate trail and sneak like a coyote beside them, sleep beneath the stars, close enough to hear the laughter at their fires. I saw myself arriving at the boardwalks of the town at dusk, finding a dog to share a bed with and in the morning, beginning my search.

It was not the fear of a desert night that stopped me, nor of being found by men not wanting to be followed. What stopped me was not knowing how to search.

I thought I might find myself among white people and then be overcome by some sweet scent, like my mother's lavender or the bite of tobacco that once filled my father's pipe. I needed to be older, keener, so when I set foot in the town I would know what steps to take and have a plan to carry me past a single sunrise.

Instead, I placed my winnowing baskets close beside those who brought back news of other places, risked their shouts at me, the brunt of their kicks, so I could hear. I wove mats and worked the mano against the grain to be near the storytellers, used what they shared to fuel my dreams of entering the world my parents lived in.

Older now, I see my efforts kept another vigil in those days: they helped me set aside the heaviness I felt at being there, alone. The burning that began behind my nose when I saw a mother spit on soft leather to wipe her child's dirty cheek did not result in tears if I thought of other things. The thickness that threatened to close my throat when a *moo'a* placed beaded moccasins on her grandson's feet or when she stroked his head in pride became determination, not despair. I always had a plan to think on, a way to keep deep feelings in a covered basket so the sight of others close together without my shadow in their way would not become more powerful than my plan.

I would leave someday. I would find those who did not mean to leave me. I would help them find me. I did belong, somewhere.

And so I gathered food, cleaned fish, scraped hides, made myself useful, and stayed out of the way. I did not challenge any rule, found comfort in dogs' fur and laughter in their licks. And in everything I did, I watched, doing what I could to keep from being traded to some band less kind and to keep from being forced to leave before I chose.

Still, I had no single wickiup to call my own until the year the Modocs joined the Paiute gathering.

We had moved before, traveling with the seasons to places of food and winter preparation. We walked south to the mountains for the pine nuts that grew on bushy trees. In the east, rabbits and some deer and antelope fell to the Modoc guns and arrows. At huckleberry gatherings, they traded rifles and knives with Klamaths and Walker River people who arrived with their pointy burden baskets full of goods. But when green shoots speared through the spring mud along the edges of the wide flat lakes near the mountain called Shasta, we returned and gathered tule roots and fished.

But one fall, I did not.

The season that cools before winter came early that year, and we traveled northeast to the twin lakes, a place I had never seen. The Modocs planned to exchange goods and dances with some Paiute bands and visiting Snakes camped there. They would speak of wars and rifles. A raiding chief named Paulina was expected, seeking warriors to join him against the soldiers.

The Modocs were not a joining people, but they liked gatherings.

We wove our way north and east, around sagebrush and rabbit brush and sturdy junipers offering infrequent shade. Our feet kicked up puffs of dust in the sand. A whole village of horses and people and dogs with packs on their backs eased through the desert like a lazy snake. We stepped over scorpions and the discarded skins of rattlesnakes that lay like long, thin shells beneath the sage. The tips of a mountain range watched us leave, a single mountain named Snow that some called Steens watched us arrive.

Like most of the women, I walked, surprised that a rustling sound in the distance could become a roaring stream plunging out of rock, a murmur like distant voices could reveal a small creek guarded by red willows and cottonwoods. We filled our tightly woven water baskets there, splashed our hot faces with the refreshing water, rested a time before moving back into the desert.

Eventually, lakes appeared in the distance, shimmering as mist settled over sagebrush easing into marsh. One lake, called Tonowama, was said to taste of salt and gave little life. The other teemed with fish and showy white birds and ducks and a hundred smaller warblers and migrating geese that darkened the sky when they lifted. Flying things fluttered with color in the waving grasses, and as they flitted through the air, unmarked children chased at them. Pink mornings that soothed like a welcome sigh eased across a sweep of sky.

Set beside a marsh with tules and reeds and dark *wada* seeds enough to feed the people, we gathered, joined with others who wove grass and mud houses and formed tule mats and willows to make their wickiups.

It was here, not far from the lakes the white people called Mud and Harney, that I found myself making a poor choice. After all my careful watching and listening, my plan for when to leave and how to stay, I made a choice that caused me to change my ways.

"A child weaves poorly at first," Lukwsh told me when I had gained some years but still acted crabby with myself for making some mistake. "Best baskets are woven from those experienced hands correct."

Wuzzie found me, lying in rocks at the bottom of the rim-rock ridge, my once strong leg twisted like a dog-chewed bone, broken.

He waited without moving so that at first I thought I dreamed him, his image rising up like fog lifts over lakes. I tried to float above my pain to see him. He waited, deciding whether to startle me awake or take me on into heavy, painless sleep.

"Reckless," he said finally in a language I understood.

He grunted, became a man with a strange voice that vibrated like wind through an eagle-bone whistle.

"Modocs fail to teach you how to climb," he said.

He did not wish my thoughts or I would have told him that it was my wish to stand at high places, to see as far as I could see, that brought me to that lava ridge, not poor training by the Modocs. I did not like places where rocks and hills or tall trees broke my eyes from seeing far. In high places, I imagined the vastness of the land my parents were drawn to, the waters where all rivers were said to end.

My wish to be above things did it, and the moccasins of tules that I wove that were too slick and did not dig into rocks well enough to catch me when I slipped.

Before I fell, half the day had passed, and I had climbed to the top of a ridge that rose from the flat desert like a face pimple that arrives overnight, pointed and out of place. The ridge overlooked the lakes and blue-green sage. Once there I hoped to see the world, wide and broad as a lake bed, as rich with interest. My heart would open as it could not do inside the valleys we walked through on our way from the Modocs' place. And most of all, in a wish I did not let myself speak of often, I hoped to gaze north, to see a glimpse of the trail, a military trail, I had heard the warriors speak of. Such a trail would lead to *tibo*'s towns and forts and camps. And closer, I imagined, to my parents.

Voices from camps below rose up to meet me. Voices of people I did not know, Klamaths, Wadadukas, Nez Percé and Teninos, some Snakes and Bannocks, Shastas, Umatillas, other Paiute bands—the Modocs, too, who brought me, like one of their best dogs, to carry things.

Lives in Pain lay resting. Long Braids kept busy with her children. Many gathered to trade, to winnow seeds, to hunt ducks and fish and dance and remember stories of the people who belonged here, land of people who called themselves Wadadukas, "seed eaters." Each enjoyed this time of feasting and gathering. No one knew or cared that I walked beyond the reach of their call; no one expected me to be there or to leave. None would notice until they needed firewood or food brought from their baskets.

A gentle wind blew strands of my hair across my face, into my mouth. The sun had turned my hair the color of a young antelope, the hue of dirty sand. Pulled back from my face, the hair came to an arrow's point in the center of my forehead. I chopped the ends too short to braid, but the shortness kept bugs from finding a place to live, and I scratched less than the dogs. Like the Modocs, I rubbed duck grease into it to make it smooth and shiny and darker, the color of my eyes, hoping to disappear among the people, make myself unseen so I could be a better watcher.

A foolish wish since my skin was still pale and I grew more slender than most of the children and had a thin face, unlike the others. And the *naba-wici* forever marked me.

Duck fat taste entered my tongue. My fingers pulled me upward as I spit the hair out. Those fingers were strong that twisted mats, stripped sagebrush and wove strands into the skirt and shirt I wore now. Few Modocs would waste buckskins on an unbelonging child.

I reached for a rock above me, higher with each step, imagining how far my eyes would see when I reached the top. My nose itched from lichen tickling it as I hugged the nubby lava rock, each step closer to the highest point. A spider ran across my fingers and I startled.

My treasure basket stayed thonged to my waist. Once discarded by a careless woman, the tule reed basket no bigger than my palm now belonged to me, to hold my meager wealth. I patted at the scrap of pink pinafore, the tiny gold chain, and a special bone shared with a dog on a rainy day.

A nosy hawk arced toward me, caught the breeze, and maneuvered out into a camas-blue sky. My eyes watched him, envied his freedom and speed and direction. He took my gaze from the sharp rocks beneath my strained fingers.

My foot slipped. I recovered, caught my breath, rested. Sun beat like a friendly hand steady on my head. Sweat trickled beneath my arms, beaded against my chest beneath my sagebrush shirt. I took another step.

I stood close to the end of my journey with my foot solidly wedged into rock. With one hand, I adjusted my treasure basket, checked the cover. I took a deep breath and reached for the top.

I was so prepared to breathe in the stretch of land before me that I almost did not feel the rock break beneath my foot.

My fingers ached at the jerk and the task expected of them. They looked as though they belonged to someone else, and then they too slipped. I lost my grip, and my legs and arms belonged to space.

Pain like a new knife sliced my body as it scraped against ragged rocks, split open skin on my arms and my sides. I slid downward, downward; lichen and broken lava splayed across my face until my head slammed against the ground. Dirt and dust sprayed up around me.

The hawk screeched, dipped high above, closer to the view I never saw, and soared away.

It took some moments more before my breath returned, pushing against sore ribs. My head ached and pounded behind my eyes. My arms were tingling, and I felt a dark, sticky stain beneath my leg pushing through to numbness. I touched the pale shaft of bone lodged beneath stretched flesh. It pushed against my skin but not through it. When I tried to move, the pain jabbed me like a jagged spear, and the fear of what this meant began to throb inside my head. My teeth chattered against themselves from the stinging breeze and the sharp edge of my bone and skin gathering wind.

No chubby-faced *hitse* stood by me while another ran to tell my mother. No father came running with worry and fear set upon his face. I had no hope for scolding wrapped with relief that I still lived.

I wondered if I could drag myself back to the village and who would help me if I did? Maybe I would die. I almost wished it, at the thought of winter coming and this wounded leg.

There Wuzzie found me.

Once he decided to become a man instead of a bad dream, his fingers felt warm, like coarse sand. He rubbed them against my prickly skin.

I startled at his touch, tried to push away, braver now that someone joined me.

"I can do it," I told him, my voice sounding unfamiliar.

It was more a prayer of hope than a description of what was. He ignored me and felt my leg again.

"No!" I tried to brush his hand away. "Please, I can do it."

Even in my pain I heard the fear in my voice, as though I knew already what fate would greet me if I could not care for myself.

But Wuzzie acted as if he didn't hear and moved his spindly fingers around my leg, his body bent over me like the crooked end of his sagebrush walking stick. He laid his stick beside my injured leg, and then he spoke.

"Stupid children should not go off by themselves into strange places." His voice fluttered, neither high nor low. He stood concealed behind an antelope skin that sheathed his chest and lower body like a valued knife. His chest heaved with effort, and I imagined him hot and wondered why he wrapped himself, then how he found me and why he bothered. But when my throbbing pain spoke again, I found I did not care to know the answers. Other things came first.

"I can," I said and tried to push myself again, fighting off the threatened darkness carried with the pain.

He stopped his hands moving at my leg and stared. Then as though remembering something important, he lifted one of the baskets from his chest and handed me a water basket made of tule twists and offered me a drink.

He gave me cool water, a surprise in this hot place. And sweet, not with the taste of lakes—spring water, refreshing and clear.

As he lifted my head, he spoke trade language words I could understand.

"You do not belong in this place," he said. I looked at him over the water jar and stared into a face as smooth as a shelled pine nut, as dark as washed jasper. He took the jar from me and dabbed at my face gently with wet fingers, a gesture so unexpected I felt tears form and fought them back, not wanting to look weak as well as stupid, frightened as well as marked.

He reached again for my leg. The treasure baskets hung crisscrossed from his chest and bobbed on his body when he moved.

"No!" I told him in the jargon, to be sure he understood. Refreshed now, I thought I must do this alone.

"Even more reckless to resist," he said.

I pushed myself up on bruised elbows. I tried to lift my leg, but the pain that followed felt as though I'd stepped into a fire, and I swallowed back a sickness from my stomach.

He grunted as if he expected this would happen. With head lowered, the little man thonged sagebrush sticks to either side of my leg. I remembered seeing him among the Wadadukas. I had overheard someone say he was *poohaga'yoo,* but I had little interest in such things. He did not seem powerful with his little size and odd shape, but I hoped he had strength enough to help me back.

Water formed in my mouth again, and I swallowed several times to keep from throwing up, the feeling stronger when Wuzzie leaned closer and I smelled his onions and herbs. He appeared grim, as though he held no gentleness, and his one blue eye and one brown eye looked me over like a pelt with some damage.

I shivered despite sweating. He bent more firmly to the task. He unrolled a tule mat he must have used for gathering grasses and roots as he moved such things aside, placing them into the baskets hung on his chest. He grunted and showed me with his hands how I should move. When I hesitated, he grunted again, then rolled me to the mat, overlooking the cry of pain that escaped before I could stop it.

Shafts of light pierced my eyes. I heard a terrible sound that frightened me almost more than my pain but I was already on the mat before I realized the scream had come from me.

With two cordage thongs he tied the tule corners, making me a bundle inside the mat, then pulled the thongs across his forehead in a tumpline like the women used with burden baskets.

"Wait," I said, my voice breathless. "My basket." What tied me to my past was in my basket I kept always with me.

"The basket," I said again in jargon, pointing awkwardly from inside the mat that wrapped me.

He looked around, but his eyes did not search much.

"It belongs to me," I said, my breath panting in effort, my voice pleading.

A great hole opened in my stomach that I believed back then could only be filled with the treasures from that basket. My eyes shamefully begged.

"Get another," he said, wiping at the air with the back of his palm. "What is of value to a small child can be replaced. Or go look yourself," he said and laughed.

He pushed me back onto the mat then reached inside one of his bags and sprinkled something into the water bag. He held my head again. I thought about resisting so I could search, could show him my strength, but the pain was too great. So when he placed the drink to my lips, I took his gift.

The mixture tasted gritty. Small flakes stuck to my tongue. I felt sleepy as he lifted me from the ledge, his breath coming hard, cords tight along his neck. He laid me flat, still wrapped like a baby in tules, then stepped away and turned his back. His body became a horse to pull me as I sank back into the mat, into accepting what I was: a burden entering winter without treasures. I could neither gather nor tend fires.

Why had he bothered with me? I would be a mouth to feed, take sparse food from an elder. I had nothing to offer in trade. The answer to why he helped me lay in a later time.

Wuzzie started off across the desert, pulling his burden behind him in an uneven gait. In a daze of pain and just before the gritty water put me into sleep, I thought of what waited for me, how I would live now, carry out my plans to leave and search. The face of the girls and their circle of stones came to me along with Spring Water's threat.

Perhaps she was right, that grim-faced girl. Perhaps my search had ended and my time for burning had come.

AWAKE

WE REACHED THE GATHERING PLACE, a dry marsh beside lakes.

The grasses pressed soft against me when we stopped, the change in rhythm jerking me awake. The smell of dying grasses and mud filled the air, and my mouth felt full of cottonwood fluff. A tall sandhill crane lifted its head to stare at the commotion Wuzzie caused by dragging me past. Drifts of swans splashed and sliced the water spiked with sweet reeds and bulrush. Usually the large birds brought comfort to me, but now their flight seemed frantic, as though wishing to leave a dangerous place.

In the distance, I could see Dog Mountain, the rock ridge I did not climb.

Wuzzie had pulled me while I slept, and now, awake, I was dragged through a crowd whose faces moved in and out above me, seeming larger than they were.

"Wuzzie finds a bone!" someone said.

Laughter followed.

My heart beat louder. My eyes had trouble seeing who stood over me, blurred from sweat or fear or Wuzzie's gritty water.

I watched the people's eyes, their bodies, young and old, some familiar, some new, as they made room for him, for me, then filled the space behind us, moving like the warp and weft of a woven, rabbit-skin blanket. Thick-tailed dogs with heads larger than the Modocs' dogs squirted between the legs of the onlookers. One sniffed at my feet. Another growled as though discovering an intruder.

Wuzzie stopped in the center of the gathering and lowered his tumpline. The sides of the tule mat opened to expose his burden—and the worthlessness of what he carried.

"Who owns this child?" Wuzzie asked in his fluttering voice.

All eyes stared at the damage to my leg.

Running Dog of the Modocs eased his way forward. He towered over Wuzzie like a giant pine over a piñon but Wuzzie stood the stronger. Running Dog picked at a tooth with a sliver of greasewood. His eyes ran over me like a night spider, paused at my dark *nabawici*, stopped at my leg thonged to the stick.

"Who would claim her now?" he said.

My eyes floated around the circle of faces. Some of the looks came from people I'd gathered food for, been struck by when I worked slow. Now their eyes promised other things as when people hovered over rabbits during the winter drives, just before they lifted clubs to stop the rabbits' squeals. Running Dog had wisdom. No one would claim me now. I felt a spider crawling up my neck but when I reached to brush it off, only wetness lived there. My thoughts raced. I must show them I could move and walk, was not as worthless as I looked.

I scanned the ground for a stick I could lean on. My leg throbbed, the pain made me dizzy, my stomach turned to sick but I struggled, grabbed the skirt of someone standing close before she screamed and brushed at me. A dog darted toward me. He stopped, his tail pointed and still.

"No one puts their claim on this one?" Wuzzie said. His voice held hesitation as though he wondered himself why he had brought me back. Dogs who were injured were left behind or killed. Marked ones might be traded, but if they were injured, lost their value…

My heart pounded. How stupid to crawl in rocks simply to see high places. How poorly I had planned. I should have made new moccasins or gone without them on my climb. Why did I choose that time to search the heights? I could have found a better way to look north for the trail. Now I might never find it, might never see a road my parents could have traveled. I was a burden basket, needing to be tended to and carried.

"I care for myself!" I said, attempting to sit again, to show my strength and defy the helplessness I felt. My elbow held me part way but my voice wavered with my words.

People laughed.

"I can work, even while I sit," I told them, swallowing back tears. "See, my hands are fine." I held them up, flapping them in a clumsy effort to show they worked. Several chuckled at my effort.

"She looks like a wounded duck," someone said to more laughter.

"Let the dogs bring her in," said another. "Good practice for them."

"I prefer dogs," I challenged.

"You caught a spirited one this time," one woman said.

I hated their teasing. Desperate, I made one last effort to stand, to resist the searing pain that moving caused. I could not even sit well by myself and the attempt to go higher left me breathing hard, fish swimming in my stomach. The look on Wuzzie's face said he wished he had not found me.

I ambled like a wounded dog, tossed myself around hoping I could stand while they teased at me, reached a hand then withdrew it, offered help but laughed when I tried to touch their palms.

"Let her be," said a woman who wore her hair pulled back freely flowing behind her neck.

She stood tall, could look a horse in the eye, almost. She looked down on me, stared a long time, and I wondered if she saw my grateful look.

She said something to Wuzzie in words I did not understand. A few people in the circle began drifting away with no more excitement promised. Then Wuzzie and the woman argued, and people turned back, seeking the distraction of other people's distress, of a woman strong enough to challenge one said to carry special powers.

The woman nodded her head toward another lodge, and I saw an older woman standing some distance away, scowling openly with arms crossed before her narrow chest. It looked as though Wuzzie made an effort to convince the hair-flowing woman of something. He spoke rapidly with his arms moving and fingers pointing. But she shook her head. Buckskin fringes shimmered on her wide chest as she talked. She nodded again toward the old woman.

I tried to think of what they argued over, tried to think of what action I could take to stay alive through the winter. My head throbbed and I closed my eyes, blocking out the jeering faces of those still standing and watching.

Finally, Wuzzie grunted some agreement and he called out to the gathering.

"Lukwsh will give a black *wehe* to the one who claims this child and takes her to his lodge until she is healed. She would take the child herself, but if her lodge expands, it must be to make room for her husband's mother." He nodded toward the older woman who I saw had one shoulder lower and smaller than the other.

In the silence, several people looked toward the old woman. Then two or three others spoke all at once, for I learned later that the woman, Lukwsh, made a special *wehe*. I wondered why this woman bothered to trade a special knife for me.

"The pale one warmed herself in rabbit skins I caught."

I heard the voice and shivered. Lives in Pain, awake now. He hobbled toward Wuzzie, his hip the source of agony given from a *tibo*'s weapon, though he could ride a horse and strike a child walking beside him with ease.

"I take her. For the *wehe*," he said.

Going with him would be like a rabbit living with a hawk. The thought brought new fears, and this time with great effort, I almost stood, the leg thonged to sagebrush stuck stiffly out before me, the pain making all of me almost numb. People blurred and turned upside down just before I fell.

The tall woman told me later it was my effort that convinced her she should try to save me. "You resisted pain and fear," she said. "Like a warrior."

She looked from me to Lives in Pain's narrow eyes. He set his jaw, glanced away first, then opened his palm toward his leg. "See, I have pain, too," he whined. "And my stomach hurts. I have to eat wild celery often to make my stomach work. A good *wehe* would ease my suffering, make it easier to strip rabbit hides for blankets. And I know this child's ways. Eventually she will walk again and help me."

The tall woman spoke to Wuzzie in words unfamiliar to me. Wuzzie grinned, motioned for her to speak to Lives in Pain.

"You can care for her though you cannot gather food for yourself?" questioned the hair-flowing woman.

Lives in Pain shrugged. "If you distrust me, take her yourself," he said and rubbed at his leg as though it hurt.

Lukwsh clucked her tongue, and her eyes darted toward the older woman who had begun to make her way closer to the gathering, her face set in a serious scowl. People moved back as though the older woman took up more space than what her thin body showed.

I smelled wet earth, salt, and dog droppings and wondered if these would be my last smell of the lakes, the last sounds from the land of the desert and sage. The flap of a great blue heron lifting into the still sky broke the silence the old woman's presence brought.

"I made an offer for the *wehe*," repeated Lives in Pain, unaware that the power of the moment had shifted. "It will not be bettered."

"She must be kept until she is well," Wuzzie said. "That is what Lukwsh wants for such a valued knife. When she is able she can be traded. Or run errands for Grey Doe or other old ones. This would please you, yes, old woman?"

The older woman stood beside him now and snorted. "What I want is a live son or his wife to care for me. I have neither."

Lives in Pain bit out his next words. "She is not worth the food she will eat until she can gather her own. I keep her until she is well. It will be your best offer."

Tears pressed against my nose. My chest tightened with the powerlessness this lying here had left me. I had nothing to give for someone to want me, no way to remain out of sight on my own. I was just a child who lived with dogs, forced like them to follow others' plans. Even with the offer of a *wehe*, only someone without trust offered to take me.

"Let me go with him," I said.

I deserved him for my foolish fall. His was an offer I could accept, anything to put away the ache of what would happen when the snow came and my leg could not carry my weight.

But the woman who offered the *wehe* cast her eyes to me, ordering silence.

"I have decided," Wuzzie said before she could speak. "She will fill my own lodge. A pale child who believes she can climb the tallest rocks may have *pooha*." He hesitated, then lifted the head strap that pulled me on the mat and turned. "She is strong to survive the fall," Wuzzie added. "Perhaps there is a reason she has lived this long."

"She said she would live with me!" Lives in Pain challenged. But Wuzzie ignored him and began dragging the tule mat with me in it, the decision apparently settled. What remained of the circle parted before him, and my stomach lurched again with the fear of this new plan, that he saw me with some power that I neither had nor knew nor wanted. He stopped suddenly, and I twisted and caught the dun color of the leather moccasins belonging to Lukwsh and the old woman who stood before Wuzzie, towering over him.

Wuzzie's blue eye and brown eye did their darting dance. Grey Doe spoke. "Do not keep her in your lodge. You risk your powers with her."

"I decide what threatens," Wuzzie said. "Not you, old woman. Or this stupid girl. But since I found her," he said with delight in his voice, "I will get the obsidian *wehe*."

"You cannot keep her," Grey Doe said again.

"No?" Wuzzie said, turning slowly to face her. He smiled then as though he expected this turn of events. "You are right, old woman. I do not share space well." He wiped a thin layer of sweat from his strangely bald head, and I wondered if Lives in Pain's plan might be accepted. Wuzzie spoke to the remaining crowd.

"Lukwsh will keep this child. Until she is well." To Lives in Pain's and Grey Doe's astonished faces he added, "But I will get the *wehe*."

Grey Doe began to speak. Wuzzie interrupted. "It is a good plan. You were wise to think of it, old woman." He nodded his head once which seemed to mean there would be no more discussion.

"You have no room for me in your lodge but can take this milky-skin thing!" Grey Doe said, turning on Lukwsh, swinging her whole shoulder when she turned to speak.

"She claims the child for me," Wuzzie reminded her, his hand in the air as if to stop her. "She does *me* the favor. And maybe later, you, when this milky-thing is well enough to look after you in your old age." His voice fluttered high and he tossed his head back. "Does anyone wish it different?"

Grey Doe glared at him, then complained beneath her breath. She turned away and walked alone back to her lodge. She scowled at Lukwsh as she passed her and let a hot stare linger on me.

Wuzzie dropped the strap across his head and acted as if he had just become awake. His face broke out in smiles, and I wondered if he planned this as it happened. He called to some men standing about. Several hands then lifted me and carried me to a tule lodge newly built. They stepped down one or two paces, and we entered the cool darkness of Lukwsh's place, for there were several black *wehe* lying on mats, shiny *wehe*, smooth, like water on a moonlit night. They laid me on a rabbit blanket and left, the furs soft against my shivering skin.

The room grew quiet with only a flutter of a breeze through the smoke hole. The woman knelt beside me. And while she did not smile, she pushed another blanket up behind my back so I could sit, and laid another under my leg which lessened the throbbing. The gesture in its tenderness told me I was safe, at least for the moment.

My mind felt tired, my leg ached with swollen pain, but my need to notice, listen, plan caused me to scan the lodge. Three or four baskets, some winnowing trays, water jars—enough to meet a family's needs, not enough to be a burden in travel—lined the edges of her lodge, circled it like a large campfire. Fresh teasel to comb out hair snarls stuck up from a willow basket that blended the colors of earth and rocks. A short stack of smoked hides filled a small space with a pungent scent. Everything appeared new, so this must have been the lodge of someone who had lost a loved one or newly joined these people as someone who once did not belong.

A cooking fire glowed low in the center, gave away pale smoke rising through the hole above. A blackened basket near the fire let forth steam and invitation. My eyes must have showed my hunger, for the woman, Lukwsh, lifted a small basket from a corner place and ladled steaming soup into it. She blew on the contents.

We were interrupted.

Lives in Pain entered the lodge like a man intending to stay. He said something in a language I didn't understand. Lukwsh did not turn to him, pushed the food toward me. Following her lead, I blew too, looking over the basket at Lives in Pain standing behind her. I ate nervously, hands and body shivering in spasms both from the pain and Lives in Pain's intrusion, his rush of words cascading over her bent back.

The woman stood finally and spoke to him, still not turning. He wanted her to listen and he stepped closer, shouting to her ear. Her face did not change, but she shook her head at his words.

Finally, she turned, snapped a phrase at him, and scooted her hands at him as if he were a troublesome dog made to leave. His finger pointed at me, jabbed at her, then caught her chest and pushed her backward. I felt my heart pound, my mouth get dry, but she did not fall.

I tried to speak, to tell him I would go with him so he would cause no harm to this lodge or any others, but the words stuck in my throat.

Lukwsh pushed back, both hands on his shoulders, her jaw set. I had never seen a woman challenge a man in this way.

"We are a gentle people," she said in the trade language so I could understand. "But we will not be jabbed at. You are not welcome here."

He took steps backward. To catch himself from falling, he grabbed the flap that covered the door opening. He snarled out more words to her I didn't understand, but Lukwsh acted as though she didn't hear him now, as if he had already left. She turned back toward me so she couldn't see him glare at me and shake his fist.

"I'll be back for you," he said, his finger pointing at my heart. "A bargain was offered. It will be kept." He shouted something more to her as he disappeared into daylight. Her face flushed.

"He is all wind," she said to me.

I expected her to tell me he was getting a headman or that Wuzzie had changed his mind. Or that she had, and that I must prepare to leave. I expected it. No damaged child was worth such trouble brought into another's lodge.

"I'll go," I told her. "He's not so bad."

"No," she said, motioning me to be still. "An agreement has been made and will be kept, but it was not with that one." She nodded her chin toward the empty door opening. "Rest now. He will not bother you again. It is my promise."

A promise? She gave me a promise? A warm and sheltered promise given as a gift? She turned back to put another warm rock into the water basket. The soft hiss as it hit the soup sounded like a sigh. A warmth moved through me that grew from more than her filling soup.

She had stood for me. Offered shelter and protection. Me. A marked child in the shelter of another.

Her eyebrows raised at me in question, and I wondered if I had made a sound, had not caught the cry of cautious joy before I shamed myself with tears.

She knelt beside me, then, sat on her heels. She touched my head gently and stroked the snarls of my hair and pulled at the bits of moss and earth collected by my fall. She dabbed at my face with a rabbit skin blanket.

Then Lukwsh did something I had longed for, something that the thought of now still causes me to tear. She began to sing.

She sang a sweet song with no words that I could recognize, only a rhythmic melody I heard women singing from a distance, songs sung to an *onga'a* in her board. Her voice eased low like a summer breeze, the sounds swooshing like grain thrown to wind, like precious seeds caught in winnowing baskets for safekeeping.

I leaned into her side, expecting her to move away, hoping she would stay. She placed her arms around me and rocked, her voice far away as though she sang of a time and a loss much greater than mine, a place where I did not belong, but her voice invited me, perhaps to soothe her wounds. She smelled of earth and dried onions and warm rocks. And no change of leaves and grasses will ever come my way without the company of Lukwsh's lilting song drifting to my mind.

Tears eased their way down my cheeks and into my ears. I sniffed, afraid to wipe my nose and eyes with the back of my hand, afraid to do anything that might send her away.

I must have slept, for what I remember next was awaking with a start to Lukwsh's back and a beaded barrette of butterflies clutching at the flow of her hair as she bent to her fire.

Someone coughed, and I wondered if Lives in Pain returned and if that was what woke me.

But Wuzzie stood at the opening. He motioned toward the sagebrush staff that lined a side of my leg and then entered, bent to unwrap the thongs that held my limb still if not straight. I sensed without knowing why that when the staff was gone, pain would stab back, and I grimaced.

The two exchanged words, and Lukwsh knelt beside me before Wuzzie crow-hopped away.

"Be strong, na?" she said.

Wuzzie returned. His skinny body broke the dusky light spilling in through the opening of the lodge. He handed Lukwsh a bowl and then disappeared. The wind from his leaving moved flicker feathers hung on strings that floated like a live bird above the flames.

I drank from the bowl. I saw the swirl in the bottom of the basket, had time to think that its maker was a skilled weaver, and then fell into blessed sleep.

In a dream I felt pressure on my leg, faces huddled over me. Lives in Pain scowled, a woman hit me on the wound sending shafts of pain and light swirling to my head. A dog talked, told me, "Drink." Wuzzie sang and wrapped me tightly like a baby in my board. Then Lukwsh sang too as I rose upward, watched from high up in the lodge, close to the smoke hole, shimmering between earth and stars.

I am light as the hawk, diving, soaring. I am far-seeing in the unfamiliar, like an owl in the act of breathing in. I am like a *wada* seed in winter, waiting to unfold, and then I plunge hard like a rock against the rabbit furs into deepest, darkest sleep.

In the night I awoke to sounds of heavy breathing close to my ear. Familiar sounds, like Lives in Pain's breath. My hand formed into a fist, waiting, my mind wide awake. The breathing stopped. I lay still as a captured marmot, willing my eyes like an owl's to see into the night. My leg throbbed in time with my heart, but it seemed to hurt less. Fingers of fear crept like spiders down my spine. I sniffed in strange smells of dampness, fish oil, duck grease, and fur, the coiled presence of someone close to me, someone not asleep.

Night as black as the inside of an antelope's stomach filled the lodge. The other's breathing began again, more shallow. It moved closer. Lives in Pain come to claim me and his *wehe?* Wuzzie seeking warmth? My head pounded into a mass of tightness. All tiny noises sounded like shouts. My heart sent up a prayer, somewhere, for protection in this Wadaduka place, and it was answered.

Hot breath, the brush of hide and fur, and then a wet tongue touched me, washed me with dog breath and relief.

"Pinenut!" I whispered to the big-headed dog as he poked a warm nose into my ear. He yawned and whined in his throat. "Shu-shu, Pinenut," I told him, "be still, now. You are safe too." I took his wide head between my hands and ruffled his neck. I could not see the dog, just felt his tawny fur as he nuzzled closer, stretched against my body, twisting, moving into comfort, lying on his back, one paw apparently pointed upward toward the stars that shone through the smoke hole. He sighed, and I heard the heavy breathing of a dog, asleep.

I must not find trouble where it does not live, I told myself, for there will be enough walking right through the opening of any lodge I stay in without me holding it in my mind before it comes.

I lay awake, stroking the dog's head, twisting my fingers in his fur. Despite my injury and uncertain future, I was as grateful and contented as on any day in my life.

What I needed most was time: to heal, to get through winter without trouble, to set my sights again on when to leave. But I was a young girl who had been lost and alone. And for the first time, all at once, I had a full stomach, a woman who watched over me, and a dog to keep me warm. What more did a marked child need?

BRIEF REFUGE

FOR SOME DAYS, IF ANYONE HAD LOOKED, they would have found me in Lukwsh's lodge with only the big woman and the dog to tend my limbs. Lukwsh said nothing about the dog's arrival, simply threw it scraps as though it belonged.

The tea she gave me took me in and out of dreams and drowse, night and day. My sleep was fitful with voices that shouted and scraped against my mind with sharp stings and sometimes softness. Once I thought Lives in Pain sat beside me in the night, but perhaps it was the eyes of hawks. The strange face of a young man I did not recognize leaned over me in a dream, tending my leg. And from a far away place deep inside my mind, I sometimes watched the shadow of children moving in the wickiup, felt their ebb and flow like water against the tule mats that lined the lodge walls. But whenever I awoke, the woman Lukwsh was always there with me, alone.

Time passed in this lodge as though walking on an uneven trail.

"You," Lukwsh said one morning after I had shared this lodge for some days. An early frost had formed on the ground outside, and I felt the coolness as she woke me with a gentle roll of my shoulder. "Up now. It is time. You have visitors, na?" She signaled with her chin toward the door opening.

Faces as dark as berries stared at me against the back drop of the morning sun. I squinted, cleared my head and eyes as Lukwsh spoke, her words bringing the faces attached to bodies through the opening into the lodge. There were three, and they stood in a line at my feet.

"Learn names," Lukwsh commanded.

I understood her, though her words did not carry the usual lilt and swoosh of the Modocs or even the Wadadukas I had met. She did not smile, and for a moment I thought perhaps I dreamed her tenderness. Then with the quickness of a hummingbird's wing came the worry that Wuzzie or Lives in Pain might take me back, that my leg might never heal, that in the spring, they'd move to root-digging sites and leave me behind before I could walk.

But I could still recall the lullaby's rhythm and remind myself not to look for trouble when it might not be there.

"This is Xali-Xali." Lukwsh said, bringing me back to the present. She hesitated before giving me a word I might know. "Um, bird. Wren," she said in the trade language. She placed her hand on the girl's head as she walked behind her, ran her fingers over her ears, down a neck as delicate as a heron's. Wren was the smallest of the three and was dressed not unlike myself, sagebrush skirt and shirt. Her brown eyes held a dreamy look as she stared at me, direct.

"Wren's are powerful," Lukwsh said. "They kill rattlesnakes in the cliffs. Never threaten a wren's nest." She draped her arms now over the girl's shoulders. "Our Wren is not so fierce, but she is strong." Lukwsh smiled at the girl, revealing dark spots from ash on her gums around snowy white teeth.

Wren giggled and placed her dirty fingers against her mouth to cover her smile. She looked my age but stronger, had been loved and cared for.

"And wrens like to fly to high places," Lukwsh continued, "so you two share a wish.

"Tiish, 'Stink Bug,'" Lukwsh said next. She laughed loudly as she stood behind the chubbiest of the three children. "The Paiute word is Po-o-o-zea," she said, dragging out the sound to the irritation of the boy. Her laughter bubbled like the small springs that rippled out of the side of Snow Mountain, brought light to her wide face. She ruffled the boy's hair while her upper lip rolled under, stuck to the top exposing her full row of teeth.

"He will receive a new name some day," Lukwsh said. "But for now he has this one because of what his body does with wild celery."

She waved her hand in front of her wrinkled nose, and Stink Bug's round face turned a rosy brown. He dug his bare toe into the earth and cast his dark eyes downward.

"And this," Lukwsh said, suddenly moving to stand behind a slender young man who held one arm crossed in front of him, grasping the elbow of the other, his finger to his mouth, nipping at the edge, "is Shard."

I did not know then the place Shard would have in my belonging, my leaving, or my life. No one told me I should pay attention, that he would someday be a stout-hearted man with wisdom to equal any. He did not strike me as someone I should carry in my mind. I noticed, though, that his body reflected interest, though he did not shift his weight to look at me.

He stood sideways to me, perhaps not wishing to expose much to a stranger. A breeze moved through the opening of Lukwsh's lodge and ruffled the eagle fluff knotted into Shard's straight black hair. Two short braids framed his face and ended below his ears.

"Where my people began, far from this place," Lukwsh said, waving her hand to the south, "there is a story."

I understood then that she did not begin with the Wadadukas, which explained her height, her narrower face, the different way she wore her hair. I thought she would tell me more of how she came to this lodge, maybe where her man was, but instead she moved to the door where she picked up a large pot made of clay. It was the only such container in her lodge. Everything else appeared to be stored in woven things much larger than my missing treasure basket, more practical for traveling than the clay pot.

"The most beautiful and strongest clay pots," she continued, "the ones that honor their creator as uncommon, come from mixed clay. The old people, they take shards of pots with chips and cracks and broken lips, and after they are old, they throw them out. The desert takes them back. Then, years later, other *kasas*, grandmothers, they gather those old shards and grind them to a powder and add them to new clay that has never known the fire. The clay comes from two places: one fired and one fresh. The pots will only hold together and be strong because they have been blended."

She ran her hand around the jar, let her fingers trace the wide lip circling the opening. I noticed a small chip in the lip.

The lodge was quiet except for the gentle beating of the dog's tail against the earth, and I could tell that Lukwsh had gone away in her mind, was remembering another time. I thought she still spoke of the pot when she said: "This one is of the new clay, blended with the old, made stronger."

But then she nodded her chin to the tallest boy, set the pot down as if it was the most precious of treasures, and walked behind Shard, her hands on his shoulders.

The boy turned to face me straight away then. His cheekbones were high, and the sun had burned a line across his cheek, just below eyes that seemed to travel far and carried something familiar in them, something warm yet distant, something deep yet safe. He did not appear interested in any translation of what she had said, understood the trader language, too. He simply looked at me, boldly. His eyes were the color of obsidian and appeared as shiny. They bore into me. Full of judgment, I thought. He opened his mouth as if to speak, his tongue wet his thin lips, but he remained silent, wary.

I decided he did not like me.

My eyes found my fingers while he stared in silence.

"And your name?" Lukwsh asked.

I looked up to her and felt a catch in my voice as I tried to speak my name, so surprised that someone asked.

"Asiam," I answered, the word sounding foreign, and I wondered for the hundredth time what my mother must have called me, tried to bring that memory back.

Stink Bug chuckled, scratched at his hide breech, and tried to say it.

"And your dog?" Lukwsh asked.

"Pinenut," I said. "But he isn't mine, just one who followed me."

"You belong to him, then," Wren said. "And so he stays."

"Unless he does not get along with mine," Shard offered, his first words spoken from his silence.

I looked around, wondering how they could decide such things about Lukwsh's lodge. I scratched at the neck of Pinenut, grabbed him a little tighter while he panted beside me, but saw no signs of another dog.

"Yours is large enough to settle his own problems," Lukwsh said.

Shard did not smile. He wore hide clothing for the cool fall, and I was surprised, aware now he must have had his first kill and then a second, given hides to his grandmother to make into breechcloths for him. That meant he was older than he looked, almost a warrior.

"They will take you into the sunshine, Asiam," Lukwsh said, stepping over the discussion of dogs. My name sounded strange on her lips. "Your leg will heal better now with moving. There are things for you to do, to make your way here. You have rested enough."

A part of me did not wish to leave the routine of this lodge and go with these new children, even though I knew my future lay in how quickly I could heal and make myself useful. For a moment, I was still a small, wounded child.

"I must make water," I whispered to her.

"Yes. Make water," she said in a loud voice. "Then you help gather *wada.*"

"It hurts," I said, attempting to stand.

Lukwsh grunted. "Not as much as it might if you refuse to do what you are told. Come now. Before Stink Bug honors you with his namesake."

She signaled the others. I caught Stink Bug in a scowl.

Tiish, Stink Bug, moved slowly to assist me to stand, and I noticed when I looked down that my leg looked different, was thinner. Twists of sagebrush wrapped around the area below my knee held shadscale leaves over the wound. Something itched beneath it. There was little swelling.

Wren moved to help and performed a small dance with her hands and her feet as she moved toward me, tapping her head, rubbing her hands. My broken leg stayed straight when Wren pushed her slight shoulder under my other arm to hold me up. Stink Bug, with stocky legs and dough-like arms, took my elbow to assist but waited for Wren to finish her movements. I noticed a jagged scar on the side of her face that grew darker with her effort to help me stand.

I had no time to consider what her movements meant as together, we hobbled to the outside, to the brightness of the cool morning. A mist drifted over the lakes in the distance. The large geese that fly as an arrow's point were overhead, calling to each other as they headed south. The reeds and grasses were browner than what I remembered before I entered Lukwsh's lodge, the air cooler. I must have been in drifting sleeps for many days.

"I take her now," Lukwsh said.

She was so tall and strong she could walk with me by herself to the waste area some distance from the lodges. Quiet, she helped me bend and squat. A marsh hawk lit on a sagebrush, lifted its feet, clasping and releasing, looked down on me with stone eyes, arched beak, watching.

"Here," she said, handing me a juniper limb I hadn't noticed she carried. "Shard cut this, for your balance." There was no tenderness now in her words. She was all distant.

The hawk lifted, too, when I stood, spread its wings, but flew low as though leading us back toward the lodge.

"He is trained by Wren's *moo'a*," she said, her chin pointing toward the hawk. "Likes to eat scraps if you have any."

I hobbled with her help.

"Sometimes the hawk is all who will talk with Grey Doe, and she has to bargain with old meat for that."

Lukwsh chuckled at her own joke. I wondered where the *moo'a* was and what caused this pulling between them.

Shard was busy chipping an obsidian stone outside Lukwsh's lodge and did not look up when Stink Bug and Wren squinted into the sun like two puppies watching us return.

"She is yours now," Lukwsh told them. "Set her to work."

Shard twisted aside to let us pass but offered no help. I thought him bothersome, but neither Stink Bug nor Wren gave him notice. Over her shoulder, Wren spoke some of her language to Shard. He disagreed with a nod.

"Brother," she said, raising her voice an amount as tiny as a seed. "Now!"

Shard dropped his knife and stood at the same time, then stomped away to Lukwsh's lodge. I thought I caught a slight grin on his face as he passed me, and it seemed she could get her brothers to do what she wished.

Like a three-legged dog, Stink Bug, Wren, and I made our way to the marshy grasses nearer the lake, Pinenut at our side. The brown and white of the hawk's tail led us on.

The effort, little as it was, tired me. "Need to sit," I told them. "Feel sick."

Stink Bug let go to protect himself from my stomach's potential heaving, leaving Wren to handle all the weight of me. I fell, pulling her down with me. My leg burned with her weight, sent sharp pains up my back.

Wren picked herself up and scowled. Stink Bug watched warily. Behind us, I saw Shard at first dragging himself like a wet hide, but he quickened his steps at the sight of Wren brushing herself off. He carried a burden basket and two winnowing trays shaped like beaver tails.

"What's the matter with you?" he scolded. "Help her up."

He thrust the trays into my hands before I realized his anger was with Stink Bug and not me.

"No bother," Wren told him. "She was going to sit anyway."

The distinctive white stripe of the hawk flitted over us and disappeared. Pinenut, knowing when to leave a tense place, sniffed his way into the tall reeds and seablight and *wada* seed grasses. Wild rye wove and bobbed around him in the morning breeze.

"Go find your new horse," Wren told Shard. "Take Stink Bug with you. Let him ride away from us girls."

Shard hesitated only a moment as if being sure she was well, then pushed at Stink Bug's shoulder and moved the boy ahead of him.

"Go," he said, and they left.

I was aware of an inner warmth that formed at my edges when Wren grouped me with herself. "Us girls," she had said, as though I belonged beside her. She was as powerful as her name said. And kind. She wanted no one blamed, no one upset with another. She smiled at me as the boys left, an encouraging smile meant to lift me up. At least I thought it meant that. It had been so long since I had seen a smile directed just at me I wasn't sure if I could tell the ones that meant softness from those with a sting.

Clatter of activity drifted from a distance along with the smell of roasting ducks and fish, filtering over the grasses. Games began in sections of the camps around the lakes, final events before people returned to their own places to winter. I hoped Lives in Pain had already left. Children slapped mud into shapes of toys, tossed rocks, and picked pebbles, and for a moment I imagined Wren and I exchanging stones and smiles around a circle, Wren and I talking and sitting as friends.

For the first time I let myself think past this morning, this healing of my leg. The gathering would end. The games would be over. I could remain. If I did my share. If I did well. And then I could move on, in the spring, when I was older and stronger and not too far behind my parents.

A sigh escaped me.

"Don't complain," Wren warned.

I felt tired and a little chilled in the harvest sun, weary from my movements though I had not gone far, full of aches from my leg pain though it was less than before. But I hadn't meant to complain, hadn't thought my sigh sounded crabby.

"You must work," Wren said, serious, her voice soft as though sharing a secret. "No family can feed someone who is lazy. And if the winter is greedy and does not share many seeds to see us through, old ones will be fed first, not you. You must know this. Your place here is like a shaky bridge," she said, rubbing her hands again. "You could be gone—like that!" She clapped her hands once. "Look at your leg. Your bridge is not built well. And there are those who would keep you from making it stronger."

She began her dance again with her toe tapping and hand rubbing, but it did not distract me from the weight of her words. This was not a safe place, yet. I could not let myself forget my plan. I had a long winter to get through and more people who wished to kick me than to help me stand.

I reached for the winnowing basket and nodded to her to place the strands of grass in them. I would toss them to the air and catch the seeds as planned. But my hands shook, more from fear of what the future held than from weakness.

The commotion from the grasses startled both of us. Wild sounds of snarls and bites brought alarm. Reeds bent and moved as if a dust devil swirled inside them, but I saw nothing, only felt my stomach sink, only heard the growls of large dogs fighting.

"Flake!"

I heard Shard shout as he ran from the sagebrush corrals toward the reeds. "Come!" he shouted again, racing past us.

He entered the grasses so tall they swallowed him, and we saw only the top of his dark hair as he moved quickly toward the sounds.

"Your dog went in there," Stink Bug announced for me as he caught up with us. He did not follow his brother into the reeds to help out.

"I know where he went in," I said, my words snapping, covering up the danger I could feel sticking to my clammy hands. With the juniper stick I stood, shaky, but on my own for the moment.

Stink Bug laughed and scratched at a belly growing out over his buckskin. His grin formed into a sneer, and he licked his lips.

"Shard has a bi-i-i-g dog," he said stretching his words and hands to show me. "Like a small horse," he said. "Flake likes little dogs. Chews them into bits, buries the bones, likes to bury bones."

The sounds from the grasses were wild with fur and fangs tearing at flesh. There is no sound quite like a dogfight with its snarls and rips and little hope of interruption. I shouted, though I expected Pinenut could not hear me, would not stop if he had.

"If he doesn't chew yours up, and it's your dog that walks out," Stink Bug said, raising his hands like a cottonwood fluff drifting into the air, "you'll be gone next," he said and smiled.

"Be still!" Wren said, "Or help."

Like a crow, Wren hopped, hopped toward the edge of the marsh. She shaded her eyes from the sun and peered toward the ruckus in the reeds.

Stink Bug snorted and walked slowly toward the sweet grasses. He did not go far.

What was left of Pinenut as he skulked howling out through the reeds almost knocked him over. But I had a glance, just for a moment. Later, I wished I hadn't seen it. The dog flashed by me, eyes bleeding, chunks missing from his ears, blood pouring from his chest. Shreds of flesh along his side exposed pink mixed with fur and mud and seeds, a section of hide flapped from his side.

"Pinenut! Come, dog," I pleaded, my hand out in coaxing. "Come."

I couldn't run to him myself, had no one to ask to do my job. The dog did not notice me or could not hear me above the howling and barking or his own pain. His tail slid between his legs, and he worked his way back into the reeds before I could even take a step. Red glistened on the grass stems where he entered. I saw reeds move a short distance and then stop.

"Dangerous," Stink Bug offered when I started toward the last place the dog had been. "Should wait till Shard comes out with Flake."

My heart pounded for Pinenut. The prickle of dread for my fragile place within this gathering hovered around me.

"Don't see Shard's dog," Stink Bug said, casting his eyes into the distance. "Maybe Flake's dead." He smiled again when he turned. "You lose," he added and walked away.

I started after Pinenut then, thinking I should not hope for good things,

I should not trust in safety. None of these were reachable for a small child. Only wariness and distance and the hope of leaving should be my companions. Anger and frustration burned behind my eyes.

"Pinenut!" I pleaded. "Come!"

I hobbled only a few feet before Shard stepped out of the reeds and grabbed my arm.

"Don't follow," he said.

I pulled myself from him.

"It is my choice," I said.

"His wounds are bad," Shard said, stepping over my challenge. "His throat is torn. If he lives, it will not be for long."

"And your dog?" I asked, the tears stinging behind my nose. "What about him?"

For my answer, the largest, blackest dog with a massive head like a bear's, larger than I had ever seen, lumbered out of the reeds and moved slowly behind Shard. He too had wounds and a torn strip of hide, and through my tears I could see that he limped. His tail hung low but wagged, his tongue was pink and panting, and he wore a victor's eyes.

"I look for him," Shard said, "after I tend to Flake. But I will not bring him back. The reeds will be a good place for him to rest, forever."

I felt Wren's hand touch my arm like the flutter of a feather.

"Winnow your seeds," Shard told me in a softer voice than I had heard him use before. To Wren he said: "Show her what she needs to do to stay alive here. I will care for the dog."

When he left, followed by the black dog, I hobbled with my stick into the grasses.

At the sight of Pinenut, I dropped beside him, expecting to be brave. I straightened his head, didn't remember seeing so much gray in his muzzle. I patted him, thanked him for his comfort on those cold nights, and thought I did well with this leaving. But then I could not stop the tears. The ones of anger at the pain he suffered, the ones I hadn't shed when I fell down, the ones I buried deep when I felt helpless, lonely, or afraid, that covered up my longing to be somewhere else. They all came then, without stopping.

"You have poor ears," Shard said coming up behind me.

"I decide," I said, wiping my nose, "not you. Now you can burn or bury him. I've told him good-bye."

"What does that mean?" he asked genuinely. "Good-bye?"

I realized I'd used an English word and had to think. "That I will never see him again," I said. "It's what people say when they leave or someone has been left behind."

He grunted. "It is not a word we have. Go now. Help Wren, and I will do this thing."

As a woman having lived through many disappointments, I admire those who set aside their pain and get their tasks completed. Only later in my life did I pause to wonder when such people eased their grief or said good-bye, or did they?

That day, I thought that I would never stop my crying as I made my way out to the opening where Wren sat waiting. I couldn't imagine how I could put my hands to work.

But Wren took Shard's direction without question and led me too. She clasped a handful of rice grass stems with one hand and sliced them in a stroke with the *wehe* she pulled from her belt. Then she hopped, hopped back to the burden basket where she laid the long white stems. "For your aching bones," she called to me, "when we grind the seeds to flour." She made a motion like washing her hands, tapped her head with her fingers, then stopped in front of me.

"He did not mean it," she said, and I thought she spoke of Shard's dog. "He will find a way to give him rest and tend to him so coyotes or the other dogs will let his bones be. Work now," she added.

Stink Bug returned and was pressed by Wren into cutting cattail heads. He lowered one armful beside me. "Beat these," he said, "if you know how." Then he hurried to follow his brother who had left the grasses with Pinenut in his arms.

A riot of noise reached us from beyond the lodges, a welcome distraction of dust-covered horsemen and the chatter of excitement. A thick-waisted woman dismounted. We heard bursts of laughter, excited voices, and dogs barking at new arrivals.

Wren paused and shaded her eyes with her small hand. I noticed a healed scar sliced below her little finger, wrapping around to the palm.

"It's Sarah," Wren said, turning to tell me in a whisper. "With news, maybe. Don't tell Wuzzie." She looked around. "It will make his day go bad."

She took a step forward, then looked back at me, a question forming on her lips. Before she asked it, the dreamy look in her eyes took over her face, and without warning, she dropped to the grass as though the earth had been pulled from beneath her.

Her slender body became a mass of motion, jerks and twists and jumps. Her small hands arched awkwardly, away from her body; her head threw itself back; her hair gouged into dirt. Sounds as of a sick person came from her throat.

I reached for her, pain racing up my leg, and watched from a distance that might be miles instead of inches as her eyes disappeared from her face, leaving white. Wet bubbles formed at the corners of her mouth.

"Lukwsh!" I shouted. "Help!"

My voice was from a small, unfamiliar child, and there were many men and women laughing and talking some distance away, conferring with the people just arriving, dogs barking, too much noise.

"Shard! Stink Bug," I tried again, louder, but did not see them or anyone I knew.

But Flake appeared like a shadow brushing past me. His presence frightened me as he bounded close to Wren and barked, short, steady barks, jumping around her, as though aware something was wrong and he should not leave. Blood sprayed from his ear wound when his barks shook his head.

Wren's jerking movements brought her closer to me. Flake jabbed toward her, then back, shoulders lowered, barking. I expected Shard to follow his dog, but he did not appear.

I needed to do something, didn't know whether to leave for help or stay with her. With effort I touched Wren's shoulder, felt the jerking move from my fingertips to my fear of being able to do nothing, of hoping the dog would not object, hoping his barks would bring help.

Her shoulder felt stiff, and her face grimaced and strained. I started to rise, to lean over her and hold her face in my hands. I shouted again and lifted Wren's arm to bring her closer, to do something well in this day of entanglement and helpless pain. I wanted to do something before this presence moved beside me, grabbed and pinched my hand and wrenched it from Wren's shoulder.

VISITS

WUZZIE STOOD THERE, a black obsidian *wehe* thonged to his side.

"Get back," he hissed, and I did.

He dropped beside Wren and wrapped her in his arms like a baby swaddled in its willow board. He began to sing.

The dog whimpered, quieted, turned, and lay down.

Wuzzie rocked back and forth with Wren in his arms while I stared, still startled by his hairless head, the bareness of his face, the way his two-colored eyes seemed to float up into his scalp with no eyebrows to separate seeing from his forehead. His voice calmed Wren, and her body stopped hopping and jumping. A string of pelicans drifted across the sky above us, and my heart began beating without running a race.

The dog rested his dark head on his paws, eyes watching Wren. He had a wound on his face and a chunk hung from his ear, but otherwise he looked little troubled by the fight that took Pinenut. I shivered and turned away.

The girl looked to be asleep in Wuzzie's arms.

"Better," Wuzzie said, no longer singing. I thought he spoke of Wren, but he turned finally and nodded his chin toward my leg. With one hand, he reached out to touch the shadscale leaves that wrapped it. I jerked at his touch.

"You will climb rock walls again," he laughed, "earn the *wada* Wren gathers for you."

"I do things, now," I told him, alert to the influence he might have in my staying. I showed him the winnowing tray. "I am familiar with these *wada*."

I wanted to ask him about Wren, why the dreamy look turned to motion then into sleep. I wanted to ask if the scars that marked her were from falls. But he behaved as though she was not present, so I kept quiet and let my hands winnow seeds.

Wren moved but stayed asleep, so Wuzzie laid her down, her cheek pressed against the soft grass, her legs curled up as though she was merely resting.

"What happens?" I asked him, finally brave.

He stared at the sleeping form, paused so long I did not know if he refused to tell me or if he too had fallen asleep. When he did talk, his words were wispy, and he moved closer to me, his breath warm on my face.

"Chosen people speak with spirits," he said, his voice promising a secret.

"Spirits?" I said. I had seen nothing, was surprised he thought some spirit might take an interest.

"Some of us choose when we will go away to meet with them; others have it happen when they are not expecting, do not do the choosing." His eyes left mine to look at Wren; his long fingers stroked her bare arm as she slept.

"It is like this with Wren," he continued. "I know this. Her spirits come often to her, cause her to give her whole body to their wish for attention. So she drops and goes to them in her mind. Those chosen must find ways to work their power, not resist or try to stop it."

"Spirits?" I asked again, uncertain that such things even existed.

He stopped stroking her arm but did not turn.

"You question me?" he asked, looking into the distance.

I fidgeted with my shirt, smoothed it, did not want to make him angry, but did not understand.

"Your presence bothers," he said then, dismissing me as an insignificant being. "If you have no spirit speaking to you, stay quiet. Get away from the one being chosen. Do not try to touch her." His face moved closer to mine. "Or you may find yourself taken up like the ghosts of those who die, who come to take the living when they get in the way."

His hand fluttered into the air above my head; his eyes opened wide and then he closed them.

The breathing of a snake came to mind, and I moved backward, beyond his reach.

"If you know the spirit songs as I do," he said in his fluttering voice, all gentle now, "you may speak with them." He smiled, but his eyes carried both fire and ice. "But only those *poohaga'yoo* like me must ever interfere."

Pride crossed his words.

"Never interfere," he repeated, his voice low now. "Never."

I had no interest in interfering nor speaking with spirits, no wish to name a trouble I could not see when I had many I could touch right here beside me. Watching him, I wondered if he put too much stock in spirits. None had given him height or a handsome face or two legs the same length.

The dog perked its ears at attention, watching, wary too, perhaps, of the shifting of this man. Wuzzie slid his brown- and blue-eyed gaze to my face, slid across me like a catfish in a murky lake.

"Such power could be taken, used for evil. It might even force you from this place," he warned.

That snake smile eased onto his face. Like a slice of quick pain, it left a bad memory. "Who knows what might happen if you meddle with spirits."

He chose to believe in them, but not me. I would look for real ways to solve my problems, real things that I could see and touch to set me on my path again, get me well so I could leave.

"Never meddle," Wuzzie repeated.

"Who meddles?" Wren asked as though arriving from a deep sleep.

She sat and stretched and gazed, the dreamy eyes the same as before. I thought Wuzzie wrong to think she had conversed with spirits. I had seen or heard nothing.

Flake stood and shook himself. I looked up to his head as I sat beside him, watching his pink tongue hang between loose, black jowls. He sneezed, his head shaking a little less blood from his ears. Wren grabbed the dog's hide and pulled herself to sit, and the dog licked at her as though she belonged to his litter.

"Did you see Sarah? Does Lukwsh know?" she asked.

Wuzzie snorted, nodded his head toward the commotion that continued closer to the camp. "Her name is Thocmetone, not Sarah. And you do well to stay away from her."

He stood, peering in the direction, but short like us, he could see little happening in the grassy area in the narrows between Lake Harney and the little one, Mud. His next words were riddled with disgust. "She does not know who she is, but I do. She is like a mind sickness that knows no cure, that traveler."

He spit, then wiped his mouth with the back of his hand as though trying to take a bad taste from his tongue. He walked in the direction of the activity, telling us to stay away.

Wren sighed deeply. "I am tired. I rest now."

"Where do you live?" I asked.

"In my mother's lodge," she said, surprised. "Now you are well enough to work, we can return. It will not make *Moo'a* happy, but we will be. She wakes up crabby and tries to give it away all day."

She performed the little dance before walking toward Lukwsh's lodge. Flake shifted when she moved and trotted with her, his shiny fur rolling as he walked, glistening like fish oil wiped across his back.

I sat alone in the center of a whirlwind. So they belonged to Lukwsh's lodge, were not visitors at all. I was the visitor, the one who could be asked to leave.

A splash and flutter of white flushed up from the lake, and I watched more pelicans ease through the air like a strand of sea shells against blue cloth. Their movement sent mud hens skittering across the water. Black terns and glossy-faced birds, mallards, then geese lifted and settled like a breeze rising and lowering on the lake. Some things were familiar here; the birds and lakes gave gifts that never changed. But much that happened felt like walking on a spring mud flat, soft and uneasy.

A chill fluttered over me. Movement would warm me up.

The winnowing tray sat beside me, and I piled seed pods in the smallest basket, lifted brown cattails and brushed them into the tray. I thought of my basket and my missing treasures and wondered if my leg would heal enough before snow fell for me to search for it.

The effort involved in standing tired me. I chose next a clumsy plan, one to ease Lukwsh's burden, Wren's too, and let them know that I was useful. I stood, picked up the seeds we'd winnowed, and started out toward Wren's lodge. And her brothers', too.

Lukwsh had raised some of the tule mats part way up the willow bends so the cool breeze could flutter the flicker feathers and bring in the last days of snowless air. Shafts of light poured inside, so I could see her kneeling and Wren's legs beside her. But a third set of knees were there as well.

The third person, a woman, spoke in Paiute with tightness and a raised voice, and I wondered if the knees belonged to Thocmetone. It sounded as if Lukwsh was being scolded, and I wondered what kind of friend this woman was. Hesitation greeted me, but my shadow crossed the opening and Wren motioned me inside before I could escape. Her small eyes touched me here and there with tender looks.

The scolding woman did not step aside when I entered, so I almost bumped her with my load and my walking stick and my stiffly held leg. Wren scampered around, made a place for me to sit across from the opening, but I stood, afraid to move. Lukwsh said something to the other woman, and as my eyes adjusted, I recognized Grey Doe, who grunted and glared at me from the corner of her eye as if vermin had entered uninvited.

"My husband's mother, Grey Doe," Lukwsh said, introducing. "Wren's *moo'a.*"

Grey Doe's face was a brown winter desert without warmth. She had a rounder face than Lukwsh and smaller eyes and carried her chin up, out, as though it challenged the air to move aside before she entered it.

But she was a grandmother, so I dropped my eyes, respectful. She continued her conversation as though alone with Lukwsh. I understood little of what she said. Lukwsh answered her in the trading language, so I made connections about the different way in which Grey Doe and Lukwsh saw the world.

"What she brings is for her people, our people," Lukwsh answered Grey Doe's words.

She moved baskets, sorting, busy twisting bulrush for duck-egg bags.

"The big war takes much from their government," she continued. "There is little left and many are hungry. If the army wishes to give us food, why not take it while we can? Some of us may be pleased this winter, if we do not store seeds enough."

She reached and removed the basket from my hands as she talked, but did not look at my face.

Grey Doe spit out a question, glared at me.

"She will earn her way. But you do not speak of this one," she said, nodding toward me. "It is Sarah you dislike."

From the corner of my downcast eyes I saw that Grey Doe's left arm hung limp, shriveled like a small child's, but she managed force with her words.

"A bay city," Lukwsh said in answer to Grey Doe's next words. "San-Fran-cis-co, na?" She said it to me as if I might know. "Many clap their hands at her, discover our people through her words. Others dance on a high platform, a stage. And Old Winnemucca goes also. Sarah is not alone."

Grey Doe's voice raised high, and she stood, began to pace, her left arm limp, swinging. Brown eyes snapped at Lukwsh, who listened, respectful, nodding while she helped me move my leg out of the old woman's way, told me with her eyes to remain quiet.

"I will call her Thocmetone if that pleases you, husband's mother," Lukwsh said.

Grey Doe's bony fingers grabbed her rabbit cape tighter around her neck. She tossed her chin my way, spit some words. Thin braids the color of singed sage swung as she paced.

Lukwsh nodded. "It may be so, what you say, though I do not see Thocmetone's skin changing color. Owls do not become wolves. White does not become brown."

Was this Thocmetone a white woman? I wondered. Or someone who traveled like the warriors, in and out, along the Military Highway? Toward the ocean where my parents went?

A grunt escaped Grey Doe's mouth, and she said something else before swinging her lifeless arm before her, using her good shoulder to push her way through tules covering the door, misery and bother mingling in the air about her as she left.

In the people's language, Lukwsh spoke to Wren. The girl's lower lip stuck out in protest, and she left, though not before the toe tapping of each foot, washed hands, and a finger touch to her head, the same dance as before. She smiled at me again, then bounced after Grey Doe, and I heard her call to her to wait up.

"She is still missing her son," Lukwsh said to me when we were alone. "Grey Doe's son lost his first wife some time ago, before Wren. I joined later with that one." It pleased me she invited me in closer by telling me some of her story.

"We brought Shard and Stink Bug back to their father's lodge from Grey Doe's," she said. "After a while, we prepared for *our* child."

She continued her work, and I thought she had nothing more to say when she added: "Wren comes in a different way than Shard and Stink Bug. She comes to Grey Doe's son and me."

Her hands became quiet as if to better hold the memory.

"Grey Doe's son, my husband…" She sighed. "It has been barely one cycle of seasons since he left us."

A flicker of grief sliced across her face, and I wondered if this was why Shard seemed to carry little warmth in his.

"It is not a good time for Grey Doe," Lukwsh continued. "And she does not think it wise for any of the people to spend time with the white-faced, hairy *tibos* who can never be satisfied."

She was quiet again and then as though to reassure me said, "It is not of your concern, Asiam." Her hand pushed the air to the ground, dismissing the subject. She stood and looked around the lodge as though searching.

But even with my few years, I knew that her last words were more hope than promise.

Lukwsh busied herself with the bulrush egg bag, stacked winnowing trays, carried them outside to the roasting fire, where I watched her tall back bend to the low flames. The tule walls and the cattail coverings over willow, the dust and the empty lodge closed around me, stifled my breathing inside, alone.

"Let me help," I shouted to Lukwsh who did not discourage my offer. Nor did she help me hobble to the fire.

The flames were low, and she stirred the *wada* seed pods I knew would turn our fingers black when we sifted, later, through the cool ashes, broke them open, and removed the tiny *wada* for storage. In silence, she stirred them slowly for even roasting, low smoke lifting to the sky as she pushed the roasted pods to the outside of the fire, took fresh pods I handed her to replace them. I beat the cattails on the ground, picked up the fuzz, and dropped it into a water basket. I had never been allowed to do more than this with the Modocs, but I had watched and learned. Now, with the stirring sticks I lifted the soaked fuzz like flour and dropped it gently into the fire. These seeds would supply for winter, keep us alive through heavy snows and iced-over lakes, along with the few ducks and geese we might gather up. Or an unsuspecting antelope.

Lukwsh stirred the roasted fuzz from the flame, and my fingers become dark with brushing the seeds in the winnowing basket, taking them from the ash-laden fuzz. It was a soothing cycle—this gathering, roasting, sifting, and storing—and we spent much of the afternoon together working in silence.

I did not ask her about Wren. I did not speak of my wonder about Stink Bug and Shard and how they all came together in the shadow of Grey Doe. I did not speak of my questions of the woman who caused Wuzzie to spit. It was not my place to ask, though I burned with questions, especially about the woman Sarah.

With the tiredness of the day, my heart began throbbing in my leg, my head nodded while I sat.

"Go inside," Lukwsh said, noticing. "You will be of no value if you fall into the fire. Eat some pine nut stew and dried duck and drink your tea again."

I followed her advice and soon slept.

When I awoke, the woman with many names—Sarah Winnemucca, Thocmetone, Shell Flower—sat across from me inside Lukwsh's lodge. She and Lukwsh pressed each other into arms of friendship and spoke together using trade talk, then Paiute and some other sounds like *tibo* words. They bent their heads to each other and chattered like sisters while they twisted tules into duck decoys and laughed, then turned serious, with no space between.

Sarah looked like a squash to me, colorful and all one size with no waist. Her mouth worked into a grin, followed by an explosion of words that made Lukwsh laugh, her lip rolling under as if stuck on her upper teeth. It sounded as if they spoke of men and babies and travel and gossip, and I pretended to be asleep, barely opened my eyes so I could watch.

What Sarah wore caught my attention next. She wore cloth clothes, not buckskin, and silver rings that sparkled on her fingers and a necklace of shiny black beads separated by smaller ones and links of a tiny black chain. At the base of her necklace hung a cross with the form of a man hanging. I stared at the necklace, was reminded of my own lost treasure lying at the base of Dog Mountain.

"You like these?" she asked me.

I startled, caught in my stare.

"My prayer memory," she said, fingering the beads. "Look closer."

Sarah's dark hair was piled high on her head, not in braids. It had been flattened some by the wide-brimmed hat that lay beside her. She stayed kneeling, her fingers touching the little beads from memory.

"From my Christian family," Sarah said in the jargon so I could understand. "Each reminds me of the prayer words. In case I forget, as happens to old women like Lukwsh and me." She laughed and took Lukwsh with her.

My confusion expanded. I did not know this Christian nor who was so old as to forget what matters. I thought they were teasing.

"You like it?" she asked.

It reminded me of something missing and I did not respond, but I watched this woman, her eyes the color of cattails, carrying her memory on her breast. I built courage to speak.

Sarah shrugged at my silence and returned to her task, jabbering in jargon with Lukwsh. She stripped and twisted the tules that would fool the ducks in the morning. The women worked, weaving in and out of quiet.

"She is like a rainbow with many colors," I told Lukwsh when Sarah stepped outside to speak with an old friend who came looking for her, to show off a new baby.

"She requires notice," Lukwsh said, agreeing, affection for Sarah in her voice.

An ache of awareness pierced me, of the soft sentiment between friends, a fondness that I did not share with any. I had not even Pinenut to tell my day to. Tears burned again, and sadness and disappointment made me risk Lukwsh's disapproval by asking questions.

"Why does she travel?" I asked, watching as Sarah cooed to the woman's chubby *onga'a*. "Does she have babies? A man to hunt for her? Why does Wuzzie hate her?"

"She is a Paiute, from Pyramid Lake. Her grandfather, Old Winnemucca, raised her. He believes those with pale skin," her eyes rested on my milky face, "are friends. She speaks their language. He took her to California, and white people raised her. They gave her the Christian name and their religion."

"Like the clay pot," I said.

Lukwsh raised an eyebrow at me, surprise in her face. She said: "She can dance on light feet with the people and stand solid on a stage in San-Fran-cis-co to share the Paiutes' story. She is strong. Blends old and new."

She was a woman who had many faces and much power and could lead people into the white world, I learned. I wanted to gain my speaking courage and stay closer to her side.

"Why does Wuzzie wish you did not come?" I asked Sarah when she stepped back inside.

"O ho!" Sarah said. "You found your voice."

Lukwsh frowned, but she did not scold.

Sarah sighed. "He does not know how many others there are beyond these lakes and deserts, how many will come and take what they can if we are nothing more to them than rabbits. Wuzzie is like old men who stay away and so they stumble on change. Younger braves and women will soon tell him what to do."

Lukwsh's eyes got large with the sound of such a challenge.

"It is so," Sarah answered her friend's eyes. "I tell them, those in the cities, that we are more than docile animals to be hunted down and shot. We are distant relatives, I tell them."

She stayed kneeling, but her arms spread wide, expansive, as though we were gathered before her to hear her story, her bead necklace bouncing on her chest as she spoke, a light in her eyes, fast walking in her words.

"You tell them we belong to the same family?" Lukwsh asked. "They must argue with that."

"They cry; tears even flow. I say: 'We are your mothers and sisters, your uncles and brothers. We belong together!' That is what I tell them on the stage in San-Fran-cis-co. My grandfather," she explained to me, "believes the dream given him years ago, that someday we would meet our lost brothers, the pale owl children who were separated from us and taken across the ocean to make their way back. When they were better behaved."

"And they listen?" Lukwsh said, hands stopped in midair, head cocked in disbelief. "Those people believe what Old Winnemucca believes, what you tell them? That cannot be so. The whites in this country," she nodded her head toward Snow Mountain, "they are not that well behaved. Who believes you?" She picked up a tule, shook her head in disbelief.

Sarah looked at her, watched Lukwsh put a tule reed in her mouth, hold it with her lips while she stripped it to the width she wished.

"I do not know what they believe, only that if they think it possible and their Christian hearts are pure as new snow but not as cold, then they may not let their distant relatives go hungry this winter or the next. They may choose not to let their government decide to kill us or hold back the tools and seeds promised that keep us from starving. That is my only reason for telling them the story. They will come to you, too," Sarah continued in something of a whisper. "And they will promise you seeds to plant and special knives to harvest heads of wheat and tell you to stay in one place where you belong, not to travel for roots or deer meat. Be wary."

She lifted one of the greasewood sticks Lukwsh had lying between them, poked it into the tule frame she worked in her hands.

"Too hard to know who friends are," Lukwsh said.

"Talk only with the soldiers," Sarah told her. "They are wiser than the agents. Get them to move the agents to bring you seeds and what you need to harvest first, before you agree to anything the agents say about the land. We have had our own problems on our reserve."

"But if they are family?" I said, confused by the mixture of people who could touch the Paiute lives.

"Even good families can have bothersome brothers," she said to me and laughed, but it sounded like a sadness.

"Soldiers," I said, clinging to the faint memory of my father.

"It is not my decision who to speak with," Lukwsh said. She moved away from Sarah ever so slightly, as though her words brought a space between them.

"Each will need to choose."

"But the army does not come this way. Nor agents. We gather our own food, make no trouble."

Lukwsh pulled a small cattail rope around the bundle of tules she held in her hand, doubling three and four of the wide reeds to form the duck decoy's body. I had seen these made before by Lives in Pain, but Lukwsh worked faster, her hands surer in the waning afternoon light.

Sarah shook her head, looked at me directly while she spread the tules of her decoy like a fan of feathers. "Each will cull, like separating ripe huckleberries from hard ones," she said. "They will spread us out like these tail feathers, separate us, make us wonder where we belong. We might forget that we are from one source."

"My people at Warm Springs signed a treaty," Lukwsh said, defense in her voice. "They do not need to stay in one place."

"O ho!" Sarah said. "You Warm Springs and your Teninos and Wascos think you have no trouble now. It will not last!" She spoke as though she had visions of some future time. The tules rested on her wide thighs; the rings on her fingers peered out from the reeds like noses beneath a threadbare blanket on a cold morning.

"The Bannocks and the Snakes do not like the reserve set aside for them or their agent who they say cheats them. Soon they will come here, wonder why you are allowed to wander where you wish while they are asked to stay in one spot. You will remember what I say when that time comes."

Sarah looked around, missing something, stopped her work with reeds, and added: "Then only the army will stand between you and empty bellies."

"There is always more than one way," Lukwsh said.

Sarah's eyes searched as though she had not heard her or wished to talk no longer. I could tell she sought the dead duck. Neither she nor Lukwsh could go further making their decoys without dead birds, without real feathers and hides to stretch across the tule frames. To fool a live, flying duck required first something of its own kind to land beside, belong with. I started to share this, tell her there were no ducks, when Shard entered and what he held in his hand by their necks made my thoughts a lie.

"Good," Lukwsh said, a smile on her face. "We need the dead to make this one look alive. It is a strange thing."

Sarah clucked her tongue, admiring the plump mud hens. She took a bird from Shard's hand, held it, neck and head down, so the fluff of the feathers fanned out.

"Life could not be recognized without death," Sarah said.

"I would try a time without it," Lukwsh said and nodded her head once to Shard in thanks.

She stood among a cluster of men and women beyond the main fire, her head bent to Sarah. Lukwsh spoke softly and then she and the men stepped back in laughter at what was said. Lukwsh smiled, and it pleased me to see this woman in a warm place, among *hitse*. No more gatherings were planned before people returned to their wintering sites, and it appeared that I would stay. Lives in Pain had not renewed his argument with Lukwsh. No one else had claimed me as their marked child. Tonight Shard and Stink Bug would roll mats on their side of the lodge, and Wren would roll hers next to mine. Wren told me of this, and it must have been their coming and going through my drift of hazy sleep and pain that I felt but did not see.

Shard appeared beside me and lifted his hand, a swift movement. Without thinking I crouched low, squeezed my eyes in habit, waiting to be hit or kicked. My face flushed warm.

"I would touch the shadscale wrap, to make it fit tight through the night," Shard said.

I expected pain instead of gentle touches.

"The leg heals well," I said, pulling away from him, looking around for his dog. I had not talked with him since he tended to Pinenut.

As though he knew my mind, he said, "The dog is taken care of. His paws were not webbed. He would have fished poorly."

"He was useful for hauling and for flushing ducks."

Shard shrugged his shoulders. "Flake fishes," he said, though I could not imagine the big dog entering the lakes to fish.

Shard eased himself down beside me as though he thought I wished it.

I didn't.

It was Sarah who I wanted to sit close to now, Sarah who moved between two worlds, both of which I lived in, though one was only in my mind. It was Sarah who I imagined could expand my plan for searching. I would find out how long she'd be here, when in the spring she'd return. If the food lasted and I lived, made myself useful in this lodge of many people, perhaps I could go with her when she went to the cities. Perhaps she would understand my wish like a deep thirst to search another world to find where I belonged.

But Sarah stood with a circle of men and women, laughing and sharing stories in a language I did not understand.

Maybe in the morning, I told myself. I will find her in the morning.

Lives in Pain hobbled on the other side of the fire, and I thought he glared through the lifting smoke. I chose not to touch that trouble. He should be gone in the morning, back with the Modocs.

Across the grass circle I watched Wren run errands for Grey Doe's one-hand commands, bringing sweets to her and a blanket to cover her thin legs while she and other old women sat in places of honor where they could see the dancers without straining. Drummers beat out the steady rhythm, the fire flickering on faces intent on the dance. I watched people pair off, step back away from the grass flattened by moccasined feet.

Only Stink Bug took away from the quiet of the moment. I had not seen him for some time. He had skill in avoiding places of work. When I did spy his chubby frame closer to the wickiups, farther from the fire, I wished I hadn't. And I wondered if what he did with the dogs was what he meant someday for me.

I watched him in unsettled silence, the sounds of the drums still beating in my ears. He poked with a stick at a litter of pups, causing growls and snarls. I started toward him. Seeing me, he stopped and disappeared into the crowd.

"What's wrong?" Shard asked behind me.

"Just puppies," I lied, not telling him how my heart beat watching the dogs scatter, defending themselves weakly against a larger intruder, one who did not belong.

STRUGGLING SPIRITS

IN THE YEAR I INTERFERED WITH what Wuzzie called "Wren's spirits," spring came early but did not forewarn.

Cool rains and early snowmelt from Snow Mountain and the Strawberries flooded little Mud and Malheur Lakes and created another lake beyond them, washed over marshes and willow-lined sloughs. The Silvies River ran swiftly, carrying gifts of winter to the Malheur. From Snow Mountain into the Malheur River, sheets of ice cracked and clattered in the night, waking us. We thought at first that someone attacked with the pop-pop of rifle shots, but it was only the Silvies' ice breaking up, announcing the spring.

In the meadows, not far from where I first fell from the lava rocks, flowers bloomed. Large blossoms of a dozen tints and sizes spilled over the plains like stained rocks beneath a fast moving stream, bright and brushed with color.

Our cluster of wickiups sat near the Silvies River on the north side of the growing Malheur Lake. At the lake's edges, in the warm spring sun, bare-breasted women squealed as they splashed and dipped their strong arms deep into reedy water seeking tule roots so tasty in spring. Dogs watched in wonder, and small children scampered about in the first warmth of the season. Older ones looked after younger brothers and sisters in their cradle boards, while others directed the moving of wickiups, helped build new ones away from the slow seeping lakes. Boys took their dogs to corner marmot pups, with plans to turn them into pets kept on a leather string. Grey Doe trained another young hawk.

I had not seen Sarah for nearly two years.

She took her leave without excitement the morning after I first met her, and I wondered if the Pyramid Lake Paiutes too lacked the word for good-bye. Rumors flew about her, though. About her travels, what she shared with *tibos* about the people, that she was too friendly with soldiers, or that her skin had turned white. Even Lukwsh found speaking of her troublesome, must have, since she rarely chose to do it.

Her absence did not stop my yearning, my wondering what her life was like, how I might find a way to travel with her to a target of my own.

Several of the young men, Shard included, had taken jobs away in the winter with *tibo* ranchers. With their earnings, they rode to Canyon City to purchase grain and blankets they delivered to us, then rode back to the "bunkhouse" at night. We saw little of them, but they remembered us, still kept us in food like a good son or husband.

When spring came, their visits were a little longer, and I hovered around, listening for stories of how they lived and worked in white men's worlds.

A blond-haired smithy they called "Johansen" showed Shard ways to fix wagons and make tools. He brought one or two for Lukwsh that spring.

"O-o-o-h. So smooth," she said of the *kapn* he handed her. "I will dig deep with this, put lots more camas in my Sally Bag."

He beamed with her praise and would have stayed longer, told her more, if Grey Doe had not appeared with her scowl.

"Take it away!" she said when he handed one to her as well. "My hands will not touch that thing." She raised her one good hand. "What that Swede man shows you to make could hurt the roots. Next you will bring us hoes and tell us to dig up the fields and plant corn. Uch!" she said turning her back, dismissing his gift. "You challenge each spring enough with the cattle your ranch-man lets graze on the prairie."

Her lip curled, her chin lifted toward me as she added, "And with that one still with us."

He had made no *kapn* for me and gave the one Grey Doe rejected to Wren. She took it with her toe-tapping dance, movements that became more complex as she entered each spring.

His gift to Wren was expected, though it did not stop the prick of shame I felt for failing to warrant his favor. Neither did it stop my wish to speak with him and question what he knew.

Flake followed him toward the place where the men worked on tule boats, getting ready to gather duck eggs. I had made peace with the dog, even laughed at his nose caked in mud from his sniffing at the lakes, liked to watch his brown eyes almost sleep when I scratched that place along his nose. I started after them.

I walked past *moo'as* who clucked their tongues, giving directions for the right way things should be done while others peeled tule roots in the afternoon sun and stacked them beside grass shelters newly built. Women handed wet roots to others, moisture dripping off tiny cold bumps along their brown arms. With bones aching from the wet spring, older girls—like me—moved the cradle boards heavy with plump babies so the sun's rays gently filtered through woven willow hoods that arched out over the babies' heads. The thinness of a long winter could be seen in the *moo'as'* faces as they watched and sang their soothing songs.

I moved with fragile force, my leg still aching from the cold that found its way along my healed bone. I hoped any who noticed me would assume I had a purpose. And I did.

"You walk as fast as you ride," I said, breathless, catching up to Shard. He looked surprised to see me, moved his head to the side as if uncertain who walked beside him. "I'm the same," I said, giving Flake wide distance between us.

Shard grunted, and for a moment my boldness frightened me. Perhaps I had assumed too much. But I persisted with my effort, trying what I'd seen older girls do to find favor.

"The *kapn* is a good one," I said. "Lukwsh likes it." The dog sniffed at me, and my fingers wiped at his head. "You make other things?"

He shrugged his shoulders. I didn't know then he carried with him the sting of Grey Doe's words, his own struggle with whether leaving was the thing to do, if blending with the ranchers to help feed the people would bring comfort or confusion. I did not occupy myself with such thoughts then.

"What do the women do?" I said into the pause that always preceded Shard's statements, as though he heard the words but took extra time for them to travel to his mouth.

"Who notices?" he said.

"Is it as Sarah told us? That some speak kindly? That they wear necklaces to remember their religion? Have you seen soldiers who are friendly, or did she tell that as a story?"

Silence, then, "Such a meddler," Shard said, a smirk on his face like an eagle pestered by a magpie. "I thought Wuzzie told you not to meddle."

"Just stretching my wisdom," I said.

He laughed. "Your meddling gets more skillful."

From a distance, Wren waved her new gift at us, then turned back to show more friends, tapping her head with her fingers.

"She does the dance often," I said.

A meadowlark warbled, landed on a blade of grass that barely held the bird's weight.

"We were to watch her," Shard said, his eyes far away, remembering a time past, "Stink Bug and I. One day we did not. She walked behind a new horse, a spirited dog beside her. The horse was not pleased and kicked both. She almost died. But Wuzzie made her well."

"Wuzzie says she speaks with spirits when she dances or falls."

Shard said nothing.

"I do not believe in them—spirits," I told him, my slender shoulders standing straighter. I pushed long strands of hair the breeze blew into my eyes.

"It has grown, the time she takes," he said. "Now that I am gone I see she adds the finger dance." His own fingers repeated Wren's movements. He shook his head.

"She says she must do it. I tried to make her stop once," I said. "But she cried."

I waited for Shard's pause then heard him say: "You must have upset the spirits. They make her complete the dance to stop her crying."

As an older, wiser woman, I know there is one Spirit, the One and only One. I know that now. And even then I questioned in my mind what Shard had said. But such things were new to me, the talk of spirits moving through some dance. The closest I had come to even sensing such a Spirit then had been one night when I had raised my eyes to a moonless sky dotted with blinking stars and wondered who had made it, had caused the glitter and the raven sky. Oh, I remembered asking once for help, behind a disappearing wagon, hoping someone would keep me from harm while I hung onto a gold chain and my fleeting memories. The Modocs came, but I did not think of them as answer to a prayer, though perhaps they were. For here I am now, a grown woman, granted keenness and a clarity about who controls all things, who quenches every thirst, who is the one true Spirit.

But then, Shard's words troubled me like the heavy snap and friction that precedes a summer storm.

"You found a way to be a good brother," I said.

He grunted, not sure what to do with my noticing of how he solved his problem.

"I can set it aside," I said, "except when she falls down. Then it is hard not to touch her."

"Who says Wren cannot be touched?" Shard asked, surprised.

I hesitated. "Perhaps it is the language. I do not speak it well yet, just trade words."

"Who tells you this?" he said, his voice demanding now.

"Wuzzie. He said I must never touch her when the spirits speak to her, when she dances or falls down."

"This is new," Shard says. "I will speak to him."

"No!" I said, clutching his arm, dropping my hand when he stopped. "Wuzzie is like an old marmot: he does not like to be bothered with young pups."

Shard's shoulders eased and he smiled. "This is a good picture of Wuzzie, one to keep in mind."

I relaxed until he added, "When I ask him why he says we must not reach out to Wren."

I wished I had not spoken, at least of Wuzzie and his spirits. I wanted to talk about what happened in the other places, to gather up news as I gathered grasses for winnowing. I would winnow the ideas, decide what would work when I was ready to leave.

Even the narrow land place between the lakes disappeared under the spring flood. The men gathered tules and cattail leaves strong enough to have withstood the winter storms and spent their mornings soaking and twisting leaves into rope, making slender, sturdy boats. Buck Brush, Oytes, and Shard and the many uncles and cousins used the boats not just for harvesting ducks and mud hen eggs but to ease their way across the narrows in high water, to go from the north to south side of the lakes, to gather up ducks the dogs had helped push into nets.

I watched the making of the tule crafts, silence required. Shard's elbows reached out like arrowheads from his hips as he stood to see what had been done. From a distance he could be selected from many by those elbows, poking out.

My eyes had witnessed the making of boats and the gathering of tules many times now, and I felt suddenly grateful, with the warm sun on my face and the smell of spring earth in the air, to live where all that the people needed had been supplied.

"Not so strange," Grey Doe said when Lukwsh handed her the tubers dripping wet from the reedy lake. "This much water has happened in my life before, that time when Oytes and Ega— when my son broke the new colts in the corrals. We could barely see the tops of sagebrush in places. Remember? Those horses tired fast."

I dropped my own roots near her, stepped back, away from the force of future words. I stumbled briefly over Flake, who shook his black, wet body and flopped hard in the sun.

"Oytes fell in a flooded corral, remember? That friend of my son." Grey Doe poked her chin to the ground.

"He landed on water instead of hard ground," Lukwsh said, brushing the wetness from her arms with her cupped hand. "Doesn't hurt his head so much."

She reached for a cloth shirt lying on the grass and covered her shivering body. Grey Doe's latest marsh hawk flew low, landed on a tule lodge, and rocked back and forth on tiny feet, waiting for a field mouse.

Grey Doe snorted a rare laugh. "He is good with horses, that Oytes." She pushed the brown tubers into a single row with her good hand. "He is a good friend to my son—was a good friend."

She turned to me to share a rare secret. "He gains power now, learns about Smohalla and his medicine. Maybe he will be stronger than Wuzzie. Wren says he comes often when she is there, helping Wuzzie with his baskets of herbs."

To Lukwsh she said: "Oytes didn't need to travel so far to find *his* wife. One of his own proved good enough for him, both times he picked. Not like my son." Her dark eyes narrowed and slipped upward at Lukwsh. I felt the pain of Grey Doe's stabs that pierced other hearts, not just mine.

Lukwsh did not bite back. She took what others gave and did not bleed from their cuts nor let their words make wounds in her soul that refused to heal.

"Your words cut," I said, as brave to Grey Doe as I had ever been.

"It is not your place," she hissed at me, her eyes angry in a flash. "Your tongue—"

"Is kind," Lukwsh said, "but misplaced."

She stepped between Grey Doe and me, made it look as if she looked for something, then said to Grey Doe: "Missing Eagon is one thing we still share, my mother."

"We could share a living place," Grey Doe said almost too quickly. "You have room for her but not your husband's mother?"

Lukwsh sighed. I had overheard this old argument often, one they had long before Lukwsh gave an obsidian knife for my meager bones.

"I have a dog in my lodge and your hawk would not be happy there."

"Shard took Flake with him," Grey Doe said.

"Your sister would miss you if you left her lodge for mine."

"She is like an old bee. She buzzes at me so that I wish to swat at her. But don't. She is older, more frail." A pause, then, "Wren could stay there and this one"—she pointed at me—"could help Wuzzie. Or maybe Stink Bug. Or my sister and I could come here."

Lukwsh turned from her toward me, and I saw a small smile open her face and light her eyes. I wondered if someone wished to swat old Grey Doe, too.

Wren appeared and changed the subject. Her arms overflowed with roots to take us from this familiar spat. Her eyes sparkled with excitement. I hoped Lukwsh would not trade Grey Doe for Wren.

"I have news," Wren said.

Her hands looked shriveled as did my own from spending much time digging deep for tubers. She had grown taller, and the two of us looked more like sisters with our reedlike bodies turning now to bumps and curves. I wore my lighter hair longer, pulled back like Lukwsh wore hers, held with a cat-tail string. It was my third year with the Wadadukas, and I remained in cautious luxury, still sleeping in Lukwsh's lodge. I tried not to distress, but found that words came more quickly to my mouth, words that sometimes took me into trouble.

Wuzzie had complained; I had heard him. Something about an owl shar-ing space and stealing power from a warrior, which Shard had become. I wondered if this could be another reason Shard had left.

Lukwsh treated me well, scolded me, and sometimes smiled if I deserved it. She seemed stronger to me than Wuzzie, though I knew this could not be.

Stink Bug had become a man now, too, and his bad manners took new twists. I had difficulty seeing him as someone who protected those of this lodge while his older brother worked away. Once I caught him holding a hot stick from the roasting fire against the paws of a dog, his wide hand clamp-ing the animal's mouth closed over its whimper, a sneer easing across his face at the dog's struggle. The scent of singed flesh hung fresh in the air. Stink Bug's eyes lifted to mine, but he did not release the squirming animal even when I started toward him. Only when the stick had lost its sting did he kick at the dog limping away, tail clutched between its legs. The salves Wren and I made from Wuzzie's baskets did little to help the dog's healing.

Wren's words interrupted. "We are to have the flower festival, *Moo'a*. You must tell us how it is."

"Who said?" Grey Doe asked, surprised.

"Wuzzie."

Grey Doe snorted.

"Because all the rains have made the flowers grow," Wren said.

"You will not be a part of it," Grey Doe told her. Her words were heavy, like those of someone who had brought home a big antelope for all to admire but only she would eat. "You with your bird name cannot hope to create a song or walk with a mate at a flower festival. Too bad your Lukwsh did not think to have a naming for you that would fit."

Her smile at Lukwsh was like Stink Bug's when he plays a trick, then blames another.

Wren's warm eyes began to swim. She blinked and her nose turned red. I swallowed back tears for her.

"When does Wuzzie say the festival—"

"Five days," Grey Doe answered Lukwsh, nodding wisdom as she turned a root in her fingers and held it up to the light as if examining it. "Those who know, know how this is. The time is set for five days from the idea." Her teeth squatted on her lip.

Wren nodded, some of her enthusiasm gone. "Five days, Wuzzie says. But it is of no matter now." She sighed, began her dance of feet and fingers, and turned away, still tapping her head.

I walked with her and noticed Flake followed. I heard Lukwsh say something in biting words to Grey Doe in the distance.

"Does Wuzzie say more? About the festival?" I asked.

"It is of no matter. We will not be allowed. Except to stand and watch."

"We can have our own festival," I told her, walking faster. "My name is not a flower. And we can invite others." The disappointment weighed less heavy on my shoulders because someone shared it.

She shook her head. "It is not how things are done. Wuzzie would be angry."

She sighed again but walked with strong steps away from the lake, along the grassy banks of the Silvies. I kept up with her. I watched broken willow branches and old leaves swirl with rapid speed past us in the mud-streaked river, pushing against the water-slicked banks. In the shade, thin slices of ice still stuck to the sides. It seemed the river came up slowly, though the banks were wide and deep, not alarming.

Flake sniffed the grasses, flushed up a cinnamon teal believed itself hidden in an eddy close to shore. The dog raced ahead, and I imagined him rushing at the fish caught behind weirs.

Red willows clustered up toward the sky like reaching fingers. Beyond, in the narrow pines across the river, a golden eagle pushed the air with her wings and dropped feet first, settling into her treetop nest. Fallen trees reached out into the cold flow on both sides, their tips disappearing like slick otters beneath the surface.

The men had placed their weirs among the roots and windfalls. When Flake wandered off toward a being in the far distance, I imagined Shard standing like a Sandhill Crane, stocky chest, sturdy legs, steadfast beside the shore, his black-tipped spear pointed like a beak, waiting to pounce on the

big suckers or small trout when trapped. Others waited and watched, con-
quering the spring catch in their own way.

"Wild Rose and Lupine and Thunder's Flower will all go," Wren said as
we walked, her mind on her shame. "They'll gather up Buck Brush's interests and Stink Bug's and Shard's and we won't even be a part of it, not like
the flowers. They will all have a good time. But you and I and Willow Basket...and Vanilla Leaf and..." she spoke names of those who shared our
winter without benefit of flowers. "We have no fragrance," she said.

"Vanilla Leaf has a scent," I said and pinched my nose. "Like Stink Bug's."

She did not smile. Instead, she shook her head as though she had water
in her ears.

"It is not the smell," she told me. "Just because deer spend hours in
vanilla leaf and Lukwsh stuffs it into hemp piles beneath our heads at night
does not mean it is a flower. Only girls with flower *names* are honored at the
festival. The rest are left to carry rocks."

"It will not be so bad," I told her. "Lukwsh says, 'There is always
another way.' We will find it."

"We are too young," Wren said, bumping me, stopping to stand beside
the river, catching her balance.

We watched a swirling stick move slowly, bounce against the shore, then
pick up speed as it rushed quickly into the current. It moved out into the center of the river and was lost to the rush and boil of snowmelt and springs.

I could see across the Silvies. It was not so wide, though broad enough
that none could cross it in the spring without becoming wet or risking cold
or illness. A water-soaked log bobbed and dipped in the faster current, shot
out yards downstream.

"Too young to talk of 'being in full bloom,' as the *kasas* say, or to make
up songs," Wren said.

I started to suggest we speak to Lukwsh and find out more, when Wren
shook her head again, like Flake just out of water. She stared at the river, her
eyes lost of excitement.

"Wren?"

She did not answer but began the toe tap dance. I chose not to interfere.
I looked upriver to the men moving to a new site to fish. I stepped on tiptoes
to spy Shard's form.

My mind stayed on other things, so I did not see Wren's moccasined feet slide closer to the grassy banks, closer to the rushing Silvies River. I did not notice until she slipped, her body sliding like an otter into water.

It happened quickly.

I could not grab her washing, washing hands. She did not tap her head, did not reach out for help. Instead she began the shaking which did not stop even when her arms and elbows hit the river and her face went under.

"Wren!" I shouted. "No! Wren!"

She did not answer. Her body shook in the water, rolled, jerked until her face turned upward toward the sky then down, moving ever farther toward the center where the Silvies rushes fastest in the spring.

I could hear Wuzzie in my mind saying, "Do not interfere; you do not know the songs," but his spirits picked poor times to speak. Wren's eyes were staring now, her limbs twitching less. She bounced against the slickened bank like a hollow log without direction. I ran beside her, kneeled down, and tried to grab her hand. Before I reached her slender fingers, her legs were swirled around, and she shot like a willful spear into the faster flow. Her eyes were glassy, staring at the cloud-streaked sky. Her shaking did not stop. Her face was washed with water as her body bobbed, then dipped beneath the surface, came upward, under.

My heart pounded in my ribs, my eyes a blur of tears. I heard a voice inside of me say, "Save her! Save her!" I did not wish to interfere, but with new courage, I challenged what Wuzzie said. And so I chose, plunged in, dipped under into a cold and closed-in world.

The river sliced like ice across my body, ached especially where my leg had healed. It rushed swifter than it looked, smelled of rot and leaves. I could not touch the bottom. I forced myself upward, grabbed a breath, shook wet hair from my face, and paddled with my hands and legs as I had seen Flake do. I was often in the lakes, gathering tules, making water be my friend. But this river had no time for play; it demanded strength and power and serious thinking.

My nose and eyes sat just above the surface, and I saw Wren, like a slender reed, beyond me, swirling in the current. My bones were cold. I felt the water's power against my legs and small arms, and knew I was too weak, too insignificant to struggle against currents and hope to win.

But it was hope I had, though I knew no word for what I felt, whispered only in my mind. "Help us." Even then I seemed to know of something greater than Wuzzie's spirits.

As if in answer, I saw a way.

Not far beyond Wren, along the other shore, a pine snag reached out into the main flow. I could not make Wren's body move that way, but in my mind I hoped it, willed it, whispered my wish. She turned and dipped, went under, floated up and swirled. Yet in an instant I saw her pushed toward the other side, just the distance of a willow branch, but enough. I paddled hard, grabbed a breath, and pushed my face beneath the water, tried to swim, turned on my back to kick and splash. I heard a barking, barking and caught a black spot racing side to side along the shore we'd left, noticed boys or men running, saw a splash, watched the current carry one black dog downstream. I turned in time to see Wren slam against the pine snag, face scraped on jagged bark.

My heart soared! I forgot the cold and numbing in my hands and legs and fought against the current. I forgot that Wuzzie might not wish her to be caught. Instead, I reached her, wet and clammy, but silent now, without a song. Dead leaves and dirty bubbles like frog's eggs stuck to her face and hair.

Careful, crying, I turned her over, watchful that the pine snag held her and did not spit her back into the river.

My fingers touched her clammy skin. Her eyes were closed now as if sleeping. I could not let my mind say it was more.

My one hand hung onto broken branches that stuck out like stubby fingers from the snag, one arm reached across Wren's small chest. I tried to make my way along the snag, the water still too deep to walk, and so I paddled with my legs. I made distances no greater than the width of my small palm. My shoulder ached, my arms. Wren's legs tangled in the branches below the surface. I breathed and rested, knowing I must get her from the icy cold, find a way to dry her, warm her, see if she still lived. In a distant thought, I wondered what my Spirit would do next.

Then Flake appeared, swimming close beside me, his soft round ears flat against his head, eyes wet and shiny as obsidian. He pulled on Wren, ripped the cloth clinging to her body.

"No! No!" I said.

I saw him push against her then and believed he could keep her legs afloat if only he swam with me. His weight lifting her let me creep my arm along the log that held us all until I got another grip, pulled Wren beside me. The log's bark scraped against the tenderness of my arm and ribs, but I felt my feet touch the muddy bottom and my pain was now forgotten.

"Now, Flake!" I told him. He stood on shore, head low, tongue hanging, ears forward, eyes alert. "Now grab on her. Get her!"

Together we pulled her, wedged her between the bank and tree crotch while I scrambled to the bank on legs as soft as wet reeds. I took deep breaths. Flake barked. Then I reached beneath and around her and pulled, slipped, stepped back, pulled again, again, like the landing of a heavy fish with no resistance until her body lay atop mine, her black hair wet against my cheek, her eyes still closed.

I rolled her off me, folded her arms across her chest, pushed the dark hair strands from her mouth, eyes, strands stuck wet to her cheek. Her lips were shriveled huckleberries. A trickle of blood oozed from her ears. I said her name, called her, started to sing a song that came from nowhere, a kind of chant I hoped would call her back, make Wuzzie forget I interfered.

Her chest lay quiet, still.

Flake barked and barked; his tongue hung red and dripping. He licked her cheeks, wet arms, legs, laid down beside her.

I did not feel her breath. "Save her, save her," was all that I could say, and I spoke into a silence.

And then I opened wide my mouth and covered hers with mine and gave her breath. I held her in my mind, kept her with me, did not let her drift away. Something made me lean across her, push against her chest to feel her air return, and so it did! I shared my breath, pushed down, once, again, again. I did not care about the time that passed, made my own dance now with Wren.

Only in a distant place did I become aware of shouting and talking coming closer. Wren was all I cared about, sharing breathing, sharing space.

Flake barked, a who-o-o-ing. He sat up, eyes alert.

Shard ran toward us, Salmon Eyes, his uncle, others.

I bent to feel Wren's breath against my cheek. I felt a flicker, the flutter of a hummingbird. It moved no more wind than a butterfly's wing, but it was there. I sensed it. It was there, and then my heart began to sing.

It was more than I could hope for.

Shard's dark eyes accused first, then dropped to Wren. He reached for her throat, his fingers gentle.

"She lives," he said, lifting eyes to Buck Brush. He removed his shirt, laid it over her, rubbed her arms between both his hands. "Make a fire," he said.

One grabbed an arm, then a leg and rubbed warmth to her limbs like a firestick. Buck Brush sang to the sounds of rushing water. Another gathered grass to start a warming fire. Someone left to look for Lukwsh.

I shivered in cold but felt only a glow from inside.

The fire burned low. The crackles held little smoke but much warmth. Wren coughed then, her body lurching. She rolled herself and liquid spurted from deep within her like a person sick of what's inside. Her skin paled, my own color. Her insides gave up more, her back pushing, shaking, until she lay quietly, breathing hard.

"What happened?" Shard asked her.

Wren sat up slowly. Shard rested his hands on her back, holding. She did not speak. Her eyes searched the faces, places all around her. She gazed at the river.

"The other side," she said, looking at me, shivering and shaking, lips less blue. "I walked on the other side."

I did not know if she spoke of what happened in the water or with me.

"We talked of flowers," she said. "I felt the need to dance, wash my hands, and then nothing. Until I am here all wet and cold. Did we go swimming, Asiam?"

"We did swim, though I did not choose it," I said to her, so happy to hear her voice, see her moving and alive.

She shook her head. "Did we, Asiam?"

I nodded my head and repeated my words.

She pulled at her ears, looked at the ooze left on her fingers. I feared the jerking again but this time she shook her ears of river. "Too much water," she said with a shaky smile and wiped her ears with her fingers. "I do not remember being in the water," she said to me and then to Shard, "or that Asiam came swimming too. Who took my memory?"

My eyes dropped, uncertain about what to tell her. "You slipped," I said. "Maybe you hurt your head when you fell."

"You were not pushed?" Buck Brush asked.

"No!" I said, alarmed that any would think that of me. "We walked, and then she fell."

"Maybe," Wren said. "But it is like I am when Wuzzie says that spirits talk with me. Tired after. Did the spirits speak?"

"It took Flake and I to bring you out, and we are tired too," I said. "Any would be tired in that water. Look how fast it flows."

"Did they, Asiam?" Shard asked, but his voice carried no blame now. Across Wren's body he reached for me, lifted my chin with his fingers until I searched his face. He dropped his hands. "No one needs to know you interrupted what the spirits said," he told me, his voice as soft as Flake's ear. "Were they speaking when she slipped?" his question almost a whisper.

Tears pooled behind my eyes. "I tried to sing the songs," I said my voice catching in a sob. "But I do not know them!" My teeth were chattering, and I held myself, felt my body rock back and forth. "I could not let her go, not in the flooding *paahoona*. I chose to save her, not to anger, not to interfere. I do what I should do."

I would have cried for Wren's life if I had not made my choice. Now I cried for mine and what I feared would happen when I heard the next words, words that carried danger and marked the peril of my choice.

THE WIND KNOWS MY NAME

"YOU BELONG WHERE WE ALLOW YOU, where I say you can go," the voice neither woman nor man said. Still shaking in my fear and cold beside the river, I knew without looking who spoke to me.

It is the announcement of my distance that will always be, perhaps the moment when Wuzzie determined that I would leave. It seems strange now when I think of it, that the same event that let me see how much I wished to stay should be the moment that marked the beginning of my leaving.

"I will tell you when the spirits talk. I will tell you what they say and where they send you. It is where *I* say," Wuzzie said with biting words. His eyes darted. "Where I say," he hissed, "not where you choose to take yourself. What makes you think you are wiser than spirits? Not to interfere—that was your instruction."

"She's mine to teach," a welcome voice said. "Or have you forgotten the black *wehe* you wear?"

Lukwsh pushed her large frame beside Wuzzie, set him off balance with her body and her challenge.

Wuzzie sucked in breath, clenched his teeth together. He steadied himself but stood silent.

I wondered what power Lukwsh had to keep Wuzzie from doing harm as she handed a blanket to Shard and placed one over my shoulders, then hovered over Wren. With touches so tender I could almost feel them, she put her fingers to Wren's face, gently caressed her skin as though making sure it was warm and responded to life. Lukwsh turned to me then, held me in the dry blanket.

I wondered why she risked her power to honor my poor being with the comfort and safety of her arms. Shard pulled the blanket tighter over Wren's shivering, but he watched Wuzzie.

"She made a poor choice," Wuzzie said to Lukwsh.

"Wren might not think so," Shard said, surprising me with his defense.

"And I don't," said Lukwsh. "Spirits cannot talk to people under water, so her being there was not their will. Asiam knows this."

Wuzzie grunted and spit in my direction. "She knows nothing. Spirits talk wherever they wish; water babies ask for things. Who knows if Wren was what they wished? Maybe they honor her by calling her to them. Maybe if she had answered without interruption she would be remembered always. Maybe her going with them would have kept them from taking away fish and ducks from the rest of the people. Who knows what visions Wren could see if her dance had not been stopped by *this* one."

He turned his back then and ordered Wren carried along the east river bank to the river's mouth and our camp at the fresh lake.

Lukwsh let him give the order. I wondered if she considered what Wuzzie said as she walked beside Wren.

I decided to tell no one of the words that told me what to do.

I became aware of a presence at my side. Shard said nothing, but he reached for my hand and rubbed the back of my fingers with his thumb. He looked straight ahead, his black eyes set like stone to the future. But the gesture and his choice to walk beside me warmed me for longer than the moment.

"I have decided," Lukwsh said later. Flake sniffed at my hands as we sat, waiting for her decision. He tugged gently on my fingers with his teeth, his eyes sparkling in play.

"My friends come, Sunmiet and her husband, Standing Tall. From where I once lived, where my mother's people stayed long ago. When they arrive, we will do more than dig for roots and fill ourselves with each other's company. We will celebrate with a name-giving."

"For Wren?" I asked.

"For Wren, who lives when she might not." Lukwsh smiled. "And you, her sister." She ran her tongue over her teeth, beneath her upper lip, raised her eyebrows in delight. "We will celebrate with *e nanooma* and see how Grey Doe and Wuzzie live with that."

A sister! She had called me Wren's sister! I could not believe what gift she gave me, how full her words had made me feel. So much excitement bubbled from within me that I felt a flutter in my stomach and a soreness.

"You swallowed *paahoona paa*." She looked me over, her eyes searching. "Fix peppermint tea. For Wren, too," she added, putting her hand on her other daughter's forehead.

In between drinking tea, we began our assigned tasks of making treasure baskets, sifting seeds, lacing sagebrush cordage into nets and tightly woven shirts, racing time to be finished before the flower festival. By mid-morning of the second day, the sun beaded up small balls on the sagebrush, and with *wehe,* we scraped clear ooze into baskets, rolled it between our fingers, and laid the soft balls on the edge of the low fire, roasting them to a perfect chew.

"Don't forget to gather some pond moss and set it to dry," Lukwsh shouted to us. "For Sunmiet's baby." She was always thinking, planning ahead.

To the sounds of dogs barking and birds lifting by the thousands from the lakes, Shard brought fresh fish that were dried by hot fires. He smiled at Wren and me, differently I thought. Stink Bug trapped squirrels far from the lake in the sagebrush and rye grasses and brought them back, flinging them to the ground, a frown carved into his face. Even Grey Doe found herself weaving tule mats at a rapid one-arm pace, her thin braids tied together in a knot over her chest to keep from being woven into her mats.

It was a grandmother's place to participate in Wren's name-giving as she had for Stink Bug and Shard when their voices changed. The people still called each other by their familiar names, but that did not take away the honor of a special naming. From the way Grey Doe enjoyed her efforts, allowed a smile to creep across her face, I knew the *moo'a* must not know of Lukwsh's plans for me.

Lukwsh grew more concentrated in the night as she knelt before the fire chipping obsidian into *wehe* of many sizes, the soft chink-chink of her blade a song heard while I drifted into sleep. In the morning I saw the pile of thin flakes as dark as moonless night, noticed her fingers and palms crossed like deer trails with slivers of cuts, and felt sad to be part of the reason for such pain.

"Some pain is given freely," she said when I mumbled something about her hands. "As a gift."

She shared a thought new to me, one to put into a treasure basket for safe-keeping.

"You make too much," Grey Doe complained on the third afternoon. The sky wore the color of snow water, and the fire felt good near my feet. I drank more hot tea, but my stomach still ached. "It is, after all, a name-giving for only one child."

She checked the fire, motioned for me to bring more sweet grass for smoke. I heard her say behind me, "At least you have found a good use for that one, putting her to work for Wren's day."

I noticed Lukwsh did not answer.

I noticed too that Wren did not dance.

Instead she moved from place to place as I did, without the strange tapping and hand washing, without the delays. She did not drop and shake, at least had not. Something had interrupted her dance. But she also shook her head as if trying to rid her ears of bad water. And she did not always answer what was spoken—unless her eyes watched the speaker's lips. I chose not to talk of it, wondered if others noticed, wondered what it meant.

The day before the flower festival, three horses arrived to the serenade of barking dogs. Flake's bark was steady and high pitched. His shiny black body rolled with effort, short neck hair and thick tail raised. I placed a hemp rope around his neck, pulled on him, told him it was fine. He chewed on the rope, stood beside me, and barked less.

The two who sat tall astride sound mounts were a handsome pair. A third horse, smaller, was ridden by a boy somewhat younger than me. A child's head poked out from behind the man, a girl's. Painted *shaptakai* rested on blankets behind the riders. Flake began to bark again. The adults dismounted amid much hugging and giggling.

Lukwsh lifted one, two chubby children from the horses and nuzzled the nose of the third in a *hooopu* she removed hanging from a leather strap over the horse's withers. The infant's wide eyes searched the newness of this place with the sounds of birds and ducks and dogs and strange people scurrying about. A small circle of rawhide, crisscrossed with sinew like a spider web, dangled from the brace of the *hooopu*, caught sunlight and dreams.

Lukwsh's friend was a woman of finer features, wore a prettier round face.

"You have come in time," Lukwsh told her.

"To be eaten by your dog," Sunmiet said, walking wide past Flake and me with a sway that reminded me of a gentle breeze moving through the tree tops. Her soft deerskin dress bore the scent of smoked wood; her waist showed the thickness caused by the births of three children. Thick, dark braids rested on still-high breasts.

"He is nothing," Lukwsh said of Flake. "All bark and some whoo-whooing. But you are in time—"

"For the giveaway," Wren told her, squeezing into the circle of activity, pulling on my hand as she moved. "For my naming!"

Lukwsh asked: *"Uhamasu tukapu?"*

"We ate on the trail," Sunmiet answered, shaking her head, her shiny braids moving like whispers around her soft face. She looked as though she had just bathed, though they arrived at noontime after many hours of dusty riding.

From my place beside Flake, I watched Standing Tall dip under the neck of his paint horse. In silence, he tended the horses, removing the *shaptakai* from their backs rather than hug and touch hands to faces of friends. His black rock eyes, one drooping, turned to stare at Lukwsh now, Wren, then me. I felt his knowing—what everyone knew—that I did not belong.

I wanted to tell him that I would belong. That my longing to leave could be gently brushed aside by the tenderness of a mother's blanket, the shared joys of a sister's smile, the warm hand-touching of a friend. "My marking does not matter," I wanted to say to him. "If I choose, I can stay."

"I could have taken more time," he said to Sunmiet, his words sour. "I am a fool to be here with brothers of enemies."

"Oh hayah!" Sunmiet said. "It is an honor easily given to be present and accept Lukwsh's *namaka*. She is of us, has made her way here. And we stayed long enough at Canyon City. Such strange men with their talk of gold.

You are not afraid to be with brothers of those foolish men or with those small yellow people in little caps. You call them what? Celestials."

"If I must be in company of strangeness, it would be better there than here," he said, still staring at me.

"You would let old wounds keep you from—" She shook her head in some disgust before dropping her eyes.

Standing Tall's face scowled.

"And the flower festival," Wren continued unaware. "You can help make the dancing place."

"It has been a long time since I saw one of those," Sunmiet told her gently, turning her back on her husband. "Ann has never." She brought the child to stand in front of her, help her through her shyness. Sunmiet's smile dipped slightly as Standing Tall walked away, heading for activity near the Silvies without a word to her.

"Some things do not change?" Lukwsh said, shifting the cradle board to one arm and wrapping the other around Sunmiet, pulling her to her shoulder. "It is like a drink of spring water, seeing you. Here," she said handing the cradle board to me. "The girls will take Aswan and Ann and—what is this *onga'a*'s name?"

"Owl," Sunmiet said and glanced at me.

"You must tell me all the gossip," Lukwsh said. "I know nothing."

"Not true in this lifetime," Sunmiet said, eyelashes fluttering in delight. She placed her slender fingers over her mouth as though preventing too much laughter from escaping.

She scooted Ann toward us with her hands. The boy chose to tag after his father.

I held Owl, the baby. I noticed the leather wrap and caught the faintest scent so common with a small one.

Wren wrinkled her nose.

"The pond moss is dry and in the bag," Lukwsh said.

She and Sunmiet giggled, and Wren and I exchanged a look, noticing how easily we were relegated to the caring of children instead of the excitement of preparations or even eavesdropping on our elders.

Wuzzie could have been chosen. He attended the event, but in recent months, his feet had taken him away to the Modocs and bands south and east. He brought back talk of mind hunger, of an angry land used up by grazing cattle, of raids and wars, of army wagons loaded with food keeping the people in some places from starving—but with a price. When he returned, he spent less time talking. He watched more from a distance.

At first, he wanted me close by, ordered Lukwsh to send me in the mornings to tend his fires, move my fingers in his herb bags as he said. He corrected me with his strange eyes and sharp words and watched.

Then he drew away, and the times I was asked to help him mix his herbs and brews or hold the reflecting glass while he plucked his brows grew fewer than the mudhens left in spring.

He would leave, ride away, his short legs almost straight out from the sides of his gelded horse. He returned with words about dead people being brought to life or about *tibos* being whisked away so the people could have their lands back.

"All is to happen through the dance," he told Grey Doe, words I overheard, words with strange meanings.

As I look back and consider all that happened next, I see now: Wuzzie did not wish me in his presence, even before I rescued Wren. Perhaps if he had been chosen, given the honor some said later was due him, what happened might have been prevented. But that is wandering in the past, something a wise woman knows better than to do.

So Lukwsh chose Thunder Caller with his loud, clear voice to be the speaker at the name-giving.

Thunder Caller was a headman whose views were often asked for, and it was an honor that he agreed to announce Wren's name. Lukwsh had not asked Grey Doe's permission for either the caller or the name.

"It is my choice," she said when Grey Doe asked. "My way to discover a new Wren."

I wondered if she had changed her mind about my place in the naming. Perhaps she could find no flower-name that fit a marked child with brown eyes and pale hair.

On the day assigned, everyone gathered in the grassy area stomped down by dancing feet. In the center of the circle, Lukwsh's baskets were stacked like woven treasures, filled to overflowing with *namaka* and items for the meal. Some sat like hungry wolves around a carcass; others smiled and waited patiently, their eyes shining at anticipated delights. The scent of roasting fish and duck drifted near the circle. Older *onga'a* waddled about, clinging to their kneeling mothers, tumbling over their fathers' shoulders leaned back in rest. All dogs were banished to beyond the circle, but Flake sneaked through, sniffed, sneezed, and found an old deer bone to chew near Shard's feet.

"Our sister Lukwsh has invited us," Thunder Caller began, standing up on his toes. His voice gave equal weight to all words, did not drop until the very end. "And we should honor her wishes to give a name to those she chooses so the wind will recognize this chi-ld." He dragged the word "chi-ld," making it two words, dropping his voice, announcing a pause.

A murmur of approval stirred through the gathering, for Thunder Caller was a man as old as Wuzzie but wiser in the ways of some things. He stood much taller, solid, like a tree unwilling to let the wind push it over, but top-heavy too, as his chest pushed out over his waist.

"So the wind will know fierce little Wren, who the river gave back," he continued, his voice thundering across the marshes, above the din of birds arguing for nesting space in the advancing dusk. His thick braids held only spider webs of gray that showed white against his shirt decorated with porcupine quills and dyed seeds tied into designs of grasses and ducks and blue water.

"In the language of Lukwsh's people," Thunder Caller continued, "her new name means 'the Curlew's Beak.' But it carries two meanings, both a bird and a flower. Two sides, as Wren has. Two worlds she walks in. The Wren that is a bird that shoots toward the stars. And one that dances with spir-its."

Silence marked approval, and it greeted Thunder Caller who stood behind Wren and announced her name: "The wind will know her now as 'Shooting Star,'" he said in Lukwsh's Sahaptin language. "Shooting Staa-ar," he repeated in Paiute.

Wren, Shooting Star, stood still as a blue heron in the center of the circle. Her face flushed. Lukwsh had pushed her gently into the circle as though she had not heard at first the calling of her name.

"Tomorrow she will go out and gather purple and yellow shooting stars. She will fill her arms with small blossoms. Their slight fragrance will become hers. Tomorrow, her hair will sparkle not with the pollen of cattails but with the tiny yellow beads of Shooting Stars woven into her braids, seeking their place." Murmurs, then silence. "I present to you Shooting Star," he said, holding his hand over Wren's head. "The wind will whisper her name, but you may say it loudly so all will know. Shooting Star. A flower that blooms early in spring, covers the grassy ravines with its purple, bobs its head low to the ground, brings brightness and direction, announces spring."

His voice dropped, finished, at the end.

Shooting Star glowed. With Thunder Caller's head nod, she began around the circle, without her usual dance of tapping and washing. She stood taller. People waved at her and smiled, gathered her good fortune into themselves. Did anyone notice her new power—or loss of it—to move without the dance?

She selected presents, then, from the basket pile. An obsidian *wehe* was given to Thunder Caller both as headman and for his help. On tule mats spread before her, Sunmiet laid out seed necklaces, doll's spoons, string figures, tule toys of horses and men, reed and sagebrush candies for the children. She handed a warm rabbit blanket to Grey Doe and another to Grey Doe's sister, who lived without a name except for how she related to another.

I caught a smile on that old one's face as she rubbed the soft fur against her thin cheeks. Flake suddenly lunged for the sister's blanket and pulled on the skin. Grey Doe swatted at his nose with her good hand in rescue of her sister. Laughter followed as the big dog let go, and I saw him for the first time with his tail low between his legs.

Oytes said to the gathering, "You scare off your suitors, Grey Doe, with that wicked one-hand hit."

"Who would want so weak a man he can't fight off an old woman?" she answered back, adding to the laughter.

A second obsidian *wehe* appeared in the hands of Standing Tall, who allowed a smile to cross his face as he looked down on little Wren, upon special Shooting Star.

Thunder Caller's voice rang out the names of people receiving distinctive *namaka* so all would notice and themselves be honored for accepting them, but more, so Shooting Star gained honor for their having been received. *Namaka* for the cooks working on the feast were set aside.

Wuzzie heard his name called, and he hobbled forward to receive a tiny *wehe* from Lukwsh, one for him to slice his dried herbs and divide his medicines. He nodded at Shooting Star. "You will be a pretty flower at the festival," he said, patting her head. Both his blue eye and brown eye fell full on her face and washed her with gentle affection. His bony fingers held the small knife. He looked like a father accepting the first kill of his son, and I believed he had forgiven Wren for not staying with the river.

"Time to eat," Grey Doe shouted, in charge now. "Then more to give away in honor of my granddaughter, Shooting Star."

Grey Doe stood with effort, throwing herself forward, her weak arm dragging behind her. She started her waddle toward the wickiup where the smells of roasting ducks put water in our mouths. She carried one end of her sister's new blanket.

I shifted with the crowd and tried not to show my disappointment, blinking quickly so no one would notice my eyes floating in tears. I understood. It is only what I deserved: Lukwsh's change of heart.

The strength of Thunder Caller's voice stopped people in their shuffle toward food.

"There is another who will receive a name this day." People turned back and looked about.

I was invisible, could not be seen. My heart pounded in my head. Would it be my turn to bear a face flushed with joy, my place to be accepted with a family and a given name?

Thunder Caller boomed out loudly for all to hear. "Lukwsh chooses a new name for the *tibo*, Asiam. The wind will know her as Thocmetone, Shell Flower. It is the name carried by our sister Sarah Winnemucca, who is of two worlds now. Asiam will be known as Thocmetone by the wind, one who rides in the white world and one who rides with the people."

Grey Doe had swung herself around at Thunder Caller's words. But before she could return like a raging bull elk, he added what could not be taken back.

"Lukwsh claims her as her own. She belongs *nano*, together, with this family."

He finished and walked with swift legs to the food.

Grey Doe's eyes bore holes into Lukwsh, and she hissed, "Does Thocme-tone know you give her name away while she lives? To white dung?"

Lukwsh's calm eyes faced forward. She did not turn to Grey Doe's glare. "She knows and is honored."

Lukwsh began to hand out items she had set aside, an act that pulled people back from the food. A precious Hudson's Bay blanket and a soft hug from Lukwsh went to Thunder Caller, dried fish for Oytes, more for Buck Brush, a rabbit rope for Stink Bug. A soft deer hide that smelled of Sunmiet was handed to Grey Doe, who snorted at the *namaka* but then took it as Lukwsh knew she must.

Shooting Star bounced happily about, handing gifts and trinkets with-out a twinge of jealousy for sharing her naming with me. I gave out smaller baskets, some with flower designs woven into them, some marked like snake skins. I saved my treasure for last.

My eyes caught Lukwsh's, and she nodded. Amid the activity so as not to bring notice, I handed Shard the work of my hands.

The decoy was made of the skin of one of his ducks, caught in nets with the help of Flake. I had stretched the skin over the tule frame, stuffed it with cattails, tied the bill, and made it with all the tenderness my hands could give. I believed it had value because Lukwsh admired it. It would be precious if Shard accepted it in honor of my name.

The usual pause was followed with his words, "You have done well, little one." His hands brushed mine as he lifted the decoy from my fingers. "It is as good as I have seen."

He turned the decoy over in his wide hands, honored it with his touch.

Before I had the courage to look up at him, let the warmth of his words fill me up, I heard Thunder Caller shout out, "One more gift." A crumb of fried bread dribbled from his chin.

People watched in silence.

Again Lukwsh nodded her head and I approached, heart pounding. She handed me a large basket I recognized as one she filled late in the night when she thought us all asleep. She whispered to Thunder Caller, who announced the recipient.

"For Wuzz-ie!" he shouted. "In honor of the *nabawici* child Lukwsh now calls her own."

My eyes lowered in respect as I handed the little man a burden basket wide at the top, coming to a point at the bottom. It stood almost as tall as he but was as light as a *wada* seed for it contained dried herbs and leaves. Cusick's sunflower for coughs, spider flower for fevers, some black tree lichen brought by Sunmiet and stuffed into the basket to be boiled to ease the aches of old bones. Wide leaves of rattlesnake plantain for treating boils and some wild lichen for bruises and even wild iris for toothaches lay deep in the dark basket. Lukwsh had even placed morning glory inside, and I understood now why she giggled when she did: the ground-crouching plant was a fine hair tonic, something Wuzzie's bald head would force him to give away.

Lukwsh had gathered these herbs and saved them from her travels between her first people and these, used them sparingly. Her gift was precious beyond measure, and she had given it for me.

Wuzzie's spider-like fingers reached deep into the basket and pulled out soft leather bags. He rubbed the herbs and leaves inside between his fingertips. He sniffed at the tiny buds and took a long time touching and smelling each bag. His eyes gave away his desire.

And then I thought I understood what secrets Lukwsh knew that gave her power: she knew his need, his greed. He had exposed himself to her and now would have to accept me and my new name if he wished to take away the basket.

It was an error in understanding, one not corrected until I was older and had been sent away. But on that day, I believed Wuzzie would be more powerful if he had never bared his inner being, kept who he was wrapped up tighter than twists of horsehair ropes. It was something to be remembered, how Lukwsh looked into him and, knowing who he was inside, stripped him of a small petal of his power.

Wuzzie turned from me and said loud enough for all to hear. "I found this Asiam and traded her away. This was a mistake a wise man learns to say out loud."

My ears burned and I felt a flutter in my stomach. Wuzzie praising me, saying he had made a mistake in trading me?

"I should not have traded you but left you," he said, glaring, "so you would not be influenced by Lukwsh's strange wisdom. But I did not," he raised his fluttering voice to head off murmurs, "so the spirits will know you as Shell Flower now, Thocmetone." Beneath his breath so only I could hear, he added, "But they will also know—as I do—who you really are."

My eyes searched for Lukwsh, to see if she was pleased he had accepted my name or angry that his words threatened to dishonor her gift. My own mind wore confusion wrapped in his stinging phrase.

Lukwsh spoke to the crowd. "I am happy Wuzzie has accepted the child I take as my own."

I understood then that he had accepted what he must if he wished to take the basket. He honored the spirit of the gift if not me, and Lukwsh returned the honor. I was proud of her wise thinking, that she had again shown there always is a way.

But before I found her eyes to thank her, Wuzzie added final stinging words.

"You must not think you are so special, Asiam," he said for all to hear. "You are simply equal to the value of old leaves no longer attached to where they belong." He let some of the herbs from the basket drift from his fingers. "You are set apart from what gives life. Decayed. You do not deserve what honor has been given you." He smiled then, that quick one that left pain. "You are traded again, this time for things dead. Perhaps these leaves speak of your future."

People talked at once, too mixed up for me to understand. Lukwsh raised her voice, Grey Doe shouted, even Shard had words to say. His eyes flashed, his mouth twisted in anger, but I did not know if at Wuzzie or at me. Thunder Caller interrupted, gained control over his people if not the flush of my face.

"A name has been given as a sign that a child is precious to another. Gifts given and received. She will be held now in another's mind with that name. That is the way with our people. Nothing can take away Shell Flower's name from the wind nor the love in which it was given. This name-giving is finished. Let us eat."

Thunder Caller earned his blanket and the *wehe* he received that day. And by the force of Thunder Caller's words and the power of Thunder Caller's presence and the honor of the headman's position as speaker for the giving, Wuzzie raised no more objections.

Grey Doe turned her sour face inward to add to what lived there. And so we ate and finished the feast with the scamper of small children racing over the gifts and toys, chewing balls of sagebrush ooze that turned their gums black. They devoured everything laid out for them as hungry dogs consume a squirrel.

Near the end of the feast, I squeezed in beside Sunmiet holding her baby in its board. With a gentle finger I pushed the little ring with its crisscross of sinew hanging from the rose brace. My heart with force turned to happy things, dreams of my own.

"You will have to come with Lukwsh sometime to visit us at Tlhxni," she said. "Little Owl will be older and more fun to play with." She let me push the dreamcatcher. We watched the feather flutter in the wind. "Many gather there to fish. It does not matter who you are or where you come from or what your name is. You will be welcome while the salmon run."

"Standing Tall...?"

"His surface is hard, but he scratches easily," she said. "He is angry with some Paiutes, those who stole and raided in the war. He lost friends when they came over the hills, killed a *kasa* who could not outrun their arrows. He does not believe those warriors were mostly from the Nevada country. He thinks Lukwsh is foolish to stay with these people when her man has died. He thinks she should come home."

She looked up and led my eyes to Lukwsh, gently stroking Wren's hair as they talked, their faces close to each other. "But Lukwsh has found her place here where she gave her heart to a Paiute and his children, had one of her own. He was kind, always kind, that man." Her eyes drifted away, and I wondered if she wished for such kindness in her life.

"Standing Tall even scowls at my people," she continued. "Lukwsh's people, who have been where we live since the beginning." She laughed, fluttered her long eyelashes. "And he says he dislikes *tibos* too, that our spirit man, Queahpama, is right about not dancing with whites." So she too had heard of the strange dance, the one that threatened to harm *tibos* but bring the people all together. "But he has learned not to stop my friendship with them, especially one *hitse*."

I thought she spoke of Lukwsh until she added, "She is like my partner, that one who lives along the packtrail where we fish. But only *my* friend. Standing Tall does not like her."

"A white woman summers with you?"

"Jane Sherar does not live at Tlhxni where the river rushes sideways in a rope-like falls," she corrected. "Not yet. But like us, she feels it. That river is a part of her. None of us lives there all the time. We come to fish." She motioned her hand to the north. "It is that way, off the road they call Military Highway. We took that trail from Warm Springs to Canyon City to ride here."

My mind wandered with her words. She had taken the north highway, the one my eyes had gazed toward since coming to the lakes. She weathered the ways and names of white people and had seen a place they lived differently than in the wickiups of the people.

"If I looked for a certain *tibo*," I asked, hesitation in my words, "I could find them? Along the road?"

"The agents do not keep their word about providing tools or blankets to us," she said. "Most leave the reservation for food. A man named Huntington tried to trick us and took land in return for rag papers." She shook her head once as if agreeing with herself. "We take care of our own."

"If I wished to find a *tibo*..." I persisted.

She turned her body to me, gave me her full attention. "If you came with Lukwsh to visit, you might meet her, my friend. She would make you not afraid to be an owl, which is what you are. Never be afraid of what you are, or you will give away the power to change it into what you want to be."

Her words floated over my head but drifted back in years later. That day I wanted only to know what hope I had for searching, so I told her what I remembered of it, the day the wagons rattled away. When I finished, she shook her head.

"Not without a name," she said. "White people give no meaning without one, two, three names. More names means more power. All their scratchings on paper command only if they mark their names there. They make some up and change them. Most do not remember who had a name before them, which *kasa* first wore it so any can know who are cousins. To find a certain white person without a name..." Her voice trailed off, and she raised her hands to the air and lifted her fingers to the sky.

"Something that belonged to them," she said, "paper marking land or a likeness they call photograph. Maybe a trinket. Or knowing where they came? Where they traveled to? You have none of these?"

I shook my head. A twinge of sadness walked across my heart for the lost necklace, the lost people that were my own. Snow had fallen before I healed enough to search that year I fell. Each spring since had not revealed my treasure basket or any link to a disappearing wagon.

"A pup never belongs to a litter if he is always wandering to other places. Others get his share of food. You have a family now and a special name. Perhaps you can search here to find where you belong."

That night I slept and dreamed of flowers, of fish jumping in the twists of a wild river, of talking with owls. It was a dream of changes and journeys to faraway places. I traveled alone. I saw buildings of stone, green leaves lining long lava caves, people with pale faces shuffling about. I arrived there tired, trying to find the reason. My heart pounded from the effort of my search. My chest filled with a warmth I imagined might be like *puhagamni,* having powers, made me wonder when I would discover mine.

I awoke alert, the dream fresh in my memory, and I tied it into my string of knots.

I had a day dream, too: a new name and people willing to claim me. A sister now to share my thoughts with and my hope; a woman who made obsidian *wehe* who stood for me and let me think of her as mother; an invitation to visit Sunmiet and ride on the military trail. And the joy of the flower festival yet to take away Wuzzie's distant words of pain.

My treasure basket was full, and I had dreams to make it overflow. I didn't know then that what we dream of is not always meant to be.

CHANGE

STOMACH PAINS AND CRAMPS BEGAN in the night and woke me. Something wet and sticky remained on my mat when I made my way outside toward the private place. A star fell from a sky as black as Flake's fur. I ached all over. Stumbling back to my mat, I noticed a strange smell coming from me. Twisting and turning took up much of the night. I finally found my stomach twisted less when I pulled my knees up, and I wondered for a moment whether Wuzzie had put something in my food to make me ill.

"You have begun your flow, na?" Lukwsh said in the morning after scooting Shard and Stink Bug and even Wren out the flap. Red streaks on my mat were her answer.

I had heard of such things and had seen Lukwsh go with her friends to willow wickiups built for this purpose and remain five days. She seemed to find pleasure in the time away. I could too, if it had not fallen on the day of the flower festival.

"Vanilla Leaf. We will ask her to go with you," Lukwsh said. "There are usually three the first time."

"She would miss the festival," I said, my voice breaking. I choked back the sob that worked its way forward as my mind said only one trail led through this disappointment. "Hers is a flower name."

"Then Grey Doe. She could do it alone the first time."

My eyes shot to hers.

"She is *moo'a*. It is our way."

Grey Doe! The woman who would not turn her weakened body to face me when she spoke. The woman who felt I kept her from Lukwsh's place.

111

The *moo'a* whose words stung with spurning. This one would take me from my girlhood into grown? My mind was as murky as a muddy lake.

But things do not always happen as we plan.

Grey Doe and I counted twenty-five days together set apart from the others.

At first I heard the sounds of laughter and the activity of the festival as though a whip cracked across my back. I expected the memory of what I missed to leave deep scars. I thought my breathing would be small and tight inside a place where I could feel both the roof and walls on my skin as I sat, like being stuck inside a narrow lava cave, curling my knees up in sleep. And when I heard the clatter of birds rising from the lakes, I feared the memory would be knotted with a woman who did not like me, instead of being wrapped with signs of flight and freedom, a way of soaring high above, just like the birds.

But I came to find "another way," as Lukwsh would say, and looked to lessons I could learn about myself, buried deep in challenge.

I learned that patterns helped my mind make a trail through difficult days, and that when I struggled with uncertainty in my future, I could bring in lessons from my past. In that way, I blended and became strong, like Lukwsh's water pot.

It took some time before I found the richness in the lessons. With Grey Doe, it felt at first as though my life was meant for mere instruction.

"The sun comes," Grey Doe announced the first morning. "Gather wood."

My feet took me along grasses flattened beside the Silvies, and I loaded my arms with branches and twigs, returned and stacked them. I went back one, two times, until I had a pile as tall as myself.

"Go again," Grey Doe said. "Don't be stupid. Take cordage with you, to carry on your back. Five stacks are needed," she said to my surprised eyes.

I had no idea what occurred when girls and women spent their time away but wondered how Lukwsh could find it pleasurable if this was how she spent her day.

Grey Doe performed her duties, though she rarely turned her shoulder in my direction. Sometimes she stood next to me and spoke as though to the tree in front of us. It took some time before I recognized that her words were meant for me. I listened, made many more trips for my five piles, strained my eyes and ears to hear the joy of the flowers feasting on their day.

Afterward, we ate.

Grey Doe made the meal, ground wild rye into flour with her one hand, added water and reed sweets, made a mush. She talked of the power of food and the hands that fixed it. Her voice wore a softness new to my ears.

"Never feed in anger," the teaching grandmother said, "or those you serve will be sick."

I watched carefully for signs of her anger, wondered whether she followed her own instruction when my stomach ached and twisted.

More wood gathering followed. I had time to think as I raised up another five stacks. I traveled farther out each time as twigs and branches became more scarce.

The time of gathering marked something new. Perhaps I would have friends, now that I had a family. Maybe a girl besides Wren would share some space with me. I thought of Wuzzie and shuddered. I held Lukwsh in my mind, the courage in her kindness.

Again we ate, a light meal without flesh. Grey Doe told me the meanings of the seeds and teas and I tried not to question her, wanted to believe she told me rightly, wasn't teasing me for later embarrassment. She showed me how to weave sagebrush and tules into baskets and spikerush into spoons. I even made some sandals from the soft, shiny spikerush stems for when snow covered the ground.

And she let me sleep as needed and even took out the grasses and leaves my body soiled and buried them on her own. Only the wood gathering was required.

Once I winced in pain, but Grey Doe did not scold me. Instead, she rubbed my back with fish oil and a kind of fungus to soften my skin. In the small fire pit near the opening, she burned a showy flower of white and gold that left a fragrant perfume. She offered me a yellow tea she said would ease the pimples from my face when I should have them. Her sudden tenderness tendered caution.

"Sit now. Keep your thoughts clean like new snow," she said. "I tell you things only women know about men and children."

I found much of what she said hard to believe, but even in the pale light of the hut, I could see that Grey Doe shared the truth. She spoke without laughter, though some of what she said caused giggles to bubble into my head.

It is a marvel to me now that a woman who lived with such distaste of *tibos*, such fears of how white would wash out the desert brown of her people, could be forced to spend a month with one, isolated and alone, and still share with her the vital information needed to carry on tradition. It must have been the role of *moo'a* overcoming her human hate.

For Grey Doe soothed and even combed my hair with a rye grass brush and saved the tendrils in a basket, the wisps of wet desert sand twisted tight beneath the cover.

Each afternoon, I began again. I gathered fuel for my stacks, took new paths. My arms bore the stains and slivers of the wood. Fifteen new mounds sat around our lodge by the end of each day. It was good work, and I had done it.

At night I fasted, and she told me, "Wait for songs."

My dreams were wild with color and movement and faces of strong feelings. I woke to my own hard breathing and aches beneath my belly, the smell of tules and the mountain cedar we sat on scented with my sweat. Grey Doe did not scowl but stirred the fire and heated tea and sang to me in words that entered in my ears but swirled and filled my body like sweet grass smoke surrounds my soul. I eased back into sleep.

As the gathering took longer, I had less time to make things. I worked on a cradle board for a child's doll; another day, a spikerush brush to scrape ashes from the fire rocks before placing them in soups. Grey Doe went with me once to show me how to thread pine nuts on the trigger of a special deadfall trap, how it could bring a rock down on unsuspecting prey, and how to skin the squirrel we found there, how to cook it, too.

"Hunter's job," she told me slicing around the animal's neck, "but a woman needs to know."

Knowledge given me not just for how to live among the people, but for how to leave, how to survive, how to take the land and make it friendly as I traveled. These were lessons I had longed for, to make me strong when I slipped away to find my people. Somehow, leaving seemed less important now. I shook away the feeling.

And always, I gathered sticks in a pattern broken only after five days when Grey Doe took me to the lake to bathe.

Even there the old one talked to me about the changes of my body, how to cleanse, be pure, and only once did I do something that threatened the fragile peace we forged there.

My eyes had wandered. I waved in joyful recognition to the familiar figure I saw pushing a boat out into the early mist. I splashed the water, shouted, pleased he had not left yet. I wanted him to turn and look.

The redness where the basket tumpline pulled across Grey Doe's forehead grew deep.

"Keep your hands to yourself, Shell Flower. You may be two people but mostly you are a woman now, not a small marked child splashing in your bath." Her words carried the familiar bite.

"I am only pleased he has not left yet," I told her, eyes lowered.

"He is your brother," she hissed and then noting she had hit some chord of fear within me she said, "Nothing more. Do not be of two minds about this. If you work to make it different, bad things will happen. To you, to him and all who call themselves the people."

I did not see myself as having that much power, but she was right about one thing. I did see Shard as one who shared my wickiup as a distant brother and one who also intruded upon my waking thoughts as someone more.

The wood gathering continued. My meals looked meager the few moments I had to think of them before falling into a deep sleep. To vary the effort, I looked for greasewood bushes that reminded me of shrubs and scrubs on my longer forays, farther out. On the warmest days I found a greasewood worm or two in the roots, dug them out, and stuffed them inside a basket.

The pine groves and marshes offered freedom, housed eagles and hawks to remind me of heights. The song birds and swallows suggested space. But I missed the others, Lukwsh and Shooting Star, who I still thought of as Wren. I wondered what Grey Doe did during my long absences of gathering. I tried to guess if she could tell when I rested my sometimes tired leg by lying in willow stands or on my stomach catching sun beneath the shade of sage, watching insects crawl through grass. I wondered if she knew that I puzzled over Wuzzie's power and Shooting Star's new ways. I hoped she did not know I thought of Shard.

The old woman acted pleased when I delivered the greasewood worms to her. She clucked about roasting them later as "flesh."

On the third bathing day, fifteen sleeps into this sacred time, I again saw Shard from a distance. I did not wave. I stayed low in the water with only my eyes and nose showing, peered out from the mist. He looked my way, his hand above his eyes as if searching, then on his hips, his elbows like arrows in their distinctive ways.

I felt warmed despite the cool water. I remembered a time when snow geese settled on the lake, and frogs and crickets serenaded dancers following a huckleberry feast. It had been a long day and my leg ached. I wondered if Shard would dance around the pole or wait until the coming of the rabbit drives in the winter to show his dancing skill, collect some young woman with his courting. He sat contented beside me, leaned back on his elbows, and looked straight ahead at Wren.

"She is your sister," I ventured.

"All young girls are my sisters," he said and I could not hear teasing in his voice.

We watched the dancers bend the tall grasses with their moccasins. A girl with flashing black eyes looked over her shoulder at him and smiled. I felt the drums beat like leg throbs. Another dancer whose belly stored many seeds but whose smile eased into straight with unbroken teeth grinned at Shard. She did not notice me, but I remembered the ache I felt when her face lit up and he left me to dance at her side.

When my second flow stopped, twenty-five days had passed, and the *moo'a* and I left the hut. Like a snake shedding its skin to form a new one, Grey Doe returned to how I remembered her best.

"Don't forget what happened here," she warned. "And that you are still only a white woman."

Behind us rose wood stacks like gopher mounds, sticks to be burned by old people who had no grandchildren or sons to look after them. I stood with some pride at the size of the brown mounds, my ability to give, to gather fuel for the elders.

"Sunmiet left you a gift," Lukwsh said when I entered her lodge after the passing of one full moon. I wondered if I looked differently to her. My eyes searched for Flake. When I did not find him, I assumed Shard had gone.

116

Lukwsh heated rocks to go into the basket to cook fresh rabbit soup. My mouth watered for flesh.

"It comes with the cedar basket that holds it," she said of the gift. "For your new name, but mostly for leaving your child-side behind. And missing the festival."

I did not want to be reminded of what I'd missed.

"She seems a good friend," I said, pawing through items on the far side of the lodge.

Lukwsh nodded. "We do not see each other often, but it matters little. It is a treasure to know you are held in the mind of another, a sign of no greater love."

The cedar basket I picked up had a forked horn's antler for a handle. Bear grass and choke cherry bark alternated to make a darker then lighter stripe, not unlike the sun streaks of my hair. Inside hid another gift: a barrette beaded with a hummingbird design.

"It is her *kasa*'s," Lukwsh said when I showed her. She rubbed her wide thumb over tiny beads. "She made it for me once long ago, but I wished it as a *namaka* to you and so it is now. From both of us. There is another, too."

My fingers made tracks around the inside of the lip and felt before seeing a tiny basket, no longer than Lukwsh's thumb. The same cedar and bear grass as the larger basket formed the smaller one that had a tiny cover as well.

"For your most precious *namaka* when you find it," Lukwsh said, "though most of what matters in this world cannot be placed in any basket." I wondered what thoughts were turning in her mind.

"What was it like?" Wren asked as she burst through the lodge opening, interrupting our words, with no familiar greeting first. Flake bounded at her side, whoo-whooing when he saw me. He lunged toward me as I put the tiny basket back.

"Was Grey Doe crabby?" Wren asked.

My hands reached around to clasp my hair and place the barrette at the back of my neck. I swaddled Flake's big head with both hands, shook his face into mine, deliberately did not answer.

"What about the festival? That is a better subject," I said, aware of a strange reluctance to share just when I had something a sister might value.

She turned with a question in her eyes to Lukwsh, and I saw the stuffing of cattail fluff in her ear. Lukwsh repeated "festival," and Wren turned back.

"Oh, it was more fun than a grass dance or jacks or even the namegiving," she said. "More fun than anything I have ever had with anyone. Especially you."

"She was different," I said, well scolded. "She did not bite as much."

"Humph," Wren said, sounding like her *moo'a*.

"She taught me things for how to survive, like trapping rabbits when I am alone."

"You plan to go somewhere alone?" Wren asked.

"It is always good to know how to feed yourself," Lukwsh said, "so you do not stay in a bad place waiting for others to keep you alive."

I looked at her and wondered if she spoke a double meaning, but she found another subject.

"You must give her all your clothing now," Lukwsh said, "to Grey Doe, since she chose to tend you in your time."

"She will look strange in what I wear," I said.

"It is our way," she said.

"I have some to give her," Wren said when she understood the discussion, forgiving me for my unwillingness to share.

"It is Shell Flower's *namaka*."

"What will she wear after she gives her clothes away?" Wren asked, my own question.

"We make things, new things, to go with her new person. What is given away will be returned, na? It is the way of our people, the way of our beliefs."

Perhaps the different clothes did it. Perhaps what Grey Doe taught me or what I learned about myself in the days I gathered wood and we were held together caused the change. Perhaps the change, the ebb and flow of my body, moved into my head. Or maybe it was the passing of the seasons and time.

Whatever, I began to see myself apart from Wren and her hunts, think more on the interests of the women and the young mothers and even the grandmothers and aunties I met in the private hut for five days each month.

Now I saw the joy Lukwsh returned with. No demands from *moo'as*, no children scampering about, no men to tend or hides to tan. Just five or six women slowly weaving, sharing laughter and understandings collected in an instant with a look or movement of a hand, all gathered in a treasure basket of belonging. No one pointed out my markings. No one called me *tibo*. All acted as though my presence was expected, and they seemed to like the way I shared my stories, found pleasure in responding to my wonderings of things I did not understand.

Later as we placed burden baskets on our backs, adjusted the tumplines across our heads, and traveled north to pick huckleberries, south for antelope hunts and piñon nuts, I was aware of how my body changed, the tightness of my clothes that pulled across my chest. My waist grew smaller than my hips.

My face, too, looked fuller in the reflection that peered out from me at the still lake in high Snow Mountain. My eyes were more noticeably round, my nose thinner and straight. I barely noticed the dark line of my *nabawici*, and once, as we traded near Canyon City, a store-keeper mistook me for a lighter-skinned Klamath. He bit his words at me and called me "dirty siwash." I was torn by hating his dislike of who I was but shamefully pleased he thought I belonged with the people he despised.

My wavering worried me.

I had a plan to leave, to learn what I needed so I would succeed. But perhaps Sunmiet was right, perhaps my pursuit of people from a distant wagon offered no future. Without the necklace or name, what hope did I have? And why should I leave to join people who saw me as a "dirty siwash," a filthy savage? Why should I walk away into uncertainty when Lukwsh had invited me to live with tradition and routine?

The answers moved farther away as I felt the joy of being part of something, knowing my hands could help, hoping someone returned the wonderings of my heart.

In the winter months when stories were told to entertain the children and keep the past of the people ever ready in the mind, I listened, memorized tales of skunk and eagle, of coyote and his troubles. I no longer sat among the children. From my mat near the back of the headman's wickiup, I noticed instead the ways of the boys whose voices had changed, those with first kills and seconds. When we prepared foods, shook out dusty blankets onto hard snow ground, I paid more attention to the stories of the women and the ways of their search, heard their dreamy wishes, listened for their lessons.

One such woman was Summer Rain, a chubby woman who did not seem to mind the paleness of my skin or my desert hair. She made plans to join with Natchez of a Nevada band in the spring and talked freely of her yearning and her expected woes. She had a twinkle in her eye, a cheek flecked with a dimple. Excitement squeezed out through her pores. She planned tricks on others, sometimes let me belong to her secrets.

Vanilla Leaf pleased, too, as she watched and listened and talked with me in the comfort of the hut or as we ground seeds together, reached for dried tubers, tied cordage into nets. She shared especially her jokes about Stink Bug and another, James, of the same age. She showed interest in Shard, too, hoped to sweeten him, I think. But she did not earn her name. She disliked the cold of the lake for bathing and so carried with her a less than pleasing scent I thought would keep Shard away.

Shard had returned to work for the rancher, though he came back often. Since the time of my flow, he had moved to his own lodge when he returned. He often took meals in Lukwsh's, provided her with needed food, but moved to the other side of the wickiup whenever I entered. While ripping at smoked salmon, legs crossed as a visitor in Lukwsh's lodge, he spoke not only of cows and bunkhouses of the ranchers but of trails away, to the big river north, to Bannocks in the East, to the falls at Tlhxni where Sunmiet and Standing Tall summered. His words, like Wuzzie's, spoke of hungry people, confusion about where gathering and hunting could happen, of change and distant rumors of death.

Happily, he had not lain any nights in a pattern at the feet of Vanilla Leaf's *moo'a*—or any woman's grandmother that I knew of—seeking approval for a bonding. No one had seen him smiling at any one woman's charm.

Instead, in his hesitating way, he shared stories of wars and bad times with people who had no food and spoke with confusion about agents who bore less honor than the army, of ranchers carrying visions of closed-in places and words with strange meanings such as "trespass" or "rivers that marked boundaries."

And he related news of a reservation being planned for this marshy place to include the lakes and lands south, Snow Mountain and the springs and grass fields, the land of seeds and sage.

"It comes with a promise," he told Lukwsh, "that we will have tools to plant corn and clothes to cover us and a mill to make lumber so we can build wooden houses."

"Close together," Lukwsh said, grunting as she stirred the *wada* stew, "near the agent and that army."

She talked with Wren using her fingers, and Wren asked then, "Will we still gather food? Harvest ducks?"

"You sell your soul, working for *tibo*," Stink Bug said, entering the conversation late. "Only guns speak loud enough."

Shard paused. "The blacksmith who teaches me, who calls himself Johnson now, he says the reserve will keep our land safe, a closed-in space, and we should not fight it."

Stink Bug snorted. "Who listens to a milky-haired man who makes hoes!"

"Cattle grazing on the grasses use up roots, change the way the water runs in ponds and streams from the mountain," Shard said. "Woolly sheep eat the grass so short the roots are startled and die. I have seen it."

"There will be a change for us," I offered, not noticing until later that I included myself within the troubles of the people. "For how we gather and keep ourselves."

Wren nodded but remained silent.

"Whether we listen to the agents or not," Lukwsh said, and I wondered if she thought of Sarah's words those years before.

"No agent will switch my life," Stink Bug said, standing to leave. "No soldier either. You women can discuss it," he said spitefully to Shard, "but men will settle this trouble." He stomped from his mother's lodge.

"Learn owl ways, Mother," Shard said quietly after a moment, "so we can live and tell stories to our children's children."

Lukwsh nodded and lifted her chin to the clay water pot. "I know how to blend," she said.

Blending was not Wuzzie's way. At the gatherings, he reported that *tibos* angered the land spirits and that the people must be wary of them. He walked wide circles around me, pulled at his chest and stomped at the ground when he saw me. It still surprised me that someone with his power should act bothered by my person.

When Shard attended the headman lodge discussions, many listened and nodded to his reasoned words. Even Stink Bug sat as if he hung on Shard's thoughts, though he spoke ill of him when he was gone.

The talking put the children to sleep, made many women weary. When Sarah visited our band again, along with her brother, it was in Vanilla Leaf's lodge she rested this time, for Vanilla Leaf's uncle, We-ah-wee-wah, was a wise man. He had been selected as a chief by the soldiers, something Sarah said the army liked, to have one man to speak all the words of the people rather than taking time to listen to many voices. Our band accepted this, but some of the people we gathered with were unhappy with one name being placed by owls above all others.

Wuzzie, too, took issue.

"We decide our own leaders," he said to a gathering while the pipe was being passed. "How can someone from there," he pointed with his head toward the proposed site of a new reservation, "know who to talk with?"

"You would have him only speak with you, Wuzzie?" said Oytes, smiling.

"No. Not with me only. Not with anyone only. That is their way, to listen to only one, and make him tell the rest. We each have wisdom." He gazed at the faces before him, both colored eyes shining. "Not like those who follow one soldier. That is why they like Thocmetone," he said in his fluttering voice to her face but speaking as though she was not present. "She will lead people like sheep to bad water because they give their thoughts to one chief, cannot think for themselves. They think she speaks for us." He spit. "I will like to be around when they discover their mistake."

Sometime during the time of gathering tubers, Sarah and her brother were asked by the army to bring us into the camp called Harney on Rattlesnake Creek. General Crook wished to make a peace between us and those who brought cattle to our land. The army would give us cloth of dark colors with splashes of the sunset, maybe some metal pots to replace our baskets, and some grain.

At the last minute, Lukwsh decided not to go.

My heart sank. I had imagined the ride to the fort, stepping inside the wooden buildings, looking through glass set into wooden walls, running my fingers over smooth boards called tables. Shard had described a dozen treasures I thought that I would see. And though I would understand little of what was spoken, just watching the soldiers, I believed, would be a wish fulfilled.

Shard went. "To charm them," he said, "we must know their ways."

"I will go with him," I said.

Lukwsh scowled. "No girl travels without her mother."

"Sarah does," I reminded her.

"She is a woman, making her own choices. That is not you, Asiam, yet."

So I obeyed and did not go. Each decided on his own as was the way. Most decided to remain. But Shard went, along with Vanilla Leaf and her family and a few others led by Sarah.

Stink Bug and Oytes and others found ways to avoid Sarah when she returned. Most would not take the cup of flour handed out from army wagons as a sign of acceptance of the peace between the ranchers and the people.

That very day, Oytes and others left the village and returned with the fire of victory in their eyes and new horses trotting behind them. They unloaded forged iron from wagons they took and later made the iron into bullets. I heard them in the evening telling stories of settlers dying of fright, while the warriors made wooden stubs of greasewood they would use later, if they needed, to plug bullet holes in their arms and bellies.

"The white settlers remain angry," Sarah told Lukwsh. "So few agree to consider a reservation. And when the army hands out food and does not shoot us, the settlers say they pay twice for our 'good' life. The raids must stop before settlers will be happy, before we will have a future."

No one responded. No one claimed the answer.

It was a time of whispers between old friends. Quiet talking stopped when certain people entered into another's presence. Long discussions begun at the lake wound up in the headman's wickiup. The air carried with it the smell of armies and ammunition, of lost ways and wars.

Shard returned with Flake to the ranch; Vanilla Leaf did not speak of their journey together to Rattlesnake Creek, so I believed their time together blameless. And despite the wedge she could have driven between us, I liked Vanilla Leaf, who willingly shared Sarah when she visited.

I was pulled to Sarah-Thocmetone, whose name I shared, pulled by the chain and crossed bars that graced her neck, drawn as a dog is led to coyotes, fearful but with an urging, knowing some connection there is offered, unsure of what it was or the danger lurking in the seeking.

"They think with different minds," Sarah told me. "Those settlers act as pitiful as trapped possums when a cow dies but have no feeling for a child who sleeps hungry because their cows have destroyed the camas." She shook her head, and the long necklace of beads bounced on her wide chest. "I tell you. At Pyramid Lake, the agent Parker calls himself a Christian. He uses the money meant for food and medicine I get the government to give, and he builds privies!" She shook her head in disgust. "While children die of strange spots."

"What we waste must be greater than what we eat," I said, thinking of the privies.

"O ho!" she said and smiled without laughter. "They drool over land like coyotes in the midst of trapped rabbits. But I go there, try to talk with them before they take away everything that is familiar, until all that is left is something held in our minds."

"The reservation…" I said, trying to form my question.

"It is the safest place for us, where the army marks the edges. They are too many, those white people," she said, adding water to the pine nut stew to thin it. "We must capture them as we do the antelope, I think. If we agree to remain inside spaces, the army will protect us. I will make them keep their promises to hand out food. My time away from my people will not be wasted." She rubbed the crossed bars at her neck. "Otherwise, we will all go the way of dried leaves, and no one will even remember we were here."

Lukwsh and Vanilla Leaf and her aunties and I treasured our time with Sarah. She could leave the world of war and tell stories as varied and brilliant as butterflies quivering across grass.

But I preferred the rare times I had had alone with her the year before my own change. I liked walking along the shoreline, picking up snails or throwing a stick for dogs who splashed and scattered fowl. At such times, Sarah noticed my impolite staring, encouraged me to be bolder. Perhaps she understood my interests and tolerated my questions because she understood the feelings that rose when things were said about you that did not describe the person you carried inside your skin.

At those times, when I felt well understood, her walk between two worlds led me closer to my own, closer to the future I would someday choose.

"They call themselves Christians who wear these," she said one time when we talked. The crossed bars lay gently on her fingertips as she spoke. "The beads remind me." She let it drop amidst other shell necklaces, beaded ones that draped around and across her wide chest. Badger moccasins left slick tracks in the wet sand as we walked by the lake. Then I could almost see what her white family taught her, the "Father, Son, and Sacred Spirit" she sometimes spoke of.

"Some are kind and wise, and their hearts do what their lips say. Others use their book to beat with. Those I do not trust."

"How do you tell?"

"Their eyes have a glassy, angry look, and they paint their smiles on thin, tight faces. Their words have a too-sweet sound to them. And their hands and feet do not match their heart. They never touch my fingers when we greet," she said, touching her hands to mine.

"But others have warmth," she continued. "They say the Holy Spirit is the fuel that flames the fire inside them, makes them move and yearn for things. They told me the Spirit had the power to carry out the Father's wish, one that burns differently in each of us. They say they can give their warmth away but will always have enough."

She bent to pick up a snail. "I think I make sense of the Father and the Spirit they speak of." She placed the snail in the basket on her side and shook it gently. "They are Creator and spirits of this world and the next. It is the Son, this Christ they speak of, that is still confusing."

"Is he a first child?" I asked.

"An only child, so spoiled." She grinned, then became more serious. "But they say he is a brother, too. And very wise, with big ears, able to listen to everyone who calls out to him. He answers by flowing inside, like a water spirit might."

She laughed and wiped the wet mud from her fingers onto her cloth dress. "They say he actually cares for us, each one, knows us by our names. Even has a task for us, like a basket we should make that is different from all others." She shrugged her shoulders. "Hard thing to think on, having a Spirit who cares enough to warm you up, with enough to give away."

"It is like a big naming, with a giveaway," I said.

Sarah laughed. "It is a long day's gathering to understand how they think."

"Perhaps they see the day world through night eyes," I offered. "Maybe, like owls, the light confuses them."

"Do you speak from your own eyes?" she asked. The smell of mud lifted up to our faces.

"Sometimes owls become mixed up if they fall into marsh grass when they belong in a tree perch or a cave," I said.

Sarah nodded. "Getting from one place to another is a trouble, but not traveling can be dangerous, too."

She stopped our walk and after a moment spoke out toward the lake, not to me. "Those warm Christians say the Spirit is the One who sets us on our journey, and we must not be afraid to listen even when we do not understand."

Her words both comforted and alarmed.

If the Owl's Son was a spirit, perhaps it was not only his ears that were large but his wisdom, too, enough to span the universe, rise higher than the eagle, swim deep beneath the streams. Perhaps it was he who talked, protected us, knew our name, and gave direction. Perhaps he was the Spirit who was with us as we moved and grew, no matter where we were or who walked with us, the One who ordered when we joined a place or when we left. Perhaps this Spirit told us when and where our lives belonged, and not the wind, or our will, at all.

THE CHARMING
OF ASIAM

A MIND CAN SING A LULLABY to itself and sleep through what it should be awake to see.

That happened the year after our names changed, the year Wren finally spent her long days in the private hut. Lukwsh spoke to *Moo'a* who permitted me to tend my sister along with Grey Doe. The time wrapped Wren and me into the folds of good friends, a gift of strength I didn't know I needed.

I tended wisely, followed Grey Doe's directions, and uncovered one puzzle from my time with her alone: when a chosen one is gathering wood for their stacks, the tenders could sleep.

Throughout our stay, Grey Doe told Wren the same things she told me. I felt relieved, though she spoke words with more gentleness to Wren. Grey Doe rarely spoke to me. She allowed me to overhear what she said. My sister would then turn to me and watch my lips as I repeated Grey Doe's words more slowly and could show my teeth to make sounds clearer. I even learned to speak well with my hands as it became more certain that Wren could speak but could not hear.

I did not let myself wonder if my rescuing her in the river had been the cause. I did not wish to think that Wuzzie might be right, that I had interfered and given Wren her silent scar.

Inside the hut built for two, I took deep breaths to calm myself, tried to imagine the walls as marking safety, not hard breathing. When the closeness felt like a covered basket, I closed my eyes and imagined a sky above me with

clouds drifting through the air. And each day that I woke and found I had endured the tightness one more time, I felt stronger, had something new to add to the treasure basket that was my life.

"Try this," I said.

Wren took what I offered.

"Chamomile tea. For your stomach," I said, rubbing mine to show her. I touched her hand lightly to bring her eyes to mine before I spoke.

"Lukwsh sends it. Later, we will crush nettles. To stop the flow."

"Humph," Grey Doe said, but she wore a satisfied look and I permitted myself some pleasure in knowing that my hands would work for healing.

Only once in the twenty-five days we remained there did I know fear. Only once did the pattern change.

It happened the morning Wren gathered her greasewood. She returned and talked about bees and small animals as was her interest. Our fire burned hot. Lukwsh had given us honey brought from Sunmiet's last visit. We sweetened cakes with it, and it sat in a basket beside the low flames in the fire pit, the precious gold liquid just beginning to ease its way from crumbly combs. A flower fragrance and the scent of clover filled the air.

"And then I saw that new dog Shard brought, with the white feet and chest, sit on a rock, staring at water," Wren said.

She wore a dress of twisted sage she scratched at as she kneeled on her rabbit-skin robe.

"He leaped in, that dog, and came out with a fish in his mouth, and he carried it to my brother!" She shook her head. "He fished by himself, that dog. He did not need a man!"

"No one needs a man," Grey Doe laughed, then scolded. "But you tell a tale. Now is not the time for stories. You are to gather and rest, think."

I shortened some of what Grey Doe said when I repeated it, and the old woman jabbed at me with her elbow. "Do it right," she said, and I did.

Grey Doe kneeled next to Wren, facing into the hut's side as she worked. Wren's knees were directed toward me.

"But it's true, *Moo'a*. It is," she said with certainty.

Grey Doe grunted and dropped hot rocks into the tea basket. My sister chattered again, settled herself, twisted back as she lifted the tea water to her lips. She sipped quietly.

At first I did not recognize the scent. It smelled like burning sage, this tea Grey Doe fixed. Then I thought it a foreign smell, unfamiliar, from far away. I thought to look outside to see if someone had let a fire pit get away while we three rested here together, but when I moved closer to the opening of our wickiup, I coughed. The scent grew strong and inside.

"Ay-ah!" Grey Doe shouted suddenly. "She burns!"

I turned in time to watch Grey Doe drop a basket. I thought she spoke of her hot water basket and tea. I reached for Grey Doe's hand, but she pushed at me and grabbed for Shooting Star. Then I saw the flames reach up behind my little sister, heard her howl in pain.

Grey Doe lunged at Wren, but her one-armed weight pushed her off-balance and Wren's ankles and feet edged into the fire. Grey Doe pitched like an uprooted tree over me, her strong hand batting at flames. Her body held me from helping, kept Wren's legs wedged in the fire.

I pushed at Grey Doe and reached for water to pour on the flames. By mistake, my hand sunk into the sweet-smelling basket of honey. I wrenched Wren forward, pulled Grey Doe with her, then both of them onto my chest. Smoke swirled and threatened to suffocate our breathing. With no other choice, I doused Wren with the sticky gold stream, grabbed for her feet and cupped my gummy hands over them. My action smothered the burning. Then I helped Grey Doe pull Wren farther from the pit.

A sizzling sound, like fish oil dropped on hot rocks, came from Shooting Star's flesh. With hands gooey with honey, I patted out flames, pulled off what was left of smoldering sage.

"What happened!" Grey Doe panted as she rolled from under us. She pushed open the hide covering to the outside, not waiting for an answer. Smoke and bad smells billowed out. She crawled out herself, still coughing.

Wren whimpered beneath my stinging hands. Her flesh burned red, and the bottoms of her feet were blistered with soot. Honey felt soothing on my burned hands, something that surprised me as I held Wren's tender feet. She winced, then added in panting breaths, "It helps."

"More honey!" I shouted to Grey Doe who stood outside, thumping smoldering ashes sparkling near the opening.

She squatted and looked at me, at us.

"It eats the stinging," I said.

"I will see if Wuzzie has blazing-star leaves," she said, in control now that the danger passed. "You," she said to me, "take the blanket, dip it in the river. We will wrap her burns. That is how it is done. Maybe I'll see about honey." Her words scolded as though I had suggested something childish, of no value.

But the honey felt good on my own hands and the stinging soon stopped.

Though we were not to be interrupted during this private time, Willow Basket spied Grey Doe leaving and knew something bad had happened. She saw the excess smoke too, so joined us.

"Soak this in the river, for Wren's burns," I told her. I continued to rub the sticky honey over Wren's red back, massaged it gently into her toes and her feet, tried not to notice how she shivered with the scorching pain.

When the wet blanket arrived, Wren would not use it, wanted the sweet healing of honey instead.

"You make it worse," Grey Doe chided her. "Do what you're told, now."

Wren agreed to the blazing-star poultice Grey Doe brought back, but Sunmiet's honey sent by Lukwsh made her skin feel best, she said.

That evening, in the darkness of the hut, I offered to gather Wren's wood for her.

Grey Doe scoffed. "She must gather her own to make the passage. The spirits would not understand if another made the piles."

"But her feet..."

"You must not deprive her of the joy she will earn by completing her tasks on her own feet. Besides," she added with her old bite, her chin pushing the air before her, "you think that honey heals? Then why worry. She will walk with no trouble at all."

I watched Wren hobble out in the morning for her early gathering, grateful the third week had passed and only one remained. I wished she did not need to travel so far to bring her wood. I thought through the night that there had to be another way.

With the silence of a marmot sitting out a coyote's eyes, I reworked the piles while Grey Doe slept. Gently lifting greasewood and sagebrush from several mounds, I made another and another, gradually shrinking larger piles, ending with many more. I hoped Grey Doe's old eyes did not notice.

"She will be angry," Wren whispered when she returned from her first forage.

"Only if we tell her. Otherwise, she will never know," I said and rubbed honey into Wren's feet, peeled dead black skin from her heels and her toes and wrapped her ankles and tender feet in rabbit pelts, fur side out. And I raised a song to the Spirit that might know my name and hers, be even wiser than the wind. I asked him to put out the flame in Wren's feet.

Grey Doe did not discover us. When she awoke, Wren would make her way back for more wood. When we left the hut at the end of the week, Wren said her skin felt tender to cold and to hot, but it felt smooth like a baby's bottom without scarring. Her feet were the color of a red sunrise, though the natural bronze color was sure to return.

When she showed Wuzzie that the honey took away both sting and scars, he snorted.

"It is the blazing-star poultice, not what that *tibo* discovered," he said.

But Wren noticed later that he kept a new tin of the honey next to his fire.

I said nothing to anyone about speaking with a Spirit or how it seemed to have listened. I kept to myself the satisfaction of knowing that what I thought of had brought some healing to a friend.

As was the custom, Wren divided her clothes between Grey Doe and me when we finished in the hut—clothes which were all too short for either of us. Lukwsh delivered her a burled bowl in honor of her woman state, and together we made new clothes from traded cloth Vanilla Leaf had received from the army's wagon. She traded for one of Wren's baskets.

It pleased me that I recognized the patterns, knew what they expected yet could take what action I thought best. Nothing bad happened because I helped Wren gather wood; nothing bad had happened because I learned to blend.

While we worked the cloth in the pale light of the wickiup fire, caught up on the gossip from our time away, Wren told Lukwsh of the honey cure and of my helping with her gathering. Lukwsh listened quietly, then her fingers touched my knee as we knelt side by side, and her eyes watered in appreciation. I let her look of kindness wash over me, let it fall like rainwater in a gentle spring, felt it refresh me, cleanse me, let myself feel loved. My heart split wider, as a *wada* seed in spring.

I think that moment I made the choice to stay, to remain where I felt cherished, where I belonged.

In the spring of the year known by Sarah's agents as 1871, I felt that I might soon be taken as Shard's wife. Instead, Thunder Caller announced that we would charm the antelope, and all attention turned to this.

Word came into Wuzzie's vision that a herd grazed not far from Snow Mountain. Headman We-ah-wee-wah announced a time of dry ground, a hard winter ahead, so the antelope would be welcome both for food and hides and would carry us through the winter.

"Ten days from now we will charm them," Thunder Caller announced to the gathering. "Each must do their part."

"Not you," Wuzzie said, his finger pointing at me through the seated crowd gathered in the headman's lodge. I sat among the women in the back and turned to see who Wuzzie pointed at behind me. I had not spoken, made myself small.

"It would upset the spirits to have someone who does not listen to them be nearby," Wuzzie said.

His bony finger pointed at me.

Wuzzie did not know I prayed to a listening Spirit, could not know. He hung on to old hatreds such as my plunging in the water with Wren. Like Shard, Wuzzie had been traveling more. But Wuzzie danced with a prophet man named Smohalla, and he told us Smohalla could raise the dead, destroy the *tibo*.

Wuzzie stood and walked wide around me, muttering about *wehe* not being of enough value for the vermin he brought into this band. I wondered, then, if he also feared me, believed I stocked some power I did not have. A prideful, foolish thought.

"We need all hands to help," Shard said, his voice deep like the man he had become. "All must listen to the drum's vibration, sing the songs." He sat not near the seat of power, but his voice carried it. The air in the lodge felt hot, close.

Wuzzie's neck jerked quickly to where Shard sat cross-legged in the circle of men.

"This herd has been sent. No *tibo* will stain the Creator's provision. South, the owls brought sickness and many have died. North, they wage war." He nodded his head in the directions, his arms folded across his chest. "It is a gift to Lukwsh that her owl is still among us. But no owl will be among us while we hunt."

"Only small children and old ones are to be left be-hind," Thunder Caller said, his last word dropping.

"Let that one remain with the children," Grey Doe said.

There was a long quiet broken by the words: "This is a good plan." Wuzzie sat back down.

"The *moo'a* can stay with the children," Shard insisted. "Neither will be harmed then or asked to do more than their share. To charm such a large herd, each young back is needed, including that of all our sisters."

Grey Doe grinned at his final word, lifted her chin toward me. Her look distressed me, but I had no time to respond.

"Who are you to know so much about antelope?" Stink Bug said.

A murmur of discontent rumbled around the gathering. Brothers speaking against brothers in the council boded poorly.

Stink Bug had grown large, carried a man's chest, a boy's puffed-up pride. I noticed Flake and other dogs dropped their tails between their legs when he walked near. He scoffed at me when I grabbed at his arm once in the futile defense of a pup. Later, I watched him move in anger against his horse, leaving welts as he smiled.

"Have you been present when we have hunted in recent years? No," he said.

From behind him, I could see his thick neck turning a reddish brown beneath the part in his black braids as he made his charges against his brother.

"Neither have I been on raids to rattle white women in their gardens," Shard said. "I have other thoughts than making their men angry enough to shoot for no reason."

"They need no reason." Stink Bug snorted and shifted weight on his wide buttocks. "It will not matter how woman-like your words are. They will still take what they wish unless we do what we know."

"It is not wise to speak of war when we have been given the gift of a herd," Thunder Caller said wisely, breaking the brothers' eye arrows.

"If she stumbles, is foolish, it will be bad," Wuzzie said. "All will be lost. Mistakes. Errors. Disobedience. All cause problems."

"It is so for each of us," Shard said. "No one's thoughts must stray from the charming. Each must say openly if we trip or make a mistake. We all know this."

"We will ask Shell Flower to help build mounds, then return to be with the children and *moo'a*. That way all are served."

All but me, I thought.

"This is a good plan also," Wuzzie agreed, "as long as As-i-am"—he dragged out the word—"does nothing foolish."

We rose and filed out from the lodge, the issue settled. But Wuzzie's words made me wonder again at my place. I thought of Shard, of his willingness to defend me. But was it as his sister or his friend, or as a future mate?

I felt a hand on my shoulder.

"Building the mounds is most important," Shard said, pressing with his fingers for me to stop. His voice flowed over me like wind whispering in tall pines on the way to the rocky crest of Snow Mountain. People passed around us, rushed a bit as the air smelled of rain.

"It is the mounds and the movement that charm them. The antelope know about one, the other is new. Both make the prong horns think they are walking to safety."

"But they aren't," I said.

A pause, then, "You will be part of what matters before you leave." Wisps of black hair found their place across his face. He shook his head, did not lose my stare.

"What I have to give is an unworthy gift?" I asked.

"Just different," he said, this time with no pause, as though he had thought about me in this way before.

We walked toward the edge of the lake, the smell of salt and mud mingled in the air. I felt a dog sniff at my hands. Smoke, Shard's new one. The dog chewed gently on his fingers, came between us.

"He does not accept you as the head of his pack," I told Shard. "You are just a littermate, someone to play with and chew." I reached across to scratch Smoke's ears. "He will not listen to you unless you act like a headman."

Shard laughed, paused. "So you have discovered the ways of dogs, now," he said.

"They are easier to understand."

I missed the dogs when Shard left, had never become attached to another as I had to Pinenut, was surprised now that I looked for Flake.

Smoke bounded into the water scattering mudhens, setting swans to escape.

"You will avoid seeing them scattered and confused after they walk through the openings and it is not what they thought," Shard said, and I realized he had returned to the antelope. "Even though it means food for the people, and I am grateful, it is always a sadness for me when I see that they have trusted us. The fright shows wild in their eyes at their mistake, but they are unable to escape, their minds lull them, make fences that trap them."

It took many words from Shard to share his thought out loud. His eyes held a faraway look, as though he saw something more than antelope charmed then destroyed.

"You risked speaking," I told him, hoping he understood what I meant.

"A brother must always talk for his little sister," he said, a smile in his voice, teasing.

I felt a flame on my neck, an irritation at his lightness for my feeling.

"What about your brother? Did you wish to talk for him? Is that why he says such things about you in front of others?"

Shard grew silent and squatted at the lake's edge.

"Who knows what makes my brother mad," he said. He picked up a stick and drew in the mud. "His anger feeds on what he cannot change. Like all of us. Maybe anger at an older brother who has no power, either." Shard sighed, then slapped his hand on his thigh to bring the dog. "Stink Bug could make a change, but he prefers to use it to stomp others."

He stood and took my hand, stepped back from Smoke as he ran out of the darkness toward us and shook himself of the wet as he panted into the night.

I resisted speaking into the silence, and Shard finally spoke, a lightness to his voice: "I should have stayed so he would not be alone in a lodge with women. That can make a man mad." I could hear a grin in his voice and a wish to change the subject as we started to walk.

"Maybe he will leave, like you did," I said, "if he can find a woman to fix pine nut stew and live without little sisters to boss around."

"Some woman's grandmother will invite him in. Grandmothers like big eaters." He laughed.

The possibility had not entered my mind before. Lying at a grand-mother's feet, yes, but moving in? Women here who married did not leave their lodges. Men joined them.

So Lukwsh *had* been different. She had come to a new place. Her hus-band had created their lodge that did not include his mother or grandmother. Only the children of his first wife. And one child together before the father died.

"Does a grandmother wait for you, too?" I asked.

The pause seemed longer than usual, and I thought of Vanilla Leaf's grandmother or maybe someone in a faraway place. And what of me, of my choices, what lodge would gather my husband to its fire if I stayed here?

"You will go away, to find a wife?"

"My father did," he said too quickly.

His hands covered mine, alerting all my senses. I felt the callous ridge from the leather reins he held when he rode, the roughness from the waters his hands dipped into for ducks and for fish. Our breaths mingled in the small distance between us. I wondered if he could hear my heart. I did not want to move. I wanted to hold on, to savor the sweet tension of the moment.

"You have gone away," Shard said and moved his wide hand in front of my eyes to bring me back.

"Being different," I lied.

"I like a spear that is unlike any other," he said, and I thought he spoke of the uniqueness of me. "One that feels good in my hands, alone."

He pulled me closer to him, and I pressed my head to his chest.

"Wuzzie will not like this," I said.

He paused, moved me back away from him enough to look into my eyes. "Nor Grey Doe. But it is not theirs to decide."

Perhaps we spoke of the antelope charming, but it felt as though these words could speak of love as well.

We walked in silence back to Lukwsh's lodge. His fingers still touched mine, though our hands were bumped by Smoke slipping between us as he moved in and out of the darkness. Shard stepped aside at the lodge opening and touched my back lightly as I bent to enter. I turned, thinking he had something more to say. And I wanted to catch the sweetness of his breath so close to my face.

"It is time your *brother* brings you back," Grey Doe said into the night. She snapped back the entering flap, broke our spell. "Your *brother*," her words hissed, "nothing more."

Shard disappeared into the dark, and I shut out the chattering Grey Doe continued in my ear. Instead, I remembered Shard's words about liking a special spear, about the choices being our own.

So I stayed with them for the beginning of the charming when Thunder Caller and Wuzzie chose two men to be the messengers to the antelope. I felt some pride mixed with worry when both Stink Bug and Shard were named.

We had traveled south, along the west side of Snow Mountain more often now called Steens. There a wide basin opened, sunk south gently as the summer sun eased out of the day. Clusters of sagebrush and rabbit brush, sparse stands of juniper and tall grasses near springs dotted the earth, attracted the antelope. A spring rain washed the desert into pungency.

In the morning, the two men chosen lit their sagebrush torches and stood back to back, then walked away from each other, marking a wide circle with their torches in the dirt as directed by Wuzzie and the headman.

The rest of us began making small houses from grasses and willows we brought with us, dragged by the dogs and horses loaded with our tule mats. Each built a small lodge on the marked circle. Thunder Caller's grass house rose in the center of the ring. Across from him, facing east and the antelope far in the distance not seen yet by any eyes, was an opening.

In the morning, they made another, beyond the ring of huts we slept in. We gathered grasses and sagebrush and greasewood and stones and rabbit brush, and I was reminded of my first days in the private hut, wondered if this too was a passage into something new.

A mound formed while Buck Brush and Oytes, who both stood taller than the rest, took the branches we handed them from our baskets or the backs of Flake and Smoke and all other dogs and ponies. Buck Brush made the mound high so it could be seen from a great distance. Thunder Caller stepped three hundred long strides and marked where the next mound on the circle would rise. We repeated the cycle, three hundred strides between, until six were complete.

No one stubbed their toes or dropped a rock intended for its place. No one lied or made errors without telling. Wuzzie pranced around, proud that no one disobeyed the rules he thought necessary so that the charming would proceed without trouble.

In the night, loved ones held each other, fell into deep sleeps from the effort of our labors. Only the dogs responded to the coyote howls that whoop-whoop-whooped in the distance.

Then the charming began.

I thought I should return to the children and *moo'a,* but no one spoke of it and I did not wish to leave. I stayed and made myself blend as best I could, bending over so my longer legs would not make me stand apart.

For five mornings and evenings we charmed.

I wanted to pay attention, but my eyes drifted to where Shard sat across the circle. Thunder Caller passed him the pipe, and each man after smoked, and then the women. Vanilla Leaf handed Thunder Caller the elk hide drum filled with her name's sake. With a haunting sound, hollow like depths of caves, sad like the call of a mateless goose, Thunder Caller began to strike the drum. At its tapered ends, the stick vibrated on the stretched hide like the flutter of a throat. I felt the tremor from the vibration deep within me, moving through my limbs. The sounds and rhythms, the spirit of the stalk, the days of building mounds and waiting forced out songs now, high-pitched, undulating sounds that carried far beyond our memories, far beyond our mounds.

Perhaps it was the drumbeat kept in cadence with my heart. Perhaps the sorrowful scent of moist sage mixed with the swimming taste of sacred smoke. Or perhaps it was the throbbing in my head, my chest, my inner being that took my mind beyond where it should go.

I left the gathering under a dark sky sprinkled with stars like cottonwood fluff, grateful to be undiscovered. Tomorrow Shard would begin the chant and march, and the next day, I would be sent away. I pulled his thoughts to mine across the desert, knew he thought of me at the moment I laid my head down on my mat.

My mind entered sleep as though entwined by his embrace, as though we were strong cordage strung together in a net. So when Shard came to me, lay in my dreams on the rabbit furs next to Lukwsh and Wren and me, I was ready for his fingers to press against mine. Sage and sweetgrass swirled about my dreams like soft movements just below sleep. Lifting arms and sinew high above our heads, I rose up with him until we twisted out through the smoke hole, embraced as one by night, soft like the winding of a rabbit rope, stretched to reach great heights.

I awoke as dawn moved soft as a baby's breath into the lodge. I lay still, not sure if what I remembered of the night belonged to sleep or real.

That morning, the sixth morning, Shard and Stink Bug walked with their torches into the desert, out through the opening across from the headman's lodge, out through the center toward the herd. They walked in opposite directions around the outer mound circle, and when they met on the other side, they stopped, smoked, then crossed again. This time they walked a new circle that was wide and reached far enough to surround the herd that until now has been known only by faith, only by Wuzzie's vision.

Shard and Stink Bug had the honor of seeing the antelope first.

The torchbearers were intent, they never let themselves be seen. They returned in the other's footsteps, then they met at the base of the large circle and reported back to Thunder Caller the herd's movement and size. They reported seeing a large herd of great value. Tomorrow, the men and boys would follow Shard and Stink Bug on their circle walks. For five more days they would walk the same paths, and on the sixth day, the antelope would follow them around the circle, back into the center between the mounds. They would not walk away or run, for they were charmed into seeing fences where there were none and so they remained, captives of the lulls in their minds.

It had always been so.

"You go now," Wuzzie said to me the night before the men would lead the pronghorns back. "Take Summer Rain with you."

I didn't think Summer Rain would like the punishment being sent with me meant.

"She can watch children," he said.

And me, I thought.

"I will talk with her myself," Wuzzie said in his fluttering voice, almost friendly. "So she will see how going now will help."

Lukwsh nodded to me, said reassuring, "We come, in eight, nine days, with meat and hides. Plenty to keep us busy."

I looked for Shard to offer something different, but he did not. No one would rescue me from what I did not want. He prepared himself to lure the antelope, that was his task. He did not remember me or what had passed between us.

I would have talked myself past this view and remembered the closeness we had shared, but I saw him speaking with Thunder Caller near the headman's lodge. Joy rose up from his deep laughter, the men pleased that the herd grazed where it was meant to be and carried large numbers. Even Stink Bug seemed to blend into the gathering of men, stood and talked and offered words that brought bursts of laughter.

Vanilla Leaf walked close and touched Shard's arm. Boldly she intruded on these men. But Shard did not seem to mind. He bent his head to her. Maybe to listen above the joking and laughing, but too close, I thought, too smiling for a man of few words.

She smiled back, her wide mouth with straight teeth, those dark flashing eyes. He shared what she said with others, and they nodded and smiled. He brought her into the circle! Her words were wise, it seemed. Shard nodded and bent close to hear her again, put his hand on her shoulder to pull her closer, her voice is so soft.

He held no thoughts now of antelope.

He pushed hair the breeze had blown into her eyes. I could almost feel the touch of his fingers on her face, the fierce shock through my being such a touch would leave left me now in pain. I tried to ignore the ache behind my eyes.

A burning welled up inside me and formed an unfilled hole of disappointment and grief. I could not take my eyes from it, could not turn away. I watched him touch the skin of Vanilla Leaf and reach inside her soul.

It came to me that Shard had only shared my sleep deep in my dreams, had never meant to make me think such feelings bridged the dream time into day.

The next choice was not of my making, or so I told myself. In years since, looking back, I know I had some place in it, was not swept along by a fast-moving stream. My mind was present. Still, my anger chose, my hurt decided. My unworthiness kept my wisdom buried deep beneath my judgment, separated from my helpful spirit, culled from my very soul.

My eyes wore a screen of seething as Shard stood talking with Vanilla Leaf. He had draped an arm around her to better bring her into the circle.

I turned toward Wuzzie and watched him talk with Summer Rain, saw how he looked up to her face as soft as sweet gum, as dark as cattails. I made judgments of my own.

Summer Rain scowled, probably wishing she had gone with Natchez, Sarah's brother, so she would not become a part of this affair. Wuzzie stood shorter than she, but he directed, told her, I imagined, that she must return with me. She glanced over his head to catch my eyes, said something to him, her mouth snapping like a hungry dog, the dimples disappearing. He squeezed her shoulder, those spider-like fingers pinching, and I saw her bend into him, her face a wince of pain. She nodded once, then, an obedient girl, and he released her.

Hot tears of imaginings of where Shard slept, whose grandmother called his name, filled the long night. In the morning, we two, obedient girls, somehow different, started back. But we were obedient. Surely obedient.

When Summer Rain suggested in her child-like voice that we make our journey an entertaining treat, it should not be so surprising that I did not wait long to consider the temptation.

"We can parallel the herd. Who will see us?" she said. "No one. We will walk as one and charm the antelope ourselves."

I did not recognize until much later how a wound could hurt so deeply and so quickly that it might require removal. I did not know that more than antelope are prone to charming by the fancy of lulled minds.

HELD IN THE MIND OF ANOTHER

"WE WILL CAUSE TROUBLE?" I asked Summer Rain. I wonder now why I bothered with the question. I had already decided that it did not matter.

It was early in the morning, before the people started out. We carried dried berries baked in pine nut cakes, the food of outcasts headed out.

"It works," she told me.

For the first time, I wondered if she, too, were out of favor, perhaps for some behavior I knew nothing about.

"My cousin Mary and I made ourselves look like an animal, and the antelope believed."

She bent over, her arms swinging in front of her, hips swaying from side to side like a cumbersome cow.

"We were close enough to see their brown-and-white-striped throats," she said, her words falling to the ground. "I could have touched the fine hairs on their black noses if my arm had been twice as long."

"They did not spook?" I didn't want to ruin the hunt, only steal a memory of some might.

She stood, hands on hips. "No! I heard them break wind, saw them blink their eyes, wiggle their ears behind their black horns."

I looked skeptical.

"It is so! Here, I will put my head in your back and we will walk, bent over, just a little way. The herd will not see us. Before the people lure the antelope back, we will be gone. It is just for a moment, just something of our own to share since we will not be part of the end."

Her dimple appeared in her chubby cheek. "We cannot hurt the charming. It is already almost finished. If it were otherwise, Wuzzie would have sent an escort with us to make sure we did not stumble or lie or do anything to warp things." She smiled.

Perhaps, I decided, I could make this charming something of my own design and hide in the fabric my pain of disappointment.

"I'll put my head to your back," I said.

I could lower my hands from her hips quickly, drop to the desert if a buck caught our scent or someone spotted us.

"Good," she said and turned to lead me in my own charming.

I bent my head, held her hips, and began to sway.

We watched as pronghorns lifted their heads and sniffed at the wind, then lowered their heads again. We were close enough to see the herd Wuzzie had dreamed of. They moved like a sea of brown and white, the color of bunch grass and sand, ripping at grasses, lifting their heads, then returning to graze. Yearlings bounded and bucked and scattered dirt as Summer Rain and I eased our way closer, quietly, walking as one.

In the distance behind us, I could see the smoke of torches, tiny wisps of dark clouds carried east. The people walked behind us, slowly making their way around the first circle, soon to surround the herd and move them toward the closed circles. The movements were so even, so gradual, taken in such small steps that the antelope would be trapped by noticing something that was different, but not be alarmed. They would think that little had changed, only some new thing now shared their range.

After some time of walking and watching, we crossed over the tracks made by walkers from the days before.

"We can go closer," Summer Rain whispered over her shoulder. "Drop down, see how far we come."

Beneath the shade of a sage we rested, lying on our bellies, eyes staring into distance. The antelope were hidden by sagebrush, still upwind of us. But if I rose slowly I could see them, throats blended from the colors of white rabbits and tawny deer. The antelope moved unaware, and so did I. I failed to see trouble in my watching, did not recognize danger in the desert.

Summer Rain raised up beside me.

"Ease back," I whispered. "We're close!"

She slid back down.

I felt a surge of power as I sat there, waiting, watching. The day felt sultry and dry, and meadowlarks warbled and flitted from the sage above our heads. Perhaps we dozed.

We did not see the torch smoke, at least I did not.

"Go closer." Her voice was a hiss not unlike a snake's and took me from my sleep.

"We'll have some good story to tell our children of how we stalked the antelope without them knowing." She sat up, her slender back to the herd for a moment. "Too bad we did not take Shard's spear," she said. "We could take a hide ourselves."

She had more bravery than I remembered. I wondered where her courage came from, until I heard her gasp. I turned to look at her. She pointed, her eyes as big as fists.

From where we had walked was not so long a distance. But it had taken us inside the circle and between the antelope and our people. Half the charmers who followed Shard were walking the circle tracks close enough for us to hear a cough, the slap of their feet against hard earth. They made better time than expected. The smoke blew close enough for us to smell.

I hoped the charmers were still far enough away they would not see us. And we were almost safe—except for one.

He was not to follow, was told to remain with the women at the mound site. But he had not listened either, and now he stood, tail wagging high above his back, barking, barking at a familiar scent. At me.

My heart pounded. I felt cold and hot at once, caught in an act of disobedience. I could not call out and tell him to stop. I could not disappear or make my scent sink into sage.

I did not know what Summer Rain would do.

Why had I done this, made a choice that put me at risk? Perhaps my presence set the charmers at risk too. I thought of Wren and the dance she could not stop or start and wondered if I had her illness, one that made me do things that were the opposite of what the people thought I should. What punishment would I attract if Shard or Stink Bug or someone else should break their stride to search for what bothered Flake and found me?

Summer Rain slid down, knees to chest, and brought her hands across her ears and head as though such moves could hide her. The sound of animals once gently grazing now clattered through the sagebrush, throwing the heavy scent of desert like a blanket on my head. A meadowlark shrieked in my ears louder than my heartbeat, louder than the sounds of antelope disrupted in their charm. Torch smoke drifted above me, and I whimpered in my huddle and hoped I could vanish too.

I felt a prayer rise up, knew I did not deserve what I would ask. Make us invisible; don't let the antelope turn back toward us or be scattered by the dog! A foolish person's prayer, spoken as though the Spirit listened even when the trouble had been invited. Make them all—people, dogs, and pronghorns—keep walking the way that they should go; keep them charmed and I will never choose wrongly again, I said under my breath.

It was a promise I knew I could not keep.

Flake barked a long time before I realized no one would search for the cause of the dog's distress. To look would break the spell that charmed the antelope. To leave the path would announce that they had thought of something other than the hunt!

Eventually Flake left, following them. The sounds of their shuffling evaporated in the wind. Flake's bark grew fainter.

"You are powerful," Summer Rain said. "I heard you praying that we could not be seen."

Her eyes bore a frightened look, though I could not tell if our close call or my prayer scared her. The two of us sat until we could not smell the smoke, then made our way as one, quickly, across the charmer's tracks, careful not to step on them, walking low, away, before the second group passed on the circle. Beyond the tracks, we dropped beneath some rabbit brush and greasewood. There we waited until almost dusk.

A vermilion sunset melted across the wide expanse of desert, settling on sagebrush. My heart no longer pounded in my head. Summer Rain's eyes searched the growing darkness and dropped in shame whenever they met mine.

Careful not to speak or get upwind of the herd being gently urged toward the mounds, careful not to mention the foolishness of our ways, we eased out of the inner circle and away. We made a dry camp along a small creek below a ridge rock.

Summer Rain said the stream was a safe place, pouring out from a spring cut into a jagged lava ridge some distance beyond us. Red willows speared up toward the clear night sky and leaned out over the fast-moving stream. A night owl hooted. It was like a refuge, this creek, and so we called it "home" between ourselves, ate dried berries, and curled up together in the cool night. I sighed relief. We were made invisible, were not seen.

We did not speak of it again, Summer Rain and I, and yet there was a bond between us not tied before. I was uncertain whether what tethered us together would keep me safe or later, bind me up.

When the band returned from the hunt, they spoke of success, how the antelope followed the people into the circle and danced and pranced and bucked but would not go out between the mounds because their minds made fences there, where the people had walked. And so they were all charmed, then killed, every one, almost all with head shots to avoid damage to the meat and hide. Arrows and the bullets of the rifles traded for by men such as Shard and Oytes and even Stink Bug met their mark.

Lukwsh wore sweat on her forehead from the weight of her work. Brains and spinal cords were saved and brought back with the hides, and Summer Rain and I helped Lukwsh and the other women bury them in the wet ground near the lakes.

"Get away," Grey Doe said, batting lightly at her hawk who raised in protest, sang his own high-pitched song. "Find scraps over there. Oh, look how he swoops," Grey Doe said. "Gets in that pile before the dogs can catch him. Fa-a-st," she said, her voice taking a slide from high to low.

All seemed as it should be.

After several days, Wren and I along with Lukwsh and Grey Doe pushed the soft organs into baskets of water and then squeezed them through a hemp sieve to ready them.

And when the hides were moist, the hair slipping and more easily scraped with rib bones, we braced four smooth cottonwood logs against each other and stretched the hides over the ends, scraped and pulled at the hair, taking all of it, taking turns dabbing at drying hides with handfuls of water and wet hair. The work took all my energy and thoughts, gave me a place to leave my anger and frustration when I thought I saw Shard stand close to someone else.

When the hides were smooth, we rubbed the mixture of brains into what the antelope gave us and said we did not mind that the leather felt like slick snot from our noses on cold days. The hides would keep us warm beneath our rabbit blankets, be available for trade. They had been given us because the people did what they were told to do and charmed the herd.

The hunt proved successful, everyone said. We feasted on roasted meat, dried strips of loin in the sun. No one knew otherwise, and Wuzzie said the spirits smiled.

Sarah did not ride our way that summer. She had married a military man named Bartlett who used sweet words, was pleasant to look upon with his yellow hair, a man who enjoyed fine horses and too much wine. The marriage was not allowed in Nevada where *tibos* and Indians were prevented from joining, and so she traveled east. When I heard of it, I was pleased for her and wondered if her soldier might know of a way to track backwards should I ask him, if I somehow found a name. I even wondered if the blond-haired man might be someone from my past. They were foolish thoughts, but thinking them gave me less time to think of what I did not have.

Sarah had found someone to share time with, someone who gave his warmth away. I missed her because she talked with agents and the army, talked of how white people thought. The summer wore on with little rain and long hot days that burned our feet and dried berries on the bushes. Some said only Sarah's words with the soldiers would keep the army filling wagons of food for those who were willing to put their bellies above their beliefs.

My own filling up came in another way. After the charming, Shard remained. He did not return to working for the rancher or the blacksmith named Johnson. I watched to see if he sought out Vanilla Leaf. But he spent no time with her.

Instead, my eyes found him as he fished at the Silvies in the summer, and my looks of longing seemed returned. I began to set aside my suspicious thoughts, wonder if my hot fury at the charming had cast a shadow on my judgment, forced me into a choice better left aside.

"Walk with me," he said in the early fall.

Beneath cottonwood trees turning the color of yellow pollen, Shard's white-pawed dog sniffed at Flake's behind. They settled differences and raced with us to scatter birds at the lake and grab up rabbits on the run. Together they circled sage hens, allowing Shard to shoot them, while Flake brought them happily back to me.

"So. My dog prefers to bring his catch to you," Shard said smiling.

"I am the better cook."

At Willow Basket and James's wedding dance, Shard put his hand in mine and we danced the owl dance together. I knew we were both thinking of the night bird and not the difference in our skin.

My eyes tried not to notice the scowl of Grey Doe nor the face of Lukwsh that like the winter lake, cool and smooth, covered unknown depth.

Instead, I touched Shard's hand, my heart beating fast as a fancy dance swirled in my head. I did not think about the future and held him in my mind no less when he just left me at my lodge than when he was gone on long journeys of some weeks. Each separation ended was like a basket empty for a lifetime, finally filled.

We began to risk more time together.

Once we rode followed by dogs to the place where Wuzzie found me. We spent some moments seeking a lost treasure basket.

"Probably part of the earth," I told him without hope, my hands scratching at the ground, moving rock pebbles. His answer warmed me.

"Some things are worth doing no matter how they turn out. Looking is no waste."

"We should climb, then, too," I said. "To see beyond the mountains where the rivers run together."

He laughed. "The ocean is farther than what you can see. Beyond even another set of mountains."

"Some things are worth doing," I teased him.

"Let's climb, then, Pussytoes." We did, carefully this time, until we reached the top. It was farther than I had ever seen.

"It is not the ocean," he said after some time of letting the wind blow against us, ruffling his long hair, tugging at my hair below the barrette. "Someday, I will take you there."

When we rode away, empty-handed, I knew that the tiny gold chain was lost forever and with it the strongest hope I had to keep on searching. The patch of pink pinafore I once wore had disappeared, too. Even the bone of a Modoc dog now belonged to the past. Nothing remained of that time before the Modocs but the knots of my memory, the search of my heart.

We traveled south to Snow Mountain on that journey. Shard extended his hand to mine and pulled me up behind him on his spotted horse. My arms reached around him, felt the softness of his belly, the firmness of his back. His black hair scented with sage swung before my face as we rode in rhythm up the ridges.

At a spring bubbling from beneath dark rocks, I rinsed the cloth head-band he wore, hung it to dry on a juniper tree while we talked of simple things such as dogs and weighty things such as war. He picked pussytoes for me, their curled blossoms like the bottom of a cougar's foot, stems like silver tules. During stops where we ate dried seed cakes, he told me of his journey near this place, how a mountain lion shared its power with him so Shard could enter life as a warrior and man.

We spoke of what might happen if we joined, became as one in a marriage of the people, which wickiup would hold our baskets. We used no names, spoke to make it sound as if we spoke of others, such as Sarah and her lieutenant, and yet we thought of ourselves. I knew the talking was of us.

To hope for more was frightening. I was afraid to speak out loud how I might feel for fear the words themselves could become jealous of the feelings, take for themselves what pleased me the most.

We rode through thickets of timber, past prairies like palms streaked with tiny rivulets of streams. The thin soil dotted with white flowers hugged rocks between green and red grasses and stretched like moss to the sides of gorges so immense my breath caught. In the stinging winds, I hugged him closer. We were one in how we saw this world, and I was pleased beyond measure to be sharing such a feast of life and vision with someone I had come to love, someone I held now in my mind.

For I had come to love him, fearful as that was.

In times since, I have heard it said that first love is the one of children, that it does not bear the weight of older woes and so is considered smaller, of less value. But I have felt such love, and when I hear of it among the young, I nod in knowing. Such love is not the kind a breeze can drift away.

Grey Doe's scowls increased in the fall. Wuzzie's looks alarmed. But so deep was our devotion, so blind were our eyes that we did not notice how the others walked beside us or how they watched us through calloused eyes. It seemed enough to know that when Shard entered my thoughts, I was also entering his.

I tried especially to ignore Grey Doe's looks. She was the grandmother who would make room at her feet for the suitor of a granddaughter and I knew she would not. For we were different, Shard and I, arrived from different places and yet had shared a lodge.

Shard spoke little of his feelings and looked with confusion when I told him of my pain the day he stroked Vanilla Leaf's cheek, the day before I left the charming.

"I have no memory of it," he said, his eyes looking into the past.

He seemed to share the truth, though why the moment was marked differently for him than me became a puzzle never solved. And while his words were few, I knew by the look of his eyes when he first saw me enter the headman's lodge for council, or the way his fingers lingered on my hand when he lifted a basket to my back, or the gentle touch of his lips on my forehead, cheek, and then my mouth, that I had been settling inside his thoughts, had been held, too, like a precious treasure.

I did not know where this filling up would take me. I only chose to let it be, let myself imagine life here with these people and this man, stopped my search for an unknown, distant future, and accepted the present that held my hand.

When the cottonwood leaves turned dark and dropped into the gaunt streams that trickled to the lakes with deep muddy shores, Sarah's brother Natchez sent word to Summer Rain that he would not join her until winter.

"He goes to the great salt lake," she told me with a sigh.

The sweet-talking first lieutenant husband of Sarah had resigned from the military, and Natchez, the brother-in-law, left to escort his sister back to Nevada following their divorce.

"She should have married one of her own," Grey Doe said, and at first I was not certain if she spoke of Sarah or of Summer Rain waiting for her Nevada man. We sat together in Grey Doe's lodge forming rabbit pelt chains. I tried to make myself small with her talk of what didn't belong.

"Her sharp tongue scares them off," Summer Rain answered. "Or maybe like moths she is attracted to bright light even if it does burn."

Grey Doe grunted. "They are more wary of changing color."

Wren touched the back of my hand, and I mouthed the words, worked my fingers.

"It does not rub off," Wren said then and tied her rabbit skin through its eyehole, dropped her rope in her lap. "See?" She showed her feet, then her hands, turning them this way and that before us.

Grey Doe motioned her to put her feet down.

Wren continued. "They did not stay pink even with my white sister rubbing and rubbing with honey," she said. She held her palm up for all to see, and I noticed also that the scar that once sliced there had faded.

"No? Look at us," Grey Doe said, pushing her chin into wind. "When we are finished with this rope, we will twist it as the white men do instead of the old way. That is how it rubs off, before we even know it."

"Is it so bad, Mother-of-my-husband?" Lukwsh asked. "The blanket is made faster. Has anything been lost?"

"Our old ways." Grey Doe yanked on the string of hides I held, surprisingly strong with only one hand.

"The old way is sacred just because it has always been?" Lukwsh said. "You do things differently than your mother because of your wound."

Her words were followed by a hush and dropped eyes. I had never heard Grey Doe's shriveled side discussed before.

"A blend of the old and new will make a stronger rope, na?" Lukwsh continued. "Like old clay and new clay make the best pots."

Grey Doe sat silent a long time before she grunted her response. "You have been too long in the presence of an owl. You forget who took my arm's strength. Quiet now, before your bloodless color rubs off on lesser beings."

Lukwsh's eyes dropped, and I saw the flash of pain that crossed them.

Her far-seeing was not appreciated, or perhaps it was her sadness for Sarah, who could think distinct, that bothered Grey Doe. I wondered about Sarah's sorrow with her sugar-word lieutenant now gone.

"Will Sarah still speak with the army?" I asked.

Grey Doe grunted. "She gives us no gifts with that effort."

"Some have gotten food and more cloth," Lukwsh said.

"What?" asked Wren, and I told her.

"It is a trick, to get us to agree to that reservation they still speak of," Grey Doe said.

"The calico is nice," Wren offered, one step behind each thought.

"Maybe her man leaving her will teach her who is safe to listen to and who should be left alone," Grey Doe said.

I wondered of my own place as Grey Doe hung on tighter to the past and showed fresh resentment of anything new.

The lakes froze over deep that winter, though in places the ice was as thin as our faces. Wind blew as though it had much to say each day. We huddled in the headman's lodge for stories that helped us forget how our stomachs growled. The horses wandered farther to scratch for grass through more shallow drifts of snow. The sky was as dark as a duck's bottom and promised wetness. Antelope meat disappeared faster than we imagined, and even the rabbits we'd driven to their deaths at the first sign of snow were all gone now, their hides warming our backs but no longer our bellies. The land became stingy with its roots and seeds, the lakes low with limited fish, the geese flew high and early. We entered winter thin, lived from the fat of our hips if we had them, grew haggard if we did not.

What We-ah-wee-wah had foreseen had come to pass. Little food remained.

Wuzzie sat in the headman's lodge. He wore a rabbit rope robe that flowed from his shoulders and spread like wings around him, covering his legs as he sat. His hands were hidden beneath the white fur folds twisted the old way with the rabbit's feet still on. He sang a song none of us had heard, could not have heard because he had just received it from the spirit land where he said he had resided, dead.

Five days earlier, Lukwsh had sent me to Wuzzie's lodge, told me to take dried nuts to him, and so I did. And there he lay, dead.

Lukwsh, too, believed him dead when I raced to her. But she saw slight breath in the coldness of his lodge, and so we stayed and built a small fire in the fire pit he had allowed to burn out. I thought of Lives in Pain's charge that a poor fire was a sign a lazy man lived inside. It did not seem to fit for Wuzzie, for even in his sleep I suspected he worked and planned.

Many took turns keeping his fire up and waiting to offer water if he awoke. On my day, Flake's tail beat against the floor, the only sound in Wuzzie's lodge filled with the scents of strange herbs and baskets of all shapes and sizes. The temptation proved too great. I looked around, touched a thing or two. There sat the tin of honey he said did not heal. In the shadow area, beyond the smoke hole, I found a burned stick, a stick Wuzzie maybe placed to his eyebrows to singe the hair away, or did he pluck them? When I bent to pick it up, I leaned over a spot of hard water and jumped back, startled by a face moving toward me, then back when I retreated.

It was my face reflected in the water that did not flow, my face with its straight, narrow nose. My face, with wisps of desert-sand hair falling across clear brown eyes, across hollow cheeks. I touched my fingers with broken nails to lips as red as choke cherries and judged what I saw—the face of a woman-child who did not belong.

After five days, Wuzzie awoke. It happened while I sat there, watching and waiting. His words startled, soft though they were.

"Get Grey Doe," he whispered.

Flake yawned at his words, stood, stretched front feet low, tail high, then sniffed at the man on the mat.

"And Thunder Caller," Wuzzie said as I rose, adding ominously, "you, do not return."

My feet took me along the paths made icy by tromping moccasins of sagebrush lined with fur. I wrapped my own blanket around my shoulders, felt the rabbit fur tickle my nose as I ducked into Thunder Caller's lodge. I delivered my message, then ran to Grey Doe.

"Wait here," she said as she threw her shoulder through the door, brushing past me.

Much activity followed. I could hear it outside in the muted sounds of feet on snow, the chatter of lowered voices. The sun came out and burned in a blue sky but offered no warmth. My body chilled beneath the blanket.

I heard voices directing the people to the headman's lodge where Wuzzie counseled about his dream-state and what his spirits told him. For a moment, I wondered if Shard believed in such spirits and thought that I would ask him, share my own questions of such things, when I heard shouts for Stink Bug.

Oytes broke into the activity as I watched from the lodge opening. He and Stink Bug were dispatched to carry Wuzzie in his weakened state. I decided to leave Grey Doe's space, chose to locate Lukwsh or Shard, did not like the gnawing feeling growing as I stood alone.

I met Shard, who touched his hands to my cheek, smiled reassurance to my eyes, but said nothing. I walked, hopping like Wren used to, to keep up with his long strides. Breathless, we entered the wickiup of the headman together.

The air was smoky, like fog rising over the lakes, and so I knew the pipe had already begun around the circle. Through the warm din, I saw Grey Doe raise her eyes at me, scowl, follow Shard as he slipped into his place not far from authority. I eased behind Willow Basket kneeling with her toddler child who peered around her shoulder now, smiling. I stretched my fingers out to the wide-eyed girl and touched her toes. She reached back, and I took her, then let my eyes look around her mother's broad backside, seeking Lukwsh, Wren, Stink Bug, and Wuzzie, identifying my allies and my foes.

Wuzzie started his song then, a high, plaintiff call without benefit of drums. It was not unlike a loon's. He sang, it seemed, for hours, though it was not so long as that. The air in the lodge smelled warm and smoky, and the scent of wintered bodies and tanned hides and children welled up in the space. Even the sweet grass smoke was not enough to keep some from sneezing, feeling their breaths thick in their throats. I felt almost dizzy and even started to doze, when the singing abruptly stopped.

"It has come to me," Wuzzie began in his voice that sounded almost as high-pitched as his song, "as it did to the prophets of my father's time, that we must rid ourselves of what does not belong."

His eyes were closed, his head slightly back, his arms forward, palms up in appeal.

"We have for too long allowed ourselves to be slowly charmed, like antelope. We permitted what is not of us to be among us and allowed bad spirits to roam. All of us have allowed this by giving shelter, food, names, and accepting what was offered. It is why the antelope did not give enough of themselves to feed us, why the *wada* were taken by the wind.

"I made it, my greed. I found it and did not walk away. I brought it here like a sore treated wrongly. So it has spread. I wished an obsidian *wehe*." Wetness oozed from his closed eyes. "I did not see how such a *namaka* would cut."

My breath came in short gasps, my chest heavy from the weight of the eyes of those who turned to look at me. My heart beat steady, not fast yet, but loudly in my ears.

"We will dance the dance that will take us from this bad state," he continued. "Our dancing will cause the earth to tremble, rocks to fall from the ridges. Snow will fall in summer, and the sun will burn up. Rain will water the dry earth. The lakes will rise and rivers flood. But we will be safe on high ground."

His talking of the dance had taken people's eyes from me, and I thought perhaps his attacks were not at me.

"We will be joined by the dead who will rise from their sleep as I was raised, as you see before you. Only the people will dance. Only the people will rise up. Only the people will live."

Then he opened his eyes, and though he did not know where I was sitting when he started, his eyes stared wide at me.

GATHER FARTHER, STAY OUT LONGER

A TURBULENCE LIKE THE SWIRL OF LEAVES picked up by a dust devil opened the flap at the door and whirled into the headman's lodge. Willow Basket twisted around to see me. Her eyes grew large before she snatched her child from me, an act that cut deeper than Wuzzie's words.

Lukwsh rose to stand beside me, and for one moment I thought she would speak for me, that her strength would be enough to keep me safe.

"Take her out," Wuzzie said to no arguing.

Dancing began almost immediately.

I could hear the drums and the singing behind me as I step-hopped to keep up with Lukwsh walking with long strides to her lodge.

"What will happen?" I whispered.

She touched her hand to mine, looked away and shook her head, as though she did not know. It was then the tightness in my chest began to choke me, to argue with the pounding of my heart.

In the days that followed, someone from each wickiup danced at all times until the people fell exhausted onto their blankets as though dead. While they rested, another replaced them in the field that turned to mud by the tromping of feet and the thaw. My sense of separation grew with each swirling body I watched.

They left me, more than sent me off, avoided me as though I were a spent dog—though someone stayed always with me.

The dancing continued into a spring that spoke to faces filled with distant, vacant eyes. We accomplished little work. I heard Grey Doe speak without a mumble to Wren that dancing to exhaustion would bring an end to all intruders, so fixing tule mats or fishing weirs no longer mattered.

Several became skinnier, with flaps of skin hanging from bones. Grey Doe's sister faced death from lack of food. Vanilla Leaf's family, who did not dance as intensely as the others, rode to the army to gather food from their wagons as they had some seasons past, but she refused even those meager rations.

"I cannot dance," the sister said, "but I cannot put anything from the *tibos* in my body." So she died.

I watched her burial from a faraway place, saw smoke rise from the greasewood and sage piled over the mound, wondered if she had believed that she would rise from the dead through Wuzzie's dancing.

My movements among the people were not challenged. I loaded my arms and back with firewood, ate small amounts from pots of watered stew prepared for all. I wondered why no one stopped me, why they let me eat when they had no wish that I would live. No one spoke when I appeared. All eyes seemed to know my presence, though they did not gaze my way. I felt as though I lived inside the thickness that precedes a violent summer storm.

Lukwsh worked beside me in the cold water, reaching deep for tule tubers that appeared in our hands smaller and less tasty than in anyone's recent memory. Some of the women chattered as they worked, talking above the sounds of the drums which were as constant as the chirps of red-winged blackbirds nesting in the reeds. Our breasts were bare but for the chains of shell necklaces, and I could see how hunger had pushed our bellies out, our chests in. The snow melting brought relief for me, a hopeful promise of spring.

The western sky was crowded often with snow geese flushing up from the water, their high-pitched cries like a chorus of concern. Redhead and ruddy ducks and birds the color of vibrant sunsets made nesting sounds, sprinkled color if not comfort into the dullness that had become my life.

Working, Lukwsh and I did not speak. Soft words were exchanged only in the quiet of her lodge when Stink Bug left or Wren, so none but Lukwsh would face an angry Wuzzie should he hear her treating me as though I belonged.

"It is so everywhere, Shell Flower," Lukwsh said in a whisper. She rubbed dirt from the grizzled tubers with her large hands. Her use of my special name warmed me, reminded me of better times.

"The land is tired this year and so does not wish to work so hard to make the food we need. We will have to slice these very thin, make them last a long time," she said of the roots filling her hands. "It is not just here, na?" she said then, for the first time speaking of the charge against me in her distant way. "You did not cause it."

"I am punished," I said.

"Among others. Even in the east and south they dance to bring the dead alive. Owls die and many others. There are more rumors of deaths than real, even among the Modoc." She did not look at me, faced forward into the desert spring. "Wuzzie's upset is not forever. When the rains come and the seeds open wide, so will he. Until then, stay off of his path."

"Perhaps I belonged with the Modocs. Maybe you should have let Lives in Pain have me. Or I could have left as soon as my leg healed and looked for my family."

Lukwsh's eyes looked wounded. "You have family here, or have you never made the choice to stay? No," she shook her head, "there is no flavor in chewing old meat, Shell Flower."

I sat still as a cornered marmot, not sure what to say.

"Do not give up so easily," she said. "While we live, there is always a place for hope."

She set the meager tubers out to dry, then faced me, her eyes serious, her wide smile gone. "You must tie knots in your memories, keep them to feed your tomorrows when you struggle or feel sad." From her own waist she pulled a length of tanned leather softened to the smoothness of Flake's ears. "Make this your memory. This cord will connect you to us, always."

The slender leather thong was not much wider than the black line of my jaw. But it stretched long enough to take the knots of my memories, knots whose touch would bring back the smells and sounds and sights and touch and taste of this Wadaduka trace.

Lukwsh's spirit of hope kept me through the spring and into early summer, the strength of her wisdom telling me I too could live despite the feeling of the growing storm that slept with me, woke me every morning.

Shard did not often speak to me. Once or twice I caught his eyes and felt a sharp pain of longing, thought he felt it too, for he always seemed aware of where I sat or stood. When he danced, he was a different person off in the distance. Perhaps he debated with demons of his own. But when he landed in exhaustion in a heap, I noticed he caught my eye before he fell. It was our closest contact.

My life felt as hollow as a fallen cottonwood covered with its own white fluff. I lay inside it in my mind, allowing the image of its decaying sides to mold around me, fighting to keep the short breath and crawling fear from consuming me before I fell into restless sleep.

All changed when Wuzzie's mind gave him a vision of a large antelope herd, south, near the stream Summer Rain and I once named Home Creek. It seemed late in the year for a herd to be there, summer already well advanced.

"They come," Wuzzie called out in his fluttering voice, "because so many have danced and abstained from eating flesh."

The drums stopped, and the stillness into which he spoke seemed as immense as the starlit sky that reached over us.

"We have kept ourselves pure. And apart." His voice squeaked in its fatigue from singing, his eyes below bare brows sunk deep in his head. "We will all go now to the place I have seen in my dream. Charm the antelope and eat of this *namaka* of the spirit." His fingers grabbed at his hide shirt. He pulled something invisible to the ground marking the ending of the dancing and the gathering.

The preparations began and oddly, included me.

"We all go this time," Lukwsh told me. "Children as well as *moo'a*, horses and all dogs. So we will not have to load the meat and hides and take them to the people. We can eat there, where the antelope fall."

"Will I build mounds?" I asked.

She nodded. "But not walk out among the herd. Wuzzie will not challenge the spirit that brings the pronghorns. Perhaps they will forgive you for being—"

"As I am," I finished for her, hoping there would soon be food enough and no need to blame a young woman for past miseries, for being only what she was.

I wondered if this charming would mark the end of my isolation.

We walked on tired feet toward our belief in Wuzzie's vision. Wren alone wore a cheerful look, and I wondered if anyone had told her what was happening. She tapped my shoulder with her fingers to point out birds of color or a snake slithering through the sparse grass. But she did not speak.

Only one moment of joy broke into the journey, like a shaft of sunlight on a stormy day. It happened on the day Shard chose to ride beside me as I walked. A burden basket filled with my few belongings and some of Lukwsh's meager supplies hung from the tumpline that pulled against my forehead. The day dawned hot and dry. Sweat dripped down my rib cage beneath my leather apron.

Silent, Shard sat astride the spotted mount that once held both of us in harmony. His eyes faced forward, though I walked at his side. My heart pounded in my head. I longed to lean into his shoulder, press my hands to his chest, tell him of the loneliness I carried, wait for his words to lift me up.

His bare leg rubbed the horse's belly and bumped me as he passed. I looked up at him, not sure of his intention. His eyes stayed forward, staring between the twitching ears of his horse, gazing toward some destination farther on. But he spoke out loud.

"It will be well," he said as to the wind.

I questioned whether I had even heard him speak.

Just before he dug his heels into the horse and sped away, he bent to touch my head. "You are in my mind," he said. "It is a promise kept."

Despite the drought, Home Creek ran fast and clear. The willows we cut with sharp knives were easily bent to shape the wickiups. After James and Thunder Caller carried the lighted torches and made the first circle, we would rest in those grass lodges, regain strength for the longer day ahead.

The second day we made the mounds, carrying greasewood and sage. From the slice in the lava ridge where Home Creek began, I dragged branches of cottonwoods and fallen junipers. Hard, dry berries dribbled at my side. Summer Rain worked with me for a time, but she had become the second wife of Thunder Caller now, given up on Natchez, so she stayed closer to elders such as Grey Doe, even Wuzzie.

My distance to gather wood was greater than that traveled by others searching for greasewood, but no one spoke to scold me. Each accepted the material I handed up to Buck Brush or We-ah-wee-wah, while my eyes searched for Shard. I found him building a far mound, taking juniper branches from old ones. Even Grey Doe, with her bad shoulder, lifted wood awkwardly for this important charming.

No one stumbled or fell, told a lie without owning its name.

As before, the charming began with the smoking of sweetgrass, the beating of the tapered drum. For five nights we sang songs to charm the antelope into thinking all this noise and gathering of people is where they too belonged. I spent evenings beside Lukwsh, walked with her and Wren to the small grass lodge recently built. I slept between the two and could almost convince myself that things were well again, I was forgiven for being who I was.

Once Wren woke in the night, cried out, said she saw dark shadows walking within our lodge. Lukwsh burned a strand of Wren's hair, her own, and mine, said we were protected from the shadows that preceded death. I believed it would take more than singed hair to protect me from a charred juniper I remembered seeing long ago.

On the fifth morning, Thunder Caller and James walked out with the torches, followed by the men and boys. They passed through the opening across from the headman's wickiup, walked around the circle of mounds, and smoked their pipes. They made a new circle to go around the antelope herd of Wuzzie's vision.

I hoped they would be gone a long time.

The women who remained used the time to gossip quietly while they rested, weakened by labor and so little food. One or two made attempts to repair a mat with a tule or find a rock on which to grind seeds for stew. Some looked after Wuzzie's needs as he sat and sang outside his lodge. Others were dispatched to gather up sagebrush gum to keep the children sweet, and to branch out, set dead-falls for squirrels or prairie chickens.

I was one of those.

Lukwsh nodded with her chin to me and motioned that I should take Flake. "Bring a rabbit," she said softly. She chipped away at a piece of black obsidian, which now left me with an icy cold sinking in my stomach. "A good stew at the end of the first day of the walking will please many."

She smiled, and her upper lip caught on her teeth as she watched Flake and me walk away. She raised her hand and held it toward me for a long time, like a blessing. Then I heard Wren call my name and rush to follow me.

It is the image of the people I choose to keep in my mind forever, not those that followed.

Our search for rabbits took much of the day, but we had success. Holding an obsidian knife between my teeth, I stripped the rabbit of its hide in one long piece, knew the pelt was prized and would someday join fifty others to make a cape for Lukwsh. We roasted the meat from the two we caught and shared small bites of one. Wren's eyes sparkled in a child's excitement as the fat dripped into the fire. She rubbed the flint pieces in her fingers without looking, as though they did a fragile dance. Grease dribbled from her chin without her wiping it, and then she showed me faces she could make to cause babies to laugh.

"You have a heart for children, Wren," I said, touching her hand so she would look at me, watch my mouth.

Her smile was full, and I was strangely happy in a moment pressed into a dangerous time.

The rabbit skins hung from hemp strings we wore about our waists when we arrived back. Much commotion stirred the camp.

"Not possible!" I heard Wuzzie shout.

"We walked where you direct-ed," Thunder Caller told the little man pacing in the dirt, kicking at the dust. "But it is not as you said."

"Maybe we did not go out far enough," Buck Brush said. He stood eye to eye with Thunder Caller, though he had a smaller chest. He said his words to the headman with soft-spoken respect.

"We saw no signs," James said, pushing his hair with both hands behind his ears. "Nothing to circle."

"Maybe your vision stream is in another place," Shard said. He wiped his forehead with the headband he removed. All the men looked tired and weary from having walked such a distance.

"Maybe we should go north, onto Snow Mountain," Shard said. He looked around to the others. "It is more likely the pronghorns would be there this time of year."

"No!" Wuzzie screamed. "The spirits are not wrong." He danced around in the dirt, his spider-like fingers pointing toward Thunder Caller. "No!"

No one challenged him or suggested he had perhaps misunderstood the spirits.

"You must go out farther. Look better for signs. That is the plan for tomorrow," Wuzzie directed with finality. He did not even see me when he stomped by.

Dread seasoned the evening meal in our wickiup. Later, at the singing and passing of the pipe, the smoke floated upward into a flotsam of doom.

That night I dreamed of high places where white-peaked mountains glistened in the moonlight, where eagles soared and dipped in cool wind. I stumbled through the air to a strange land of rushing water where leaping fish shimmered against the backdrop of tall, red rocks. Pale hands reached out to me. Unknown people with eyes like Wren's looked up, and when I touched their faces they were transformed and I expanded, drifted upward and away, into familiar, into my own. I awoke rested.

The men and boys went out earlier in the morning with Wuzzie walking close behind Thunder Caller, closer to the choices. At the far circle we could see the black smoke of the torch drift and disappear in wind.

"It will be better this day," Lukwsh said. "Sometimes we must work harder, to better appreciate a gift when it is given."

"Let us make *namakas* then," Grey Doe suggested, and we each began in our own way, twisting tules, making spoons, sewing precious cloth. Wren made a tiny spikebrush spoon, the size for child's play but perfect, like her smile when she showed me. Later, she twisted tules into a small horse and dog.

"Toys," she said and smiled. I barely noticed the jagged scar on her cheek.

I worked on making tule baskets to hold water, a smaller one for treasures, and thought I'd offer one to Wuzzie. But when the men returned again, even later this time, I understood that no *namaka* of mine would be enough.

Their faces were lined with dust and dirt collected by their toil. They did not look at us as we were ordered into council.

"Someone has lied or stumbled or done a foolish thing and not told it,"

Wuzzie said when we assembled. "It is the only way to explain."

The thought crossed my mind that Wuzzie could have been mistaken, made up the dream to have a place for us to go, a hope to follow and keep us working and alive. It was a fleeting thought, one quickly taken back for fear it would be noticed as a foolish thing. Just my being here Wuzzie might find as the reason the land coughed up no herd.

"Whoever has something to tell must do so now, before it is too late," Thunder Caller called out, his eyes scanning the gathering.

A deep-buried silence followed.

Each seemed lost inside, looking for wrongs that might have offended. My eyes were cast to the ground on which I sat, searching myself for something I might have done besides being who I am, as I am. My thoughts searched deep, reaching to my depths as though my memories were hands digging in the water for tule tubers.

I did not at first hear Summer Rain speaking in the voice of a woman married to the headman. When her words finally reached me, I knew within an instant that the burden ahead would not be borne by any basket I could carry by myself.

"—to walk as one," Summer Rain said. "We crossed the tracks the charmers made." Her voice cracked. "She chose to do it. Made me do it."

Great racking sobs interrupted her breathing now and halted for just a moment her stinging words. I felt my face heat up, heard my heart pound steady, ever steady, though so loud I feared my head would burst. All moisture traveled to my palms.

"She is a bad spirit," Summer Rain continued, her voice a whine. "Very powerful. Not even the dog gave us away. She made us invisible to his eyes, your ears, so you did not—"

"That hunt went well!" I heard myself breathing hard, my words spoken to the men of the circle, not Summer Rain. "You took many hides and much meat. Remember? Your bullets hit their mark."

I turned to Stink Bug, Shard.

"None were lost and—"

"Do not tell us what to remember," Grey Doe snapped.

"You do not deny Summer Rain's words?" Thunder Caller asked in wonder.

"I would not have done it by myself. I am not so brave as..." Summer Rain's words drifted like smoke into wind before being silenced by her husband's eyes.

"It is my fault," Wuzzie said into the chaos, raising his voice and his hand, settling matters and my life. "And I will mend the hole in this net." The group remained silent as he stared at me. "I will think on what must be done to make repairs. Tomorrow we will meet again," he said with a flick of his hand to his chest. "That is the plan."

Each filed out to his own lodge, filled with his own thoughts.

Mine were consumed with anger at Summer Rain, who did not need to speak, at Wuzzie, who did not need to make repairs, at myself for being who I was, doing what I did. I looked to see if Lukwsh's eyes accused me...or Shard's. Lukwsh would not meet my gaze, but Shard did. His eyes rested on me with sorrow, not accusation.

I did not sleep that night. Instead my eyes searched the wickiup for signs of safety. They sought memories of tender moments, baskets filled and emptied, of gifts given and received. My fingers sank and twirled in the thick hair of the dog who lay loyally beside me, his breathing a comfort to my short breath, eyes puffed with tears. They did not look into the future, those eyes, did not waste their time in hope.

Sometime before sunrise I felt the presence of another kneeling beside me on my mat. I turned to give a startled cry, but he placed his hand over my mouth and leaned to my face. He whispered in my ear, his breath warm against my cheek. His words were tender, strange, spoken without anger but with force.

"Each time," he said, "remember this: gather farther and stay longer. And when I signal you, that time, do not return. It is the only way."

Shard's words had no meaning. But I set understanding them aside when I felt his lips press against my forehead, his fingers outline, seem to memorize, the contours of my face and mingle with the wetness of my tears. He touched the tip of my widow's peak, brushed my hair back from my face. His eyes glistened in the murky morning light.

"I will hold you always in my mind," he said.

"Only in your mind?" I asked bravely.

Flake nudged beneath his hand and waited for the pat he wanted, giving Shard a momentary pause he did not fill with words. Instead, he leaned into me, his lips found mine and pressed against me with a tender yearning. Soft kisses moved to my forehead. He held me close to his chest.

"What will happen?" I asked, moving back from him, though I would have stayed in his embrace forever. "What do I gather?"

He shook his head. "Trust me in this, Shell Flower. Just remember what I told you." He held me a while longer, and something told me to memorize the scent of tanned hide lingering on his skin, the feel of my cheek on his chest, the sound of his heart to my ear. One last kiss to the soft place beside my eye.

Then he left.

My fingers lingered at my temple, the last place he had touched me.

At the first seep of eastern light washing over the rabbit brush and sage, Lukwsh moved about, stuffing things into a small treasure basket—dried seed cakes and berries. I saw her slip Wren's flint inside and some items too small for me to see. She must have felt my eyes watching her for she motioned me with her chin, and I came to her.

"First, we bathe you," she said.

"Why?"

She shook her head, motioned me to silence. I stood and held my arms out. Warm water squeezed from a chamois ran over my shoulders and breasts, ran like an escaping river over my hips, my legs. The water was scented with wild rose hips, scented as for those who are washed to prepare their bodies for a journey to another world.

My heart picked up its pace; a finger of fear worked its way up my back. Goose flesh formed in tiny bubbles on my skin, though the lodge felt warm. A small fire heated the water.

Lukwsh rinsed clean water over my hair and squeezed it through the thickness. Behind me, she twisted my hair into a single braid, a dried shell flower woven into the center, Sunmiet's barrette at the base. Then she dressed me in the softest buckskin I had ever felt. I wondered what made her decide to bring it. I wanted to ask, but she would not lift her eyes to mine, would not let me read inside her thoughts. I wondered when she tanned the hide, sewed on the shells and seeds. Would it have been what I would have worn when I invited Shard to my lodge, made Lukwsh a *moo'a?* I could not ask; she would not answer.

Lukwsh motioned me to hold my arms out again, and she wrapped a cord around my waist, secured beneath my skirt the basket she had filled, patted the flapped cover so it did not bulge. The soft buckskin shirt hung over my hips, molded itself to me like a friendly child. Flake sniffed at the buckskin fringe that fluttered along my legs.

Satisfied, Lukwsh touched my fingers to hers in a caress lighter than a whisper.

"Why?" I said, my voice hoarse, my future pushing through this present pain.

She shook her head. "I cannot say. Wuzzie wears many faces. Just do as you are asked." She smoothed the hide over my shoulders, brushing some imaginary thread from the skirt. "Do what you are told."

I watched water pool behind her eyes and wanted to ask her more, but she silenced me with her hand.

"I made a good bargain, na?" she said, her words thick with tears caught in her throat. "Always remember. It is not possible to live without a good knife, and you were more valuable than one carved from obsidian."

Her sadness spread over me like the slow rising of a river.

I tried not to think of Wren's dream that spoke of future death as I walked out into the sunshine, out into the circle. Wuzzie sat at the center of a gathering planned before, without my knowledge, palms upward, arms outstretched. In his high-pitched singing voice he called me forward, signaled Thunder Caller and Stink Bug to help me sit before him in the sand. A curlew screeched in the distance.

"This is the plan given to make repairs. When this is complete, rain will come, the earth will shake, rocks will fall from the ledges, the antelope will appear, and the dead will rise. But owls will die. We will help the spirits make this happen."

His eyes opened like a flash of lightening burning into mine. I remembered the day he found me, how I wondered if he was a nightmare or a man. Now it did not matter.

"You will gather as you did when you made the passage from being a child to a woman," Wuzzie told me for all to hear. "And when you are finished, your spirit will rise in the wind." His fingers fluttered upward.

Is there a dread so heavy a being cannot move? Is there a fear so loud, so noisy that no other sound can enter in one's ears, one's mind, one's thoughts? A fog stole my thinking, put heavy pressure on my breathing. Wuzzie's world swam before me and made my stomach ill. My clouded eyes searched for Lukwsh, for Shard, for safety.

They found Shard, caught his glance. His eyes spoke sadness and something else. He nodded his head so slightly I almost did not see it, but the movement brought me back to words he had said: "Gather farther and stay longer. And when I signal you, that time, do not return."

His eyes moved back to Wuzzie, and mine followed, aware again that the scrawny man spoke.

"I have chosen the place," Wuzzie said. "Around this, you will bring your fuel. It will be set before the headman's lodge in the first circle. My *wehe* will mark the spot."

The circle parted for me in silence. I was amazed the circle parted for me. I was still alive, could still be seen. My feet felt heavy, my head lowered with a burden too large for any basket.

Even in the deep ravines some distance from the camp I could hear the drums. Like a heartbeat, they drowned out the frantic feelings that pushed up toward my throat. I could not let myself think of what they meant, the ending that they promised. I could not let my mind go past my task to "gather farther, stay out longer."

The red willow growing beside the stream bent but did not break easily. I looked inside the treasure basket and saw a small knife, but I decided cut branches would be noticed when I brought them back. I might be searched. So I laid the basket down, hid it for a later time, marked the place.

I took a long time gathering, then walked slowly back.

Thunder Caller was the first to meet me. He took the pile from across my shoulders and did not meet my eyes. He said nothing, but I wondered if he thought my load light for such a long time spent in gathering. He laid the branches around the obsidian *wehe* Wuzzie had laid in the sand. The pile of sticks reminded me of Wren's small gathering after she burned her feet and the way we eased her pain.

Beside Wuzzie's knife stood a pole they had pounded in the ground.

As I dropped a second armload at the pile, Stink Bug greeted me. He grinned as he patted the pole affectionately and stepped back from the brush.

"It will not be such a hot fire," Stink Bug said, "but with the green willows, it will burn a long, long time." He scratched his fat thigh and smirked.

My return to the ravine took me longer. I walked as though through thick mud, understanding now the magnitude of the coming sacrifice.

I caught a glimpse of Wren watching. She did not turn away when I looked; her eyes carried a deep sadness, like the losing of a friend. She smiled and waved a child's wave, and I wondered what her words might be if she had no word for good-bye.

Flake bounded beside me, brushed at my legs. His presence warmed me as he wagged his tail and jumped before me, head lowered in play.

"O Flake," I said into his pool of brown eyes, so grateful for his presence.

I heard the shout—"Flake, come!"—as the dog turned with me to look. A flame burst inside me like a hot rock dropped in oil as I recognized the caller. I watched Flake abandon me for Shard.

Why gather farther and stay longer? Why hope Wuzzie's mind would change? Why not just let them end this struggle quickly? I felt as empty as a broken basket.

I made three more gatherings, going farther out, remaining longer. The wind picked up and I recognized the feel of late afternoon. Stink Bug managed to stay close to the pile, picking at his teeth with a stem of dried grass, his wide mouth still set in a smirk.

Shard walked between us as though sent to shield me from my fate. His eyes were filled with a feeling I had not seen in them before, a look that turned to strength as he caught my gaze. He looked east, then north, with a slight movement of his chin and the promise of a smile. I took it as the signal.

I memorized everything about his face, his eyes, his nose and mouth, how the sweat stained his headband, how wisps of hair stuck to his cheek. I caught the way a smile moved across his face like a gentle sunrise lighting the desert. He bit at his fingernail as though a boy, then brushed at his eyes as I turned away.

My feet wanted to race away, but I forced them to walk no differently than if I'd just been sent for seeds. Some dried sagebrush lying close to camp I placed in the cordage strapped to my back, showing evidence of my efforts. Like a sage hen grubbing for bugs in the desert, I walked and bent and picked up sticks, walked and bent and picked, heading ever steady toward the source of Home Creek, toward the cuts in the deep ravine.

Beyond the sight of camp, I dropped my cordage burden and shoved it under some willows. I uncovered my small treasure basket, and while strapping it around me, began to run.

THE RHYTHM OF DISAPPEARING

MY SENSE OF TIME DEPARTED.

I reached the narrowing where a stream pressed out of the ground as a seeping spring but did not know how far it flowed from camp. Still, the sound of the drums no longer beat in my head, only the rhythm of my message: *Gather farther and stay longer and do not return.* Fallen logs stretched across the spring, scattered between rocks and boulders broken from the ridgecap and resting against each other, most larger than a wickiup.

Beyond them lay the narrow opening of rock that spired upward higher than the tallest pine tree of my memory. Like smoke moving up through a hole to the stars, my feet and hands would need to carry me upward through jagged rock, along narrow ledges using shallow footholds, upward to rolling grasses taller than my being. My neck ached with looking.

The water pressing through the grass felt cool and tasted sweet. The splash of it felt good on my hot face and neck. A breeze cooled as it drifted across the water and announced that night would soon settle.

I had not eaten all day and reached now for a dried cake, surprised that in the midst of this I could still savor the bite. I took a moment to wonder. I wondered who would follow, how long I had. Maybe no one would be sent. Perhaps they meant it as a simple way to rid themselves of me. That thought cheered me, made me wonder if that was why I gathered alone. Perhaps

Stink Bug simply sat by the stick pile to frighten me, to make me want to leave, to force me from the people's presence. I let my mind consider the idea that my life had little risk, let it roll around like a sweet meat, giving me time to get used to the taste before it became bitter with truth.

I wondered what they were doing, Shard and Lukwsh and Wren, whether they thought of me. I even reflected on Flake and the piercing pain of Shard calling him back, as though his own dog was not enough, as though I did not deserve even the comfort of a dog. The hollowness of my chest told me my wonderings were of no value, that I had no time to mourn.

The sun set; the wind laid. The ridge cap cutting into the purple sky needed scaling. It was the next step. The ravine narrowed and going up—to get out—appeared the only way. It was not a task for nighttime, not even with a promised moon. It would be best to travel under stars once I reached the upper, smoother ridge that eased gently back toward Snow Mountain and the lakes and to the world beyond, whatever world I chose to walk toward. Even the thought of what lay beyond caused my breath to shorten.

"Think of climbing the rocks. Just get over the rocks," I said out loud, surprised at the strength of my voice.

I could not climb them then, not that first night. My limbs were suddenly exhausted.

Beneath a fallen cottonwood I removed my basket, stirred up the tree's fluff like old snow, bent again to drink my fill, then nestled down to a restless, dreamless sleep.

The moon had already been up some time when I heard the noises, loud enough to wake me from an awkward, aching sleep, yet too faint to recognize and name.

A rabbit scampering in the fallen branches? No, something larger.

My mind jolted awake. Sounds thundered in my ears just beyond my face. Swishing sounds, something moving through the dry sage beyond where the ravine narrowed before the spring seeped. The air felt cool. I could hear the gurgling of Home Creek formed up as a stream beyond the spring. The moon shone bright though not full, so bright the junipers cast shadows on the sage, made the willows dance upon the water.

My heart pounded, my breath came short and shallow, my tongue thickly dry. My body knew to fear before my mind could name the source.

Two men on horseback cast shadows, moving as a bad dream without effort through the sage. They approached the boulder-scattered area, dismounted, and tied their horses to a juniper. They jumped across the shallow stream, stood looking, began to weave their way through the tumble of boulders, their feet slipping on the smaller rocks, the sound carrying like an angry grumble through the desert night. They had no reason to be quiet. Did I hear them actually exchange words? Did they speak my name? Perhaps they came to tell me all was well, the herd found, and I could come back. Perhaps Wuzzie planned this sequence all along. Hope inched its way inside me. I watched from my concealment near the log, wondered if I ought to stand, to just call out.

But Shard's words beat their rhythm in my head: Gather farther, stay out longer, and do not return. *And do not return.*

They dipped out of sight, moving slowly around the boulders, but kept coming like a cramp at night.

Searching, searching for a hiding place, I scanned the boulders, looked for washes, maybe caves. Heard their voices. My shoulders pushed up against the cottonwood log. I eased sideways, then on my belly, pulling with my elbows, made my way toward the opening of a rotten log. I reached inside.

My fingers felt hollowness beyond what I could reach. A rotten smell lapped at my face. I crawled inside a burden basket. Tightness pressed around my face. Too close. Too tight. I could not catch my breath. I eased back out, gasped in cool air, felt rotten wood clutch my hair.

Search, search, fingers frantic, find nowhere safe, hear their voices, coughs, know Stink Bug's laughter carried by the wind.

The log alone had been provided. I turned back. This time I pushed my feet first against the narrow, wet and rotting, felt it close around my back and belly, skirt slipping upward. The log scraped my shoulders, dropped stinking smells and creeping things across my bareness. Only scant room, only enough to pull my head in like a turtle, arms tight beside me, face to wet and rotting, angled toward the ground. I closed my eyes.

I could not feel the basket at my waist, did not feel it still attached. I had lost it! I heard them in the distance and prayed they had not seen my shadowed movements, prayed they could not hear my heart beat, hoped they thought I had scaled the ridge.

My eyes pinched closed, as though to make me smaller. The rotting smell spread through me, overpowering. The snake that lived in small places crawled up inside my stomach, moving to my heart, my throat, threatened to shut off breath.

Think sky and trees, imagine open spaces, lakes and birds in flight, a field of flowers, shell flowers, a sign that I was loved.

I heard the footsteps coming closer, stopping near the fallen log. All senses turned to sound.

"She could wander by this light," Salmon Eyes said, clearing his throat. "Keep on going."

"The ridge would challenge a weak girl," Stink Bug said. "Maybe we passed her? Maybe she hunches beside the stream someplace."

I heard the soft swish of moccasins on grass. The log remained quiet but for the pounding in my head.

"Ayah! Look here!" Salmon Eyes said.

Stink Bug snorted. Quiet, then: "She was here."

"We climb rocks?"

I imagined them scanning the rocky ridge, eyes stopping at the top. If they started climbing where would I go? The desert would reveal me in the moonlight.

I heard movement, and then wood creaked. A kind of panic seized me. I shivered as I felt the tree bark groan beneath Stink Bug as he sat. He was right above me, closer to my being than he had ever been since the day he helped me from Lukwsh's lodge to sit in the sun. I imagined his wide bottom spread across the log that hid me, his bare flesh beneath his breechcloth pressed against the rough bark, and I almost laughed. How strange that terror can breed a laugh.

I made my mind a splinter sticking up into his soft flesh, making him miserable with irritating pain. He shifted his weight. The log held.

"Rest," he said, grunted, his own breathing hard from the effort of his search. "Such a slug will not go far."

"She could have used this. Stupid girl can't even hang onto her treasures."

"Greater trouble than a bad agent," Stink Bug agreed. "Lukwsh made a pet of her. Shard, too."

They sat quiet, doing something. I heard Salmon Eyes's voice come from a slight distance, heard him make water while he spoke.

"If we go back without her..." His words were spoken with the weight of dread.

"Let Summer Rain go in her place, another stupid one who tested the antelope."

"Summer Rain has no worries about burning," Stink Bug said, "not sleeping in Thunder Caller's lodge. My brother has more to worry over."

A long silence followed.

"Will Wuzzie accept his offer?" Salmon Eyes asked, moving closer to the log. I heard scratching on the thin space that separated me from them, carving or marking the log or pulling on rotted bark. Could they hear me breathe?

"Leave the basket," Stink Bug answered finally, softly. "Let her spirit take it to her in its own time. Maybe she will not die as quickly as with the fire." He grunted. "I will miss hearing white skin sizzle in those flames, but she will die before she reaches wherever it is she is going. Or my brother will, or both. We leave it to Wuzzie."

I heard crunching and creaking as the log breathed with his departure, hoped his movements drowned out the whimper that grew in my throat.

Salmon Eyes argued briefly, wanting words to say when they returned with empty hands. Stink Bug made some offers, said I had been taken off by spirits, my belongings left behind.

"We say we found her basket and some bones with meat on. Not bring anything back she might have touched."

Salmon Eyes seemed satisfied. I heard someone yawn.

"Wait till morning?"

Stink Bug coughed and spit. "We can make some distance yet. I would like to scratch myself on my own mat by morning."

"Clouds, west. Maybe with her gone the rain will come, as Wuzzie says."

"It would be a better sign if the herd appeared. Then my brother's offer would be accepted, and I would be rid of two thorns that have poked my backside for as long as I can remember."

I heard someone make noises like a stretch and hoped the moon was not so bright they could see my crawling tracks. I heard swishing sounds, moccasins on water-pressed ground, voices growing duller as their feet slipped and crunched against rocks. I listened for horses disappearing in the night.

Long minutes passed, maybe hours. My breath came in deeper, quieter sighs. But each time I planned to move, I imagined them turning back, finding me, knowing all along I hid beneath them like a buried soul left in a rotten grave.

The soft patter of raindrops dribbled on the log like a child tapping fingers on a drum. Tears pressed against my cheeks. Stink Bug's words rang true then: my leaving brought good things to the people, a rain to water the parched earth, to fill the streams, bring the ducks.

In that moment I grasped the meaning of the rest of Stink Bug's words.

Shard must have offered up himself to keep me from being found! Someone else would die at the log near Wuzzie's *wehe!* The weight of Shard's offer, the price of his gift was so large, so beyond what I could measure, that I could neither grasp the meaning nor keep thinking the thought. The terror of my closed space became stronger than the fear of what awaited me, of what I must learn to live with once I left. I opened my eyes.

The moon burned bright, sneaking out between dark clouds that spattered rain in unplanned places. Enough light to see, to make my way. Stiff and cold and numb, my limbs refused to move. For a moment I believed I would simply die there in that log. I even thought I wished to. But Shard's words carried greater weight: *Gather farther, stay out longer, and do not return.*

I eased my shoulder inch by inch to pull forward, opened my eyes to the light beyond.

I scraped my arms and pulled myself out to face a pale light fragrant with freshly washed sage, dark with crying clouds.

Unworthiness threatened to steal the thoughts I needed to survive, and I remembered a lesson from my passage time: routine. Follow a routine. Be an arrow heading toward a mark.

Soft rain fell. I pressed spring water to my face and lips, squeezed rainwater from my tangled hair. I left the ants and larva in the thick of it, no time to comb it with my fingers or reset the barrette. A quick brush took sticks and bugs from my torn dress, and I shivered with the thought of where I had spent my night. I stared at the hollow log and allowed myself a fleeting sense of pride at having conquered—when I needed to—such an overwhelming fright.

I looked for the basket and found it dropped beneath the log. Inside, crumbs of dried cakes stuck to my wet fingers. I patted the ground, found another cake or two dropped there when they tossed the basket. I licked only the crumbs, savoring them one by one. The basket held more, but I laced it to my side, pushed now by the need to get away, to not risk someone's swift return. Routine. Routine. Straight as an arrow. *Gather farther, stay out longer, and do not return.*

I slapped a handful of soft mud on the cuts and scrapes left by the log. The rain stopped. I took one last long drink from the beginning of Home Creek and began the ridge cap climb, heading east to end up north.

It was not unlike the time I reached as a child for the high place on Dog Mountain and later fell into Wuzzie's charms. This time would be different. It grew darker in the shadows, but my moccasins were of hide, my feet and fingers strong enough to pull me up, hold me steady.

Sharp, rough rocks scraped against my legs. Each step was a thought first, a movement second. I spoke quietly to the snakes that made their beds in the cool of flat rocks my hands reached up to.

"Snake, snake, snake," I chanted quietly before I reached my hand up, "I'm too big to eat. Too big to eat." I breathed relief each time my face pulled up even with the rock and no snake awaited. Once I caught a glimpse of a tail slithering deeper into the rocks. Another time, I jerked from the scamper of a lizard or scorpion leaving tracks across my wrist.

Wind picked up mats of my hair, blew pale strings across my face. Instead of raindrops, sweat trickled along my forehead and into my eyes. On a solid foothold I stopped and lifted my skirt to wipe my eyes.

In the distance, far behind me, looking back from where I came, I sensed a follower. I saw nothing moving low among the willows. I squinted, my heart pounding, breathing hard from the effort of the climb. I could not afford time spent in wondering, must keep going: *gather farther, stay out longer, and do not return.*

Rocks dribbled from my scrambling, pushing, pulling with every fiber of my strength. Each time I gained a foothold, I moved with greater hope, stretched across rock cuts, reached, pulled up to narrow ledges, resting, panting, pushing, pulling. The climb took time and all the strength I had.

On a ledge, I gasped only for a moment and hugged the side. I listened to the rocks move, waited to hear someone panting ease up behind me, feared whoever chased me—if someone chased me—might know an easier way, even meet me at the top. I shook my head. My imagination followed me, the spirit of my guilt. I was too frightened to return, too weak to rescue Shard, did not yet know what led me on.

At the top, I pulled myself over the ridge rock and rolled low onto grasses growing tightly to the edge. No time to celebrate, no one to share my momentary joy at having climbed the ridge rocks in the moonlight-spattered night.

Beyond stood tall grasses. I eased myself upward toward dimples filled with juniper and scrawny pines. No time to wait. I ran, grasses cutting at my face, my hands, as I pushed through them, too scared to turn around. I darted quickly into sagebrush, pushed back rabbit brush and bunchy grass. I located a cluster of trees with broken branches and made a wide berth, made it look as though my body left the grasses in another spot. I stepped quickly, barely missing a small pond of brackish water. I splashed my face and decided to rest.

The ground softened near the water. With my hands I dug in the wet earth, gathered sage and slender boughs. I lay down in the impression and rubbed my legs aching from the effort. Finally, I pulled leaves and limbs up on me and made an arch I could see through.

I reached to pull my hair back and felt no barrette. Lost somewhere in my efforts. I closed my eyes. It had been two nights since I had slept, one night since Shard had pressed his lips to my face, a lifetime ago.

The sun burned high in the sky when my sticky eyes opened, my arm numb from the position it held me in for sleep. Drool pooled on my arm. I slowly scanned my surroundings. I saw nothing to fear. Neither rabbit nor deer nor human. I tossed back branches, sat and pulled my treasure basket to the front and removed it from my waist. I reached inside for a cake and took the time to see what other treasures Lukwsh had sent.

The basket held a tiny *wehe* like the kind Lukwsh gave to Wuzzie at my naming. Smooth, black obsidian with a streak of rust running through it.

Two edges. It fit the palm of my hand, and I thought of her words, of the importance of a good knife to my life.

At the bottom of the basket a strip of cloth curled. It had the markings of a headband worn by Shard. I lifted it, buried my face in it, breathed in his scent, and swallowed back tears I could not afford.

Beneath Shard's headband lay another gift: a piece of flint for fire and a tiny tule dog Wren had twisted just the day before. Could it have been only the day before?

Something from each of them had been sent, something to knot into my memories. I wondered then if my soft leather ring of knots was stuffed inside, but it was not. Still, I emptied the basket into my lap and discovered something more.

I held the thumb-sized cedar basket made for me by Sunmiet, the cover like a fingernail, still attached. Would it hold a tiny *wehe?* Some herbs, perhaps? With little effort, I pried off the woven lid and turned the basket upside down in my hand.

It was a treasure basket almost without equal when I felt the smooth, gold chain that had once been worn about my mother's neck, once swung against my childish chest.

When had Lukwsh found it? Or had Shard? Why had they kept it from me, given it now? Did they wish no remembrance of the child they called their own? Or maybe they had sent it to speak to me of what was past, of where I once belonged, and what might be my future.

It had been cleaned and shimmered in the sun. I turned it over in my fingers. Hadn't Sunmiet said a search without a treasure, a name, or likeness would be wasted? But here, perhaps, I held what I needed to find my family, after all.

The thought of family delivered a piercing pain.

I shook my head of it, felt instead the smoothness of the chain against my fingers and recalled the touch of Shard's hands against my jawline, the softness of his breathed words. Perhaps it was sent to remind me to come back, to see if I could save him from the consequences of his care. Or were the treasures of the basket but an ending of a refuge freely given, but a refuge only, not a place where I belonged?

The smallest bubble of joy welled up inside me as I thought of who I called my family—Wren and Lukwsh and Shard. But it formed itself into the deepest sobs of loss and longing, wonderings and wounds. So much I would not know, could never tell them or myself. So much behind me. My eyes swelled in the sobbing; my breath came in gasping starts deep from my stomach, caught like a frightened wail born in a baby's chest.

The chain dripped between my fingers and fit back into the basket. I wiped my nose. Splashed water on my face. A faint smell of smoke drifted then disappeared, and I wondered if the scent was real, perhaps marked the mounds, the presence of a herd, the ending of Shard's life.

The sun had moved. I had not noticed.

Only one cake remained. Soon I would need to gather berries, make up something to lure a rabbit to a dead-fall. I must have left the area, though I do not remember how or why I moved. I recall spots of green amidst the desert, moving from spring to spring. The ridge land sloped to the north. I headed in that direction. Once there and dropping down, the river from Snow Mountain would let me follow it to the lakes and then beyond, though I did not know to what.

I spent a second long rest near a spring in what I hoped was a safe distance from where I started. To get there, I crossed over man-dug ditches that marked a boundary. Cattle mashed around the seeping spring, causing dark water to puddle in the tracks, making the clearest water shallow and framed by mud. I had trouble reaching it. In the distance I could see the shape of animals with the look of dullness radiating along their long horns. They idly munched. Their presence meant ranchers came here, had marked a field with their ditches and tried to mark the land. I wondered if Shard's blacksmith Johnson helped with these cattle or if a less friendly rancher set them to graze here. I scanned the horizon for signs of men and wondered if I should stay.

Still, it beckoned as a good place to rest in the heat of the day, and I wedged myself far enough from the water to avoid being trampled by a cow, close enough to watch all who might venture near the spring.

I did not sleep well and awoke with the sense of being followed once again. The sun threatened to set as I scanned the horizon behind me. Nothing moved. I had no reason to wear my dread like an old threadbare blanket tossed around my head.

My feet took me from there with all quickness, skirting the edges of tree clusters, dipping into shadows of cool, avoiding open spaces, resting as dark overtook the day. I ate one half of the last remaining cake, rolled each dried berry around on my tongue, savoring it like the most precious of tastes. When the moon rose to my right, casting shadows, I moved out again, eyes directed toward the bright star that shone over both my head and the lakes I knew I should reach in a day or two. My eyes glanced behind me. The hair on my neck bristled until I turned, but I found nothing.

I felt so small in this still, vast country I moved across alone. I imagined myself standing on one of the stars that twinkled above me as I walked, balancing and looking down at the sea of grass and sage. I knew I could not recognize even the slightest speck of myself from that distance. I wondered if a herd of pronghorns had been recently charmed. I wondered if I could see what followed me if I looked down from that high sky.

Toward dawn of the third day, I awoke to rustling in the grass. No time to run or hide deeper. I reached for my treasure basket and grabbed the sliver of a *wehe*. I would make my stand there, tired of being prey. My heart pounded, my throat felt dry. My stomach ached in hunger, but all were set aside to see if the being crawling like a snake through grass would kill me or try to take me back.

I waited, squatting on my heels, *wehe* ready, and watched the grass part.

"It's you!" I whispered in amazement. "It's you!"

He thrust himself upon me, bowled me over with his weight. A joyous bark greeted me. A hemp rope, torn, still dragged behind him in the grass.

Flake's big head pushed against me, weak in my joy. He rolled against me, licked and barked. I savored the softness of his muzzle on my throat, cherished the wetness of his tongue on my cheek, cried into the ruff of black hair around his neck. He whined, then whoo-whoo-whooed, head thrown back in triumph. He pushed me again. His tongue hung to one side, and his big chest heaved with his breathing. I wrapped my arms around him, held him close enough to hear the slow beat of his heart.

I scanned the horizon behind him, suddenly wondering if he had come alone. It was a fleeting thought. He was the last of who my eyes would see of what I left behind. I knew this. I scratched his neck and felt a collar, soft with nubby knots.

"My memory," I gasped. "You brought my knots of memory." Lukwsh or Shard or Wren had tied it as a collar, must have kept him back so none could follow him to me, let Stink Bug come out first and fail.

To the west, tips of mountains rose in the far distance. The land rolled like a vast bowl toward them. To the north stood more hills rich with huckleberries and the promise of my future. I would carry this place in my mind, tied into the knots of my memory. But it would be only that now, not someplace I would call my own. I did not let my mind wonder if the fuel I'd gathered just three days past had been burned around another. I chose to believe that Shard would find a way to outwit Wuzzie, would not give up his life for someone so unworthy as me.

Flake's big paw lifted to my shoulder as I sat. He pulled at me. I untwisted the ragged hemp rope.

"Kept you tied, did they? Didn't want you trailing after me? Fooled them," I told the dog.

He cocked his head, then pushed back and lifted his leg to scratch at his neck.

"Stink Bug lacked your nose," I said, burying my face in his fur. And his big heart. "He'd never get this far. Only you could find me." I actually laughed out loud, amazed at how the dog's very presence lifted me and gave me new hope.

Rested now, Flake whined impatience.

"I know," I said, gazing at the horizon, considering the land we traveled, the future we faced. "I know. It's time we moved." I draped my arm over his broad back and patted his shoulder. "Time to leave, that's certain. We will head to the lakes, pick up a water basket at the camp. But after that, Flake, where do we walk after that?"

FULL CIRCLE

ON THE SIXTH MORNING OUT, the final day of the charming of the ante-lope—if all went well—I knew that Shard had died.

I felt chilled over my bare arms. A breeze wisped through the shreds of my buckskin and twirled between the tangles of my hair. New tears formed against my eyes, behind my nose. I did not know where the water came from to flood my face. It did not press in a caress against my cheeks. I thought the pond that formed my heart would soon run dry, but each new thought of loss discovered more.

The certainty that Shard was dead brought pain that cut the deepest.

I had dreamed of him the night before. I talked to him in words crisp and clear, though I do not remember speaking. Rather, soft impressions and feelings moved between us.

Flake and I had nestled down beside a juniper, brushed the hard blue berries from where we wished to lay our heads. In another day, we would be near the lakes and could pick up baskets, rework old food caches to see if some crumbs remained. The night did not cooperate, the moon hid behind a growl of clouds. Along the far horizon, lightning spiked the earth, expos-ing clusters of clouds embedded within larger shadows spilling toward fragments of dark, open sky.

My sleep came quick and deep.

Shard arrived in the dream almost instantly. He told me to hurry on, that he would follow if he could, that we would meet again after a charming of the future. I did not understand him, argued with him, said I should turn back, tried to convince him I could rescue him now that rain had come and the herd had been found.

"Wuzzie will change his mind. I can make him," I said. "I have a power-ful Spirit who walks with me. See? I have lived these days when I should have died. I cheated death. There must be some reason."

Shard paused just as he would have, then nodded his head. "There is reason," he said.

Then in my dream his eyes turned tender as a rabbit's and pooled with water. Those eyes left his face to watch me. I had to look up to see him then.

"Where Wuzzie lives is not for you, not now. You have a reason. Find your place away."

I whimpered in my sleep. Flake pushed against me, warming me with his dark body stretched next to mine. A roll of thunder furled across the vast sky like the sounds of antelope thundering between mounds, between fences made by minds. I willed myself back into my dream, unable to let Shard dis-appear, clinging to him as a wet hide, clutching at his form as the last leaf of aspen flaps hopelessly against a winter's wind.

"The journey," he said, "is like a charming circle." His gentle voice hov-ered at the edge of a sob. "Our paths will cross again. We will wander wide and far but always with direction. And when we meet again, I will recognize you as having been there with me all along."

"And me?" I said, crying now, trying not to for fear that I would wake and he would go away.

"This is a promise: I will hold you in my mind, and someday we will walk as one."

The dream ended then, and his name would not be spoken by my lips until the mourning time had passed. I knew he was dead.

My hands stretched out to hold him, instead seized wispy air. Deep sobs burned my chest and woke me. And even though I knew it was a dream, knew my crying could not bring him back, I seemed powerless to stop the tears from flowing, could not make my sobbing cease.

Flake nuzzled me, let me cry into the fluff of his neck until my eyes were swollen and pinched. He whined and nudged, licked at my face hugged to my knees. His wide tail beat against me as he stood to protect me, facing away.

For a long time after, I simply sat. Flake decided to wander a short dis-tance. He sniffed at night birds, lifted his head to watch me. My arms clasped in rocking around my knees. I watched lightning through a prism of tears, spied shafts of rain sweep across parched sage. My neck tingled along the gold chain I wore as lightning flashed close.

Flake returned. I clutched at his collar, fingering memory knots. My mind memorized the knots that marked each word, each touch, each look that passed between us. Beyond, where the sky opened into a cloudless raven black, the full moon broke through. A lance of light raced across the sky and pierced the last of raindrops seeping into night. Then like a flower opening to the sunrise, pressed into quiet, an arc of color formed, so soft, so light, so like familiar things I loved—the shades of still lakes, faded sunsets, pale pollen, and shooting stars. It sprawled across the sky, this pillowed brilliance of the night, spread itself from earth to heaven, then disappeared from sight, its course a memory, a savored memory washed upon my heart. It faded to morning light. I treasured it, that rainbow of the night sent to warm the chill and remind me of a promise.

In the morning, I moved at a gentle lope along a deer trace I hoped led to water. Flake panted at my heels. My mind lived far away, distant, trying to decide where I would go once I left the empty village by the lakes. My thoughts were interrupted by the strong memory of the dream, not asked for, but arriving just the same. A coldness chilled my skin despite sweat beading above my lips. Without thinking I reached for the gold chain I wore again around my neck. I held smoothness between my fingers with only the memory of his love and a faded flicker of hope.

Flake barked behind me. I turned to see his tail lifted high, still, his neck hairs stiffly arched along his back, brown eyes locked in stare. How could he know I thought of death?

"It's all right, Flake," I said, patting my thigh so he would come to me. His tail dropped to wag. His big head lowered in embarrassment.

A golden eagle screeched high above us, dipped its wings, set its talons as it plunged to the ground. It rose in a moment, a plump rabbit still squirming beneath it as it flew north to an unseen nest.

Together, Flake and I killed a rabbit, too, and used its innards to comfort the dog. Wren's flints gave up a low flame. I roasted the meat, shared it with the dog. He took a small bite from my hand, his mouth gentle as cotton-wood fluff, his teeth tugging at the meat but leaving me always with the final bite.

At the lakes I walked as though among the dead. Only bird sounds stirred the air that settled around the lodges like old gossip, stale and distorted. It seemed years had passed since I walked there, touched his hand in friendship then in love, let Lukwsh trade an obsidian knife for me.

Flake helped me unearth a small cache of seeds and a forgotten one that allowed me to eat my fill of dried duck buried between layers of grasses. Filled, I moved between the mats and wickiups like a silent spirit, unnoticed, touching familiar things of others and my own. A small water basket with its cords of tule twists lay wind-tossed beside a lodge. I tied a leather thong across my head and settled the basket on my back. Beneath an old rabbit robe, I found the larger basket given me as a gift from Sunmiet when I became a woman. I decided not to carry either, though both would have comforted as I left. Instead, I found a spear point I could fish with, more dried cakes, a stash of pine nuts, and a small burden basket I slipped onto my back.

I made one circle walk around Lukwsh's wickiup, leaving touches upon a rawhide rope, her rabbit blanket, her clay pot with the chipped lip. "Blend," she had said. "Take what power you are given and blend it. You will be stronger." Sunmiet's cedar basket stared at me, and in my looking I considered: I could seek out Sarah to see if she could help me use the gold chain to find those I once thought I could not live without. She lived in two worlds, might help me live there, too.

Or I could make my way toward Sunmiet's place, Tlhxni, where owls and dark-skinned people mixed as one.

It was as good a plan as any.

"Perhaps I'll meet her friend there, the *tibo* named Jane," I told Flake, not knowing that finding who I was mattered even more.

The dog plunged into the still shallow lake, swam about, his black nose just above water. He surged out and ran toward me, shook himself of the wet, and panted, ready.

At Wuzzie's wickiup we paused. Flake stuck his head low, sniffing below the hide flap. I considered stepping inside to destroy what he left there, to let him know when he returned that someone who hated him still lived.

A shiver of anger thrilled through me, burning like bad fish swallowed. Wuzzie. Because of Wuzzie I had to leave. Because of him, my life tossed about like a stick on spring water. Because of him, the one I cared for had been asked to die.

I pushed open the flap to the wickiup and entered, my anger cutting through the fear this place breathed out. In the cold darkness I felt—or heard—*Do not let what Wuzzie does choose for you. Be grateful for what is.*

I suspected my young imagination, tiredness, and sporadic food were really speaking, but with the words, I backed on out, backed away from this whole empty village that once held me in love.

"We will go without Wuzzie's potions or his herbs or his dances," I told the dog, feeling stronger with direction and a plan.

Slowly, we made our way north, through the dried grasses already looking stronger from the bursts of rain my leaving brought this portion of the desert. We passed the narrows between the lakes without getting our feet wet so shallow were they, not yet refreshed from the rainfall in the mountains. Pelicans gathered on the mud flats far beyond us, their whiteness like ice along a river's edge.

I left it all behind me, hoped to find my reasons somewhere else, blend in, be strong, maybe find the past I longed for.

We went north, toward Canyon City country and the river they call John Day's. I skirted the small town, not wanting to be shouted at by the men using words I did not know and whose faces leered like Stink Bug's or scowled like Grey Doe's and Lives in Pain's. Flake and I moved beside the trails most traveled by shiny-eyed miners, kept ourselves in the ripples of land, away from the ranches raided by our band. I bypassed stands of juniper dulled black and red by an old fire. I hid behind juniper and pine, watching, walking, resting in the day hours, moving most at dusk and dawn. We stepped untroubled beside the streams and rivers and followed their meandering only as a trail to somewhere else.

A ripple of activity caught our attention on a ranch where stages stopped. Stacks of grass hay dotted the distance. The black posts and dead junipers that surrounded the new-looking house exposed remnants of a past fire. Several soldiers with their dogs lounged on the covered porch.

For just a moment I thought of walking forward, attempting with my hands to tell them who I was, see if old English words might come back. But I heard them laugh heartily, sitting on boards with legs that tipped as they leaned back against the wall or dropped forward with a thud.

Flake growled low, and so we slipped on by.

A pack string of loaded mules wove its way along a dusty road. More pairs of soldiers passed them, moving toward the lakes, and I wondered if this might be that highway Sunmiet spoke of! Dalles Military Highway, where soldiers moved between the city of The Dalles and Canyon City and perhaps a future reservation. I overheard words I did not understand, and thought of the man in uniform who taught me to answer, "As I Am." No name. No likeness. Only a gold necklace. I fingered the chain, but something told me not to show it to anyone, especially people riding along a lonely dirt highway.

We veered northwest along a fork of the rock-lined river. I learned later that the man whose name it bears was once *Kahkwa Pelton*, "lost in his head," and needed help to rid the strange and strangling spirits that moved inside his mind along this stream. I wondered if my Spirit might be gone, left behind. Or would he leave me like *Kahkwa Pelton* if I could not learn to live without the people? I walked this trail before. But this time *I* left, was forced to. It surprised me that the pain felt no different, cut just as deep as when others rattled along the ruts away from me. But I was older now, had a keener edge, and knew what took me time to learn before: I must seek the ones I thought would love me above all others.

Only years later, as a wiser woman still, would I discover that on that very journey I would find myself.

There were edges so narrow I could not walk beside the water. Rocks jutted out into the channel and forced Flake and me to climb above, keep the stream in our vision but farther away. Stands of dense pines blocked the sky. Rocks of reds and greens separated by strips as dark as Flake rose up like wide rainbows of rock. In places, the boulders crumbled to a pale powder that puffed up as green dust as we walked. In the distance, I saw men dressed in suits and hats pounding with small hammers, holding up chunks of the tinted rocks and strange bones, excitement in their voices carrying across the still, lava-rich lands. Their mules pawed restlessly at men who were not miners, not looking for gold. Something from a story told in a wickiup came to me, of places north, where leaves are pressed into rock, bones of shaggy-haired cats are caught by stone.

"Do not go near this place," Wuzzie warned. "Only bad things will follow."

"We have traveled too far, Flake," I said, not wanting to test Wuzzie's views. We turned west into the sun and into my future.

For a long time, we passed by small herds of mule deer, and once, wiggling my hands above my ears, I almost charmed a fawn beside its mother. It walked toward me with precise pauses and exaggerated movements of his arched neck and head as though each step were a beginning and an ending in itself, not part of a forward path. His mother snorted a warning, but he, curious, tendered on until I could look into his eyes, my fingers still fluttering at my ears.

I stared.

He startled, spun in one fluid movement, the black tip of his tail flipping as he darted after the doe. I laughed out loud, a sound so strange to my ears I almost did not know it. I felt a twist of guilt.

The trail Flake and I paralleled meandered north with the river. We traveled daylight hours, so few people marked the dirt roads. Those that did made noises ahead of them like porcupines scrambling up trees, providing warnings for us to hide. I made small fires, found myself unfilled by the few berries I picked from sparse bushes. I wondered what Flake lived on, felt his ribs beneath my fingers. I tore slices from my hide dress which we both chewed to answer the growling in our stomachs.

In a rocky area where I could see the ridge cap but had no plans to climb, we spent the night, warmed by the rocks holding the daylight heat. I dreamed of a steaming antelope roast, smelled the spit of duck fat dropped in the flames. My mouth moved to the chewing of tiny seeds, the mash of pine nuts soft between my teeth. At dawn, I heard the baby cry.

I thought I dreamed, but Flake growled low, hair rising behind his neck. After a time, we moved quietly beyond the rocks, circled around where the sound came from. I peered down into a treed landscape separated by sparse grasses, short shrubs for browse. Tall tamarack trees felled by the wind leaned against each other like skinny men suddenly tired, full of unbalanced spirits. A lone deer moved there, thin, a back leg as slender as a reed dragging in the dirt as it moved, head bent to browse, nose lifting to catch scents in the air.

I grabbed Flake's collar, felt the low growl in his chest, told him, "Quiet," in a whisper. We watched.

Nothing happened. We did not see people nor hear the baby cry. No sign of travelers besides us two. I almost let Flake loose.

Suddenly, a pale creature the color of sun eased past us, entering low and left, like a sleek-muscled dog. It dragged a long, thick tail, and wore its small ears pinned to its round head. It's muzzle sprouted whiskers thin as spider webs. It paid us no mind as it eased its way to the deer, a soft, snake-like hiss pushing out of its mouth. I had never seen one before but knew its name from descriptions, had heard they took cattle and even small children.

Flake pulled and lurched against my hand. I held him tight as we watched the thing spring. In an instant of fluid motion, its huge paw curled down across the deer's shoulder, leaving four tracks of blood. The deer could barely startle the lunge came so quickly, full of fur and power and motion and blood. The whiskered animal cried like an unanswered infant.

Flake lunged and chewed on my hand holding the leather necklace against his will.

The deer's legs twitched, then stopped as the victor ripped at its throat, then its flank. To the sounds of death gurgling, the cat ate its fill, turned its head once or twice to scan around, face smudged red against the deer's tawny brown.

Finished, it sat, brought a pale paw to its mouth and licked, looking soft and friendly, its stomach extended out like a once crabby baby's, satisfied.

It stretched low, then sprang as though shot from a bow toward a tree felled by the wind into another. It moved up into the branches, and I saw its tail hang low in the distance, twitching softly. The cat licked her face, then eased her way back down, making her way to a rocky ledge instead. Its eyes closed within minutes into gentle sleep, a moment of softness cradled in the midst of vicious death.

Flake jerked on my hands, sore where the leather thong cut into the palm. I could not even speak to him, made some effort at using my hand to signal him quiet. His throat harbored a low growl that stopped as I started to move, slowly, easing our way toward the felled deer. Much meat remained on the deer's carcass, and with Lukwsh's small obsidian knife, I took some, cut the loin almost untouched from the deer's back. With the hafted knife between my teeth, I hung the length of red meat cut back from his spine and draped the flesh around my neck. Then with quick, quick movements I had seen Grey Doe use, I sliced strips from the shoulder. My eyes scanned quickly as I worked, sought signs of sudden danger. From the corner of my eye I watched the sleeping animal, willed it to share its kill without a struggle. The cat slept.

Flake buried his head in the deer's ripped side, lay down, and tore at the meat held between his paws.

Satisfied, we slipped out low to the ground over the rise from which we'd watched. I placed the meat in the burden basket, and we made our way quickly, crossing the river to swallow our scent.

The roasted venison tasted as sweet and soft as sage gum, and we both ate our fill, Flake threatening to lick the juice from my chin. I dried more for travel so the deer meat could last several days.

With a fuller stomach, I had confidence to spend time stripping sage-brush and some willows to form twists and coils to stick with pitch to the bottoms of my thin moccasins. I made sage rope into cordage to trap ducks that swam along the river banks close to gravel bars appearing like long spears in the water. Flake startled the ducks into the crude nets, and I strangled one, then two, skinned them and kept the hides and roasted the meat.

I wondered if I should just stay, form a lodge of sagebrush, and fish and hunt with Flake. Surely, no one followed. Perhaps this was the place where I could spend my days, not search for Sunmiet's *tibo*, not worry about walking in a world with owls.

For the first time since the charming I allowed myself to feel satisfied, capable, trust there were some choices for me, both a future and a hope.

So my downfall should not have come as a surprise. Bad things always follow after good in my life, meant to keep me humble.

It was midday, warm. We had stopped to drink and refill the water basket. Flake chased butterflies that flitted through the grasses beside the river.

Cattle tracks punched into broken river banks, sure signs of settlers. The cow's feet left puddles that collected familiar seeds that were soft but tasty when I put tiny fragments to my tongue. High lava rocks not unlike the ridge I once fell from lined the river. The day grew hot and still.

Along the lower ridges, shallow caves promised protection and cool. Wuzzie would have sought "cave power" found in sacred places.

We made the short climb toward an opening in the rocks, and I heard the buzz in the grass before I saw the rattler.

"I do not wish to breathe snake breath, Flake," I told him.

Flake barked at the coil, darted forward and back, set the snake straight as to who was in charge of this space. The snake eventually slithered out of its twist and into the grass. Because it left us unharmed, I thought the danger past.

The birds' silence came to me first, as though some wind had swept through and stolen all their voices. The air lingered, as stagnant as an old pond, the sage intensely fragrant.

From my perch in the shallow cave, I could see the river wander through a flat area lined by nubby rocky ridges the colors of rainbows. In the distance, the cattle grazed on the river-fed grass like cranes in a sea of green. Then the cows began to run with their tails up high, fanning out in all directions. I had seen horses run when flies became unbearable, but these cows kicked and jumped, then clustered into groups and ran again like ragged rays parting from a once friendly sun.

Flake whined, panted, stood up, sneezed. He walked beyond me, but came back when I called. A cluster of ducks lifted up as though startled, but nothing else moved as they flew into the sun.

Those were the memories of warnings.

I heard the sounds of the rocks like someone scrambling over them in a hurry, watched a small chunk dribble downhill, gain speed. My mind told me no animal could be above us, cause such sounds, but the rocks kept coming. Could people climb there? Had I missed an easy ascent from the other side? Who had followed me? Why did they bother? My heart pounded, my body tingled as though struck with willow sticks all over.

I shook and shivered in my fear, could not walk out to see for sure who might be above me. I watched cattle running, running as if wild. Even grasses moved outside the cave within the stillness of the wind. Flake broke my hold on him and raced out.

"No!" I shouted, hoping none but him would hear me. "Come back!" He barked at me. "They'll see you!" I shouted with a whine. "Stay here. Oh, please stay here!"

I started after him then but could not make my feet be steady. My fear, I thought. I grabbed the sides of the shallow cave wall that moved like gentle waves. I yelled again for Flake, my voice barely rising above the falling rocks.

But he was gone. He had moved on down the ridge, then turned back to hear me. He stood, watched, his ears perked forward in a question, his eyes locked onto mine.

So we did not see the boulder high above us break, bounce like a hollow gourd, crack like thunder, hit here and there before it struck him on the side.

The rock stayed only seconds before bounding on, resting finally in a mighty splash close to the river's edge. A shower of rocks, some smaller, some larger, gouged the ground as they rolled and bounced and beat the dry earth like a hollow drum. They landed beside the dog, bounced well beyond.

My mind still could make no sense of who could push so many rocks and make the grass move without wind, how the cave could keep me stumbling so I could not reach my dog.

The cave wall calmed. My eyes skimmed across the cattle grazing like quiet children, pawing the grass for seeds, no sign they ever ran in all directions. No rocks rolled. Birds flitted and flew. The grass lay quiet.

I did not wish to see the still, dark form before me.

There remained not even a moment to be with him yet in life, to rest his soft head in my lap while he could hear my words. I talked to him, said his name out loud, smoothed the fur of his ears, his head, his bleeding side. My buckskin felt cold beneath his head, and when I lifted it, I saw blood oozed onto me. The air moved his thick fur that now covered stillness; his eyes stayed open into stare.

The boulder had twisted Flake's neck in a strange angle not fitting for the friend he was. I straightened it, my fingers slippery with his blood, and buried my face in his fur.

I told myself later that he would not have wished to live with all his wounds and damage. I reminded myself when I felt the surge of loss well up and burn my chest that he was just a dog, not some precious child, not a parent or a mate, not a valued friend. A dog, just a dog. And still, I could not stop the ache of losing him, of wondering why again I would be left, yet must go on.

As best I could, I dragged his heavy body to where the rock that struck him had dug a depression in the earth before bounding and careening to the river. Through tears I told him I was sorry that the rock should form his final place.

My limbs did not feel the growing numbness until later. I worked, gathering rocks, and in between my breathy sobs my mind repeated, "You are alone, now. Flake is gone." And I would have to stop awhile and cry.

When Flake's form was almost covered, all except his massive head, I lost all hope to carry on, perhaps because I knew my calls lured him to the boulder's path. Wuzzie had promised his dancing would bring the shaking earth. He had warned me what would happen if I disobeyed. I had no hope in running off to nowhere all alone to search for people no more real than misty memories.

I decided to bury all that I had with him, let my life end as Wuzzie intended.

I wrapped the scrap of headband over the dog's eyes so he would not stare at the rocks or woman-child who caused his death. The burden basket with what venison remained I laid beneath his muzzle. The duck hides filled the space in the dog's head crushed in by the rock. Even Wren's tiny tule dog, her flints, I laid there beside Lukwsh's knife, the tule water basket, the spear point. My hand brushed against the soft hide that remained of my dress and I lifted it over my shoulders, laid it over him.

I started to cover up his head when I spied the knots of leather.

"Trade," I told him.

Small rocks ground into my knees as I bent over him. Bumps of cold formed on my skin. I felt myself shake. I removed the gold chain from around my neck and placed it in a clump near his, the gold glittering against the shiny black fur.

"I do not belong to the love this necklace promised," I told him. The knots slipped over his ears, easily, into my hands. "If I should live, it will be not because of anything I did, not from the treasures of the basket given me by others. I live only to remember. The mistakes I made, my pride, my unwillingness to bend, how I harmed others. My knots of memory go with me from where I once belonged."

I draped the knots over my head. With my hands as claws, I covered Flake—his head, the gold of the chain—with the sparse dirt and pebbles. At the river's edge, I found grasses easily pulled and dry sagebrush and laid them on his grave. My stomach was a hollow core. I finished the mound with larger rocks stacked high until my arms ached and my legs wore scratches from the rocks' sharp edges gouging my legs as I carried and walked.

I had no tears left.

The night air turned cool. I huddled outside the cave, collecting warmth, hoping to die before morning.

It was not to be.

Instead, I awoke shivering, my stomach growling, my body wishing to make water. I hated myself that such needs should wake me, force me to remember where I was, *that* I was at all.

I made my way to the water's edge, dipped my hand, drank, and returned to the edge of the cave, waiting in my place beside the dead.

How many days passed like this I do not know; the days drifted into each other like leaves collecting and moving in a slow stream. But one morning I noticed movement in the dry grasses close to the base of the ledge. Something bobbed and wove yet did not move away, stayed just beyond the weeds. It continued without stopping, changing only to grow larger at times, as though it had wings but could not fly. As though in a trance, I moved toward it.

I felt like the fawn I'd charmed and wondered if I had been lured to the curious that harbored harm. My head buzzed from the sun and hunger. Perhaps the weaving was not there at all. As I moved closer, I saw the thing had eyes circled with a ring of brown. And it had wings that it pulled around itself, its head bobbing as though blind. It was a young owl.

It lunged toward me when it heard. High above us I spied a smaller cave and the remains of a nest that must have shaken loose in the earth's quaking. The bird jabbed at my feet, missed completely, and I realized it was blind, the sunlight taking away its vision given only for night. I picked it up and wrapped the wings over its eyes. It felt warm in my hands, soft.

"You don't belong here," I told it, stroking the smooth feathers. The bird struggled; its talons poked at my hands. It gave in.

"You belong where you can do what you were meant to," I said but heard the words as though spoken to myself. I carried it into the darkness of the cave, set it down. It kept its wings over its eyes by choice until I stepped back. The weaving and bobbing stopped, and it lowered its wings and stared, moved from side to side on its slender feet, moved deeper into the cave, away from danger. Its strength returned. It had found its place.

As though walking in a sleep, I backed out and made my way to Flake.

"I have things to do, Flake," I told him, rolling rocks near his head. I hoped he would forgive me for robbing his grave.

My fingers clutched the dirt-laden buckskin, and when I pulled it from the earth, it resisted me. A yank toppled me backward. I sat back up, breathing hard, still clutching the buckskin. Beside it, glittering in the sun, came the necklace, too.

"You give this back?" I asked the dog. A breeze ruffled a section of fur I had uncovered. "I take it, then," I said, pushing dirt and rocks back over him, "since it belongs more with my kind than yours."

I brushed off the buckskin dress, which was more like a shirt now, so many of the leather strips had been cut and chewed. I slipped it over my head and pushed the wide opening to stop at my waist. In a cluster of sage, I stripped bark, rubbed my fingers raw with the pulling and tearing, and rolled it against my thighs, twist after twist, weaving the strands together until I had enough. I eased a slice in the center of the sagebrush material, pulled it over my head like a man's poncho, and tied a belt with the thong of knots that once circled my throat.

I paused at Flake's grave.

"I go to Sunmiet's place, but I will not forget who you are and what you gave me. And I will be as good a friend, Flake, as you were to me."

I stepped back, stood awhile longer. It was not saying good-bye, but the speaking of a promise.

I followed the river north. I had nowhere else to go.

Several days passed before I reached the place where a road broke off and split west, away from the wide river, toward a chain of snow-capped mountains in the distance. It was still the Dalles-Canyon City Military Highway, I believed, but now it rolled across prairie land dotted with tall grasses. Deep, wide ravines promised the breaks of another major river. Sunmiet said she lived in the shadow of such mountains strung like white shells against the sky.

Where the trails separated, a small building with a hitching post in front attracted many travelers. I sat and watched from a distance as people came out of it, mounted up, and traveled the direction from which I'd come. Several Indians rode untroubled beside armed soldiers. The Indians had guns too. I looked to see if the Indians were free to leave. It seemed so. Their bodies simply blended together as they disappeared in the distance. It was the first place I ventured where owls and Indians rode together, and I believed I must be close to where I needed to be.

I headed toward the mountains, passed through sultry winds blowing over sagebrush and purple lilies blooming in a single slender stem that shot up from the desert floor. My feet kicked up dust on a trail around a treeless ridge. It was wide enough for narrow wagons, though there were few tracks but those of horses. The sides rose up steeply, leaving me no place to hide if a rider came my way, but I met no one. I noticed only areas where rock had recently fallen, been gouged out like the boulder that felled my friend.

I followed the twisting road until it took me above the promised river. Fierce rapids plunged against rocks that shot spray far beyond the river's edge. White water rushed through steep, rocky banks. Farther on, the stream narrowed, twisting past a rock wall that cut into a blue sky as though sliced out by Lukwsh's knife.

Then I saw what made the roar I heard: a falls, twisting like a rabbit rope through cramped boulders, forcing the river to spill and fall upon itself before plunging to flat rocks below. Empty platforms, like log rafts hung in the air, extended out over the water, but otherwise it was quiet, with no sign of people, and so I believed this could not be the place Sunmiet spoke of. Where she lived would be activity, she promised, fishing and families gathered for the season.

I stood for some time listening to the water, watching sea gulls dip and dive to the pools of fish clustered in the winding water below the falls. I stood and stared, lost in the noise and splendor splashed before my eyes, lost to the sadness that had joined me as companion.

So at first I did not notice the being who came to greet me in this place so unfamiliar, cautiously came to meet me, prepared to take me to another world.

PASSAGE

THE SMALL, REDDISH-BROWN DOG WITH POINTY EARS advanced with hair standing, head lowered, mouth still. It stopped and stared. Behind him, on the ridge we shared, I detected men. Sounds of chopping reached my ears, though no trees broke the view. Voices carried over the ravines like straight arrows in still air.

I did not wish to encounter others as I did not believe this was the place that Sunmiet said. I wanted to move on.

More voices. I saw one or two men with rugged tools of iron like those brought back in raids by Oytes and Stink Bug. Men, through the mist of rabbit brush and sage, emerged from around the bend. Others followed, moving like beetles, slowly but with purpose. Some stopped and chopped at sagebrush; some pulled at roots and stacked the pale green in piles. For a brief moment I stood with Grey Doe and the time of my passage.

Behind them, I heard the whistles and shouts of encouragement said to horses and mules pulling wagons of rocks and dirt. I thought I heard a jumble of English, something else. A steamy warmth rose off the road as the men put their backs to their work, their shoulders glistening with sweat. Bodies of dark colors and light bent to tasks together, laying rocks to make the road wider, give it a place to go, or so it seemed.

A low growl rising from the dog regained my attention. Though not large, he wore a fierce look. He rolled his lips back to reveal black gums and large teeth. A short-legged dog compared to Flake, he almost crept on his belly toward me, wary, as though uncertain of my smell, my being.

"Here dog," I said.

His ears perked forward and he stopped, twisted his head and sat, panting in the heat, watching me. Two tan spots like thumbprints marked areas above his eyes. The same light color lined his muzzle and throat, his chest, the insides of his squat legs. He had an unusual *nabawici* but appeared neither frightened nor lost. I promised myself to behave the same.

I walked toward him and he stood, tongue hanging. He let me put my hand out to his nose, smelled the back of my fingers, and then he lowered his bony head and invited me to run my palm between his ears. His soft fur brought with it a piercing ache of what I missed.

The dog tolerated me for just a moment, then shook as though I were a fly. He trotted toward the men and looked back as if to see if I would follow.

I looked over the side of the road, seeking a way to keep on going but still avoid the men. Too steep. They had picked a strange place for a road, carving out deer tracks, through sparse grass and sage, around exposed ridges. It seemed to go nowhere, circle dance with the river. I looked behind me. I had to go forward, just keep going and hope they let me pass.

The men stopped their work to stare as I followed the dog. I noticed some of the lighter-skinned men scowled at me. One or two placed eyes on me that seemed to pass through the sagebrush and buckskin clothes that hid my skin burned dark by the sun. I wondered if like the dog they were aware of my scent before they even saw me.

A round-faced Indian with hair sliced short beneath a dark hat saw me and pushed his hat back. An eagle feather honored the hat band. He shouted something to another man who squatted at a mule's hoof.

That one turned to look, then stood with the ease of someone small, though he filled up the sky. His eyes wore a look of question beneath his flat-top hat casting a shadow over an intent face. A dark beard with spider webs of white rested on his broad chest and covered portions of a vest dyed the color of dried raspberries. He pulled on his face hair, buttoned his coat with one hand, then said something to the short-haired Indian, who joined him as he strode toward me.

Their eyes spoke questions.

The man with the vest could look fierce, I thought, his jaw set in seriousness. But his blue eyes were as gentle as a fawn's. He squatted down to me, so close his breath brushed against the bones of my cheeks. His voice had a deep rhythm like Lukwsh's lullaby, and he spoke words such as *ye* and *sure* that carried no meaning to me but sounded as gentle as a summer rain.

Perhaps it was the eyes or my tiredness or not caring any longer what pain awaited me, who knows? I did not bolt and run, did not set my feet to search for Sunmiet's place.

"You need something?" the Indian said in words I could understand.

I looked up, surprised.

The owl said more I did not understand, except I heard the word *Jane*, and my heart began to beat a little faster.

I had made Sunmiet's "Jane" bigger in my mind, someone who would recognize me for what I was. But I did not let myself hope long, remembering that Sunmiet's friend did not live at the river, she said, would only be found with them fishing when the salmon ran. I saw no one fishing.

Both men talked in low tones. Finally, at the big man's direction, the Indian brought a horse up beside us, and I felt my eyes get wide as I watched him step into the stirrup from the left, the white man's way. He extended his palm to me. The owl's eyes reassured.

When I hesitated, the big man motioned and the Indian turned the horse. Then the big man made a cup of his hands and motioned for me to step inside his palms, to mount the animal on the right, as an Indian.

The gesture caused my eyes to water in the wonder at this kindness, this recognition of who he thought I was.

He raised his palms again, and though I could swing up onto the horse as I once did in joy behind Shard, I accepted this man's offer, felt light as a *wada* seed as his fingers pressed around my blistered feet and lifted me up.

I sat on a good horse behind a man I did not know.

The dog mounted next, with no help at all, landing in a soft plop in front of the Indian.

We rode the twisting trail down, winding in and out along the edges of ravines as large as any I had seen since leaving Steens Mountain. Rocks pierced the sky across the river, a wall of rocks that looked like horse-hair ropes on end, so high they made the sun set early in this canyon. I took deep breaths as I rode deeper into the ravine, away from safe heights and hills.

We approached the river roaring through stone walls. Long, nubby rocks like fallen cattails sliced into the river. White water surged over chunks of granite, formed a frothy boil as the river spilled and dropped. A roar like a wind reached my ears, and I saw water twisting and plunging, swirling beneath a narrow bridge we rode across. I scraped my memory for something of Sunmiet's description but did not find it.

I had not seen the falls nor the bridge from the road above, nor the low building surrounded by a rock fence where we stopped. The Indian dismounted and helped me down. The little dog already panted at my feet. He scattered chickens and guinea hens pecking about.

"No, no," he said to the dog who looked as if he wanted to herd the chickens toward a fenced pen. "Not now, Bandit," he said and squatted low to scratch the dog's head.

Standing, the man reached for an object like a metal basket hung upside down near the opening of the fence. He hit it with a stick, causing a sound so loud and clanging that my ears protested with pain. The clanging continued until I felt him beside me, prying my hands from my ears.

"No danger," he said.

My eyes opened to greet a tiny woman with chestnut hair pulled straight back from a face the shape of a duck's egg. A strip of white cloth pinned over her dress held tight her tiny waist. Despite the heat, she hurried in quick-quick steps from the porch as my head rang with the clanging.

"You...old...Bandit." I recognized these words.

"Missus says, 'Either go out and stay with Mr. Sherar or don't go out at all in this heat.' She talks to dogs," the Indian told me with a smile, and I knew then I would like her.

She dabbed at her forehead with a corner of white cloth, fingertips tapping at perspiration. Her words to the dog were quick, carried scolding as she looked from the dog to the chickens, but she grinned and scratched the dog's belly as she squatted to talk. When she bent to him, I could see her hair knotted at the back of her neck, held by a beaded barrette.

The dog panted, sat satisfied. It pleased me to see she had words for the dog. It gave me time. Bandit yawned, and the woman faced me.

"What...Peter?" the woman asked.

"Bandit dragged it in," Peter said first in jargon, his dark eyes twinkling. Then he translated to the woman.

She answered him with quick-bitten words that I thought from her tone would take the twinkle from his eye, but they appeared to be friends, these two. She watched me, her tongue clucking gently, her eyes like a new fire on a cold day. I thought of Sarah's Christians with their flame inside and wondered which box this white woman would fit into.

Finally, the dog content, she stood, hands clasped in front of her, and boldly studied me while the man spoke.

Then her hand came to my chin and she touched me, and I did not jerk back. She said something to my eyes as though speaking inside of me. The man nodded. To me in jargon he repeated: "She says you carry sadness. Wants to know your name."

The request surprised me, for I had begun to see myself as indistinct, someone who could simply disappear, someone barely here, whose sorrow and her person lay hidden deep within.

And what name should I give her? Shell Flower, the name that meant I once was loved? Thocmetone for where I spent my life? Or Asiam, the one who made mistakes, was banished for her being?

"Asiam," I answered her in truth.

"Alice M?" the woman asked.

The Indian, Peter, shook his head. "Ashiem," he assured her, shrugged his shoulders as though it was not a word he knew. "She does not get it. Say your name again," he said to me in the trade jargon.

"As-i-am," I repeated, eyes down.

"Al-ice-M," the woman repeated, then when I did not answer, she said with certainty in her voice, "Alice M."

What did it matter what they called me or who I was? Not even the wind would know my name nor should it.

"I am Mrs. Sherar," she said just as I said my new name to myself. "Jane Herbert Sherar." She continued talking, but her name stayed in my ears. Could she be the Jane of Sunmiet's speaking, the one who might help me find out things I wished to know?

If there had been Indians fishing, camped on the river's banks, I would not have wondered, been surer of this place. But she did not live at the river—that's what Sunmiet had said—only felt at home with it.

I would ask the man, Peter, when I could. He translated her words to me. "She tells you I am Peter, the foreman. You met her husband, Joseph, on that 'road of his.' She would feed you. You look all bones."

My body felt no hunger, though I had not eaten much for days. I said so. He said something and she looked at me, squinted then grunted.

"Go with her," he said. "She is a good woman."

She motioned me to follow her inside the rock wall and enter the building. My steps shunned the clanging thing, and I looked behind me to see Peter catch up the reins of his horse and head toward the barn, past sagebrush fences lined with drying coyote hides. Chickens squawked and scattered.

The house was made of boards as though a wagon floor had been dismantled. I had never seen a wooden house from inside out. A long table with stiff chairs set tight to it squeezed the room. Over the table hung a giant spray of glass and shiny gold metal, a Shooting Star in late afternoon, and I wished that Wren could see it. Like a rabbit's den, several openings led from this space, but the doors were closed. Most had small markings on them.

On the walls between windows hung likenesses of people not present, such likenesses that might have helped me find my mother if I had them.

She motioned me into one of the smaller rooms. It held a mat on legs covered with a white blanket. Beside it sat a small table topped with a bowl. Pale cloth fluttered at the window that looked out onto a steep rock wall.

While her hands waved and her words rushed out, a slender man with narrow eyes like slits of dark mud shuffled into the room. His eyes searched the floor. He wore cloth the color of summer sky, and a single dark braid swung over one shoulder, shiny against his blue shirt. The woman spoke to him and he backed out, returning with a basket made of wood filled with steaming water. He glanced at me without warmth, looked at her as he poured the water into a metal log she had dragged, sweating, into the room.

The man grumbled something. Her one word response proved sharp enough to make him drop his eyes again. He glared like a cornered marmot, almost losing his blue hat as he backed out, barely avoiding the dog who scooted by him to lie at my feet.

The water steamed up. "Tub," she said, pointing to the water.

She dipped her hand in it and jerked it quickly out. Her long skirts swished past me and I peered around the door to watch her in an adjoining area lift a tail that forced water into another metal box. She dipped the wooden basket into it and poured that water into the log.

"Well," she said and pretended to rub on her face and shoulders with a white bar, smelled it with a deep breath, then dropped it into the steaming water.

I stepped closer to watch it sink. When I turned back, I saw a glass next to the bed like one in Wuzzie's lodge. In it reflected my image.

I jumped back, startled by the thin cheeks, eyes like rocks sunk into months-old snow, tangled strands, missing places and mats of hair, dirt all around my mouth, cracked lips, as dark and as thick as my eyebrows. Even my *nabawici* lay hidden beneath the dirt. Sores oozed from the side of my nose. One eye appeared swollen and draining, the other held an empty, distant look, though it could have been caused by the ripples that moved in the glass. What I saw in that mirror did not look like Asiam. It must be this Alice M.

This woman had not even winced when she saw me; nothing crossed her eyes in judgment.

She motioned me with her hands, but I could only guess at her meaning until she slipped off her shoe, turned, removed her dark stocking. She unpinned the white patch from her dress, started to work the tiny buttons. With one quick movement, she hiked up her skirt and dipped her toe into the water. She looked back at me, spoke.

She stepped away from the tub, held her arms out, motioned me to do the same. Closer to me now, she began to pull the shredded sagebrush from my breast. I clutched at my clothes. She backed away, a look of regret on her face.

Only the presence of the dog moving closer to me kept my feet from bolting out the door. But should I be frightened of people who lived with dogs? Yes, I told myself, remembering.

She chattered like a magpie, motioning with her hands, and suddenly a great tiredness washed over me from the watching and the listening and the wondering, the uncertainty of it all. And when she motioned to me again, I permitted it, held my arms out like a child, asking for her help.

Her touch was gentle as she lifted away the shredded sage, slowly, kindly, careful not to bump the scabs and sores that marked my body like angry welts. She seemed troubled by the circle of knots tied around my waist, not sure what to do with the dirty string. I lifted it over my head, wrapped it like a precious gift inside my fist. She tapped the little table next to the bed and I set it there, placed my memory in a knotted circle on a stone-topped table.

She did not seem offended by my odor which I noticed in this small, warm room. Instead, she pushed her sleeves up beyond her elbows, dipped her hand into the tub, and pulled the bar out.

"Soap," she said and rubbed it against a cloth she then stroked gently along my jaw, pressed against my cheek below my eyes.

Her hands touched soft as a lily pad, gentle, not unlike Lukwsh's, especially the last morning when she had washed and dressed me, prepared me for my journey to another place and time.

The woman leaned close enough for me to smell her breath, sweet like bee's honey. It reminded me of healing. Tiny beads of perspiration glistened beneath her nose.

I stepped into this tiny lake, turned and sat, slid under. The metal felt cool against my neck, and I could feel the warmth fill every crevice of my body, wash over every ache and exposed sore. It was unlike soaking in the lake, different than the sweat lodge heat that went deep inside while sitting surrounded by a circle of friends and steaming rocks. But I had stepped into a different place, must gather strength from both old and new.

I leaned my head back, let steaming water soothe.

She squeezed warm water from the rag. It foamed softly over my shoulders, slid down my back. The air felt sultry. A heaviness wiped over my eyes. I fell asleep.

Fingers pulled at my scalp. I felt my hair pulled upward, crossed *wehe* flashed by my eyes. I grabbed at the bearer's wrists, held her, twisted, water splashing against her dress forming dark stains. The woman startled. She was strong and wiry. The dog barked. She shook her head, said something in a pleading voice, her eyes moaned pain into mine.

I searched the room, frantic, and found the door. I let her go, grabbed the tub's wet sides, tried to stand, slipped and plunged like a wounded calf in water. The dog barked and lunged at me. A hot anger with myself flushed my face, anger that I slept.

"Alice! Alice M!" she shouted. Her words, so strong, forced me to look.

If she had gazed at me in that moment, she would have seen someone with mouth open in amazement. But she was busy, showing me on herself what she would do with a crossed *wehe,* pulling at her hair as though slicing through unseen tangles. Then she pulled a strand into the *wehe* and she snipped. A lock of her chestnut hair floated gently to the floor.

"Scissors," she said. Her eyes wore that pleading look again, offered apology, and she handed me the weapon—a place for fingers first—if I chose to take it.

My fingers slid over the cool knives, then reached to stiff mats of my hair. I could barely pull them through the knots. My heart beat slower with my decision. I handed back the scissors, motioned with my hands for her to cut and snip—but not cut short—then slipped back into the water.

The smile she extended seemed to light her face. Wisps of hair clung to her cheeks, and she wiped her eyes and forehead with the back of her hand. Her voice began again the pleasing chatter as she talked to the dog. His skinny tail pounded the floor at his name, Bandit. She called me by name, Alice M, a word I recognized in the flow that drifted and moved from her mouth like sweet rice grasses dancing in the wind.

There was something soothing about the chatter, something I had not known I missed, another loss wrapped in my separation from the people. Someone always talked there—aunties cooking, telling stories; uncles twisting tules for the duck boats, chiding their wives and sisters. Digging roots, drying salmon, skinning ducks—whatever people did, they did together. Children, cuddled or chastised by aunties, uncles, older sisters, and their parents or grandparents, sat in the center of things. At the gatherings, the weddings, the feasts, the rabbit hunts, a dozen voices might be talking all at once. Even babies put to sleep were kept within the chatter, a cloth laid across the board's brace to block out sight but never words or laughter.

And in the din that I had just begun to be a part of before being forced to leave, within the ebb and flow of words and laughter, the families of the people wove a shell around their children and each other, a shell that gave protection and said they all belonged.

I pressed away tears.

She tugged as gentle as a dog's lick on my hair. I closed my eyes, amazed that while an owl I did not know pulled at my hair with crossed knives, I lay naked in a lake inside a wooden lodge.

My journey to this new place had taken away my strength, and for many days I lay on the soft mat, my hands in fists like still brown clubs against the snow of cloth called sheets. Inside my skin I felt as though two women quarreled. One said I was the cause of so much ruin and should let my body drift away and die; another told me, Listen: *gather farther, stay out longer, and do not return.*

Every day the woman helped drag the "tub" to my room, filled it with steaming water, and encouraged me to step inside and seep away sores. I did this only when they left me alone to stare out at the rock wall while the water washed away the layers of Asiam.

Mrs. Sherar, as she was called by Sung-li, the man in blue who brought in strange foods with a scowl, sat every day on the side of my mat, my bed. She talked with me in foreign words I could not understand but whose tones were as warm as the touch of her palm on my forehead, as soft as the pillow she fluffed at my head, as comforting as the arms she wrapped around me when I let her. She had the body of a small woman, but her hands were large, like Lukwsh's, and bore the red knuckles of hard work.

I did not believe she was that much older than I. She had no lines on her face and all of her teeth. But she treated me like a child, not unlike the ways I watched over Wren. Her tending seemed to feed an unnamed hunger.

Her husband, the big owl I met on the sidehill, came to stand beside her as she spoke with me at times; his arm held her to him as though they were one. Wide fingers pressed gently into her shoulders, and when they left, he stepped aside so she could move her wide skirts first through the door. He followed her out like a woman would from the lodge of the people.

When Mrs. Sherar stopped smoothing the sheets over me, touching me gently, or bringing in bowls of steaming stew, I could hear her bustling in the cooking room, her voice loud, followed by the scurried feet of Sung-li and the clanging of pans. Outside, stagecoaches ground to a stop. I heard people talking, horses shake their heads against their harnesses, listened while they brought in new teams, noted the sounds of different voices of each day, periods of quiet broken by the rushing and meals, returning just before night.

And through open windows, day or night, I heard the plunge and shudder of the falls, a sound so constant it became like air breathed in, like the chatter of ducks on the lakes, the cackle of geese rising in flight. At night, I lay awake listening to the noises of sleep, sometimes watched the stars and wondered if Shard watched this same sky, too. My head shook, ashamed at this hopeful thought when my mind said he was dead. Sleep then became a slow insect and made my pillow damp by morning.

The woman, Jane, had eyes the deep blue of huckleberries, surrounded completely by white, like dark rocks in snow. At times, they reminded me of a *moo'a* hawk as she looked at me, not letting any detail escape. More often, they were a doe's eyes, watching, to know and protect.

She gave me a cloth dress the color of the curtains and motioned for me to sleep in it. At the foot of the bed lay a dress of cloth with the feel of warm ice. Marked with slender stripes of green and gold, a row of tiny buttons reached to a stiff black collar close to the neck. I had yet to wear it. I had yet to get up.

"Peter...here...Alice M," Mrs. Sherar told me one morning several weeks after I arrived. He stood in the doorway. She spoke to him at length, and I was surprised that I picked out several words before he told me what they were.

"Mrs. Sherar wants to know if you are feeling stronger. Are you well enough?" He used his hands some to make sure I understood.

I nodded my head once, indicated yes.

"When will you, then, get up?" he asked.

I answered him in silence, for I did not know.

"She wants to know if people look for you."

I glanced at him and wondered what he knew. But then I realized he asked if someone might be missing me, wonder where I was, someone they could tell with joy to find me here, to claim their lost child bearing a *naba-wici*. His question brought a stab of regret.

I shook my head.

"You can stay a long time, Mrs. Sherar says. And when you want, she will listen. She worries," he continued, his hat brim sliding between his fingers as he spoke. His nails were clean. He paused to hear what the woman wished him to say. "You do not eat much, do not move about. She says no one gets well unless they eat and find a place to challenge their mind and their hands."

"My stomach is startled by the food," I told him, to focus on something I could explain. "There is so much and so soft and different."

"Your belly will accept in time," he said. "She wonders what ails your mind."

How to tell him that I wanted to accomplish something, find Sunmiet, continue my search, maybe live in a place where all could blend together? How to tell him that my mind was tired from too many challenges, too many recent pains? What words to use to let him know how weary loneliness could be?

For the first time, I even wondered if Sunmiet would welcome me—if this was her place—wondered if she would open her arms to a woman-child who harmed her people, who had been washed and dressed for death, yet had cheated it and escaped.

"Sunmiet..." I said out loud before thinking.

Mrs. Sherar squinted her eyes to the word I'd spoken, spoke rapidly to Peter.

"She wants to know how you know that one. Sunmiet."

I shrugged my shoulders, wary, not wanting harm yet hopeful.

Mrs. Sherar spoke quickly, and Peter added, eyes dropped down, embarrassed to be speaking of these subjects, "*Her* Sunmiet prepares for a baby, has put another in its board. She comes in spring to fish, as always. Is that the one you know?"

"Does she have a baby named Owl?" I asked him.

His eyes showed surprise and he nodded, though Mrs. Sherar grabbed at his arm, wondering what I'd just said. He told her, and her eyes lit up.

"You share a friend."

A smile spread across her narrow face as Peter finished.

"She says you will be well by spring, ready to greet Sunmiet if you rise now, take in clear air and sun. Grow strong in winter. And if you wish, this good woman will help you find things for your hands to accomplish."

Perhaps my Spirit spoke to her on my behalf. Or maybe something in my eyes told her what else might make me well, for Peter relayed her next words that settled around me like the chatter of friends.

"This inn welcomes travelers, Alice M, but they are free to leave, continue their journeys much farther than here. Some come looking for things;
some are here just on their way to somewhere else. You are welcome, whatever kind of traveler you are. Or you can go when you are ready."

In her offer of such freedom, I found I wished to stay.

Through the fall and winter, Mrs. Sherar discovered things I could accomplish, though wearing the silky dress was not one either of us claimed. My
shoulders and waist were wider than the dress she gave me. My feet would
not squeeze into the thin leather with hooks and ties she had set beside the
bed. Instead, I wrapped my string of knots around the cloth-like sheets I had
been sleeping in. She smiled at that, nodded her head as though understanding, and in a day or two, Peter arrived with soft leather skins formed
into a dress and moccasins in my size. A part of me at first resisted so rich a
gift. But I remembered the naming and the honor I would give by my receiving it.

"My woman, Sumxseet, makes it," he said, handing it to me, moving
his hands, repeating the motion like an anxious friend. "And when you are
ready, you will wear it to show her how her hands make you look."

My hands were put to work, and my mind recalled things. I watched
men work on a mule's leg, made note of a poultice I could make, then took
a walk along the road, branched out into the ravines, the dog at my side. I
selected familiar roots and asked Peter's wife for certain leaves. With my
mixtures, I tended animals brought with cuts and sores to the barn. A soft
ooze of wild iris eased the pain of a bit held too tightly; yarrow soothed a
swollen joint. Mrs. Sherar asked for what would help a bee sting and
accepted my offer of mullein, mashed. Oat straw ground with a mano eased
the tooth pain of a buckaroo working on the ranch, and I found that the
bounce to his feet as he left without pain brought lightness to my walk as
well.

Inside the inn, as they called the house, I told Mrs. Sherar how to make
yellow-jacket soup, a delicacy she found tasty, though she would not tell the
travelers its name. In the night, I collected cicadas and locusts and stripped

them from the shell to fry crisp in pork grease as a surprise in the morning.

Mrs. Sherar even asked me to help out Sung-li, a task of interest, though his scowls reminded me of the spiteful words of Grey Doe and the uncertainty of Wuzzie with his seething hiss of power.

My mornings were announced by musters of peacocks strutting through the yard as they crowed away snakes. In the apron I took to wearing at times, I gathered clutches of eggs, helped churn the butter. Days when hundreds of sheep made their way across the bridge, I helped count them for the toll. One stick for each ten who passed by bleating, ten pennies times the sticks stuck in the bucket that held the money.

Long walks up the road toward Tygh Ridge delivered me to Mr. Sherar, who worked each day to keep his road strong. I brought him a forgotten bit of venison jerky or a note sent by Mrs. Sherar. Each journey brought me small *namaka,* like a sight of wild turkeys nesting in firs or the mastery of a barn owl tearing at mice in the rafters where the stage horses were changed. At night, when the moon rose over the falls, shimmering, I found I slept at a faster pace now. I dreamed often in my new language.

My days carried me on swift feet, surprising me with how quickly the language of the people disappeared and with it many thoughts that once formed like honey around my memory knots. The names of things surrounding me were all words the owls use, words of English said with ease. I learned the names of foods, most so unlike what I had eaten in Lukwsh's wickiup that I could not make them fit my memory. I understood the names for objects inside the house, the barn, the words for weather, the rush of water, the speed of horses and of time.

More difficult to learn were words for feelings, to describe the fullness of my heart when Bandit jumped onto my bed and curled there to sleep or when I came into the "kitchen" to see the Sherars in warm embrace standing before the window, watched them turn to me without embarrassment and smile, open wide their arms as if to pull me in, make no clucking of their tongues when I did not.

Almost everyday I heard Mr. Sherar say, "I love you," to his wife, and I watched the way she lifted her face to his, the way she leaned into his chest as he stood behind her to push her chair in at the table.

"I love you," seemed to make them smile, go deep inside, block out any others in the room. These words had not been said to me, but something in the Sherars' faces reminded me of a young man who told me that the sun rose in the light of my hair or set in the quiet of my eyes. I remembered a touch of his hand as we walked beside a lake, the way he held his arms, elbows out, then reached to invite me in to be held against his chest as softly as a sigh. I did not have the words to say that what we felt was love—he never said it—and yet I knew it by no other name.

Nor did I have words in English for what I felt when travelers stepped off the stagecoach and walked past me as though I could not be seen, some not even grunting in recognition that I carried in their bags stuffed like sausages with their belongings.

And I had no words to tell the Sherars about my fear of Sung-li, who chanted to his kitchen dolls at night in his room beside mine, or how he slammed his cleaver close to my fingers when I arrived to help him with the meals.

All the feelings, good and bad, brought up memories of those missing, of Lukwsh and Wren, of love once realized and lost. And of Wuzzie and Stink Bug and the strength of their wishes to send me away, take Shard, too, from their midst. I found no way to share the thoughts and memories with anyone who had not seen the wickiups, had not known the joy and sorrow of the people of my past.

I did my best to gather strength from blending.

My skin paled, shadowed by the bonnet Mrs. Sherar insisted I wear, at least within her sight. Only my wrists stayed browned by the sun.

My hands kept working; my body gathered strength.

Winter dressed the reptile road in white. Even in the deep canyon, occasional snow forced us to push through drifts to tend the cattle, horses, mules, and sheep. Mostly the ground stayed brown and frozen beside the river. The hilltops were covered only partway down with snow like white frosting dribbled over Mrs. Sherar's ginger cake.

In early December, I noticed a great stillness of birds and animals. It brought back a memory of silence followed by cows racing in strange ways, rocks falling with Flake beneath them. This silence, too, preceded a massive shaking of the ground. Rocks and boulders tumbled down ravines as though pushed along by raging water, some splashing like the tails of a hundred beavers warning of intruders.

Inside the inn, I heard dishes rattle, felt trembling beneath my feet, though only for a moment. Then all returned; all life breathed deeply as before.

Days later, Mr. Sherar said over coffee that an "earthquake" brought a rock slide on the Columbia in northern Washington. "Stopped all the river traffic," he said. "Caused quite a mess at those fish wheels and canneries."

"I wouldn't wonder," Mrs. Sherar said. "Unfortunately, not much slows them down."

"Ye can count on it bringin' the priests and pastors, maybe take more folks to God, sure," Mr. Sherar said.

Mrs. Sherar clucked her tongue. "Smoholla might just get some converts of his own with that dance to bring back life."

She handed her husband a spoonful of soft, fresh-churned butter. He spread it on the warm bread I brought him from the oven.

"Didn't Peter say he predicted this quake?" Mrs. Sherar asked, spoon held to the air in thought.

"Sure, now, someone did predict those rocks and the quake. Course I put no stock in such things. Be predicting Sunday follows Saturday if we're not careful and claim it some new thinking!"

Their words shook something in me, and I trembled that Wuzzie could make the earth break so far away, remembered his dreams of how he said the world would end and my part in it.

The Sherars marked the passage of a "year" with a celebration, shot off guns as though gathering ammunition held no worry. Later they invited me to a place where a man wore a long dress. A neck cloth the color of wild iris and a necklace bearing the crossed bars hung around his neck, and I gazed at them without shame, wanted to touch them, perhaps show the man my chain.

"We'll be reading from Jeremiah," he said, his voice large inside the building.

He boomed out words read from a large, black book before many people assembled, sitting. His wide sleeves billowed out like pillow slips as his arms raised to the peaked roof.

While I did not understand his speaking, I noticed warmth spread across the people's faces despite seeing their breath in the cold air. Candlelight flickered and reflected in their eyes, and the smell of wax grew stronger than the scent of wet wool of the capes and coats. I felt the warmth some myself when we all stood, lifted our faces, and sensed the vibration of a hundred whistles and drums coming from a small wagon pumped by a woman's feet, pounded by her fingers near the front.

We began to sing. And while I could not join them in their words, I saw the happiness on people's faces, the lightness in their joined voices, and I felt filled up, needed to wipe my eyes, pulled a cloth from the white muff my hands were buried in.

Mrs. Sherar saw me dabbing at my eyes. She leaned across her husband, gently pushed down the book he sang from so she could see me. Her bonnet cast a shadow in the candlelight that washed along the walls.

"Happy New Year, Alice M.," she whispered. "May this be just the best new beginning, ever."

The words "new year" held little meaning, but "new beginning" sounded like a breath of joy spoken as she touched her gloved hand to mine, patted it quiet as a dog's paw.

The building and its high ceiling echoed back the music, filled the cavity of my chest with words and rhythm. The sounds seeped through my skin, made my body tingly like a lightning storm captured inside. Tears formed again in my eyes. The deep tones of pipes were like a flutter through my feet.

And when I thought my heart could hold no more or burst, one more gift was given, great beyond all others.

My Spirit spoke.

I am here, he told me, though I heard no spoken words. *Here among these people, here wherever you are, here whenever you should call my name.*

For the first time in a long time, a bubble pushed at my heart, my face, and formed into a smile I did not try to hide. I was not alone! I did not know his name yet, this Spirit that still spoke. But I was comforted, filled with joy. For he traveled with me, brought water to my soul, gave me hope and other people, work to master, and a song.

WAITING TO UNFOLD

MY BELONGINGS WERE MOVED to a room closer to the Sherars as though I might be family. A bed warmer appeared between the sheets, placed there by Sung-li each night before I slept. I awoke, rested.

Throughout the winter my hands were given tasks they completed. I worked, quiet, talked to no one of my Spirit, simply puzzled that he traveled with me, learned different languages, too. My eyes watched how people tended each other, touched and talked, recorded what caused smiles to form or frowns, how they learned to fill each other up or take away.

Mrs. Sherar reminded me of Wren the way she moved so quickly, mostly filled with joy. Over dark water they called coffee, she and Mr. Sherar spent early mornings at the "dining table," talking, sometimes scowling as they planned their day, heads bent together. Inside the house, they often folded their hands and lowered their eyes in what Peter described as the posture of their prayer.

I noticed that the small woman could give her husband words to make his face turn sober or cause his ample beard to bounce in laughter upon his chest. His eyes spoke to her with tenderness I remembered from Lukwsh's eyes, saw again when Peter spoke to Sumxseek when I visited them. And while I saw no children of the Sherars, I expected Mr. Sherar to call her *piawabi*, as all happy fathers call their wives when they have found such fullness.

Peter became the bridge between my people and these. He and Sumxseet opened wide their wood home built north of Sherars'. Like the Paiute people, they did not extend an invitation, just assumed that I would come when ready, drop in when it suited.

They greeted me with "*Uhamasu tukapu*," and I knew that I could eat there, have my needs met.

A trail led me to their place. Snow covered the ridges, like a white lace collar set against a blackberry-dyed dress.

"This dress fits well," I told her, thanks wrapped in the words.

She grunted appreciation, looked at the stitching. "Room for you to eat more," she said. "This tread will stretch."

I laughed with her, turned to meet George, their son, who spoke English and Sahaptin, the language of Peter's people. He spoke Chinookan, too. Here, I did not need to worry over words.

"Three languages inside one head," Peter said with pride, nodding toward his son who is a man, his face reflecting warmth. "He helps Mrs. Sherar with the books and writes the names of workers Mr. Sherar gives her. Most have Indian names his mouth will not pronounce, and so he gives them new ones."

He tapped a pipe shaped like a bathing woman against his boot heel as he talked. Sumxseet frowned at him. His long fingers picked up tobacco that clumped on the floor.

"My mother gives me a white man's name—Peter," he told me, tapping new tobacco in the pipe-woman's belly. "She says it comes from their holy book and is a strong man who makes mistakes but finds a way around them through a Spirit." He sucked in on his pipe. "The mistake part is me." He smiled.

"Like all of us," his son said.

George sat in a wooden chair oiling a long rifle on his knees. His dark hair, short like his father's, fell forward toward his face, casting a shadow from the oil lamp sitting on a white cloth at the table's center. The weapon was not unlike the one once shot by Shard. Real bullets, not those formed from the iron of wheels taken in raids, sat in rows on the wood table beside him. I wondered if George had made wooden plugs to fill the holes such bullets might make in him.

"And I take 'Lahomesh' from a Frenchman I once worked for," Peter

continued talking about his name. "Mr. Sherar pronounces those two well.
I have no problems." He struck a match and lit the new tobacco. "But his
tongue twists around many Indian names of those who build his road. But
he tries, which is more than most white men trouble themselves with."

"'Alice M.' Pretty," Sumxseet said, asking for information in a polite
way. She had softened dried huckleberries with water heated on a wood
stove, topped it with a clop of soft cream skimmed from a large glass jar of
milk. She handed it to me. She had sweetened it with honey. I tasted summer
when I swallowed.

"It is the name Mrs. Sherar gives me. She does not understand my
words," I said.

"Oh?" Sumxseet encouraged.

"My name before is a girl who makes mistakes, hurts many people," I
added softly.

"Oh? You do not look dangerous," Sumxseet said.

"There are no plugs to fill the holes I left. Leaving the name behind is
not so bad a plan."

"Tlhxni is a good place to search from," Peter said, stepping into my
meaning. The draw on his pipe caused a soft whistle to form at his lips. "My
people have fished here for as long as I can remember, taken salmon and eels
and trout. In the summer, many families camp here. They bring their children from boarding school at the Warm Springs Agency." His chin pointed
west. "Years ago the children were taught only by their parents and grandparents, aunties and uncles."

He took another draw of the pipe, his fingers gently holding the woman
carved from smooth white stone.

"Now it takes on the name of the big man, Sherar, who will build roads
and bridges, bring people here who have never touched foot along this rocky
river before. But changing its name does not change what it is, what it has
always been. It is not the name that makes the difference. You will find this
out, Alice M, and then you will feel at home wherever you lay your head."

I hoped he was right.

I waited for spring, the salmon run, and Sunmiet, hoping in her presence
I would find direction.

In June of the year called 1873, almost a full circle of seasons from the day I wandered down the Bakeoven Road to Sherar's Falls, Mrs. Sherar took me as a surprise to the camp across the river she calls Deschutes.

Like a *wada* seed in winter, I waited to unfold in Sunmiet's presence, sure that seeing her would tell me what next to do, would open me wide. Their camp had been steadily growing during the past weeks. From the windows of the inn, I watched experienced Warm Springs and Wasco men tie ropes around their bellies, step out over the falls onto platforms, their wide hands holding huge nets they lowered to the water, then pulled as though against a greedy spirit to catch the silvery salmon.

"Sunmiet told me it had always been called The River by her people," Mrs. Sherar said as we rode two horses across the narrow bridge, then north. "We call it the Deschutes, of course. Sunmiet says we are notorious for always changing names of things, as though that makes them our own. I suppose she's right. There is a power in names."

I remained quiet, still wondering what *notorious* meant, then not caring in my excitement over seeing Sunmiet.

Sunmiet's face lit up in smiles when Mrs. Sherar and I splashed our horses across Buck Creek to the open field beyond. Tule mats and hides covered the lodges that dotted the spring meadow like tea leaves on a table of green. She smiled wide at Mrs. Sherar as we approached, but her brown eyes opened with question when she realized who rode with her.

Like sisters, they hugged, arms open to each other. Then Sunmiet turned to me, a wetness forming in her eyes as she reached out, held me, her arms warm around my shoulders. Her touch felt tender, filled a need.

She and Mrs. Sherar talked and giggled like young girls, called each other by their names. Sunmiet's eyes darted to me with questions she was too polite to ask, while my eyes watched them, listened to the English words they shared.

"I expect another by this time next year," Sunmiet said, patting her stomach.

"You always did like a good time. See how you've made it a habit!" Mrs. Sherar said, squeezing her friend again in happiness. But I saw also sadness in those huckleberry eyes.

"It is the only time Standing Tall carries wood in," she laughed. "Why I take an extra day or two, not just to get close to the newest one but so its

222

father will stay around, do 'women's work.'"

For a time they spoke quietly, using many English words unfamiliar to me. I made out *Modocs* and *war* and *warriors* and *scouts*. Mrs. Sherar gently moved the cradle board on her knees, quiet for a time while the youngest child of Sunmiet formed bubbles in its sleep. Sunmiet worked at tying tiny beads into a design on leather spread across her lap. I ached with wanting such a friendship, someone to share myself with no matter where I lived or slept or wandered.

In this quiet, sharing way, they passed the afternoon, good friends catching up on lives, sharing stories and a meal.

When Mrs. Sherar rode the short distance back to the inn, I stayed, prepared at last to make connection with my past.

In the trade language, Sunmiet told me of the battles involving the Modoc's Captain Jack. People had died. White settlers increased in their anger. I wondered if Lives in Pain still lived.

"One Paiute joins them," she said, and the thought of Shard escaped, living somewhere else came to me, then faded in an instant. "I do not know his name."

I wondered where her knowledge came from, but without my asking she told me of the scouts of Teninos, Wascos, others of her people hired by the army. "They say they have special spirits that let them disappear while you are watching them. They come up in other places, find hiding places, reappear to help the soldiers."

"You believe this?" I questioned.

She shrugged her shoulders. "It is what is said. Somehow they stay alive when others die, come back sharing more news than at root feast."

"And all Modocs are dead?" I asked, thinking of those who rescued me and marked me as lost.

She shook her head. "The scouts let women and children make their way at night out of the lava caves they fought in. Not even the soldiers heard them. But the rest they hunt down. There is no hope for them."

Badger, her baby, fussed. Sunmiet gave him the tail of an eel to suck on, held it while his lips moved like a fish's against it. His tiny tongue pushed against it; his face wrinkled into cry. She nodded and set the eel tail aside. She took him from his board and placed him at her breast.

"Standing Tall says it is sweet revenge they take for the raids the Mod-ocs made on this place, when they took our horses and sometimes children they gave in later trade." She looked down at the nursing child, stroked his dark hair. "I do not think their deaths will solve any future problem. Just promise more. You came to speak of wars, then?"

I shook my head and lowered my eyes.

"I did not expect to find you here, Asiam. Or is it Alice M?" Her eyes looked into mine, but I said nothing.

"They have made a reservation by the lakes," she said. "The army brought in food and blankets, though Wuzzie brought in better. He led two good antelope hunts. The people are fat, though not happy with the fences drawn on paper by the agents around their *wada* seeds and water."

"You know of Lukwsh and Wren? They are well?" I asked, too fearful to ask about another.

Sunmiet shook her head once in agreement. "I thought one day Lukwsh would send word of a blanket wrapping between you and a special one."

She must have seen the pain the mention of this memory brought because she did not continue, breathed quietly. Her long eyelashes fluttered, nervous.

I had planned words to say to Sunmiet, to explain. That I had left on my own, had decided to reach out as Sarah did to enter two worlds; that I had a task, too, to find my people, the ones who first left me behind. But her mention of the stronger state of the people since my leaving and of what I once longed for took my words away.

My heart was heaviest because she had not spoken Shard's name. Her choice confirmed his death for me, for her people never spoke the names of those who died until the mourning time had passed.

"You have been there. Know about Wren...and others," I said after moments of silence.

"Only what I hear," she said and shrugged her shoulders.

Her older children came in, then, and sat on the mats. Badger finished eating, and she rewrapped him, tucked the blanket tight around his chubby arms, made sure the black moss pillow had an opening to rest his head. She laced the strings with one hand and hummed a lullaby as the baby fought not to close his eyes, gave in.

"They are well?" I asked.

She set the board down on a stack of hides and reached for her bead-work, a hummingbird half finished, her fingers always busy. She pushed a red bead onto her needle and held it with her calloused finger.

"Much change comes to the lakes. It is said there will be a war there to punish raiders. Or perhaps they will band together with the Snakes and resist the soldiers. Or maybe go quietly to the reservation. Either way, it will not be well for a band with so few warriors."

So few warriors. Her words confirmed my fears.

I had planned to show her my gold necklace, to tell her that I had some-thing now that linked me to my past and did she know a way to use it in my search. But the talk of wars and what might happen to my people—the people—and the cloud around my leaving made me itch to go.

It was where I thought my journey from the lakes would take me, join-ing Sunmiet's band. I believed that here I'd blend, could forget about my shame but still belong with what had become familiar. But Standing Tall entered and said through his silence and his eyes what I already knew: this would be no place to leave my shame. I was still different, should go.

"You will come tomorrow," Sunmiet said.

Standing Tall grunted, scooted Ann and Ikauxau from their places, folded his long legs before him. Sunmiet rose.

"We should have many fish to make ready for the drying racks," she said. She set her beadwork aside to serve her husband wind-dried salmon, broke off another piece she handed to her oldest son. "If Standing Tall does his part," she added and smiled.

"Mrs. Sherar has tasks for me. Men come to form a new bridge and I am asked to help with cooking. Travelers come, too. There are animals to tend…"

"Hands will always find worthy tasks," she told me. She held my fin-gers gently as she spoke, turned the palm over, and I wished so much for her to tell me what to do, where to go, where my life belonged.

"It does not exist in one place or in other people," she said. "What you look for is not found out here." Her arm arched wide to indicate her lodge, the land surrounding, the people of my future and my past. "But here," she said, fingertips tapping her heart. "And only you will know it by its name."

I felt her strength and a warmth flow into my fingers, into my soul. She spoke next of more than hands when she offered encouragement for my journey, all that anyone can really give another.

"You must travel on your own, trust the trail and your Spirit. They will take you and your hands where you belong."

I started to share my deepest fears with her, ask specifically of Shard, when I heard the cry rising from outside, my intentions interrupted.

"Sturgeon!" the voice shouted with happiness. "Sturgeon!"

And like others in the tule-covered lodges, we tumbled out to verify the news.

"A sturgeon! At the falls. Bring your backs and hands, and we will have a feast!" the boy shouted, sent by his elders to gather hands in strength.

Standing Tall out-distanced each of us with his long legs and had already tied the rope around his middle by the time we reached the river's edge. A long line of men and boys braced themselves for the effort at bringing in the huge fish larger than a yearling so rarely seen this far from Nch'i-Wana. A wide Indian, a Hupa called Fish Man, had walked down close to the falls, ropes tied to him but still his feet were firm to move across the rocks slippery with spray. From this closer view he shouted directions, and nets were tossed, looking more like children's string figures extended into rivulets of runoff than the heavy cordage meant to snatch a large fish from the river.

Shared effort landed the fish that required fifteen men to pull it up the steep bank. Someone brought a gun to shoot it, to take away its suffering out of water, and a cheer rose up that sounded much like a song and prayer of great appreciation for what the Creator had provided.

"Now the work begins," Sunmiet told me. "To dig a pit that large will take some time in this rock place. But yum-yum! When that fish is buried and cooked, we will have a feast not equaled for some time. You go," she told me, her hands motioning me away. "Tell Huckleberry Eyes and her husband and all who stop there to plan on eating fish without bones this night."

And so I had a reason to disappear, not talk further of my future, to take uncertainty and old sorrows with me while I gathered others for the feast to follow.

On the day the men laid the beams across the river forming the new bridge, Mrs. Sherar shot the kitchen, Sung-li left, and a new direction through someone named Ella came into my life.

I had a part in it. I was not just an end result created by another.

Through my words, Mrs. Sherar learned that Sung-li refused to steam the plates as required. We kept busy at the inn with many men earning honest sweat working on the bridge, at noon breaking to eat large bowls of potatoes, slabs of ham and beef, wiping up their gravy with thick brown bread, holding their sides in honorable burps. So many men worked—some from the reservation came to help—that long boards across sawhorses were set outside to form tables beside the river. Mrs. Sherar and I raced in and out putting food on the table. Sunmiet and her daughter Ann helped serve. A chubby woman named Bubbles, who wore a whining voice and a proud marriage to Standing Tall's brother, poured hot coffee into cups. An old *kasa* took cold lemonade from a side pool at the river, grumbled at the dogs lying too close at their feet. No one sat except the men, who laughed and joked and relived the morning with their words.

After their meal, they returned to lay the second bridge beam. We women cleared the plates, whisked them to the hot kitchen where Sung-li reigned.

Sung-li was not happy. He scowled or whistled but did not speak as we brought in plates and empty platters. I noticed he dipped the dishes into soapy water but did not rinse them as required by Mrs. Sherar.

To help him, I heated water myself, struggled with the heavy iron pot on top the wood-burning stove. But when he saw my plan, he grabbed the hot pot with the edges of his apron, took it outside, and splashed it against the rock wall, steam rolling back to each of us from the red rocks.

"My kitchen!" he shouted at me, stomped back into the room, slammed the pot on the table smashing several tea leaf dishes with his anger.

My feet stepped back. My eyes watched him leave soap and sum on plates he stacked. He tossed me a towel, told me to wipe. I shook my head and then ran from the room as he advanced, a cleaver quickly lifted to his gripping hand from the butcher's block set in the middle of the room.

Outside, I decided to warn Mrs. Sherar.

"Sung-li not steam," I told her in a hurried voice. She struggled to make the connection, but when she grasped my meaning, she set her mouth in a line as straight as my dark marking.

"He knows how I feel about that. People will be sick for heaven's sake! Well," she said, determined. "I'll be right back. Wait here."

I obeyed for a moment. But remembering Sung-li's eyes, the grasp he had on the cleaver, I ran for Mr. Sherar, who left his bridge and walked with me rapidly with only my words: "Sung-li! Mrs. Sherar!"

Mr. Sherar took strides requiring three or four of mine. He made me wait outside the kitchen, but in seconds I heard Mrs. Sherar shout her husband's name, saw a cleaver's edge slam through the dining room door, then heard a gun blast followed by the shattering of plates and pots and pans between the crack of splintered wood. The scent of burnt powder stuffed my head, and I heard my heart pound loudly as I slowly opened the kitchen door, expecting to see death.

Instead I saw the rock wall behind the house through the hole Mrs. Sherar had placed there with the gun still smoking in her hand. Sung-li hung from Mr. Sherar's tight hand like one of his kitchen dolls behind the oven. On the floor lay a thousand shards of dishes.

"That's one way to steam the dishes," I heard Mr. Sherar tell his wife as he lifted the pistol from her hand.

"Yes. Well. My daughter always did do things a little differently," a woman behind me said, startling us all.

We turned as one to see who had spoken and found two women dressed with dark pelisses meant for calling.

By then, a dozen other buckaroos and Peter's men had gathered like metal to magnets at the sound of the gun. Mr. Sherar handed Sung-li to them, ordered the small man off to The Dalles with final words of warning to those traveling with him: "Make sure he leaves the cleavers!"

Mrs. Sherar's face had been flushed pink, but now she paled. She spoke with precise words to me but in front of the two women: "Alice M. Please take Miss Turner and her companion to the parlor." The shaking in her voice seemed to come more from their presence than her encounter in the kitchen.

I led the women to the darkened room used only rarely, waited while they floated around the room with their smooth-soled shoes swishing on the carpet. I watched the oldest one look through a hand-held circle, peering inside a cabinet holding "fine china" or so she said. I stepped back outside where I was told to go by Mrs. Sherar. "Outside, dear. Help clean that kitchen, would you?"

I left, wondering about the women.

My hands were stacking dishes, puzzling over what I'd seen and heard. Something felt familiar, though I had never met these women. I memorized each person, the look on their faces, the color of their hair. Then I remembered. The younger woman wore a necklace of a dozen beads or more, similar to one once worn by Sarah.

Ella, as the younger woman was called (though her other names were Susan Turner), remained with us when the older woman left. They spent some time in the parlor, and when they emerged, Mrs. Sherar's face flushed again and carried another layer of sadness. The woman left, and I watched Ella step outside the inn.

She gave directions to some men, and I saw wet spots beneath her arms that darkened her jacket the color of choke cherries. Tucks of slippery cloth of her blouse ended where her lighter-colored skirt began flowing over humps and hoops that cascaded like the water falls to the floor. Two hired hands lifted her trunk from the back of the buggy while she watched.

Mr. Sherar helped the older woman maneuver herself onto the buggy seat. She made a little bow with her head, the green plume of her hat dancing forward in the wind. She nodded at him as though they'd met before and once shared deep conversation, then slapped the reins against the bay's rump and rode away. Mrs. Sherar did not even wave to the older woman when she left, and I wondered if she didn't say good-bye because she planned to see her soon again.

"Mrs. Herbert is her mother," Ella told me speaking of the woman who left, "not mine."

Ella had invited me into the bedroom that would be hers, placed sweet-smelling clothes into the dresser drawers. Her blond hair curled softly around her face. She had probably lived fewer years than I, but she seemed at ease in this place, acted older and wiser.

"Mine, too, these past years. I don't remember much about my real mother." She bent her slender body to her trunk, lifted out lace and freshly laundered skirts. When she turned, I saw the bulk of her yellow hair bound beneath a circle of cordage not unlike a duck net. She saw me looking at her in the mirror.

"It's a snood," she said, patting the netting. "I can do your hair like this, if you'd like." She shrugged her shoulders when I did not answer.

She removed a dried herb spray still fragrant from between the folds of a red and black striped dress with a frayed hem. Tiny petals barely visible fluttered to the carpeted floor. Fingers with chewed nails picked them up.

"Tidy, tidy, the sisters always say."

She sprinkled the petals back into the trunk, looked up at me, embarrassed, a perfect dimple forming in her cheek as she smiled.

"You're a quiet one, aren't you?" she asked, looking at me in the mirror, and for a moment I wondered if we might come to know each other, might share fingers pressed to each other's face in friendship.

"Beautiful widow's peak," she said to me, then bent to straighten clothing in the drawer.

"'A clean person has a clean heart.' That's one of their favorites," she said next, "along with 'cream rises.' And about adversity and trouble they'd say, 'Rise above it, child' or 'Laugh and the world laughs with you; cry and you cry alone.'"

She held her hand to the air as though speaking to a group, the way Sarah did when she spoke of San-fran-cis-co.

"They had a hundred of them. Funny how they pop into your head at the strangest times."

She did not seem frightened and yet her pace and pitch reminded me of magpies, chattering.

"Here, sit beside me and tell me about yourself," she said. She patted the bed next to her, smoothed the yellow stripe of the Hudson Bay blanket as a place for me, and I wondered if she really wanted to know or wished through her words, instead, to buy distance, cover who she was with words the way I did through silence.

"Of course they also made us memorize dozens of scriptures," she continued as though she had not just asked me to sit and talk. "'God hath dealt to every man the measure of faith,' Romans 12:3. Or how about 'nothing shall by any means harm you.' I like that especially, myself." She stood, placed some lace squares in one of the two small drawers at the top of the dresser then stopped, hands widespread in the air before the mirror. "'Notwithstanding in this rejoice not, that the spirits are subject unto you; but rather rejoice, because your names are written in heaven.' Luke 10:19 and 20."

Half of what she said escaped me, her words running together like a team of unbridled horses. But I heard the word *spirits* and something about *names*. Still, before I could ask further she had moved on to other thoughts, other actions.

"I guess I'm ready for what comes," she said. "Neither work nor worry can keep me from the future." She sighed deeply looking into the mirror, leaned into it to pinch already rosy cheeks marked with a dimple, then turned. Fingers with red knuckles smoothed her skirts over narrow hips, clasped each other in front.

"And I promise after supper to slow down enough to let you talk. You're sure a quiet one, Miss Alice M. Interesting clothes you're wearing, too."

She was true to her word and following a meal of corn bread, fried locusts and some of my fresh-caught trout seasoned with joyous smiles and hugs between Ella and Mr. and Mrs. Sherar, we did talk. Or she did, mostly, back in her room.

I learned her mother once nursed Mr. Sherar back to health following an accident near Canyon City while Ella was a toddler. And some years later, Ella's mother died leaving a wish for her and her sister to join up with the Sherars.

"Not to be," she said, circumstances with the name of Mrs. Sherar's mother, intervening. And so her sister lived with a family in Eastern Oregon while she lived instead with Mr. and Mrs. Herbert, Jane Sherar's parents.

"Our Lord bounced around some, too, as a baby," she said. "Sent to live with Egyptians for years. Guess that means we can live in strange, new places, too. Sometimes when we feel we're in the wrong place, that's where we're really supposed to be. While he was hiding with his parents, evil men killed babies just to find him." She shivered with the thought. "Glad I don't have to live with someone's death on *my* conscience!" She giggled then covered her mouth, dropped her eyes in a look of shame. I did not know where her look came from, but the words reminded me of my own.

"Mrs. Herbert is a good woman, though demanding," she said, changing the subject. She lifted the necklace of glass beads from around her neck. "It's sad she and her only living daughter do not get along, and I know it's all over me, but I'm powerless to do a thing to fix it. 'All in the Lord's time,' as the sisters would say. And now Mr. Herbert has passed on. He was good to me, like a father. And she plans to marry once again and does not need an older daughter just returned from St. Mary's school hovering over honeymooners. She has a son to hover over, anyway. I'll miss Baby George, all right," she added, her fingers twirling the beads. "He's actually almost grown, just hates being called 'the baby,' don't you know. But this will be a good place for me until I marry. I suppose that's what you'll do here too?" she added almost as an afterthought. "I notice you're staying in the family quarters…"

I wondered if she thought we might be rivals over the Sherars' affections or of some same man; I hoped she might become my *hitse*. It had not occurred to me to wish to marry, find someone *here* who might form with me together. I had other things to take my time.

Ella's eyes drifted over the room, took in the starched lace curtains, the flower-painted water pitcher and bowl, the glow of linseed oil on freshly polished wood. She touched her snood again, opened the little bedside drawer, fidgeted finally into the silence.

Still, it was her wondering what my plans were, why I stayed here at this place that caused her to pause and me to bravely take the next step in my journey.

Some might say it foolish to ask a magpie important questions, that they do not listen well and give poor answers. But looking back, I think we shared a bond—two without mothers, two on a journey somewhere else—that let me trust this woman-child.

Into that silence of a young woman on the verge of change, I put my question, hoping she would answer.

"I wish to know your Spirit's name, the one people speak of when they wear the crossed bars and beads," I said, nodding toward the drawer where she had placed her necklace.

"Land sakes!" Ella said, then slapped her hand over her mouth as though she'd bitten her lip. "I do apologize for my profanity." She removed her fingers. "It's just that I didn't expect such a considerable question from someone who looks so, so…"

"My mind isn't," I answered, not wishing to be discounted.

"No. Of course not, I didn't mean that. It's just that I thought you were much younger, wouldn't be thinking about such things. At least I'm sure *I* didn't until not long ago, not even with all that influence of the sisters. It was just a place to go to school." She smiled, "Or so I thought."

"So what is the name? That Spirit?"

"I guess you'd say his name is Christ," she answered, said in a tone as though he were a close friend not yet introduced to someone new. "But people call him by lots of names. Holy Spirit, Savior, Son of God. He is God, too. It's like he's all in one." She patted my hand as she continued, warming to her subject. "Confusing at times, I'll say that. I just call him Lord."

"What do you have to promise so he will talk to you?" I asked. "What does he demand if you make mistakes, cause another person harm?"

She looked at me, hesitation on her face. "He doesn't *demand* anything. Oh, he wants you to put him above all others. But I mean, I don't *do* anything except believe in him. Anyone can talk with him. Once, long ago, I told him I was sorry for all the mistakes I'd made. Listed them on my fingers. Well, my toes, too," she said and smiled. "All the bad things I'd done and things I'd said that hurt people. And I asked, 'Can you take all that on and free me up?' I didn't have to sacrifice anything, not really."

"You did not wait for him to find you?"

"I thought of it as someone held captive and then told to leave. All the old things were forgotten and forgiven. And future, too, as long as I kept talking to him."

"This is not within my understanding."

"Doesn't make much sense, does it?"

She began unlacing the high-top boots she wore, so her next words were spoken into the floor, muffled. "Oh, I don't mean to say I don't still do regretful things. I still hurt people's feelings with my tongue. And I get discouraged. And I often feel lonely, do you?"

She didn't wait for my answer.

"But this Spirit, the Lord," she continued, "he can't be pleased by just making perfect decisions. He isn't interested in that. Boy that feels good!"

she said wiggling her black-stockinged feet, and I was unsure if she talked about her toes being freed from her shoes or the generous nature of her Lord.

"He gave us this gift, see," she continued, pointing with her shoe as she talked. "He was dead three days. That's why the crossed bars have a man hanging. It's him. How he died. But then he came alive. That's the other cross, an empty one."

"My chain had an empty cross," I said, the memory coming from nowhere.

"Did it! Where's it now?"

"The crossed bars are gone, but I have the necklace. I hope it will help me find my mother or father."

"Do you know where they are?"

"I do not even know who they are. Or were."

"I know where my mother is," Ella said, quietly, "and that I'll see her again someday because we both believed in the same things. It helps me when I feel like I don't belong anywhere. I know she's there making me a home."

The discussion had gone into a place unplanned. I had not meant to discuss my longing with a stranger, had not thought her words would touch that thirsty place inside my soul. Maybe the gold chain I wore was a bridge not to my parents anywhere in this world, but assurance for finding them in the next. I think that's when my searching for them really shifted, when I began another journey.

"And that nothing God wants to have happen," Ella had continued to talk, "can be ruined by other spirits or people or events. He's in control of everything. But for now, we have to live in this life." Her eyes gazed around the room. "And it could certainly be worse."

She looked me in the eye, then, and I did not lower mine in shame. "He's there," she said. "But don't ever talk to someone that doesn't sound like him." She whispered, as though she shared a secret, "That could be trouble."

"How would I know?" I asked. I thought of Wuzzie's power, the water babies, the spirits of the rocks and trees, the marshes, the spirits of the dead who hovered or came back when names were spoken out of mourning. The possibilities for error were as endless as the cotton fluffs falling from the trees.

She sat quiet for the longest moment. She put her shoes together in a tidy row beneath her bed, clasped her hands in her lap, and sighed before she answered. "I guess you just ask him to let you know, hit you upside the head like an ornery mule. Get your attention in case you wander off listening to the wrong ones. And keep near, of course, so you'll recognize his voice when he calls your name."

"Keep near?" I could not imagine that such a powerful Spirit would call me by name.

"You know. Sing your songs. Or pray. That's how he turns you around. And you listen to him, to his words and the ones written about him. And the sisters say he speaks through places and people and troubled times, too. Why, coming to live with the Sherars was something I had prayed for, for just years! Something I wanted so much and figured I'd never have. Then when I least expected it, here I am! Maybe just for this conversation."

She smiled, patted my hand gently. "Just be a good listener. Mother Superior would have my hide for not remembering the exact words of one of her favorites, Romans 8:28. But it's another promise that if we listen and do what he asks, everything will turn out well. Just find the purpose he has for you and trust him to help you accomplish it. That's all."

She shrugged her shoulders, put her palms out as if to say, "It's as simple as that."

I was stunned by the magnitude of the gift that Ella spoke of. And while I added only silence to the conversation that continued about her plans for the next day and beyond, I remembered what she told me as the most significant of the knot of leather memories I still wore around my neck.

ATTRACTIONS

FOR SIX YEARS, I HAVE LIVED AT SHERAR'S BRIDGE, watched it grow, gain a flour mill, warehouses, a toll bridge to pay for work the Indians do each day on the road. At times, I surprised myself as I blended old ways with new, was reminded of Lukwsh's pot fired with old shards and fresh clay. In the pot I was becoming, I recognized flakes of uniqueness if not beauty; a keen edge if not wisdom; strength, despite the broken chips that marred my past.

By day, I helped with simple things such as making beds, weeding tender vegetables I planted in a plot beside the house. Peach trees planted near the inn announced spring with their fragrance and a gentle rain of blossoms. In a natural ledge high up in the rock wall, Mr. Sherar directed men to carve out a wider space and filled it with dirt so after climbing tall ladders, we planted a sweet grape arbor halfway up the rocks, safe from curious deer and chewing rabbits. At the far end, Mrs. Sherar permitted me to cultivate and harvest herbs and special plants that eased toothaches, brought poisons out of boils, helped sleepless people find rest after a long day's travel. My hands were helpful. My longings lessened, and my pot felt full.

The Sherars invited me to leave the river some, join them and Ella on buying trips to Tygh Valley, The Dalles. Once or twice we steamed to Portland, making our way along the Columbia. For the first time, I heard the swish of wheels that lifted a thousand pounds of fish to canneries that dotted the wharves like sticky flies to uncovered salmon. On board the ship, a few women nodded their heads of plumed feathers, treated me as though I did not look awkward or out of place wearing a *tibo*'s dress over a beginning bustle. Total strangers tipped their hats to me and smiled. Ella and I both blushed at this gentle state of being noticed.

"You're eligible young women," announced Mrs. Sherar. "Careful who those smiles attract."

During roundup and sheepshearing, a dozen buckaroos or more filled up bunkhouse beds, ate hearty meals I helped serve three times a day. Sometimes, after supper, they held their hats in hand and asked me for advice as I dropped a fishing line into the river, brought home strings of chubs. The presence of my company seemed desired—or perhaps my fishing skills.

Like kindles of kittens, travelers stumbled off stages on their way to and from Canyon City and points beyond. I anticipated their wishes, ignored the looks of curiosity they gave me when they saw chains of colored beads grace my neck or commented on the beaded belt that held the split skirts I liked to wear not just for riding.

Visitors and buckaroos, travelers on a steamship, Sunmiet's people across the river were all curiosities to me, formed a tapestry of blends, all shape and light and color, not unlike the photographs I saw in one of Mrs. Sherar's books painted by someone named Renoir.

I watched these visiting people with my eyes. I smiled. I saw how they used their hands to speak to bolster up their words, how quickly they made decisions, acted as though each new day belonged just to them. I did not unfold myself to them, never sure how much acceptance they would grant to a young woman who wore a dark mark from her past and carried it with her.

Still, I opened up to some. A seed needs water. It was an act permitting both satisfaction and some sting.

Most guests at the inn spoke as though I was not present, did not exist, was just a spirit hovering to pour more coffee, clear their bread-wiped plates. When they left, I wiped up snow and mud left by their boots set at the door, slipped cattail fuzz (to dry up moisture) inside moccasins Mrs. Sherar asked all guests to wear when they slipped their feet beneath her table. I was like a moth near light, wanting to be close to gather in the news they brought yet fearful of the pain they might just speak of in their conversations over biscuits and broth.

It was how I learned of the people's devastation in the spring of '79, overhearing while waiting on tables at the inn.

"President Grant done gave them redskins some of the best rangeland in the territory, that's what caused it all," said a rancher from John Day country as he cut fresh venison at the table. "Marshes and lakes and that bottom land along the Silvies. Best grass in the territory. They tried to wrap it up inside that Malheur reserve. Wasn't enough space left for those of us who've done the work, carving out a living there on that less than God-forgotten land. Not to mention how it cut into our duck huntin'!" Bursts of laughter from the other guests settled down as he continued, warming to his subject, fork poking the air. "Got nearly a hundred acres fenced in now. No easy task with them Indians skulking around all these years. My granny still aches in her hip from an arrow wound from back in '68."

"That's why there's the army. Did their job, I'd say," reported a banker from the east.

"Yep. Put poor Lo in his place at last," said the rancher, and I wondered what had happened, what the army did. "Parrish, that first agent? Way too soft on them. Taught 'em things only a white man should do, like blacksmithin' and buildin'. Hired away my best man, Johnson. Never did understand that. And then ol' Parrish couldn't manage those siwashes. Too kind, from what I hear." He wiped juice from his chin. "Now Rinehart knew better. 'Treat a dog like a human and they'll treat you like a dog.' Can't accuse Rinehart of treatin' those dogs like humans!"

"Agents can make or break the reservation, you know. That's our experience taming eastern tribes."

"Paiutes. Snakes! The lot of them. Phooey!" This from a woman with fat cheeks fluffed like a hen on a chair across from the banker. "My husband—he's a military man—stationed at Fort Harney for a time. Those redskins give themselves fancy names, they do. And why should they? Just crude people, really. None of them, in fact, have a place on this earth except as interesting history. I'm surprised they camp so close here." She poked her fork toward the river where Standing Tall and Sunmiet camped. "Must be tame ones."

"Not many o' those left," chuckled a lawman through his thick black mustache. "Old Henry Repeater made a good Indian out of a whole lot of 'em. Course having some of their own act as army scouts didn't hurt none."

"That and the weather. They never should have gone along with those

Bannocks. Even with old Sarah there to interpret, they should have figured something was up. She actually did the army's work for 'em, bringing in that whole band without a shot! No offense, ma'am," the rancher said, nodding to the soldier's wife, "but Genr'l Howard took his time covering those attacks near Canyon City. If they'd a met up with the Umatillas like they planned, we'd all be speaking Paiute now 'stead of the King's English."

"The army made up for the delays," the woman answered.

"Hard to believe as many redskins survived that march as did," the lawman said, leaning back in his chair, thumbs tucked into a stuffed belt. "I wouldn't want to make that trip over the Strawberries during a warm summer, let alone travel two mountain ranges and five hundred miles in the dead of winter. They're tough. Give 'em credit for that." His chair flopped back on all fours. "More coffee, Miss?"

"Dead's what most of them are, squaws and children all," reported the rancher. "You cold, girl? Shivering like a poplar. Ended up marching even those who stayed home from the war. Anyway, that's what shoulda happened long before it did."

"Heard some fellow bought his wife a white mule for a wedding gift and on the way to Canyon City lost the lot of his stock to a band of those siwashes, including the mule." A pause to wipe a dribble of jam before the traveling miner continued. "Found half the white mule cut away on the trail some days later. Only part of the stock—or his wife's weddin' gift—he ever got back!"

Guffaws followed. The army wife covered her mouth with her fingers in a fit of modesty. The subject changed, chairs scraped against hardwood floors.

I was at a loss to speak. A heavy stone hit my stomach. My mind sought memories and voices, the whistle of a grandmother to her hawk, a young man fishing with his dog, finger-talking with a child no longer able to hear. These were people hard to control? I pushed back a sense of helplessness, swallowed, felt a mix of anger and despair that sent me running from the room.

Mr. Sherar had learned some of it when he found me later near the falls, eyes red, fingers squeezing the leather knots draped around my neck.

"They're calling it the Bannock War but sure if the Paiutes didn't get the

240

worst of it," he said. His voice was soft and low. "Not unlike the Irish takin' on the Brits. Word is the Malheur band never intended to fight, just wanted that agent Rinehart to make good on his word. 'Stead they ended up shot at and herded into the Rattlesnake Creek fort like cattle. I'm sorry, Alice. They marched them to Washington Territory couple of days after Christmas. Most Bannocks high-tailed it to Idaho. Strange business."

I felt a well of sadness that spilled onto my cheeks. I wondered who survived and who lay dead. I even fumbled with a pang of pity for Wuzzie's loss of power, his loss of face, if he still lived.

"Ye knew some of them, Alice?" he asked, and when I nodded he said, "Thought as much. Took them to Fort Simcoe, near Yakima. Lots of casualties, I'm afraid. Especially to the women and wee ones. No blankets, they said, and people already starving. Gets cold in January."

"Those who live...?"

"They'll hold them. Prisoners of war, of course. More like walking dead. Who knows what ruin took their minds on a march like that?"

"Perhaps death was a gift," I told him, sounding dull even to myself.

"Sure and it is to some," he said softly before I fell back into a silence.

I had days and months to wonder if Lukwsh and Wren, Grey Doe, Willow Basket and her baby, and all the rest survived. I pushed down the shame I felt that I was safe planting, weeding, harvesting in season, warm in winter, unfolding as a seed myself while I heard how they were forced to live—or die—like falling leaves scattered by fierce and evil winds.

Without knowing it, they had blessed me in sending me away. I did not endure what they did. And so the stone of guilt hung heavier around my neck. All old losses hovered around my bed at night, wetting the pillow and my face. Only exchanging thoughts with the Spirit allowed me to fall fitfully asleep.

In the mornings, I woke, still seeking to forget. *Does your crying help? What work is there for you to do?*

"I can hope for them," I said and prayed that through Sherar's Bridge, my labors and my songs, I would be ready for my purpose when I found it.

My hands occupied themselves, a way to make the mind forget. Outdoors, I tended animals and their injuries. Neighbors brought their ailing cats or dogs my way to see if I could offer them some comfort or a cure. And once word spread about a bullsnake I claimed named Slick, visiting children always asked if they could watch me call him from the grass. They giggled and gasped with wonder when I struck a spoon against the ironstone dish, watched Slick's diamond skin outline his slither from the bushes beside the house. Easing, without hurry, he made his way to a bowl of sugarmilk I saved for him.

"How'd ya teach him that, then?" said a boy with brown dots on his nose.

"When I leave the bowl outside," I told him, "I see him come, once. After that, I always tap the sides. He teaches me!"

"I didn't know you could tame snakes," the boy challenged.

"He is not mastered. Just chosen to trust I will not harm him." The boy gazed at the snake. "Marmots can be tamed, though. If they are taken young in spring and treated like a pup. One will follow you on a string and be your friend."

"How d'you catch 'em?"

"Let your dog help," I told him, remembering the joint efforts of a shiny black dog and me. "Pick a place to corner them when the mother is missing."

My heart lifted at the look of wonder that crossed the boy's face, the way he skipped away, shared these secrets with a friend.

My efforts with animals required no great skill, only special ways of listening to how they looked or moved. People told me what their "Freddy" did before he hurt his foot or what "Little Napoleon" ate before he became so ill, but those words did not speak as loudly as the tiny ways the animals talked. Their eyes, their whines and barks, or the way they set their bodies, moved their feet, the feel of their fur, the wiggle and warmth of their skin. Their language was not silent, but like many people, only missing words.

When Mrs. Sherar told me there were books that I could read that might help animals heal, I was stunned. So in Portland, she took me to a cave-like building full of musty smells and quiet carpets and people bent with muffled coughs. She read to me in a whisper experiences of a healer put down on paper, not just remembered in a mind! Memories of people I did not know, would never know, things that happened in a time no one alive could still remember. We were allowed to take the book, to borrow it, she said as the ideas inside it did not belong to us.

On our return trip, I held the book like fine china on my lap, gloved fingers pressed across its pages. Ella said as in passing, "God's words are in a book."

My eyes looked to Mrs. Sherar's to see if this was true, and she nodded her head. Twice in one day I was stunned. That such a sacred Spirit took the time to write things down for simple souls such as mine was beyond my comprehension.

I learned to read, then, sitting next to Sunmiet's Ann and others in a class conducted by Mrs. Sherar, helped out by Ella.

"Let them teach needlework and farm chores at that reservation school," Mrs. Sherar said, her nose raised as though she had smelled a varmint behind the butter churn. "We'll spread your minds, not some manure from the calf barns."

We gathered daily for a time to read. "Cor-o-na Coff-ee Blend," I said, my finger moving along the name of the green tin Ella carried from the kitchen shelves.

"What is 'blend'?" I asked, and she told me, to my delight, a word that had strong meaning in my life.

"Roy-al Bak-ing Pow-der?" read Ann, handing the dark can to Mrs. Sherar.

She nodded. "Excellent!" as happy in our learning as in her teaching. Stories from a children's book soon found their way inside my memory. Once I even read a Scripture verse all on my own that Ella showed me, though I still struggled with its meaning. "Let all that thou doest be done in love."

And then we worked on making letters, writing words ourselves that someone else could read. Mrs. Sherar was a demanding teacher, enlisting Ella in her cause. But they encouraged, were a patient pair. They also had no difficulty with us peppering our lessons with our Indian phrases.

"Learning those words makes us students, too," Mrs. Sherar said and told me later it was one small way she could take revenge on the boarding school teachers who would not let the Indian children speak their language while at school.

"It is only the very strong who do not forget the words that allow them to communicate with their *kasas*," she told me sadly.

Only the memories of the very determined are not washed away with time.

"We are all students," Mrs. Sherar reminded us as she rubbed out the words on the dark writing slate at the end of our lesson, "and should always be. No matter where you are, no matter how frightened or how bored, there is always something new to learn, something to help yourself with. Or someone else."

Sometimes in the evening while I mixed dried herbs quietly at the dining table after the guests had all retired, I wondered at my staying in this place beside the river as though I waited. It reminded me of the time I waited for my bones to heal, how that happened because others tended me, brought me food and water. There could be no greater sign of loving, I told myself, than having healed bones to show or noticing the way a painful edge of memory was worn down to dull by the kindness of another.

I watched the Sherars, observed the ways they tended each other, the intricate thread they wove all through their lives. In an evening they might argue with the vigor of the ninth pig at suckling time over some small thing they later did not remember and then laugh while they tenderly massaged each other's aching feet before the nighttime fire. Then as though they sent a signal without words, they decided together to say goodnight, douse the lamp, and head for bed. They filled each other up, and I was pleased for them, felt a lonely ache inside myself. I pushed aside the feeling, didn't want to think that my listening Spirit wished for me to go through life alone.

I watched other families, too, saw Sunmiet's grow, and in one night learned that the gathering of Sunmiet and Standing Tall had shattered. I had no means to comfort Sunmiet when her husband struck her, cut her, marked another victim of his "corn spirit consumption" as Ella said. I did not know what to say.

Sunmiet escaped from their camp to the Sherars' inn where Mrs. Sherar gave her what she needed: a friend and understanding stated without advice. But Standing Tall's *wehe* sliced a pain she never healed from, though she lives still beside the river when the salmon runs. I could do nothing, could not stop Standing Tall from disappearing on the very night their youngest child was born. I was not even present.

How odd it seems to me now that all that happened on the night I first thought of being married to an owl, though not the way I did.

I was charmed at first. All of us were.

It began when a red-haired someone claiming the name of Dr. Crickett arrived on a Wheeler Stage, all smiles and sparkling blue eyes despite the muddy conditions of the road, the rugged trip down the grade from The Dalles. He carried a crying cat he called Spirit in a cage.

Unlike many whose loud and boisterous ways sent me quietly inside, I loved the flood of this man's words that reminded me at once of several people gathered in a wickiup together, sharing joys and laughter. His great laugh bubbled up from his large belly. His eyes were dressed with childishness and joy. And while his clothes looked a tight fit, legs cut high above his boots, jacket sleeves shorter than his shirt, he knew so much and willingly shared it with me—with all of us—I soon forgot his oddities. And of course, the cat calmed down as soon as we released it from its cage. Oddly, it just wanted to be held.

This Crickett made it easy to ask questions, to answer those he asked of me. I could unfold myself with him because he built no barriers to his heart.

"Doctors have to be good listeners," he told me and touched my hand, a pleasing feeling I did not mistrust. "Good ears are more important for healing than good hands," he said, wiggling his ears with his fingers.

He was to spend just a night or two on his way to somewhere else. And this whirlwind left on the red-and-yellow Wheeler Stage. Then when the morning dishes were all steamed, I heard the cat wail in its cage and saw it carried once again by Crickett striding down the Bakeoven grade, returning to this place as though he had nowhere else to go.

The light feeling his returning brought me held confusion in it, too. His presence captured all my thoughts, and I wondered if this was why I had not moved on, was meant to be here for the meeting of this Crickett I had suddenly attracted.

I was of little use to Tai, the new Chinese cook the Sherars lured away from the Canyon City mines. I felt muddled in my daily routines, spilled herbs.

Mother Sherar smiled at first, scooted me out, and said, "Go! Have a good time," and it seemed to please her that I did.

And so this Crickett—who called himself Spike—let me show him my special walking places along the high bare mountains of Tygh Ridge, my private fishing haunts, silent sites to sit and chew a fresh-baked roll, swallow cool iced tea. I loved the snappy cast of his bamboo rod dropped into Eagle Creek, could sit for hours watching the quiet way he worked a deep hole of the White River or how he drifted his hand-tied fly of bucktail and silk thread into the shady Deschutes to lure out a trout. My eyes caught the way the red hairs of his wrist glistened in the sun and water when he dipped his net to take his catch. There was little about Spike Crickett I found I didn't like.

It was no mean feat that I accepted he might like me, no easy task to let myself begin to care for someone as I once had cared for Shard, no simple chore to say the name of one my memory holds and trust my Spirit prayers to protect me from any ghostly harm for having done it.

Ella falling in love with Monroe Grimes and planning their wedding only added to the fluff of fantasy that filled the air that summer of '79. It culminated the night the four of us (with Spirit, too) drove two buggies up the Tygh Ridge Road to a dance in the Nansene Hall.

My head was so sparkled with the joy of his laughter, the tenderness of his touch on my back as we danced, that when he suggested at sunrise that before heading home we should take a runabout to The Dalles to snatch a marriage license, I agreed, "Swept off my feet," as Ella said.

We brought ourselves back with me still sparkling to tell the Sherars that more than one wedding would be planned. They did not take kindly to the idea, thought it too soon, too unpredictable. They were wary, I suspect, and maybe feeling odd, too, since I was of an age to marry and did not belong to them. Or anyone.

And then before we even had a chance to give ourselves a moment to reconsider, the sheriff came, called Crickett an impostor, a charmer, a patient not a doctor who would have to leave with him.

It was a terrible morning, though the sun was bright and brought out the green lichen on the red rocks. A photographer, Jesse Shep she said her name was, noticed the effect of light and shadow and asked to have her camera unloaded from the stage for one quick photograph of her fellow travelers.

Everyone obliged, and the sheriff even relented, took the cuffs off Crickett so he could stand like other men for one last time.

It was not a choice I would have made for Crickett, not ever, even when I realized that the charming circle had been crossed by the reality of his making. Because before the sheriff could put the cuffs back on him and take him back to the asylum—Spike plunged into the swirling river and was gone.

"Twas a mind sickness," the sheriff ventured, though no one asked. "Fellow never did no harm. He'd get real sad, so quiet his family couldn't talk with him. Other times, I guess he stayed up all night, chattering, thinking out loud, and in the morning he'd be waiting over other people's beds, scaring them to death when they woke, a red-haired giant staring back like a cat! Tells 'em all these grand plans with his nieces and nephews and shoppin' while his aging mother walks behind him puttin' everything back. Quite an interesting case, they said. Sorry to have lost him. Should have left him cuffed."

It might seem strange to some, but I asked the photographer for a copy of Crickett's likeness.

"It'll take some more time to develop," she said, a little rattled I think from being a witness to a death. "I'm opening a studio in Portland. Come next time you're in town. What was his name, so I can file the negative for you?"

"It wasn't Crickett," I said and started crying.

She reached out to hold me. But her care for me as one woman offering comfort to another, or the arms of Mrs. Sherar as she walked me to the inn, or the firm hands of Mr. Sherar as he held me to his chest and stroked my head could not remove the weight I carried, could not set aside the guilt attached to me.

One more loss because another stayed for a time with me. He could have traveled on to where the sheriff might not have ever found him, but he had stayed, for me.

One more disappointment. He had charmed me, wasn't who he said he was, and I risked believing him. I thought that we belonged, one to the other. How could he do that? I wondered to myself. What was wrong with him? With me, that I attracted such distress? I had thought Crickett was the answer, was what my plan was for, to partner up with him, become his wife.

But I was wrong. I had misunderstood, or perhaps I had made it up.

I would belong to no one, I decided, then no one could charm me, no one could send me away, slice my heart two ways. I would not belong. That was the safest place.

In the days that followed, Mrs. Sherar watched me from the corner of her eye. She found moments to speak of subjects better left unsaid. She spoke of losses while we churned. I think to help me know that other people lived with wounds well hidden.

"I had three brothers and sisters who died very young, within days of each other," she said. "It was the worst time in my life. I still miss them. And my mother...I know it was hard on her, but she accused me of causing it. And I hadn't." Her voiced defended as though she were still a child.

"Maybe she looked for someone to blame besides herself," I said.

She looked at me, and her expression held surprise. "Perhaps you're right, Alice. Perhaps you're right."

At the river, she would sometimes start a conversation that would lead to wondering how I was, whether I could talk about my Crickett yet without it salting a hidden wound. Seagulls squawked at each other, plunged at the base of the falls seeking salmon bits and bugs.

"Sunmiet says we must forgive ourselves as well as others," Mrs. Sherar offered. She tossed a line into the river. "I think my mother did not forgive herself, let alone me. And I have work to do in that regard." She sighed, dabbed at her eyes with her apron. "Knowing doesn't take away the sting, now does it?"

We sat a time, and I suspected she wanted me to talk, yet she let me hold the silence. She spoke then of other disappointments, her unfilled hopes.

"You know, Joseph and I think of you as, well, almost as one of our children. At least your being here, walking down Joseph's road, is like a quiet answer to something we both longed for. You will always have a place here, Alice, always belong here. Nothing will ever change that. Not anything you do or say, nothing. I hope you know that."

I believed she meant it, and her acceptance gave me confidence to speak of those that I had loved, some who cared for me, who I had failed. I told it as a kind of warning to her, to not hope for much from me, for my presence promised harm. Spike Crickett was but one sign.

"But you can't think you caused his death? It was his choice to stay behind that day. It's what he wanted. We can't be responsible for other people's choices. Being answerable for our own takes time enough."

And then I told her, softly, about Shard, who gave his life for mine and how I harmed the people by my disobedience. And now this Crickett who had left this life because he came back to live in mine.

She did not turn away at the depth of suffering I'd caused others, held me close instead, and I felt the stone of shame I hung around my neck feel one pebble lighter.

"So there was a first love," Mother Sherar said as we walked back to the inn, arms linked like young girls. "I didn't think you old enough to have cared so much. But then I fell in love with Joseph when I was just fourteen."

We were followed by the cat, wishing to be held.

"I think that's good," she said, handing the cat to me. "I know it doesn't feel that way now, but loving Crickett was a gift, one you invited and honored with your acceptance. What you must remember is not that he deceived you or 'charmed' you as you put it, or any of us. Or that he had a mind sickness you couldn't cure. You didn't do one thing on this earth to make it worse. But that he loved you and wanted only the best for you." She stopped then, turned me to her so I faced her piercing eyes, her mouth, her words. "And you gave something to him, too, Alice, by loving him so deeply before he died."

It was a strange feeling to be a part of someone else's filling, taken from what seemed an empty storehouse of my own.

"Each ending is also a new beginning," Ella said one evening just before we lowered the lights to go to bed. "Like a circle, really."

It was a memory knot from her sisters, I suspected, though at first I could not hear her words of comfort and new hope, could only see the charming circle and the consequences of it being crossed.

But I looked for the new beginnings.

Crickett's passing gave me practice in my praying, to take away my grief, not let me think I caused only pain.

"It isn't your fault if someone chooses to end their life," Ella told me, patting my hand.

She knew so little.

"And if it were, you've already been forgiven for it anyway."

I think of moving on. *Gather farther, stay out longer, and do not return.*

Above the river, east, beyond the rolling breaks, I rode several miles on a good mule I traded from Mr. Sherar in exchange for my work. He was sure-footed, this mule, made his way around the boulders tumbled in ravines, walked in quick-quick steps where deer browsed, then twisted toward Hollenbeck's point. It was a spot that Peter said still showed the marks where immigrant wagons were held back by juniper logs years before. And I could not ride by there after that without looking for the gouges that marked the bunch grass ridge and shallow soil, though thirty years had passed. Some marks of troubled times lasted a lifetime.

On top, past the Buckley place, I rode into dimples of land, noticed plowed fields of homesteaders beginning to dot the distance. By evening, I turned the mule, faced west, and was free to watch the sun set against the white mountains. The wide expanse reminded me of the desert. I surveyed the red and creamy streaks melting like butter across the horizon, spilling across the ravine of green grasses that flowed like a river marsh and marked this place.

Mother Sherar had found this marshy spot, directed me to what she called the Finnigan Place located along the Dalles-Canyon City Military Highway on the east side of the river. It was not far from Ella and Monroe's ranch, and so she often rode a little farther past their place when she visited them, to this green river at Finnigan. She did not yet own the land, but had set her heart on it. Stages still changed teams there, stopped for fresh spring water, the green grass available to stock like an oasis in a desert land.

I rode alone that day to let myself enjoy the high, wide-open spaces that flowed like a lake beneath the Cascade Mountains. There I watched the wind make waves across the grasses that grew breast high, reminding me of the marshes near Malheur. Fed by an underwater river, the area stayed green long into fall when every other piece of ground in the area was covered by a hot and drying brown.

The cat named Spirit traveled with me in his cage of willow tied behind my saddle. He liked the ride, I decided. He let the breeze blow his long gray hair back around his flat nose, round face. "A Persian look," remarked Mrs. Sherar, who tolerated the cat, preferred the dog.

Dogs' ears always stood alert when Spirit was around. The cat used his charms, walked close to Peter's cattle dog, lifted and sassed its long tail beneath the dog's nose as it swiped by him on the way to water and food. Spirit came to a whistle-call, not unlike a dog. He slept often on my bed, my chest mostly. And at the first crow of the peacocks, if I did not rise, Spirit pushed his paws ever so gently on my eyelids and tap-tapped, pulled back, and waited. If I was too slow to open up and see his green eyes staring, he tap-tapped my eyelids once again, a dance he continued until I said his name and opened wide my eyes to celebrate the day.

He was a great mouser. And as long as he was held often, he did not wail or whine even when forced to ride a mule while lying in a cage.

We rode often to this Finnigan Place the spring after Crickett met the water, the year after the Wadaduka people were forced to march to Yakima. My feet sank often into the green that reminded me of soft mud when I once dug for tule tubers.

I rolled my bedroll out, made a circle marked by powdered lye to keep the snakes from crossing, and built a low fire inside the circle. The cat joined me in the bedroll, and I counted the stars that flickered until I fell asleep.

I found this Finnigan a dwelling of welcome, a place to heal, made all the more so when I discovered roots that were familiar.

"These are *tsooga*," I told Sunmiet.

She had joined me the next day, she on a slender horse, me on my mule. They grazed now side by side on the lush grass, the horse hobbled, the mule, herd bound, willing to stay close by. Children and other gatherers from Sunmiet's people dotted the side hills, too, above the grassy field. The soil was skimpy on the sidehills, barely covered rocks that stuck like noses out from the ground.

"Our willow sticks dug these near Dog Mountain," I told her, my chin pointed to the foliage. "I am surprised to find them here, so far from the lakes."

"Oh hayah!" Sunmiet said, the fringes on her hide dress and the ends of her long braids brushing the ground as she squatted. "We find good roots in surprising places."

Yellow and purple flowers, low green and pinks crept over the pebbled earth. A faint smell of wild celery brushed the air, soft as a baby's breath. Geese called in the distance, heading north.

"This one you show me?" Sunmiet stood, sank her *kapn* into the ground still soft, not yet baked hard by east winds and sun. She leaned her root digger back, bent to pull at the short green foliage, lifted the hard, dark tuber from the earth. "You call *tsooga?*"

"Grey Doe used that word."

"It bears the name *lukwsh* in our language."

"Lukwsh? Like her name? It is the name of a root that you know, too?" I am pleased with the connections, flooded with a thousand memories Lukwsh's name can bring.

"We are like a large family," Sunmiet said, "scattered everywhere, like the roots. Some know us by different names. But we are nourished by the same sun and water, began with the same Creator." She brushed at the root, raised a musty smell of wet dirt, inhaled it. "We argue and disagree and gossip about each other like magpies. But if anyone is troubled, we defend them as our own."

"Not if they belong to different bands," I said with some bitterness. "Look how the scouts led the army to the Modocs, how others helped against the Wadaduka. Some hurt without intending, but still hurt. No," I said with certainty, standing to look at the cold snow glistening on Mount Hood. "If they do not belong, they are sent away and not invited back."

Sunmiet bent to dig another root and placed it in the woven Sally Bag that hung at her waist. She risked a thought then, spoke it barely above a whisper. "I am sure Lukwsh would be pleased to see you, if she lives, no matter what has passed between you."

Her eyelashes fluttered on her high cheekbones, in nervousness, I believe, for having suggested something so directly, not using the gentle circle ways to help me find my thought. She retrieved another root, rubbed the black skin off between her fingers, scattered the seeds it bore to replenish the land.

My mind stayed quiet.

I watched red-tailed hawks dip into the air above the lush fields that flowed like a river toward the road. I heard their high-pitched whistle as they eased beyond, dipping and diving in a dance that took them along the green ravine for as far as my eyes could see. Sunmiet pointed to a scrubby juniper where we could sit in shade, then started walking toward it.

"I am not welcome," I told her. "This is something that I know will never change."

"'God began,'" she said, and I was surprised because she spoke as though from something memorized, "'by making one person. And from him came all the different people who live everywhere in the world. God decided exactly when and where they must live. God wanted them to look for him and search for him and find him though he is not far from any of us.'

"You have heard these words?" she asked, sitting down with a gasp of air. She continued when I shook my head no. "They are what I remember from a reading, from the Christian's black book. But it sounded like words we believed. Maybe I have even mixed the words, but the meaning is the same. I think they are said for you, Asiam. We are all of one family whose steps are guided, if permitted."

We sat for a long time before she spoke again. "You would be forgiven for whatever it is you believe keeps you away, Asiam. Perhaps your leaving was your path. Maybe for you to help them find their way back, their tools to find how God wished them to be."

"They are a memory in a place where I do not belong," I told her, wishing it were not so.

"Sometimes our memories charm us, Asiam," she said softly, stroking the cat who jumped into her ample lap. "They keep us inside fences of our own making."

I felt the breezes of a hot spring day. We sat side by side in a silence broken by Sunmiet's new direction. "We must look for tools to take such fences down, Asiam, or we will end up like pronghorns: dead inside a charming circle we were too frightened to walk beyond."

HAMARTOLOS

Red Moccasin, an Indian twenty years old, who lived a few miles above the agency, committed suicide Monday. The reason for so doing was a peculiar one, and is calculated to overthrow many opinions as to an Indian's character. His sister, who lives in Idaho, had entrusted two or three horses to his care. Being offered a good price he sold the animals and was accused by a half-brother, who lived near, of stealing the horses and appropriating the money obtained therefore. His heart was nearly broken at the accusation against his honesty and he immediately rebought the horses and returned them to his sister, proof that the accusation was false. But even this did not soothe his lacerated feelings and the knowledge that he, an honest Indian, had even been suspected of thievery, so worked upon him that he committed suicide. This shows that poor Lo, contrary to nearly all opinions regarding him, sometimes possesses a sensitive nature, a conscience, and a feeling of self-respect, which cannot bear insinuations against his character. —*Grant County News,* Canyon City, Oregon, 1887

"ALICE, HAVE YOU SEEN MY STETHOSCOPE? I'm sure I hung it on the... ah...thank you. My one poor brain would be lonesome if I had another."

"As your thumb," I said to his laugh.

It was Dr. Thomas Crickett speaking, smiling. He counted on me, during the rare times I left Sherar's Bridge to visit him, to find things he misplaced.

"As always, you rescue me. Now then," he said, holding my shoulders so I faced him. "Let us get our breakfast and then perhaps I can convince you to come with me to the wards. The patients seem to perk up so when you come by."

He is called to care for those with mind sicknesses as best he can in the confines of a hospital's brick buildings in Oregon's capital city.

"If it's what will please you while I'm here."

"Good. Good. Though just having you here is a spree. Only wish it happened more often, Alice."

His smooth hand with shiny nails lifted my chin. He ran his left thumb along my dark marking hidden by the wax and face powder I put on when I visited. I looked into his hazel eyes which expressed more than a wish, looked like a demand.

"You promised, Thomas Crickett."

"I know, I know," he said and dropped his hands, disgusted with himself more than with me. "But then I see how their eyes sparkle when you bend your ear to them. How much more animated their drawings are when you stand next to them. They take your comments. I know exactly how they feel because I feel the—"

"We agreed."

"We did, but I didn't expect it would take so long to win you over. Six years!"

He became aware of my silence. His deep voice added more gently, "I'm not accusing, Alice. Truly, I'm not."

"It has worked, I think." My eyes were not on his, examined instead the hemline of my silk dress, the pointy toes of my uncomfortable shoes.

"Yes, it works," he said and sighed. Then changing his mood to lightness, he kissed me gently on the nose. "And I am still luckier than most."

He smiled then, his mouth a pink line buried in a tangle of graying mustache and muttonchops. "I overheard some men waiting at the ferry in Portland yesterday. One said, 'I hope I look as good as you when I'm eighty,' and the other said, 'If you're lucky, you'll be dead by eighty,' and they both laughed."

He put on his frock coat and began to button it, still awkwardly manipulating his right hand, minus a thumb. "I intend to live that long and resist the gout and wind in my stomach and hopefully feel lucky when I'm eighty."

He bent to pat the cocker spaniel, Benny, and brushed lint from the dark wool of his pants on the way.

"I'm a lucky man, truly, aren't I Benny ol' boy? Afterall, I was just a short, fat round man when I wooed your mother." He swooped to lift the dog.

"A fluffy man, Sunmiet would say."

"Fluffy?" He patted his wide stomach that needed no stuffing when he played Saint Nicholas for the children on the wards. "Fluffy, yes," he confirmed wiggling his eyebrows up and down to the dog who panted happily, barked one short greeting. "Your observations never cease to amaze me, Alice. All the more reason I invite your company today."

"I accept," I said touching the abalone combs that held the braid of my hair piled high on my head. I leaned to kiss his cheek. The dog squirmed and jumped down so nothing stood between my husband and me except the separation of our lives.

I'd made the bed in our home—his home—that sits on the hospital grounds in Salem, brought his pipe around, slipped my arm through his as we descended winding stairs, my smooth leather shoes sliding cautiously on carpet, thinning like my husband's hair.

When with him, I wore the leather shoes, the corset that bound my insides tight beneath my added bustle. My clothes confined my body as the tall firs and pines confined my spirit when I spent time in this region of rolling hills, thick underbrush of brambles and berries, and the shadows of majestic timber.

Together, we entered the dining area splashed with light mottled by a spring shower and the huge fir grove just outside the french doors. "It amazes me it can rain while the sun shines," I told him. "Rainbow weather."

"We take what sun we get, even if it comes freshly washed. Especially after the winter we've had. I doubt we saw the sun once the entire month of February! Did you?"

"It is one thing I most like about Sherar's Bridge, how much the sun shines even with snow on the ground."

"You get your share of fog, though," he said. I nodded agreement, grateful we had moved on to speaking of ailments and the weather, subjects without tension, promise, or reminder.

One of the patients had placed hot biscuits on the table, a platter of eggs and bacon for him, and already strained the hops tea I liked to break my fast when I came to this wet valley on the west side of the Cascade Mountains.

The frail-looking man with hunched shoulders served us and smiled and nodded politely when I asked his name and thanked him for the tea.

"Mr. Kaiser will be leaving soon," I suggested to Thomas Crickett when the inmate backed through the dining doors to the kitchen out of sight.

"Has left," my husband told me. "Several times. Lasted almost six months last time. Totally trustworthy here. I think he'd stay out longer if his family could handle the occasional melancholy. They startle about when he seems to want private time, closets himself away. End up recommitting him. As soon as he's back here, helping on the wards, talking with the kitchen staff, chatting with new patients, whatever, he seems to do fine."

"What would he need to feel as at home away from here as here, I wonder?"

Thomas Crickett looked at me, the surprise and admiration of his eyes shot an arrow of warmth into my heart. "And doesn't that just say it all," he said.

He slapped the tablecloth beside his plate, causing Benny to lift his head from his pillow in the corner. "Exactly what I've talked with Superintendent about, that this has become home for him, a place he thinks he belongs and needs to have. We've got to find a way to take the qualities that work here, out there." He nodded his head toward Center Street's sounds of delivery wagons, dogs barking and men shouting, people helping each other get unstuck in the muddy side streets. "That's his real home. Dr. Lane thinks I've lost my mind." He shook his head. "Common sense, that's all it is."

He put his knife and fork down, reached to hold my hand, the stump of his thumb pointing like a pinkie to the tin-pressed ceiling. "Well, perhaps you can help me find a better way to say it so the trained mind of a single-thumbed-surgeon-turned-mind-doctor will have the same level of under-standing as a young wife just visiting her husband!"

"I will do my best," I said with a small bow and tipped up my Wedg-wood china cup steaming with hops tea.

Mine was the strangest life which began on New Year's Day of 1881, when with Susan Ella Turner Sherar Grimes as my attendant, my name changed once again. This time to Mrs. Thomas Crickett.

It was not without some pain I took those steps.

Something lured my future husband to Sherar's Bridge the fall following Crickett's death. He was a smallish man, the real Dr. Crickett. Older than me by several years, his hair had already left him just a tidy row around his head and a few brown whispers across the top. I first greeted him as he stepped off the stage coming from The Dalles. "Pretty Dick" Barter drove the rig, and Dr. Crickett seemed none the less for wear, a rare sight for a first-time passenger delivered by Dick down Tygh Ridge at breakneck speed.

The other passengers were ushered inside by Mrs. Sherar, but that one remained behind. The little doctor—as I fondly came to call him—removed his bowler hat, held it gently in his fingers, one of which flashed a shiny ring. He brushed the dust from his pants with his hat, and I noticed his right hand worked without a thumb. He straightened, stuck a lower lip out to blow some dust from his spectacles still perched like a butterfly on his wide nose. His face, clean shaven, revealed the pale skin of someone not blessed with work to take him much outdoors.

"I'm Thomas Crickett, M.D.," he said, bowed slightly.

I must have blinked, surprised by hearing the name of someone so recently deceased.

"I believe you have a cat of mine," he said, his voice surprisingly deep. "Or so I've been led to believe by the family of a former patient who stopped by this way some time back. It seems he took my luggage, my cat, and even used my name." He lowered his voice to a whisper. "I hope he had more fun with it than I've had lately."

I didn't respond, simply stood wondering why he'd be coming now to see the cat.

"I'm sorry he met an untimely demise."

"He died," I said.

"So he did." One bushy brown eyebrow lifted. His lips the color of choke cherries formed into a gentle smile. "So he did. And said much more directly by your words, I might add. He was a good man, and I'm sorry he chose to take his life. It's always a tragedy when someone loses hope."

He did not condemn. His hazel eyes with flecks of brown were bright and kind and lacked the arrogance created by intelligent men missing compassion. His face wore a mixture of curiosity and care.

"Spirit's near the front porch," I told him, pointing politely with all my fingers, hoping my disappointment at losing the cat's companionship didn't show.

"Spirit?" he asked. His eyes followed my hand, then caught my face. "Oh, so that's what he called him. I'm sorry if you've become attached. I really should have sent word I'd want him back. Once I heard for sure he'd been brought here, I did try to come, but I just couldn't get myself away from the hospital."

He whistled then, and I saw the cat jump from the rock wall surrounding the inn and bound to him. He squatted low and swooped the cat up into his arms, burying his face in the fur. "O Hamartolos! Hamartolos!" he said. "How I have missed you!"

Spirit—or Hamartolos—licked at the man's nose, eyes, pushed his head into Thomas Crickett's neck, bumping and biting. Even from a distance I could hear the cat purr-purring in satisfaction. Dr. Crickett held him away from him for a moment, looking into the cat's face, the long gray tail twitching, urging return to the man's chest.

"Not a bad alias, 'Spirit,'" he said. "But you're still Hamartolos to me! I do appreciate your looking after him," he said then, "and of course I'll want to pay for his care."

"He paid for his own keep," I said. "I will take your bags." I wanted to avoid seeing this exchange of devotion between feline and man, to begin dealing with new loss.

"Oh my, no! I can take that myself," he said, moving the cat with one hand to carry him under his arm, reaching for his valise in the other. "But I would appreciate knowing where my room is and who I have to thank for the wonderful care of my Hamartolos."

"It is a name I have not heard before," I told him as we started through the gate in the rock wall toward the inn, "this 'Hamartolos.'"

"Greek word," he answered quickly, and I could tell he liked sharing the information. "Used by an archer to mean the arrow has missed its mark or that a traveler has left a familiar road and gotten lost along some twisted path. Certainly fits for this one arriving down that reptile road I just came on!" He laughed again, looked back at the dust-covered stagecoach.

"Some translate the word as 'sinner.' Actually, that's how it's used by the Greek Christians. I thought it had a profound sound to it—Hamartolos— like something to be shouted from the stage in a Greek tragedy, not to mention the variety of meanings about taking different trails. Cats certainly do that, now don't they? So it's what I've called him. But Spirit's fine, too, if that's how you know him. I think the names are compatible, however different."

And that was how the courtship—such as it was—of two compatible though very different people began.

Thomas Crickett, M.D., had eastern degrees made possible by his deceased mother's estate and his being an only child growing up in luxury in Boston. He studied Latin and Greek as part of his medical training to become a surgeon. He'd worked in eastern hospitals and had a good practice, he said, when not six years previous, just before his fortieth birthday, he'd lost his thumb to an infection that had started out so simply, then could not be stopped short of amputation.

"Affected both my work and my pleasure," he told me, holding the thumb out for us to look at like it did not belong to him. "Can't play the oboe now either nor shoot birds the way I like. But at least I didn't need it for this new science of psychiatry. May even help me understand better the deficits people think they have."

He worked with Drs. Hawthorne and Loryea at first, in the East Portland Clinic in the medicine of working with people's minds.

"Strange business, really. Quite a challenge for people trained in surgery. Dr. Loryea believes we must actually model how we *live* with our patients," Dr. Crickett shared with us that first supper. "He plays with the children, invites inmates—though I prefer to call them patients—to his home to share meals with his family. They live right there on the grounds, you see. Even pets are allowed." He smiled at the cat curled in the early evening sun beneath the foliage of the corner fern. "There are quite a few who have missed Hamartolos—this Spirit."

"So it is not a difficult place to stay," I said, "like living in a home." We had moved to the porch outside, and at his request I stayed to share the porch swing with him. His slender fingers held a paper fan to move the hot evening air from side to side.

"Like a home?" he said, then chuckled. "If you read the *Oregonian,* you might wonder. But the state investigators who report to the legislature each year always give us a good review. The rooms are spacious. We've only restrained one person at all this past half year and that was a sailor dropped from a Portuguese ship who couldn't seem to tell us what he needed. Batted at invisible things, he did. Netted him a nurse with a black eye before we subdued him." He chuckled to himself, saw the look of uncertainty on my face. "Oh, she's fine. Truly. Just an elbow landing where it shouldn't have. Poor fellow felt worse about that than about being in restraints for a few hours, I'd say."

Before us, near the falls twisting like a rabbit rope through the basalt boulders of the river, a blue heron stood, one leg hidden, waiting for the perfect moment to dip its slender beak into the water.

"Must be like living in another world," he said. "All new environment, food, people, smells. I'm not at all sure we do them justice bringing them to such strangeness. They don't see the world the way we do, can't seem to make sense of ordinary things. Fragile, like porcelain cups some of them. Others strong as oxen but with minds of little children. Something they've seen or where they've been's affected them, I suspect."

"*Kahkwa Pelton,*" I said.

"Excuse me?"

"A Chinookan word. It means 'Like Pelton,' or 'out of one's mind,' foolish, like the one they say was first found confused in this Oregon place."

"Fascinating," he said, turning to look at me. "However would you know that?"

I shrugged my shoulders, too soon to share too much.

He fanned himself and me, grunted in question, then continued. "Dr. Loryea believes in giving patients lots of time and kindness, hopes that will help them step back into the world they left but see it through different eyes, hopefully stronger eyes."

"Perhaps they look at what is offered and decide it is more frightening than where they are," I said.

"Well, that is a dilemma now, isn't it? An insightful observation at that."

"Perhaps bad spirits speak to their souls."

He looked at me, adjusted his glasses, furrows in his forehead. "Well,

that province of healing has been discussed in some foreign clinics we corre-
spond with. We haven't had much luck in using the spirit as a healing source.
Or to quiet some of those terrifying voices our patients tell us about, but who
knows what might work in the future?"

I thought of Wren, of Wuzzie and his dream-like trance.

"It is one of the things I like about this work," he said. "The possibilities. The hope. Have you lived here long, Alice?"

"Almost eight years."

"And before that?"

"I stayed...with friends."

"You work here? It seems you're family and yet...or am I prying?"

I looked at him and his many questions, not sure if I found his interest
annoying or some effort at alliance. His eyes held an earnest look and genu-
ine interest, and so I trusted what I saw, heard my Spirit say, *Tell him who
you are.*

"I do some work here. Also some healing of my own."

Cicada songs washed over the canyon, competing for our attention with
the sunset. Spirit lay sleeping draped across Thomas Crickett's pants, the hot
breeze from the man's fan brushing the hair of Spirit's tail.

"I'd say we were all in the process of some kind of healing," Thomas
Crickett said, seeing past the meaning of my words into the fabric of my
heart. "Human nature to be wounded and still survive."

Thomas Crickett stayed at the inn for only a week that first time, then
made his way to the river every month or so, staying a day or two. He fished.
We walked and sat some on the porch.

"Couldn't leave the hospital to find his cat," Mother Sherar said once,
her voice a mix of joy and tease, "but he's had no trouble making it here
since he found you, even with Dick's wild driving."

And then one day Thomas Crickett, M.D., asked if I would marry him,
come live in Salem as his wife.

I had known somehow the request would come and wondered how I'd
answer. But my own words surprised me when I heard them said out loud.

"Yes. I will marry you, Thomas Crickett, but I will not charm you. You
should know of who I am."

"You sound so serious, Alice," he said, smiling.

We had taken a buggy to Finnigan, packed a picnic lunch of slabs of cold beef spread with whipped oil and egg and pressed between home-baked bread. The scent of it and the fresh blackberry pie wafted up from the covered basket setting before us while we lounged on the blanket.

"What could a little thing like you have possibly done that bears the weight of such a heavy voice?" he said.

He pulled a pipe from his vest pocket and tapped tobacco into the bowl. *"Hamartolos,"* I said.

He looked up, searching for the cat, then by my face realized I had used the word for more than just to call a friend.

"It is a way to describe me," I said, the words difficult to breathe out. "I took a twisted passage, missed the target, as you say. Made choices that caused harm to people who had kept me as their own. And when everyone was injured by what I'd done, they forced me to leave. I made my way here, to Sherar's Bridge. I did not die along the way. But someone did." I grew quiet. "A friend offered up his life for mine."

"Did they take it?" Thomas Crickett asked. "Your friend's offer?"

"I believe that this is so. Only a small attempt was made to bring me back. And I have learned since that the people found a good antelope herd after I left. The people teach that something must be given up to soothe the spirits. I have wondered about this, whether such pain is required. But I believe they took my friend."

He sat quiet for a time. "But surely you could find out for sure? I mean, you wouldn't have to carry such a burden."

I shook my head. "Sometimes, in the deepest place of my heart I still hope, still pray that he found another way. Maybe my prayers are answered and he has gone on to live a good life. But I cannot go back. They told me to leave—he did. In this, I will obey."

"When did this happen? Years ago, I'll wager. Why, they've probably forgotten the whole thing by now. Where were you? What band was it?"

"It does not matter now. I have walked a twisted trail, was asked to leave, to not return. I caused much unhappiness. It is something you should know about me."

"Is there someone you could contact? Who told you about the herd? Maybe they'd find out for you." He became aware of my silence. "Oh, here

I am, fixing things. It is a habit I have, trying to muddle into other people's lives. But it seems so sad to not know. And so much has happened since then; you've made so many *right* choices. Surely no one but you thinks of yourself in *hamartolos* terms."

Thomas Crickett grew quiet to match mine. He picked up my pale hand in his and let my fingers pet the cat who had made his way to us. His silence signaled acceptance.

"I do not believe that I can leave here yet, Thomas Crickett," I told him. "At least not for always, not every day. There is something here I am supposed to do."

"Can I help you with it?" he asked, eager, then pushed both hands to the air in protest. "No fixing things. I understand."

"Once I drifted like a seed carried by the wind, waiting to be planted, always trying to belong. Now I am planted. I do feel as though the pot that is my life is full. But I have not borne fruit. It seems that here is where the sun and rain will bring me into harvest, and it will not matter then what has happened in the past."

"Your work here, what is it, exactly?"

"It is not easily described, Thomas Crickett. I find pleasure in making the calves stand firm after a bout with scours or stopping a cat's cough or relieving a horse's bellyache." Hearing it said sounded so small, so insignificant. "I believe I am of service to the Sherars. Sometimes I am asked to heal people, their cuts and wounds. I tend the gardens and direct those who prune the peach trees and the grapes." I shrugged my shoulders. "It is what I think that I should do."

"Of course I'd want you with me, Alice," he said, leaning back, elbows on the blanket. Fluffy clouds billowed into a sky the color of Malheur Lake. "A person's work, well, it matters, is a big part of who they are, I've found. Lord knows I felt adrift when I lost my thumb. I felt, well, not whole, not complete. It was finding my work at the hospital that brought me from my own slump."

He sat up then, took my hands in his, and lifted both thumbs to his mouth, kissed them.

"Work has a healing quality to it that defies the mind," he said, "however small the hands doing it may seem. We've even proposed to the legislature that there be a farm connected with the hospital, so people can grow their own food, look after land, see the accomplishments of their hands over a season of time. Haven't been too successful convincing politicians that such will work, but we're trying. So I know about having a sense of satisfaction. And if that's here for you, at your river place, now, well…"

He rubbed his cheeks with my thumbs, and I could feel the roughness of his smooth face, the softness of his lips, smell the sweetness of his breath. Beads of perspiration were on his brow, and he reached for his linen to dab at his forehead, his hairless head.

"I have come to care for you, Thomas Crickett," I told him.

"And I, you, my Muffin." He placed his arm around my shoulder, let it lie gently, waited for me to lean into the crook of his arm, to rest my head on his chest. "And I am so grateful you find some small pleasure in my company. Just sitting beside you seems to fill me up."

"I would visit," I said. "But we could wait, until I know for—"

"Perhaps you could remain here until the children come," he said moving me away from him to look into my eyes. "You would want children, wouldn't you, Alice? I know I am somewhat older than you, but I'm not yet fifty, and I can care for you and any little ones we'd be blessed with, truly."

I found myself strangely silent at the thought of children, then warmed by the idea, remembering Sunmiet's babies, Willow Basket's little one.

"I would like children," I said, "sometime."

"Then we're agreed. If those would be your terms, I'd accept them, knowing I'd have at least some moments with you. And when the children come, or perhaps if you completed your…finished your work first, well, then you could join me. And before then, for visits, a week or two at a time?"

"If it wouldn't seem too unusual to you, Thomas Crickett."

"Oh my, I have no worry about the unusual, Alice," he said, smiling, holding my hands, thoroughly delighted. "I know people who are married whose wives live in Boston, and they haven't seen them in years. And some whose husbands have been in the gold fields in California or South America who send home script and Valentines so full of love and encouragement that their wives speak as though they'd just met."

"Perhaps the distance helps," I offered.

"Might allow fanciful thinking to fill in empty spaces," he said. "But I don't think one's presence is the critical thing to keeping a marriage quickened. It's what's up here that does it," he said, tapping his head, "what one thinks about. And here," he patted his heart. His eyes sparkled with eagerness. "Certainly I've seen the ravages of alliances that have not worked, though people have seen each other every day. That's what I work with, actually."

"People who see each other every day who lose their minds?" I asked.

He laughed. "Poorly stated. No, damaged relationships, regardless. The pain of disappointment, failed dreams, seeing ourselves reflected poorly in another's eyes. Many people can't let go of poor treatment by another or forget about past wrongs so they can move on. They choose to live with sadness."

"Perhaps they do not believe their happiness matters," I said.

"They're forgotten souls, most of them. People who believe no one loves them and so they fail to love themselves."

"So you will not object to my staying here for a time? Not think me selfish?"

"I'm the selfish one, to want you with me. But if that's what it will take to have you accept this old man, allow me to change your name to mine, so be it," he said.

"And I would like to share yours. It is always nice to have a naming."

For six years I traveled at least five times a year to share my husband's work and time. And he traveled once a month to visit mine.

Sometimes, in the summer, we took trips east to walk beside the lakes I once called home, slip beneath the fences of the ranchers, hoping no one will see us, shout us away. Hawks who have never been tamed fly high above us. I escort Thomas Crickett, show him how I once walked with Shard and Lukwsh and Wren and Willow Basket, the whole band, perhaps one hundred or more, even Stink Bug, holding nets of tules while we walked to move the rabbits to their deaths.

"Only in the winter," I told my husband. "And then we killed the rabbits immediately so their meat would not be tired. And stripped their hides with our knives in our mouths so the rabbits could give us warmth for winter.

Fifty rabbits for one coat, and many hours of work to sew them. But they were as beautiful as the pictures of a king's cape you once showed me. And warmer."

Once when Thomas Crickett and I walked south of the lakes, we came upon a stack of carcasses many feet high. "Are these from one of your rabbit drives?" my husband asked. "There must be a thousand of them!"

"We always took the meat, dried it, and made something of what the rabbits gave us with their deaths. These piles belong to others. Ranchers rescuing their crops. Their hides went for nothing. Most meat, for vultures."

None of the people were there in places where I once belonged. Only a tiny reserve existed closer to the fort, and I did not recognize the people there. I read the Canyon City paper, looked for evidence of those I might know, but those who were imprisoned lived a scattered life—those allowed to leave.

It might have been a torture for us to travel there, but I had listened to Thomas Crickett talk of healing. I remembered Sunmiet's direction to look for tools to break the fences of the past. I looked for glimpses of Grey Doe's or Lukwsh's life, hoped once to encounter Sarah's band in passing, maybe even Sarah as she moved from the Nevada reservations to Yakima where most Wadadukas still remained.

But I felt relief when I did not see Sarah or her friends, faced no questions about why I now lived a life of ease while nothing of their familiar lives remained.

My husband became a fan of fossil beds and unusual rock formations, and so we traveled to the marshes through the rocky areas and I thought, once, that I had found the rock pile where I buried Flake. Though uncertain, Thomas Crickett stood with me over the grave and let me lean into him, helping me hold the memory.

He did not press me, this husband of mine, did not question my devotion to him or my care. We had not been blessed with children, and so when I was with him, looking out on fir groves and rolling green lawns of the asylum, I could give him all I had to give, respond to his requests with no interference as I did that day when he asked me to share his visit to the hospital wards.

"Something different about today?" I asked.

"Hmm," he mumbled between bites of pork. "A new patient, just arrived from Fort Simcoe. Where they marched the Paiutes after the Last Northwest Indian War. You remember."

"I will always remember."

"So you will." He reached for my hand, patted it. "But for the grace of God, you would have been there too. Hungry, defeated, marched those hundreds of miles. In January! Just the thought makes my blood boil."

"All Sarah Winnemucca's words had no meaning."

"They meant something, all right. General Howard got his Paiutes, the raids stopped, and Sarah kept her grandfather and brother from dying in the Steens. Something to be said for that. Think that's why her grandfather called her the Chief."

"But the ones who lived still lost everything, trusted her to help them out."

"They couldn't even carry on their songs if they hadn't lived, Alice. They have some choice at least, in life's deliveries, as we all do if we choose to live, to manage what we're given. Now, I didn't want to tell you this just yet, but the government has begun letting them go."

I turned to him, surprised by this news, and wondered why I did not know. I read the papers, kept my ears open for any mention of the people or their lives.

"Just this spring. They're being allowed to return to their old reserve. Or other reservations that'll have them. There's very little left at Malheur. An unfriendly agent, Rhinehart, I think it was, there some years? No one wanted to go back to that man's orders. Been paid but had no Indians to agent, if you can believe that government scam. So the land's going back to the government. Anyway, I doubt many will return there even though they can get some small acreage back. I've heard Warm Springs has been approached."

My mind flew to the rainbow of plumed birds, the drifts of swans that settled on the lakes, the snow geese, mud hens, herons, the grasses weaving in the wind. All lost to the people. My stillness told my husband that this painful subject was now closed. He persisted just a moment more.

"They won't be in prison any longer," he said softly. "It'll be better for them. They'll find someplace to belong."

He had walked to the sideboard, filled his cup with coffee, returned to sit beside me.

"How I wish you would have gone there and spoken with some of them. I can't believe they hold you accountable for any of their misfortune, just a child you were! O Alice, I just wish…" He watched my eyes get large with meaning. "I know. You were asked not to return. Well, you didn't, though it seems to me your past has marked your trails for long enough you may as well have.

"Let me change direction," he said, fisting his napkin into a clump. He pushed his chair back and put both hands on his ample thighs to stand, pulled me up, looked at me straight across, eyes above the spectacles, twinkling. "I need you today, Mrs. Thomas Crickett. Will you come with me to meet this patient? She's a quiet one. Rather frail. Indian. Afterwards, we'll have lunch later in the children's unit. You always like that."

"Yes, I always like the children. How is the one you call Michael?"

"Such a charmer, that one," he said, laughing. "Can't see the value in having those Mongoloids live here, if truth be known. They're quite smart, you know. Easily trained. But the gardens and housekeeping would suffer if they stopped coming here. They really make the place run! Michael especially, so active, bounces like water on a hot spider, but I like his energy."

"She is Paiute? Your new patient."

"Oh, no, no. She's been at a hospital in Washington. Steilacoom. Long before the Bannock War they tell me, but she's an Oregon Indian they've determined, and Dr. Lane said we were forced to take her here for a time. Says we'll see if we can make some headway. String bean of a thing. Hasn't said a word. Has a patch over one eye she won't let anyone touch. Can't gauge her age."

"If you think that I can help," I said, pleased by the prospect of entering into my husband's world as someone with resources to share.

"Good. Good. Just what the doctor ordered. Let me get your cloak. You never know when this Oregon sunshine will be chased by rain." He placed the dark wool around my narrow shoulders and said, "Oh look! A rainbow!"

He opened the french doors, and we walked out through groomed lawns, my leather shoes dipping into spongy April earth, to get a better view of the colors. A complete rainbow arched over us, disappearing into the fir grove.

"Have you ever seen a rainbow at night?" I asked my husband.

"Not ever. Would be quite a sight, I'll wager."

"That it is."

He took my elbow, and followed by Benny, the cocker, we headed down the cobblestone path. I skipped a bit, danced around a puddle, while Thomas Crickett held my hand.

"Oh yes," he said, "now that I see you do a jig over that water, it reminds me. She has another unusual specialty, our new patient. She does a charming little dance that seems to seize her day."

HEALING

Skeeta Ike, a Piute, became despondent on account of family troubles and ended his existence by eating wild parsnip at Fort McDermitt, last week. The Indians seem to think that his squaw bewitched him and they will probably send her spirit to meet his.—*Grant County News,* Canyon City, Oregon, 1888.

"YOU KNOW," MY HUSBAND SAID as we made our way to the nearest three-story building of a hospital that now housed more than five hundred patients, "a saved mind is a sober thing."

I walked quietly beside him. He had more to say.

"I find it fascinating that the Greek word meaning to save, *sodzo,* also means 'to heal.' And the word *phren,* 'mind,' when put together with it is translated as 'soberly'—a saved mind or a healed mind. That's what we're about here, I'd say, helping people become sober, having healed minds, don't you think?"

"The temperance ladies would approve," I said.

"That they would." He chuckled.

"You would make a good teacher, Thomas Crickett, the way you put thoughts into new skins."

He squeezed my shoulder. "I fancy myself one at that."

A flash of discomfort crossed his face, and he stopped a moment, pressed his fingers into his stomach.

"You are not well, Thomas Crickett."

"Just a little indigestion," he said, catching his breath. He adjusted his glasses. "Kaiser puts a little too much seasoning on the pork chops in the morning. Perhaps I should pass that by tomorrow, just eat eggs and hash. I'm fine," he said again and shook his head, blinked his eyes, smiled at me in reassurance.

We stepped into the foyer of the largest of the hospital's wings. Pale pink greeted us from the long walls, the high ceilings, even the floor. Swirls of green in the linoleum broke the pink at our feet as did the black seams that marched like river canals down the center of the just-waxed hallways.

But the sights of Thomas Crickett's world stayed with me less than the assault upon my other senses. Sometimes grieving greeted me, mournful songs in words I did not understand, sometimes cries like kittens lost in rainy weather. At times the plinking of a player piano repeating itself to the thumping of the foot pump pounded against my ears like wind chimes buffeted in a gale. Once or twice the music disappeared in the crooning of "I'll Take You Home Again, Kathleen" or some other song spinning on the phonograph sung by voices as unmatched as dogs and cats.

I heard consumptive coughs, the grinding of teeth, and occasionally, screams howled out in rhythms like the clang of the dinner bell at the inn, almost as inhuman, as out of place for healing. And always, the chatter of expressions that reminded me of quarreling magpies or the settling down of irritated snow geese near a rice-laced lake.

"I am always greeted with the feeling of a too tight bow string," I told him, "like something stretched that will snap."

"There's that, all right," he said.

Smells worked their way to my senses: of old food and pots of stew; of cabbage cooking that brought ancient memories to mind; of wastes; of bodies seeping worry and despair despite my husband's permitting the unheard-of practice of patients bathing more than once each week. Smells of cloths not cleaned, carbolic spray and calomel, of candle wax and lye, kerosene, and sometimes, as though totally unbelonging, the freshest scent of cedar from boughs hung on the walls.

That latter scent gave me the greatest sense of rest in this foreign place. It brought in the land, made this cave of bricks and pink a broader place so I did not feel closed in.

"The nurses do their best," Thomas Crickett said to the wrinkle of my nose I did not realize had formed. "We have way too many patients for the building and not nearly enough tubs or staff. Wish we'd elect a Grahamite as governor. We'd have to put up with a platform of more vegetables, whole wheat crackers, and less meat, but regular bathing would be considered a necessity instead of the luxury our elected officials seem to think it is today. It's an old story," he said and sighed.

"I think less heavy food might be better, Thomas Crickett," I told him. "The patients seem to be more active when they eat potatoes without gravy or have light vegetables or nuts instead of stew. I could show them how to make piñon stew. Maybe toast and tea for breakfast instead of always eggs and oatmeal."

"Could be, could be. But we have budgets. And potatoes go much farther than peas for filling up grown adults, m'dear." He patted my hand with affection and dismissal of the subject.

At Thomas Crickett's office, we left my cloak, his hat. He tapped tobacco in his clay-lined ivory pipe and lit it, filling the room with a pungent scent, covering for the moment the less appealing smells. He ruffled through some papers on his desk, picked up one or two, and we headed down the long ward that was really just a wide hallway opening to a room flooded with sunshine, filled with patients of all shapes and sizes, all manner of missing mercies.

"Sometimes this room makes me think of a pink sunrise over the lake, full of all different kinds of birds, talking and primping and floating about."

"It is a sobering place," Thomas Crickett said. "So far our using this day room by both sexes has worked well, even if it's a bit unusual. I think it helps to have some semblance of the real world, not isolate everyone into seeing only men or only women all day long." He nodded with his head, steered me with his hand to my back in the direction. "There she is, by the window."

My eyes found a small woman dwarfed by the ladder-back chair that held her like a duck's egg on the edge of a ledge. She wore a calico dress that floated over her frail body like the linen I used to cover herbs to keep them from a freeze. It bunched up on the floor, burying her feet. Her hair hung in thin strings down her back like frizzed corn silk stained by ash. Small ears poked through; long fingers twitched on her lap. And while her face rained wrinkles as of an older woman, her hands were without the brown spots of age.

She appeared to be gazing out the window toward some ducks pecking on the lawn, but as we approached, I saw that the eye not covered by a patch did not seem focused.

Gratefully, the player piano just beyond her stayed silent and several patients seated with nurses doing needlework or playing checkers or looking at pictures in a magazine called *Life* spoke quietly. No one shouted, yet. Only a young woman dressed in a nightdress and holding a baby doll cried on the sofa between two well-dressed guests who hovered over her like the parents they probably were.

"Just sits and stares mostly, though her record indicates she had some words at one time. Supposedly connected with Bannocks. No family to speak of," Thomas Crickett told me.

Something about the woman seemed vaguely familiar until I realized she brought back memories of Lukwsh and Wren. But more, the familiar despair of her posture, the sense of not belonging, that was what I recognized, remembered in the pit of my stomach.

Thomas Crickett talked while biting his pipe. "Records say they call her Wuzzie."

I looked at him to see if he made some kind of joke without knowing, but his eyes spoke sincerity.

"What?" he said, removing his pipe. "Did I say something wrong?"

"It is uncommon. The name. Perhaps more familiar where she came from."

"It's what's listed," he said, pawing through his sheaf of papers, pipe returned between his teeth.

He motioned to one of the nurses who seemed to be waiting for his signal. She came to stand beside him, her blue-and-white-striped dress swishing behind her, hands folded gently in front of her white apron until she took Thomas Crickett's papers and pipe and stepped back as crisply as the pleats pressed in the bodice of her dress.

He pulled a chair up in front of the woman called Wuzzie.

"How are we today, then?" he asked. "Interesting ducks out there, aren't they? Do you like ducks, Mrs. Wuzzie? Busy little fellows, aren't they?

I'd like you to see her little dance," he said to me as though she were not present. "Maybe you can make some sense of it. She seems to look right through me."

Then to her he said, "Perhaps you'd like to walk outdoors, get a little closer to those ducks?" His voice sounded deep and gentle, his words sincere. And yet I thought of ferrets, how they pushed and probed and meddled.

"Let's try that, shall we?" he said and stood, gently cupped his hand beneath the woman's arm as if to lift her up.

The noise level in the room rose slightly. Words from people at the checkers table were clipped short where seconds before they had been calm. I noticed a man shuffling across the floor bump into a chair, disrupt the person seemingly asleep there, create a shout of protest. Suddenly, two women, painting, disagreed, and their voices increased in pitch until a nurse stepped forward attempting calm.

In that same instant, Wuzzie's fingers stopped twitching, her chin lifted up so slightly yet set like stone in the profile view I had. I saw the cloth at her feet move almost like a breath exhaled and felt her tension more than saw it as Thomas Crickett closed his hand beneath her arm to gently force her to rise.

I felt her shivering inside, invaded, set to bolt and run or die from fright like a sleeping fawn stumbled upon by a hunter. I wondered if everyone in that same room could feel it, feel the tingling as if a lightning storm had entered each of us.

"Thomas Crickett," I said to him in calmness. "It would please me to sit beside this woman for a moment before you step outside."

"Oh? Would it? Well, certainly." He released the woman's arm, looked about, motioned me to the chair he had in front of her.

The room calmed. The woman settled like a sunset. I saw her fingers start to twitch again, and something in the high cheekbones, the gentle arc of her eyebrows, the clench of her lips, softened, reminded me of the life I left.

"I choose to sit beside her, not in front," I told him, sliding the chair so I sat on her right, near the eye not patched. "Sometimes looking closely in a person's eyes creates more challenge than intended, as with frightened animals." I spoke to her then in Chinookan since I did not know her language, her story, or her song.

Thomas listened restless, looked around, smiled at the nurse. I focused on Wuzzie's hands. They continued to twitch, but I saw her blink her unpatched eye, a hazy brown. I caught it shift to glance at me as she heard the jargon words. She dropped her gaze as quickly as an otter slips into the water.

"What did you tell her?" Thomas asked, his voice a whisper.

"That we can sit until she is ready to move on."

"That could take some time," he said, irritation allowed to simmer in his voice. "I'm not sure that's a promise we can keep here." Then in a lower voice, "There is a law now against speaking any of the native languages."

"A person must know you are willing to be with them where they are before they will trust you to lead them somewhere else," I told him. "And they must hear it in words that have some meaning." My bustle settled into the chair. "I am willing to spend the day."

"If you start this, you'll need to be willing to spend more than just *this* day," he said in warning. Suddenly he grinned, as though some good thought had just settled in his head.

I nodded agreement, rose and moved my chair to what I believed a respectful distance from the woman.

"Could take months," Thomas Crickett said and turned. From his nurse, he took sheaves of papers and read rapidly through them. "Don't suppose it can hurt any, but be careful who hears you speaking her tongue."

"Nothing else has worked," his nurse said, speaking for the first time. "I can get her to come with me for meals and into her bed without trouble by just using a single English word or two, but that's it. I think she hears fine."

"All right then," Thomas Crickett said to me. "I'll come by later, take you away for something to eat, if you like. If you need anything, let Arlita here know. She's new but knows her way about asylums. This is my wife," he said by way of introduction. "A specialist in healing in her own right. I certainly don't think she's dangerous," he said, looking at Wuzzie though he kissed my forehead.

He picked up his pipe and walked out. I was hopeful Arlita knew his spoken worries about being dangerous were over Wuzzie, not his wife.

"I'm just over there," Arlita said, pointing, "playing checkers." She stood a moment, looked at Wuzzie's stringy hair broken by the leather strap to hold her eye patch. "That probably should be cut sometime today," she said, and I remembered my first tubbing by Mother Sherar, the terror of the scissors.

"Hair is very…special, something private," I said quietly.

"It'd be easier to keep clean, shorter," Arlita said.

"Perhaps cutting could wait until she knows you better."

Arlita considered this suggestion. "I've enough other things to do anyway," she answered indirectly and swirled toward the checkers group, hands clasped again, her long skirts swishing behind her day-bustle like a bulldog following its master.

We sat in silence for a very long time, Wuzzie and I, watching ducks waddle past the windows that extended from ceiling to floor. We could feel the room cooling off as the sun eased across the sky, leaving the room in afternoon shade.

Sounds changed as patients moved about or left for a meal. Chairs scraped against the floor, feet shuffled to offices with doctors on staff. I overheard smatterings of conversations that might be heard anywhere people gathered: a steam ship, a feast, in the Umatilla House for dining, at a basket social—the voices of a kind of family chattering about the day.

"Wasn't it '62 that Grant replaced General Halleck?" This from a checker player with a mop of red hair.

"Nope. Had to been '64," answered a white-haired man whose hand shook as he reached for his checker move.

"You sure?"

"Was the year Rachel and I got married, and I said I'd got my own general, didn't need Grant. Almost lost the wedding night war after that comment." He chuckled.

"You sure it wasn't '62?" insisted the red mop man.

"Hey, I'm foolish, not forgetful."

I wondered if perhaps I had entered some wrong place, considered why these people should be staying here at all, they behaved so reasonably, so much like travelers or guests at Sherar's Bridge. Like Spike had been.

And then I heard a wild shout and discovered that the argument was not contained, that somehow being right about the date had created some fearfulness, some tension that took the two men talking past a conversation into argument, then outrage.

"It had to a been eighteen and sixty-two!" Red Mop shouted. "You're always trying to trick me. Whole place trying to trick me. I won't be used like that." He picked up the checker table and threw it, blue and white chips scattering across the linoleum like cockroaches surprised by light.

Arlita jumped between the men and spoke in calming words to Red Mop. She put her hand behind her, palm down, to quiet Shaky Hand now agitated, shifting from foot to foot, shoulders hunched, chewing his nails then wringing his hands as he stood behind her. Other nurses ushered patients into calmer areas of the room, took away the tension that an audience could bring. A youngish doctor strode in, talked gently now to Red Mop, who lifted his hands and scowled, then charged from the solarium followed by the doctor, gone until another day.

"I'm not senile," Shaky Hand repeated when things were quieter. "I know when Grant replaced him. I'm foolish, but I'm not forgetful. I'm foolish, but I'm not old."

Through it all, Wuzzie never moved from her position on the chair. Her fingers never stopped their twitching.

I returned the following day to simply sit, and for several days, then weeks thereafter. She sat always in the solarium, already there when I arrived, but Arlita told me she had washed her hair, had moved twice to different chairs once the nurse had left the ward.

"I think that's progress, Mrs. Crickett," she announced, "don't you?"

"Perhaps I should come earlier, see if she will walk with me from the ward. I never saw her dance."

"Let's try for eight, shall we? Just after breakfast?"

And so I did, and for the first time noticed how very frail, how small she was. The leather shoes they placed on her limp feet looked out of place, made Wuzzie unsteady as she moved beside me down the waxed floors of the hall.

"I have an extra pair of moccasins with me," I told Thomas Crickett that evening. "I believe they might just fit her, though she is so small."

My time in the large room beside this woman took me back to sitting in a winter's wickiup listening to stories, watching, listening. I could almost hear the songs and chants, know how Coyote's foolish ways would teach the children, wonder again how Skunk would get his scent sac back, admire the

way the storytellers created the pictures in our heads, kept the parents listening, until the children laid their cheeks down and sank into restful sleep.

"Wrong season," I told myself. "Must not think of skunks and porcupine stories when no snow is on the ground or we'll have ourselves a
blizzard."

I wondered what fences kept her in this quiet prison, remembered what
kept me in mine: fear, shame, dishonor, a sense of being neither loved nor
needed, having little value. Whatever they were, we were weaving something
together, she and I as we sat. We forged tools as Shard once did, tools I hoped
would take these fences between us down.

In a strange and indescribable way, being there was something I was sure
of, something I believed I should be doing. And so I stayed.

I sent word to the Sherar's Bridge post office that I had been detained. I
asked for Carrie, the Sherar's niece arrived from Nicholsville, New York, to
send me the folded buckskin dress from my bureau drawer. Carrie worked
now at the inn and wrote with the package sent that all was well, though she
reminded me that she would marry in the fall in Nicholsville and not to wait
too long before returning to Sherar's Bridge to see her off.

"I have to say, Alice," Thomas Crickett said, "that I am a little grieved that
after all the years of asking I never convinced you to stay more than a week
at a time. But this one, Wuzzie, keeps you here for months. Not that I'm
complaining. I should lift the woman up and spin her around for giving me
time with you. Almost like a honeymoon it's been. I'd say this Wuzzie has
some power even if she isn't choosing to use it."

"Power over me," I told him, smiling, "but it is my choice to stay. I am
interested in her healing, in how God will take her from this statue she is,
give her motion and life."

"God is it you think will do that? I suppose you're right, in the techni-
cal sense. But it's you who've put your energy into her, your efforts that'll
complete the circle I think a healthy person needs, the communion of mind,
body, and soul."

"God breaks our *hamartolos,* then gives the healing. So we will know
peace."

"You're becoming quite the little theologian," he said and smiled. "Think I'll take you to a few less lectures by Dr. Condon and a few more about fishing and food."

"Oh, Thomas Crickett! You say the kindest things."

He laughed then, raised his glass of wine to my tea cup in recognition, belched, a grimace like a warning taking the smile from his face.

"She has created her own world, I suspect," said my husband over dinner one evening in 1890.

"Like she is under a spell," I said.

"Good description. By the way, Kaiser is back after another attempt at life in Salem. Did you know that 'Salem' is an anglicized version of the Hebrew word for peace? *Shalom.* Did you know that, Alice? No? Just found that out myself. It's a blessing word, said at the beginning and end instead of good-bye or hello. Look at all this food!" he said, delighted, the subject changed to his favorite.

Kaiser had set out platters enough to feed a family of eight, but it was just for two of us that night.

"The Wadadukas have no word for either," I told him. "They believe life is a circle. We can always hope to meet each other again so no need to say good-bye. It is a pleasant thought."

"Interesting," Thomas Crickett said. "That farm has certainly paid off in good food."

His words brought the picture of the fields and barns and gardens, sheep, pigs, and cattle that provided the asylum's food as well as a place for hands to make a difference.

"Hard to know what will penetrate it," he said, and I realized he returned to the subject of Wuzzie. His face looked flushed. He belched and apologized. "Same with all the catatonics, which I'd say she is. Or locked herself away from some traumatic event, most likely. I still think the prognosis is good since she hasn't always been like this, supposedly. Good to see her walking with you outside, taking care of her personal needs. Seems like the posturing, the way she holds her fingers sometimes, it's like her hands were dancing now that her feet don't. The longer she remains silent, Alice, the less hopeful I am. You should know that." He shook his head as if shaking out the subject.

"You are not feeling well, Thomas Crickett," I told him.

"I'll be fine. Just that indigestion bothering me again. Should take off a few pounds too, I suspect." He patted his soft abdomen.

"More rest would help you, Thomas Crickett. You work too hard."

He continued eating, and I thought then that his dedication to his work was one reason I had grown to love him. I have watched my husband give his care to patients and staff, write and send the papers that were needed to keep this asylum that is a small town moving forward like a lumbering animal, watched him pace before a legislative meeting, seen his eyes water in tenderness as he scanned a room of patients he had come to care for as his family, helped them unearth their enemies, then find the strength to leave. I admired my husband greatly.

"You are seldom missing hope," I told him.

"Hopeless? Never. Some things are just worth doing," he said. He crumpled his napkin in a ball. "Whether they turn out well or not."

"My friend said that once, that looking for a lost chain was worth it even if we didn't find it."

"Hmm. Working here is like that."

"As is sitting beside Wuzzie."

He reached for my hand across the table and held it. We sat quietly together, sharing silent burdens before I added, "But the healer must care for himself so he has enough to give away."

Thomas Crickett squeezed my fingers, and his look told me he appreciated my concern but would change little in his life to reduce it. So what he said next came as some surprise.

"I'd court you at a steelhead stream," he offered, eyes twinkling, "if you're willing. Have Kaiser pack us a picnic lunch?"

"It is a good plan, Thomas Crickett," I said, standing to kiss the top of his shiny head. "I will get my rod before you change your mind."

Thomas Crickett took me fishing that very day along the Santiam River. It was the first outing we had had since seeing Carrie just before her wedding.

We rode out in a sporty buggy, Benny sleeping at our feet. "Old age slows you down," Thomas Crickett said, nodding to the dog. "That's what I feel like doing, really."

"Let's stop then," I suggested. "I've no need to fish. Just wanted to see you out and quiet for a day. Give Benny a chance to play. Let's lay the blanket and let you rest."

"The steelhead are running," he said. "Still want to get you to one of the coast streams, too. That Coquille River. You'd have a fight there with one on."

"I have always wished to see the ocean. To see where Home Creek and the Malheur and the Deschutes and the Columbia all pour together."

"We've never done that, have we? Next summer," he announced, committed. "Won't be able to drag you away before then, I'll wager. You're more wrapped up in this work than I ever was."

"It is good work to do, Thomas Crickett. And I am grateful."

"You're inexpensive help," he said and laughed. "Making good progress with your Wuzzie. Who would have thought that some lonely Indian woman would have made my life so rich and full. Guess we never know what form some gifts will come in. Wuzzie. She's the one who truly gave me you." He bent to kiss me, and I felt my heart full.

My husband, Thomas Crickett, M.D., did not land a steelhead trout that day. He snagged one with his streamer and shouted for me to watch the split Tonkin cane rod bend like a rainbow from his hands to the crystal water where the fish resisted the catch. My husband whooped and hollered as he made his way along the shore.

"Hope the gut leader holds!" he shouted, letting out silk fly line, reeling it in, waiting and releasing, making his way, lifting his rod over his head to push his broad chest through brambles.

Benny barked and barked. Thomas Crickett shouted back for me to watch when the big fish jumped out of its watery world into the foreignness of the air.

"Bring the net!" he yelled.

I watched his fishing hat bob from the other side of the brambles. I laid my pole down and grabbed the net.

Thomas Crickett remained out of sight, but I could hear him enjoying this sport of skill and capture, knowing he would let the steelhead go if he should finally land it on the sandy shore, perhaps a pause for picture-taking with the Eastman.

I made my way through brambles. On the other side, a quietness met me, broken only by the chatter of robins flitting between willows, a dog barking in the distance. White clouds fluffed their way above the water, promising a later thunderstorm. I smelled mud and Russian olives.

I thought he must have walked some distance, let the fish take him where it would. I smiled, thinking of him doing what he loved. I followed his tracks along the shoreline, making my way sideways through more brambles. I expected to see the sun sparkle on the taut, wet line, hear him shout to me, signal me with his hands.

Instead, I heard the dog's quick, quick bark of something wrong, noted the Tonkin cane beside the water, saw my husband sitting in the sand, his hand clutched to his chest.

"Thomas?" I dropped beside him, kneeling, his face as gray as the shoreline, his eyes deep sunk with pain. I loosened his tight collar, unbuttoned his vest, pressed his head to my chest.

"Stupid thumb," he sighed. "Couldn't get a good hold on him. Lost him, Alice." His breaths came in short gasps. "No need to worry. Just need a minute."

"Oh, Thomas." I felt the tears stinging in hot streaks down my cheeks, could see he lied to keep me from worry.

"First time you ever called me Thomas," he said in wonder, gazing up at me. "Today. Without the Crickett. Sounds nice. Like we're friends that way."

"You are my friend, my most wonderful friend. Did you ever wonder?"

"Not really," he said, breathing harder now, his voice coming in gulps, his face pinched in pain. "Just thought…when you started calling me by my first name…it would mean you were ready to really stay…really love me."

They are the last words my husband of nine years said to me before I felt his body stiffen, sensed his spirit rise above me as I held him, powerless to save him, in the sand.

I had taken to speaking in Paiute words to talk about the weather, the birds that bounced the fir branches when they flitted away. It did not bring her voice nor much change in the rhythm of her days, but the words seemed to give comfort to her. Her shoulders relaxed.

The Wadaduka words brought comfort to another: to me, a healer being healed.

I sat with other patients, helped the nurses who had been like family in my husband's death. My presence was a familiar sight to families visiting. They watched me take out chamber pots, bring in fir boughs to capture something of the outdoors, fresh. Sets of towels and china, books and stereopticons once in my husband's living room now filled these spaces on the wards, made the lives of patients easier, added interest. I had given them, I thought, so Thomas could still touch these lives he cared about, but found I kept him near to me as well when I walked the halls he'd cherished, let my eyes fall on familiar things that once carried his scent.

Most of Thomas's things I gave away when I moved out to make room for the new physician.

"Not much of your things to pack, Missus," Kaiser said as he emptied out the wardrobe from our bedroom. "Know about that. Makes it easier to move on."

And so I wondered if I never gave my all to Thomas Crickett, somehow kept myself from loving him as fully as I could, always kept myself packed lightly, unencumbered by possessions, prepared to leave.

I stroked Spirit, moving back and forth with me, living full-time in the asylum, there to catch the sun, offering purrs to soothe a troubled soul, then off to Sherar's Bridge to soak up sagebrush air.

No, I gave all that I could find inside myself to give, gave it all to Thomas, loved him not as Shard, but loved him still, the most connected I could be to another living being. But I could have told him more, that much shame I carried. I had not known he wished to hear the words.

I found comfort in continuing in the shadow of his work. My thoughts fell often onto Wuzzie even when I was not with her. I thought that reaching her would be the final gift I gave my husband, that good man who gave so much to me.

I prayed for Wuzzie. Told no one.

I rented a small room not far from the asylum, thought of it as temporary until the time my Spirit told me to move on. But Wuzzie pulled me, stretched my willingness to stay beside another until her heart was ready. I watched her make no alliance with me or any others.

Until one day.

Wuzzie had touched her forehead as though her head contained some pain. It was some months after Thomas's death, a cool morning. The sun did not feel warm and clouds threatened, making my own head pound. Wuzzie's action reminded me that dizziness and headaches meant spirit trouble to the Wadaduka, ghosts whose presence called for the Wuzzie I remembered from my past.

"Perhaps you need a *puhagammi*," I suggested, "to take away your bad spirits." I said it gently, almost without thought.

Wuzzie's head jerked to me, her brown eye glared.

I looked away out of respect, but my heart pounded encouragement. She knew the Wadaduka language, had understood the word. She still stared, her fingers twitching, but she said nothing, made no new moves.

"Yes, perhaps a *puhagammi* could bring some comfort," I suggested again, pushing myself closer, the distance of one seed this time, looked closer to her unpatched eye. She did not seem to look straight through me. I saw the change as progress.

On a day long into fall, I noticed several patients making baskets with slender reeds, and I gathered some, spread them on the table next to Wuzzie's chair. In doing so, I bent my face to hers. I was thinner than any previous time, had no interest in food, no one to share it with. I wore no waxy makeup, spent my evenings reading, taking walks to grassy places, to lectures, concerts, or struggling with the words of Puritan prayers.

But something flashed in her eye as she looked at me with a kind of recognition, and I felt pleased she acknowledged my presence, sitting with her as the hours went by. I smiled, sat back down, and began the makings of a treasure basket, surprised my fingers still remembered the way to twine two cords together to create the center that must be perfect to make the basket balanced and then whole. I felt delight as I made the working surface grow with each twist to the right.

My own basket so engaged me that at first I did not notice that Wuzzie's hands had picked up the slender reeds, were weaving too.

What she created stunned me. My stomach tightened both because of what it brought to mind and because she had made it.

Complete, she handed it to me. She did not watch my face. Into my open palm she placed her creation and then said the first word I had ever heard from her: *"Namaka."*

"Yes," I breathed, my body tingling. *"Namaka.* Gift. Look!"

I raised my voice to the patients at the table next to ours, showed the nurses. "See what Wuzzie makes."

They murmured notice before returning to their tasks, unimpressed with the magnitude of her gift.

I turned the weaving over in my fingers, just beginning to put words to something deep inside that hearing the peculiar sound of Wuzzie's voice had tapped. I turned the gift slowly, making sense. She had woven a small dog, not unlike the one Wren hid for me inside the treasure basket buried now with Flake.

"It's lovely," I whispered, afraid to look at Wuzzie. The reeds spoke through my fingers, touched a memory, pushed to an understanding of why fear clutched at my throat. Her gift had signaled one fence might be taken down. Why did my heart beat, then, with sudden fright?

"Namaka," she repeated, her tone more insistent, her fingers pressed to mine.

And then she spoke in a voice so familiar, a voice so powerful from my past that I could hardly grasp the meaning above the throbbing in my chest.

"E tumatza'yoo!" she whispered, leaning to me, her bony fingers on my wrist, now working up my arm.

"Help you? How? I..." I swallowed hard; I could not breathe.

Then in words spoken like a prayer she told me, her eyes directly staring into mine. *"Ka suda nosena wunayoo."*

Her claw-like fingers no longer twitched, no longer wove the reeds. Instead, they moved to cover trembling in my hand. Then she added one more word to make the tears push to my eyes, my palms and arms so wet with sweat that I could smell myself. I heard my heart pound in my ears so that I was not sure she truly said it.

"Thocmetone," the voice sang out, fluttering above my pounding heart. "Shell Flower."

It was my name this Wuzzie spoke, my name she said, her hands on mine. Thocmetone, the name once given me in love.

COMMUNION

Praying Piutes. The Piute Indians were in the habit of paying annual visits to the California coast towns and some of their women married Spaniards, which made them acquainted with the Christian religion.... Several of their leading men and women were baptized each year. Their own religion is not a bad one, and from it to any orthodox Christian religion is but a short step. Strange as it may appear, they are a praying people. *The Princess,* Sarah Winnemucca's book, is full of instances where her people were assembled in prayer, and she herself was wont to pray to the Great Spirit whenever she got into trouble—prayed aloud as she fled before her enemies on a wild cayuse across the deserts.
—*Grant County News,* Canyon City, Oregon, 1890

"WHO ARE YOU?" I whispered.

The woman, Wuzzie, sat silent.

I willed myself inside her spell to find the truth, terrified at what I already knew, had determined in an instant, a hundred details making sense at once. Wuzzie lived alone. Wuzzie kept apart. Wuzzie had no eyebrows, no hair, neither woman nor man. Wuzzie had a voice both high and low. Wuzzie had no history with the band, still grew in power for his mystery—her mystery. Wuzzie knew the ways of charming. Wuzzie willed me far away and then was sent, herself.

The woman, Wuzzie, reached up to brush her fingers across my face. She stroked the marking on my chin. Her touch felt gentle, like the tender touch that lifted me from the rock ledge with a broken leg, helped trade my meager body for a precious obsidian knife. My hand fluttered to her fingers like a scattering spider, brushed against her palm in the Indian way of greeting.

"Who are you?" I whispered again, violating the taboo of questions, peering into eyes that carried recognition for the first time, something old and strong passing between us. The answer to my question lay in her eyes.

"Thocmetone," she said, still making sense of me, then, *"E tumatza'yoo. E tumatza'yoo."*

Her voice shook, but it reached to a place inside my soul, a place once so familiar in its sadness that I almost did not recognize it as the other side of joy.

My heart pounded. I searched her face still wanting to be sure, wondering how I could have sat beside her for this time and not known. I shook my head with the strangeness of it, the futility of wasted anger, fear, and shame. I had blamed so much on the Wuzzie of my memory, given all that power from the past to a shriveled woman of the present.

Her hands clutched at mine, and while I recognized now who she was, a part of me wanted certainty. So I told her with my Paiute words that I would lift her eye patch to see if what was beneath it was the color of a summer sky.

And so it was.

Her eye did not focus, showed damage, streaked and pinched with scars of a wound not treated properly before it healed itself. She startled, shifted her good eye to me, and we touched across the time of separation, shared a hundred burdens with one momentary stare.

I could almost hear Thomas tell me in his teaching voice: "Latin word *com* means 'burden,' a sharing of burdens, and *union*, of course, means 'a coming together.' Perfect description of what should happen in this asylum. Two people, one better able for the moment to bear a burden and in doing so, brings the other along. They come together and are the stronger, able to know each other fully, solve the problem, and then move on."

He did so like solving problems.

Commune with Wuzzie. Is that what I'd been doing these past months, without knowing? Sharing burdens?

She shriveled smaller as I put the leather patch back. Her mouth pinched as though someone had taken stitches to tie it shut. Her jaws clenched. I was embarrassed by my intrusion to her person, my need to know. I was well beyond my skill.

"Let me get someone," I told her, rising, looking for escape.

Her hand grabbed mine, stopped me.

"I'll find a doctor," I said.

She clutched tightly, as though clinging to the reins of a green-broke mount she feared would leave her far behind. But she did not speak again, simply stared at me, and then resigned, she sighed, dropped her hand and head, and returned to silence, growing older as I watched.

I sat back down, frightened now the moment had been lost. I stayed beside her and she settled, sinking into the chair as though no great thing had just transpired. I turned the tule dog over and over in my trembling hands, wondered at this gift, my fears of knowing and yet not.

My eyes sought out Arlita, but did not find her. The others were not people I felt attached to. I was uncertain whether they would believe me when I told them that Wuzzie had the power of words.

I never missed my husband more.

I so wanted him to know of Wuzzie, knew he'd have the answers to what must happen next. The thought of Shard, too, pierced through my agitation and despair, burst inside me like a damaged water basket. How I missed him in that moment, longed for the refreshment his presence would have brought. Tears threatened to pool behind my eyes as I listened to the distant sounds of burdens being borne by other patients, the startling shouts, unnerving laughter, the shuffling of slippers down the hall.

I willed the tears away. Shard and Thomas would have taken action, not sat and wept. Perhaps this was the way each stayed with me, became a memory of comfort, not of loss.

Thinking of what they would advise gave me direction in the morning. It came to me in my small room while I poured hot water into herbal tea and smelled familiar scents.

"Benny," I told the cocker spaniel resting at my feet, "we will spend some time in the past, but I promise we will not stay there. Just use it to make a trail into the future."

The dog lifted one eyebrow at the sound of his name, watched as I fingered the scent of smoked leather knots of memories still worn around my neck.

"As Mr. Sherar would say, 'We'll whip our weight in wildcats, defeat this enemy, sure.'"

The dog wiggled his short tail, raised his head at the hope he must have heard in my voice.

"Arlita," I said at the asylum, "something happened yesterday. With a patient." I nodded my chin toward Wuzzie, seated quietly as always facing the window, her palms up in a posture that would permit a winnowing basket to rest easily upon her fingers.

Arlita waited for me to tell her, hands folded tightly over that apron I wondered when she found time to starch. I took a deep breath and said: "She spoke to me. In the language of my childhood."

Arlita's eyes widened. "Wuzzie spoke?" Her voice moved from astonishment to doubt. "You should have told someone as soon as it happened. Never mind. What did she say?"

"That she needs help, for a bad dream."

"Law sakes alive!" Arlita said in an unsettling whisper.

"And..." I wondered how much to tell this person things that would open up my past.

"And what? Spit it out!"

"I believe it is possible that I know this person from a time before. I may even know some of her bad dream."

Her neck arched away from me; her hands squeezed themselves against each other. "And you just now realized it? How could that be? It's so unlikely that anyone here would actually know a patient."

"It cannot be, if what my husband said was true about where she came from or how long she stayed before arriving here. She could not have been in the hospital before the last Indian war if she is the one I remember. She would have been *in* the war itself, taken from her homeland near the lakes and marched to Yakima and then imprisoned."

"But to have sat beside her all this time...are you certain you have some experience with her?" Her look turned cautious.

I took a deep breath. "She spoke my name. A name given me in a special ceremony that not even Dr. Thomas knew."

Arlita looked over my shoulder at Wuzzie, back into my eyes, searching. "We'll check her records," she said. "Perhaps contact people from her previous hospitalization. Meanwhile, you stay with her, just as you always have." She turned to leave then stopped, her wide skirts rustling at the quick change in direction. "What were you doing differently yesterday?"

"Weaving. With reeds. I wove a treasure basket and she made a dog. Like ones the children play with. She gave it to me and said 'gift' in the language of the people."

"Good. Get the reeds out again. And talk with her. In your language, if you think that'll help. Law or no law. Let them prosecute us for speaking a native tongue." She clucked her tongue in disgust. "I'll talk with Dr. Adams. His is the kindest way. Not taken to quick judgments." And she left to find him.

Beside Wuzzie I sat close, as family, held my memory knots in my hand. My fingers wore the scent of leather as I told the stories from the knots, shared a part of me so personal yet in words I hoped would give her images of snow geese thick in flight against the spring sky, the smell of tule tubers lifted from the soft mud of the marshes near the Malheur, the rustle of wind in the willows. I spoke of children playing, laughing, of Wren squatting beside a winnowing basket, of Lukwsh's warm fire roasting sagebrush gum outside her wickiup. I talked of Flake, the way he sneezed and flushed the ducks to the nets, chewed on my fingers and mentioned a hawk that followed a grandmother.

Like a careful elder, I related the library of my memory, attempted to capture details of the way life moved before I went away, before I walked as one.

Wuzzie did not speak. But she sat taller as though aware of what I told her. When I stopped, she turned to me, and the line of eyebrow that met above her nose pinched less, marked pleasure on her face.

On the following day, I braved the knots that talked of leaving, of losing Shard, of Salmon Eyes and Stink Bug and their chase, of all the shame I felt at having hurt the ones I loved. I recounted the quaking earth, my anger and my sadness, my time of waiting beside the rushing Deschutes River.

She still chose silence, but as I spoke of finding strength with the most powerful Spirit who had words that promised he would never leave, did not demand a sacrifice for making errors, who wanted only love and trust, I saw her face soften, noticed she chose not to clamp her jaw.

"This Spirit chooses to walk with us," I said, "stays behind when people we know are gone."

"The record is a little vague," Dr. Adams said as we stood in the foyer of the activity room. I recognized him as the doctor who came to rescue Red Mop the first day I sat beside Wuzzie. He held a ledger-looking book that recorded events of interest to his patients.

"It does say she came from Washington Territory but not a hospital. From Fort Vancouver. They probably had an infirmary there. But it says she's a Bannock Snake, out of Idaho. Nothing about being—what was it you said—a Wadaduka or a Paiute person."

"Could Thomas have read it wrong?"

Dr. Adams paused, read, shook his head. "Nothing more than that." He pawed through the sheaves of paper brittle now with age, moving them left to right as he read.

"Look there," Arlita said, stopping him. "On the back of that page. Something's stuck to it."

She pulled at the fragile page delicately, as if separating cooked artichoke leaves, until she held a thin page from the past in her hand.

"Ink's faded into the back of the other page some," Dr. Adams noted. He paused to see what he could gather up. "Some reference here to relatives." He read again while I wondered if I could be mistaken. But the name, my name, so few would know it.

"A Mr. Parrish," Dr. Adams read, "says he used to be the agent at Malheur, sent a letter on her behalf, it looks like." His eyes squinted at the script written on paper so thin I could see ink letters like veins beneath pale skin. "Apparently when they herded everyone into Fort Harney, before they marched them to Fort Simcoe. Doesn't say exactly why he's asking. Mixed-up, too, because Parrish calls Wuzzie 'him.' Somehow, what got transferred with her makes it sound like she's Bannock. And it looks like she never went to Fort Simcoe. No mention of it. Just the infirmary in Washington Territory at the Vancouver Barracks."

I held my tongue, did not explain, still too uncertain. I listened to the sounds of patients walking past us, the crackle of cool linoleum beneath their feet.

"That's what this letter is about?" Arlita asked. "Nothing about others who were with her, someone we might still find or contact?"

Dr. Adams sucked on his lower lip, his teeth reminding me of Grey Doe's as he squinted over the record. "Not really. Wait. Someone asked Parrish to intervene, have her sent to Fort Vancouver with a few others instead of Fort Simcoe, though it doesn't say why. Let me see if I can make out that name a little better."

He held the letter away from his eyes. "This ink fades and smudges so easily."

"Let me," Arlita said, reaching for it. "I'm familiar with hen scratchings of doctors so this should be no challenge."

Dr. Adams grunted good naturedly and turned the letter around for Arlita.

"Here, in this paragraph," he pointed as she studied the page.

I watched them pore over the words, but my mind returned to the year of the land quaking, the year I made my way from Stink Bug, Shard, the Wuzzie that was a man. Only a few seasons separated those events from people leaving the rhythm of land they were familiar with, the cadence of moving and traveling, seed harvests and hunts and living on the Malheur Reservation, a place that no longer existed.

Sarah Winnemucca had written of it, too, published a book about the people and their plight that Mother Sherar had sent to me from one of their trips back east.

Even with their choice to blend, it had not been enough for the Paiutes, who had chosen to live as owls. They'd been herded like cattle—the agency Indians who had not raised a fist in fight—made to stand and sleep and starve in snow up to their bellies beside Rattlesnake Creek. The food houses at Fort Harney stood empty feeding five hundred people, and the new agent, Rhinehart, the Methodist minister agent, did not respond to requests for stores of food and clothing. Women and children had only threadbare blankets. And then they were ordered north, Wadaduka people, to prison. A blizzard near Canyon City stalled them. Women, children, and the elders, moving slowly north, broke bark from trees to eat the soft layers beneath. They died anyway, tossed stiff beside the road while the agent Rhinehart wrote angry letters to the government about "his Indians being taken away" and what should he do "with 65,000 pounds of beef that now would spoil."

I am lost to my remembering, recalling without effort the anger I had felt on reading Sarah's English book. So I did not hear at first what Arlita offered when she looked at me after deciphering the agent's letter.

"Please say again," I said.

"I think it says Shard," she said. "See here. Shard Johnson. He's the one the agent writes for. Says he's asked for special treatment of this Wuzzie."

My head began to spin.

"Does the name Shard Johnson mean something to you, Alice?"

"Not possible," I said. "The Shard I know is dead."

"What year would that have been?" asked Dr. Adams, unaware that my world had gone awry. "Maybe this was written earlier."

"The year of the quaking earth."

"He died in '72? Well, can't be him then because this letter was written in 1879. Unusual name, though."

"There were many Johnsons in the Malheur country. One was a black-smith. Shard worked for him," I said, my voice sounding far away even to myself.

"Know lots of Johnsons myself," Dr. Adams said. "Portland's full of them."

"Indian people have taken last names of those they admired. Perhaps this Shard did that," I told him.

"It's the 'Shard' word I thought unusual," Dr. Adams said. "Never heard of it as a name. Doesn't it mean a piece of something shattered?"

"Something once useful that has been broken, yes," I said. "And when blended with fresh clay creates new strength." A world once kept tied up in my memory knots began unraveling.

"There are some others here too, Dr. Adams," Arlita said, bringing her inquisitive eyes back to the thin pages of the letter. "Look."

"Asks that he—keeps mixing that man and woman business up—that he, Wuzzie, be kept with Lukwsh and Wren when he's sent to Fort Vancouver. Guess he wanted those two women together. But this Shard wasn't asking to stay with them. Humph. This Lukwsh woman was his mother."

His eyes lifted to me, this Dr. Adams, then he suggested I take a seat.

"You're pale as a fresh-washed bed sheet, woman! What's the matter?"

I moved briskly to the Methodist Church, my feet splashing without notice through water pooling on the boardwalks. Only later did I realize my wet shoes would remain so throughout the concert as I had neglected to bring my change of slippers; my cloth purse swung empty on my wrist.

The DeMoss Lyric Bards were playing banjos, coronets and singing that night, and I had need of great distraction, a wish for music to take away the startled thinking that had seized that day. I slipped in beside an older woman who nodded her head at me politely, added a smile of encouragement as she patted the seat beside her while I removed my poke.

"They haven't started yet, dearie. Haven't missed a thing. They say they've played for the Russian Czar and even sung in Switzerland, and they're right here. Imagine! I like the message they always give, myself," she added, leaning toward me.

I nodded my head absently, acknowledged her presence, then buried my face in the paper program, though I did not take time to read the words. My world still spun from my afternoon.

Dr. Adams helped me to a chair, and Arlita brought me water. Both stood like night owls caught in daylight, staring at me in wonder.

"Survives hearing a woman talk who hasn't said a word for years and then about passes out from a letter more'n ten years old she says is written for a dead person!" Dr. Adams said. "You know these people?"

I drank the water, sipping slowly both to be sure I did not drift away and to ration time to think.

"I did know them," I whispered. "But something happened. Years past. They helped me leave. And Shard…well, Shard died. Is dead." I said it with finality. "He died the year of the quake. In my place. Because Wuzzie ordered it."

Arlita gasped. Dr. Adams scratched at his face, seeking sense.

"But he couldn't have died then," he said, "not the year of the quake, or he wouldn't have been alive to secure Mr. Parrish's help those, what, seven years later. Must be some mistake, Mrs. Crickett. Either you've got the date wrong or this Shard didn't die when you thought he did. He was still alive, at least in '79."

"Maybe Wuzzie can tell us," Arlita said, "if you really want to know?"

I trembled at the thought and the insight of her question.

Wuzzie would not speak of it, even when Arlita asked. A part of me expected that; it was too soon. When she did, if she did, it would be in the language of the people. And so I sat alone with her again, our hands on green willows I had cut fresh from beside the Santiam River.

"Pussy willows," Arlita called the ones with fuzzy buds waiting to unfold.

Wuzzie's hands were moving quickly forming a treasure basket, and I wondered when she learned to make such women's things having spent much of her life living as a man. Who had taught her how to twist the willows? Had a mother placed her fingers over Wuzzie's as a child, showed her lovingly what to do? Or had she been like me, learning with her eyes, watching others, always seeking recognition by her actions, always longing to be loved for just being who she was?

Her fingers threaded the long strands, and for a moment I was taken back into the time of moving with our Wadaduka band, dogs loaded, making our way to the mountains for huckleberries or south for piñion nuts. We filled our burden baskets only with essentials, carried the baskets on our backs with a tumpline tight across our heads. Shaped like a funnel, the bottom of the basket left little room for stuffing burdens, while the top opened wide so someone could walk beside and see how another's burdens pulled against a tumpline, caused an aching head, and they could better reach inside the opening and lift a portion of another's burden.

"I made a long journey," I said. "Like a seed blown by the wind. It took me to you and then Sherar's Bridge and now here, to be with you. You came another way. But like a seed, there is more to unfold with the right water and wind. I can help you from your bad dream. And you can help me from mine. But you must speak with me. And with the others who are here to help you make your way."

Our hands worked in rhythm side by side with no words to break the silence. But she made a treasure basket that day, not a burden basket, though she wove her willows into a basket larger than most. Wuzzie held it tight when Arlita came to take it from her. She shook her head and clutched it.

"It will be a comfort," I suggested.

"No harm in it," Arlita shrugged as she motioned Wuzzie to her room. As she shuffled out, Wuzzie looked over her right shoulder to see if I still watched. A look of pleasure eased into the crinkled crease of her smile.

So I came to this church where Thomas Crickett often took me to hear quartets of strings or choral groups who filled the air with joy. "Music always soothes the weary soul," he'd said, and so I had come to hear a concert, to put my thoughts aside, listen to the music and the ministry that followed, hoping I would have direction.

It was a night of hopefulness despite George DeMoss's overture which included a detailed rendition of "General Custer's Last Battle" which seemed to me to glorify the army for their errors. But "Sweet Oregon" and "Glockenspiel" and the banjo band and even George De Moss's playing two coronets at once delighted me, though they were not enough to stop my thoughts of Wuzzie and her secrets, of Shard, and wondering about his.

Between numbers, the DeMosses, who had a home not far from Ella and Monroe Grimes back near the green river of Finnigan, shared their walk of faith. George spoke of a seed so small it could hardly be seen, and as he described it, I saw a black *wada* seed, smaller than a dot yet when put together with a thousand more could make a meal.

"Faith," he said above the coughs of his audience, the scraping of slippers on oak, "is accepting that God has plowed a new field for you, torn up all the weeds and dug out all the rocks. And you can plant that field the way God wants you to, not the way you remember planting it before. God makes you new to do all things with him.

"If you have faith as a grain of mustard seed...a mustard seed." He pinched the air. "Imagine how tiny that is. Well, our Lord himself promised if you have even that little bit of faith, almost impossible to see, then no harvest will be impossible for you."

They closed the program with a song that sounded like chiming bells. But it was their gospel tune, right before it, that moved my eyes to tears.

"If you believe and I believe and we together pray,
the Holy Spirit must come down and set God's people free."

I did believe and knew what I must do.

"I will be back," I told Wuzzie the next morning. "But I must make a journey to find out. It will not keep me there. And I leave Someone with you when I go."

Wuzzie acted as if she did not hear me, but she changed the posture of her hands from palms up to gracefully resting one on the other in her lap. I heard her whisper quietly, "Help me."

"I will. It is a promise that I make. And going now is one way I can keep it. But Wuzzie, you are not alone here. I have asked the most powerful Spirit to keep you safe, even in the night. He will set you free, Wuzzie, if you let him."

She turned her head to me, sighed, did not move her hands.

"And Arlita knows where I am. She can find me if something happens. But this I must do next." I brushed her hand, even stroked the side of her face, two touches which she did not resist.

The train rattled its way north, steaming and spitting through the lush fields and tall timber. In East Portland, I boarded the ferry across the Columbia, remembering a time when Thomas Crickett waited here to pick up visiting dignitaries, talked with steamship captains while their crews unloaded passengers and round-top trunks. The day turned brisk, the wind causing me to hold tight my poke to keep it tied beneath my chin.

A cab on the other side was familiar with the road to Vancouver Barracks and took me there after a brief argument about why a lady would be traveling unaccompanied.

"I have reasons," I told him, "and I can pay," a phrase that caused him to tip his hat to me and help me on board. He slapped the reins on his horse's back and started down the street.

He chattered, commented on the scenery as he drove, then: "Took President Hays to this place, I did. Was in '81. He and his wife inspected the barracks. Met with the generals, and Reverend Wilbur from Fort Simcoe came. Even that upstart Sarah Winnemucca. Had the gall to talk to the President, make him cry even, she did, raving on about the poor state of her people she was teachin' here."

"She had a school?"

"She did. Taught them Bannock kids, the Princess did, afore she left south. Started a school there I've heard."

I did not know what I expected to find at the Vancouver Barracks, but not an empty guardhouse.

"All the prisoners of that war have gone, ma'am," the lieutenant in charge told me. "Most transported to Fort Hall in Idaho some years ago. Others to the Walker River Reservation in Nevada. Last one left about four years back. All that's here are some upstarts of our own, just waiting trial. I've heard, though, that some of the Indians got allotments near the old Malheur Reservation. I doubt many from here would have gone there, Bannocks and Paiutes not exactly being on speaking terms, now are they, ma'am?"

"I would see the records of who was here and where they might have gone."

"Well, I know you would, but I don't think I've authorization for that, ma'am. At least not where they went. But the list of prisoners, that's available. And then there's another whole list at Fort Simcoe." He turned to search the glass case that held a ledger book of names. "Most of those folks went in leg irons to Oregon. Who knows from there."

I watched the soldier scan the glass case, being helpful, and for just an instant I imagined him as my brother might have been, serving in the army, maybe with this bright young lieutenant. I wondered about my father seeking his new beginnings, and if there still might be some way to find them, learn their names. I shook my head. There was no sense to dwell on that search. My gold necklace offered the best answer, telling me I would find them in another time and place.

But here, now, was a search I could complete, find out why Wuzzie arrived at the asylum and who else might be alive to claim the memory of that time and free her from her prison.

My eyes scanned the tiny names written in an army clerk's fine straight hand. Single words mostly, sometimes with a chosen second name, mostly Indian, sometimes carrying Christian tones or familiar names given by a white. Bannock Joe, Paddy Cap, D. E. Johnson. No S. Johnson was listed. There were other names, some vaguely remembered, people who came and went, who belonged to the wider band of people and spent more time in Nevada and the East.

Then I saw them, the names to make my heart soar: Lukwsh and

Wuzzie. I permitted myself only a moment of regret that I did not come here sooner.

"This is your list? All of them?"

"Think so, ma'am. Might have missed some, but this should cover it."

"And you cannot tell me where they've gone, each one?"

"Sorry, ma'am. Like to. But policy is I can't without an order." He lifted his palms up in the helpless gesture of a child.

I imagined what their lives had been like here in this foreign place: rainy, wet, no familiar roots, no lakes or marshes or cackling geese to tell them they were not abandoned. The picture troubled me. I could not shake it even as I stepped inside the cab and headed back toward the river.

I crossed back to East Portland, spent a restless night, and in the morning took the train along the Columbia to The Dalles. The next morning, I drank hot tea in the Umatilla House before boarding the ferry which took me once again to Washington State.

The stage ride to Fort Simcoe began the next day and ended with an army officer less friendly, not even willing to let me look at names of former prisoners. He carried the same message about the releases: "Not authorized to tell you where they've gone, individually. But as a group, I'd try Warm Springs. Land grab there back in '82, '83 or so. Lots of locals taking over unused reservation ground. So those mortal enemies, the Sahaptin-speakers and the Paiutes, agreed to share some space to keep the whites out, maybe even wives!" He laughed, didn't notice my scowl. "Must be working some. Haven't heard of any new Indian wars. Almost had our own up here making those Paiutes learn to live with Yakimas. They speak a kind of Sahaptin, too, you know. Never had much time for those seed eaters. Had to put 'em to work digging canals. That kept 'em out of trouble. That and Father Wilbur. Never needed the army to show force as long as Father Wilbur skulked about."

He grinned at this remembrance, coughed uncomfortably when I did not smile nor share his views. He escorted me to the waiting cab.

I was not daunted, was encouraged, in fact, by my discovery at least of Lukwsh's and Wuzzie's names. And I had a plan and knew that hope exists when one can see just one more step along the trail.

"*En,* a Latin prefix meaning 'to be at one with' as in 'encourage.' Isn't that a fine word, Alice?" my husband had said after one of his long days at the asylum. "So small and yet it carries so much force, such power. To-be-at-one-with courage. Sounds so strong, so sure, next to such a little word. What are some other words? Let's see." He strutted around the room, poking air with his pipe. "En-lighten would mean being-at-one-with the light."

"En-circle. To-be-at-one-with a circle," I told him.

"Yes! You've got it. Completely surrounded, at one with a circle. Totally whole."

"Like walking a path that has no beginning or end."

"Like that, yes. I do so love the way words come together," Thomas had said, pleased with the joinings.

I felt at one with the circle that had been my past, I decided, as my head bounced against the leather pillow of the afternoon stage heading south out of The Dalles. At one with the path I walked with my Spirit. I did not know what lay before me on this trail, but I was encouraged. I could face both the future and the past.

THE TWENTIETH KNOT

A GATHERING

Last Sunday afternoon 'Skookum John' and Mrs. 'Skookum John,' excursionists from the Warm Springs reservation, accompanied by half a dozen braves and the usual number of dogs and cayuse ponies arrived in our city, armed with a permit from the Indian agent to remain absent from the reservation until September 1st. They were waited upon by a number of citizens, each with a frown on his face and anger in his eye.—*Grant County News,* Canyon City, Oregon, 1891

"SUCH A JOY TO SEE YOU, ALICE!" Mother Sherar said as I squeezed myself out of Pretty Dick Barter's stage to stand before the inn. The midday sun burned high above us, alone in a brilliant blue sky, casting an unusual warmth for this late September day. Mother Sherar held me at arm's length, looking me over, delight in her face, her eyes like black marble, searching.

"You survived the ride down Tygh Ridge! I always think that alone is worthy of a celebration, not to mention its bringing you home."

Dick tossed down soft bags from the top, carefully lowered my Tonkin cane rod while he sparred with Mrs. Sherar. "Don't you be complainin' about my driving. I've been on that road with you, and I wouldn't share that experience with any brave man, let alone an innocent woman!"

"Oh paw!" she said to him, waving her arm good-naturedly in dismissal, and then to me, "You've become quite the lady. Still that baby face. Never thought I'd see you in puffs and pleats. And in purple! The rage, they tell me, and it looks so good with that dusty blond hair of yours, thick as yellow jackets on a persimmon. Kind of perks up those pale cheeks, that purple does. Well, listen to me prattle on. Come, come, let John here take that bag. That's what a chore boy's for, isn't it, John?"

She did not wait for him to answer, but hurried in her quick-quick steps toward the inn. She told two other passengers who had exited the stage before me to remove their shoes and put on a pair of moccasins left at the door.

She took my arm in tow, then turned back, eyes searching. "Did you bring Benny? Don't see him. Always room for another dog."

"He stays in Salem. At the asylum. My week is full of travels. I think he would resist the cage."

"Might howl the way Spirit used to," she laughed. "Wait till you see the size *that* one's gotten. Sure keeps the mice down. So glad you decided to let him stay with us after Thomas's death. He'll be as delighted as Joseph when he comes back from that road of his. You'll brighten up his day, sure, such a nice surprise."

In my old room I felt myself a guest, hung my jacket on the hook, paused for a moment before the mirror. A younger face than what I felt stared back, not like that of a woman who had experienced slightly more than thirty years. My eyes had a tiredness to them but reflected hope as well. Few wrinkles lined my face. I placed my tongue behind my teeth and made my cheeks and eyes and mouth relax. My hair, the color of wet desert sand, was piled high, held in place by ivory combs, the widow's peak a perfect name at this time of my life, a *kooma yagapu*. My fingers traced the marking, touched the knots of my memory draped beneath my pleated blouse. I sighed, hopeful I could face my future tied up with my past.

A soft cry and pressure against my skirt announced Spirit. "You remember me!" The cat eased his way back and forth against my leg, tail up and twisting. He allowed me to lift him, sink my face in his aging fur that smelled of juniper and sage. He nibbled at my chin, a view caught in the mirror that both delighted me and gave me warmth.

Mother Sherar busied herself with passengers' comfort, shooed me out the door. Freed of duty, I walked through the rock wall gate, past the silent dinner bell, to the ladder that reached to the garden ledge high in the rimrocks. I held my long skirts up as I climbed, one handed, my fingers sure on the rungs, always pleased to be above a place. There I sat among the sweet grapevines recently harvested. The arbor flourished. They had made few changes from the way I cared for it. Mother Sherar told me they had plans to build a huge hotel, three stories high. This rock ledge would be the garden entered from the third floor, across a little bridge. Fanciful thinking, to know so far ahead how something will turn out, trust yourself enough to build a garden years before the hotel.

And yet I wondered if I have not known this time would come for me, known it since the day I listened to my Spirit Lord and leaped into the Silvies River to rescue Wren. Since then, since the day Wuzzie first found me challenging, my feet had walked a strange trail that, like Mr. Sherar's toll bridge across the Deschutes, was always lined with hope, even if I did not always recognize the railings.

River sounds washed over me. The water of a hundred streams plunged to the basalt rocks below the falls before me. Empty fishing scaffoldings jutted over the white water while rivulets of river poured beneath them like sparkling braids, making their way back to the main stream. Above, on the talus slopes, I saw men work on the twisting road that still reminded me of a lazy snake in need of constant tending. I hugged my knees, wondered if what I hoped to find in searching would give me help for healing Wuzzie or be a salve for her wounded healer.

"It has been a long time," Peter said when I knocked on his door in the waning afternoon. He was fresh from the road crew, his hands a lather of strong-smelling soap, his dark hair now dusted with gray. "We have wondered how you make your way. Have you eaten?"

"I am well," I told him, nodded to Sumxseet, who smiled at me then returned to pressing dough at her table. "It will please me to join you for fry bread and some of Sumxseet's huckleberry jam. I brought you fresh grape jam and butter that Mother Sherar sent."

Sumxseet smiled, took the gifts. "Good."

"I always feel better when I am near water," I said, walking to the window, peering out through the rippled glass that looked out over the Deschutes. "Almost all my years have given me some time near rivers and lakes. Not yet the ocean. My husband and I planned to go this year." I paused. "But plans change."

My eye spied a wolf spider on the window, one who lived without a web.

"We are sad to learn that death visits you again, so young," Sumxseet said. Flour had settled itself on her cheek. Beads of sweat glistened on her forehead. She looked frail; her legs were thin like young trees, and she wore moccasins over long black stockings that disappeared beneath her often-washed dress. They were elders now, these two.

"Perhaps it is better it comes when I am still strong."

"Perhaps," Sumxseet answered. "Our son George and his Carrie? They have lost four girls. Born and then died. Only their boy lives. But the mother is young and still has courage enough to try again."

I nodded, politely exchanging information about others, how the road work progressed, Peter's growing herd of cows and horses, their work together with his son. Sumxseet dropped the dough into the hot oil. We watched the bread rise quickly into crisp, then sat to eat it, pulling delicately with our front teeth, dipping chunks in fresh beef stew with vegetables they had rescued from the rabbits in their garden.

"I am here to help someone," I told them finally, knowing they would be too polite to ask. "A woman who I used to know at the lakes near Steen's Mountain. She is *Kahkwa Pelton,* though I believe she carries seeds to become well."

Sumxseet grunted as we cleared the table together. "A foolish, feeble-minded woman would have no place here if she once stayed at Steen's."

"She has no history here or with the Wascos that I know of. But she is old now and lives inside a spell that I would help her out of. I am looking for some people who were with her at Vancouver Barracks, some names I know. To see if they came to Warm Springs the years I lived mostly in Salem. Or have gone on to Walker River or farther south. Maybe back to Malheur."

In my telling it, I saw the futility in the search, even with names, even with likenesses, even with artifacts such as letters. The possibilities of where they might have gone and the time passed too long for me to hope to ever find them now, a second family gathered up and lost. I resisted the thought to scold myself for my delay in searching.

"Some of those Paiutes came here," Peter said, sinking into a chair of stretched hides, his meal complete. "They crossed the big river in leg irons, dragging heavy balls of iron. After the war. At The Dalles, the agent had the blacksmith cut them off, ordered wagons so the men and women and children could ride. Both coming and going, those people were herded. Like cattle." He shook his head. "Most went on to Nevada country, some to Burns. Thirty or so came to Warm Springs, to the south end, as far from the agency as possible." He searched for his tobacco pouch, patted his shirt pocket to find it. "But they make hay there. One repaired the sawmill. Some worked the sewing machines and taught at the school. Most are near Seek-seequa Creek. They married and live around." He shrugged his shoulders. "I know a few."

I took a deep breath, came to sit beside him on a small leather stool. I hugged my knees and felt tiny as a child. "Probably they are not the ones I look for."

"It will not hurt to speak their names."

I swallowed. "One is Wren, a woman my age. Thin, kind, always smiling. She had small scars on her face from falling often as a child. She is probably married now, an old mother with children." I made myself sound lighter than I felt.

"With a fry-bread stomach," he said, laughed, then grew serious. "That one is not familiar." He lit his clay-lined ivory-woman pipe. His eyes moved to Sumxseet for confirmation, and she nodded. "Is there another?"

"Lukwsh," I said in a whisper. "She is a special one, named for the root. She lived once at Simnasho or Warm Springs. Her mother or a *kasa* came from the southwest, her father from here. She stayed here. She is a tall woman who makes fine knives and who married a Paiute man who died and left her the children of his first wife, and his mother, Grey Doe."

"This is the woman who is acting foolishly now?" Sumxseet asked. "I can see why."

"No, that one's name is Wuzzie." Sumxseet's insights into families caused my face to smile. "I know where she stays."

"The one named Lukwsh seems familiar. She was a friend of Sunmiet?" Sumxseet said.

"Yes! Is she here?"

"I do not think so, only that once Sunmiet rode to the Malheur Lakes to see her, an old friend. I have heard nothing since that time. But they do not fish as we do, those Paiutes, and there is bad blood between them and Sahaptin-speakers, so people from that desert lake place do not come here much."

Disappointment must have visited my face for Peter asked in gentle tones, "What of the children of this Lukwsh's husband? Do you wish to find them?"

"Wren was one; she belonged to both of them. And there were two sons, his sons. The one living is named Stink Bug. And I have no wish to find him." Disgust rose in my voice and I softened it. "Unless he could help me find his mother."

"And the other?" Peter asked, exhaling his pipe smoke.

"He died the year the earth quaked, the year I came to Sherar's Bridge. They called him Shard."

Peter was quiet for a time. "I know of no Stink Bug," he said, then took another puff on his pipe. "And if the Shard you speak of died, then…this cannot be him. But there is a man. Works at the mill, at the agency. I have seen him when Mr. Sherar and I rode there to order lumber for the flour mill on the White River. He fixes things." He sucked on his pipe, held the smoke, and then exhaled. "His name is Johnson. His first name, though, is Shard."

"He is an Indian?" I asked, my voice as quiet as a secret hope. "Not the blacksmith from the Malheur agency or the one who makes leg irons for prisoners. Or one who cuts them off?"

Peter shook his head yes in answer to my most important question. "He is Paiute," he said. "Caused some unhappiness when he said he could repair the sawmill that broke down. And he could. He may know about your Lukwsh and the others, again?"

"Wren. And Wuzzie."

"I go to the agency. Maybe tomorrow. You could ride along."

"It is a good plan," I said.

But in the night, another plan formed, a safer one.

I worried that the millwright would have no answers and my search would need a larger circle into Nevada, Idaho, places east, and my hopefulness would drain. And I shuddered at the thought, carrying with it a mix of whim and worry, that it might be Shard: a fear he might not wish to see me, a longing that he would.

"Mr. Johnson may not wish the bother of a woman's visit," I told Peter in the morning. "But it would please me if you could ask him if he knows the women named Lukwsh, Wren, and Wuzzie." And then I added, "And maybe, ask also of Asiam."

"You did not mention this Asiam." Peter lifted one eyebrow as he turned from checking the cinch of his saddle. At my silence he took the stirrup onto his horse. "Nor Alice M."

"And if he remembers her," I said, politely stepping over Peter's words, "please ask if he would wish to see this Asiam again, to help the healing of another."

I wait, that is what I do now.

I steamed the breakfast dishes, helped chop nuts and whip cream for the lunch salad, gathered carrots from the garden. My feet took me to the calf barns. I walked beside Father Sherar, who moved with a cane but whose plans and ideas still flowed from him as if his body were inhabited by a younger man. We spoke of lambs and fleece prices, not letting the "depression," as he called it, get us down; of someone named Edison; of toll collections at the bridge and how much money his roads could eat. I was present in these conversations, added and listened too, but most of me stayed distant, waited to hear the hoofbeat of a horse.

Mother Sherar chattered comfortably over tea and biscuits taken at the dining table after supper. Soft moccasins sat lined beside the door, a range of various sizes for passengers to wear.

"Ann works here now—"

"Sunmiet's daughter," interrupted Joseph stirring his tea.

"She knows that," to him. To me, "She has children of her own already."

"Off at a funeral this week."

"In Washington."

"Yakima, to be correct."

"Now don't be spoiling my telling, Joseph Sherar."

He cast meek eyes at her, yet wore a look so full of adoration that I ached in envy, dropped my eyes to not intrude.

Mother Sherar was unaware of his look of love, continued talking as though on a moving train. "An older auntie died. Peter owns land there, did you know that? Anne still hopes to see her father someday. Maybe she will in Yakima. Seeing him again would please us all, really, though what we dream about is usually quite different if it ever really happens." She was thoughtful, and I wondered if she spoke for me. "Funny, how even ornery people are missed when they're gone. They leave an empty space. No one to bounce off of, clarify what you're really thinking. Ornery people do that for you." She sighed. "Makes me think of my mother."

"I think her ornery spirit lives in you, Janie," Joseph said with a twinkle in his eye that attracted a biscuit from her hand.

"Will you stay now, Alice?" Mother Sherar asked me. "It would please us. Spirit's right at home here, liked being left after Thomas's death. The room is yours for as long as you'd like, you know."

"We've missed ye, girl," Father Sherar said. He leaned to pat my hand.

"When I first came, I did not know when I would leave. It is like that now. Something inside will tell me, if I listen."

"Know that feeling, don't we, Mother?" Joseph said, stretching to stand. "Some things just call ye and ye have to pay attention or all your life ye wish ye had and never feel filled up."

"It's how we got here," Mother Sherar said to me. "In what some would say is a God-forsaken canyon. But I claim it as my own, what Sunmiet says is my place of belonging. And so it is, since I was just a child. Feel God's presence here more than any other place on earth. Not once since we moved here have I wondered if we did the right thing. Not that it's been easy. But I've never wished to leave. God has given us everything we needed, right here, hasn't he, Joseph?"

"Aye. That he has," he said, smiling at his wife, pulling her up.

"I wait for Peter," I told them, "and learn from him where I am going next."

"How old were you then, Alice? When you first came here in what, '72? I guessed about eleven or twelve."

"I had fourteen years then, or maybe more. The knots I keep in memory tell me it must have been some time like that."

"Fourteen," she said, her voice wistful as though remembering with pleasure another time. "Lots can happen to a fourteen-year-old girl." She cast her eyes to her husband, who held her gaze.

"Enough to last a lifetime," he added and wrapped her in a hug.

I spent a sleepless night; each waking spurred a prayer. The moon rose full, a harvest moon. It cast its glow on all the plantings, tending, taking time needed to bring a seed to fruit.

Toward mid-afternoon of the second day, I lifted the split Tonkin cane rod from the rack and walked to Eagle Creek, upriver, pleased I thought to pack the rod. My mind had been of no use, my fingers, neither.

A part of me wished I had gone with Peter so I would know my next step, make plans to leave for Nevada or back to the asylum. Another part thought I should leave, now.

I did leave Spirit sleeping on the porch, envied his restful mind, hoped fishing would ease mine.

Eagle Creek rushed over rocks and willow roots, the water making sounds like rainwater pitchered over my hair, flowing into buckets I bent over. I cast the silk line and not the lure, watched the water take it to itself, embrace it. I could almost feel Thomas Crickett's hands on mine. He held this rod so often, loved its balance and its sureness, not believing its expense was an extravagance but a necessity, needed to blend fisherman and rod as one.

The fly sunk below the surface; the riffles took it, made it disappear. The gurgling of river over rocks reminded me of the sounds of Home Creek, the Silvies River, and the Malheur, a hundred knots of memories, listening, seeing fish leap, a glistening black dog sending ducks to nets. My moccasins hugged the wet rocks; toes grabbed tight like fingers.

A tug on the floating silk. I set the hook to secure the pink-sided trout, felt it pull against me as it identified its error. The fish arched in the air, splashed itself and water across a canvas of choke cherry trees and cinnamon rocks. It plunged back into river, pulling deep, deeper, taking line through water then into air again, never quitting, never too afraid to leap or dive in deep, whatever it might take to free itself. I followed it along the rocky shore, wishing for the waders I had seen men wear to take them closer to the fish, let them be one with the river.

I had none but stepped into the icy water, held the line taut against the arcing cane, felt the surge of water swirl linen heavy against my legs, so strong I almost lost my balance, felt the line pull against my arms. I made small adjustments, watched the fish take line upstream, then down.

The effort consumed me, as I hoped. The fish and river seized all I had and gave to me a tiredness in my arms and legs, wind and cool spray on my face, the scent of rabbit brush in bloom. The effort ended in a satisfaction as I stepped backward onto shore.

And when I reeled him in, we were both gasping. The fish lay, his one eye staring, body heaving. His tail still flapped. He lurched, one last hope to take him back to water.

"Such a fighter! You deserve a second chance," I told him, squatting to remove the hook, my fingers slippery with his sleekness. "We all do. Even if we don't get it."

I held the thick body in the palm of my hand, felt the fish gain strength again as I pressed him gently under water. I dropped my hand beneath him, spread my fingers until I felt him come to life, buoyant in the water. He swiveled off. I watched him dive and disappear. My hand made a shade for my eyes.

"Maybe our paths will cross again sometime," I said, almost shouted to the disappearing catch. "Remember me then as the one who set you free!"

"You speak to fish in words I hope you say to me."

I was startled by the voice, though I had prepared to hear it from the moment those years ago when I turned to see him watch me go, felt his eyes follow me well into the distance; from the time I heard him speak to me in dreams out of the pillowed brilliance of the nighttime arc; from the instant I heard Dr. Adams read his name from fragile paper and I believed he might still live.

Prepared, and yet I carried only a seed of hope, only a tiny mustard seed of faith. Prepared, and yet I stood overwhelmed by the depth of feelings that washed over me, the sense of being opened, like a *wada* seed that waited, then unfolded to a world of water and warming sun.

"It pleases me to hear you," I whispered and turned slowly toward the words.

I was aware I shivered, only partly from the wet moccasins and drenched skirt the fish left me, the cooling breeze of dusk.

He dismounted a big bay, tethered it to a willow as I watched. His body spoke experience in his wider chest. He wore jeans and leather boots and a white shirt with thin blue stripes. The starched collar pulled against his throat as he swallowed, which he did as he started toward me, eyes never leaving mine.

He was taller than I remembered, though not by much. His hair was short, like Peter's, but long enough to rest against the collar of the long suit coat he wore like someone accustomed to it. A small feather braided into shiny strands fluttered from behind his ear. Instead of a red band circling his forehead there was a mark, and he held in his hands the wide-brimmed hat that made it. Little scratches, like spider webs, eased out from his obsidian eyes, but his face was otherwise as smooth as a well-worn saddle.

Shard's mouth melted into smile. "I look for pussytoes, couldn't find them. You will accept this instead?"

He offered me his hand to help me step over the boulders and time that separated us. He set his hat down on a nearby rock and reached for me.

I gave him first the Tonkin rod.

"It is a fine piece," he said, and I wondered if he, too, was surprised by my hesitation. He turned the rod over in his hands and rubbed the silk lacings.

"You made a good catch," he said, nodding his chin to the river, "even without a spear or dog."

"It belonged to my husband," I said.

He nodded. "The man called Indian Peter tells me of the widow Alice M., the woman who searches. Then as he speaks of you, of how long he knows you, the marking on your face, even before he speaks the name of Asiam, I know." There was a catch to his voice, and he paused to clear his throat before saying: "I am pierced," he put his fist to his chest, "like an arrow with the knowing." He looked away from me, across the creek as though taking in some strength. "The woman, Mrs. Sherar, tells me I can find you here."

He held his hand out to me again, the rod gripped tightly in the other. "Come. You have gathered far and stayed out long enough."

My fingers slipped then into his grip, firm and strong from arms strengthened by carrying heavy iron, from finding satisfaction in his work. His calluses closed gently against my fingers as he gave balance to my steps. And after all the years of waiting, wishing, bearing secret hopes, his touch felt almost painful, weakening, like the slicing of obsidian, clean and keen and sure.

And then I stood before him, and he folded me to his chest. We stood against the sunset, close, as one, the Tonkin rod a gentle pressure in his hands across my back. His chin rested gently on my head, and I could hear his heart beat, smell his sun-dried shirt. Water pooled behind my eyes, and I was taken by a shaking and a rush of sweetness that spread through me like a plunge into the deepest lake, filling me to my very soul.

He spoke, his voice vibrating in his chest like a drum against my ear, and it sounded so like music that at first I did not notice what he said. When I did, I felt confused, for he told me what I carried in *my* mind but claimed the thoughts as his.

"It has been a long time to live with what I did not do for you," he said. "A long time to wait to ask forgiveness. But I am grateful the moment comes at all."

I had nothing to forgive him for.

"The shame is mine," I told him, my voice spoken into his shirt.

"What shame do you carry?" he said, moving me gently back from his chest.

"You stood in my place, for my foolishness. I wanted to just be a part of you and instead..." I looked up at him, noticed a scar along his neck. "You wore pain for me. I believed you dead. Only a miracle lets you stand before me now."

"Who tells you this?"

"I heard Stink Bug. He said it to Salmon Eyes the night they searched for me to bring me back. Stink Bug said that if they did not find me, you would die instead. That you had made an offer Wuzzie accepted."

He was very quiet. "You heard them say this?"

"I lay, frightened, hiding in a cottonwood log, not moving even when the spiders crawled up my legs." I shivered with the memory. "My shame is that I did not leave the log to save you. Instead, I ran. It is my dishonor that I found happiness in my life while believing I caused the death of someone else."

I could tell by his silence, the tighter grip with which he held me, that an unbeckoned memory had come into his mind. But he said instead, "It was good you allowed yourself joy, Asiam. Grieving should not take away your hope, only be a pause to remember what was good." He was quiet as though thinking. "There was no plan for me to die," he said softly.

"Why did Stink Bug say that?"

"They must have known you were there, hiding in the log. What greater torture for you to live and to think I died." He shook his head. "They came back to tell me you had. So each could mourn deaths that lived only in Stink Bug's curved mind." Anguish laced his words. "I accepted what that one said. He did not come back for several days, told us your bones were seen, scattered by mountain lions. Salmon Eyes confirmed the story. Even described what your treasure basket carried. Lukwsh said the things she put there. He must have found it. Told all he left it there for your spirit to take with you when it would."

"If I had only come back with them—"

"You were a child! More than me."

"Not in how I felt for you before I left," I said, "though I lacked the courage of a woman."

"Oh, Asiam." He folded me into his chest, the sound of my name on his tongue as sweet as rose hip candy, overpowering the torment of his words. "I was not strong enough to disagree with Wuzzie. I should have stood beside you."

He looked out over the stream, and I saw we were two people caught within a charming circle inside fences of our own making.

"Stink Bug created a lie. He thought it would last a lifetime," I said.

"Took his secret to his grave. More powerful than Wuzzie in this, in sending you away." He sighed as though he did not understand the ways of powerful ones. "And those who loved you learned to live without you. Even Flake disappeared. Wren said he had gone to be with you."

"He did."

"Flake found you? So you did not travel alone?"

"Until the earth quaked. We traveled at night. Slept together in the days until we reached John Day's river. We traveled well together. I thought someone sent him, he wore the knots.... But he died."

"We felt the quake. Big boulders tumbled from the ridge cap near Home Creek. Only for a moment. Enough to make us listen more closely to Wuzzie. The rains came then. The antelope let themselves be charmed, and it went well with us, for a time. But nothing stays the same." He led me to a large rock where we could sit beside each other. He laid the fishing rod on the ground beside us. He noticed me shake.

"You are cold," he said, and bent to squeeze the river from the hem of my split skirt, made a cup of his hands to massage the water from my hide-covered feet. A meadowlark warbled behind us, perched on sage.

"If it does not hurt you," I said, "I would know more of that time, of what happened."

He sighed and sat beside me, tossed some stones toward the water. "Then there were more raids, and we lost warriors. Some of us went back to work for the white ranchers, but even if we did not raid, we were targets. Soon we were like taut bows looking for arrows of our own."

"I read some of that in news sheets."

"The army came. Said safety waited for us at the Malheur Reserve. Johnson worked there. And a man named Parrish, who people said could be trusted. We needed papers to leave, papers that said we were not raiders." He patted his suit coat pocket. "I carry them now. They said we could learn to feed our families without taking cattle from others, arguing over lands. In the end, many went.

"Lukwsh and Wren worked there. I learned machinery and iron work from Sam Johnson. We all broke the land and planted with Mr. Parrish's help. Two thousand acres in wheat, he told us. Mr. Parrish was a good man. We harvested one crop with only Lukwsh's knives. The Washington fathers refused to send us tools. Women sewed. Wren helped the White Lily, Mrs. Parrish, in the school. We did what we could. Sarah came some to speak the words between us until we learned English."

He stood up, paced a distance from me toward his tethered horse stomping impatience. He rubbed the animal's nose, seemed to gather courage, and returned.

"Then the government sent Mr. Parrish away, gave us this Christian." He spit in the dirt and I shivered. "Rhinehart made slaves of us, put our crops into locked sheds. Only those who worked as *he* said could eat from it. If we wished to give some to those who still gathered seeds beside the lakes, give gifts to those who needed it, he locked the doors twice. It was not what I remember from Sarah's words about the Christians. It was a bad time. And then the war." He took a deep breath. "But that is over. Today, you are a gift." He lifted my hands. "One I do not deserve. And I want to hear of you, which people you allowed to love you, help you along."

Stillness overcame me. Where to begin in the circle of my memory knots?

"Night comes," he said then into the quiet, to save me. "We should go now." A breeze moved the feather from behind his ear. He bent to retrieve his hat, my fishing rod.

I moved as if to stand, but he had stopped. His arm surrounded my shoulder, and he pulled me up to him.

"I thank God for you, Asiam." His voice was thick, deep like a drum-beat in my ear. "Thank him that you are real, beside me, and not some lost dream I will wake up from."

He lifted my chin with his fingers then so that I could look at him, gently rubbed the dark line along my jaw, the markings of a lost child, now found. Just before he bent to brush his lips against my own, he spoke the words I never thought my ears would hear from him, longed to, to know that I was loved, was worthy and belonged.

"And now, if you will have it," he said, "I will take you home."

H O M E

We understand that a few Piute Indians intend wintering in this city and supporting themselves by doing odd jobs of any kind. Some of the Piutes are very industrious and well-to-do.—*Grant County News,* Canyon City, Oregon, 1891

"WHAT OF THE OTHERS?" I asked, still not wanting to speak much of my ways, a feeling of hesitation separating us like a woven willow wall. He had pulled me up behind him on his bay. The evening breeze chilled against my wet legs, but my face burned hot resting into the rough wool of his coat. He carried the Tonkin rod in his right hand, the silk line moving like a fine web in the breeze. Yellow rabbit brush sent up puffs of color and strong scent as Shard maneuvered the horse through the shrubs.

"Wren is gone," he said, his voice tight, bound in sadness. "She did not survive the journey from Fort Harney." His words came from far away, and I was glad I did not have to see the anguish in his face. "My sister had no fat stored on her to resist the bitter cold. We had few blankets. Wuzzie tried, gave everything to her, but it did nothing. Even the army's coats they gave the men were not enough draped over her in the snow. One morning, she did not wake up. Her face was as spring ice, so thin and cold. They would not wait for us to have a ceremony, so her bones are there, still. Scattered by the dogs and high water of John Day's River in spring now."

"So Wuzzie's water babies took her anyway," I said.

He twisted to look at me. "No...no water babies took her." He turned back. "Lukwsh still lives."

"She does! Where?"

"I hunt for her, keep her in venison and choke cherries." I felt his grin as he sat straighter, took a deeper breath against my arms. He seemed pleased to speak of happy things. "And she keeps my house."

"She is at Warm Springs?" I asked, pleasure coming from knowing that she lived—and that his mother, not someone else, kept his house.

He laughed. "She'd have long arms to tend me from anywhere else. Yes. She's there and would come to see her Asiam, but she doesn't travel much now. One foot she lost to frostbite on the journey north. Some toes later— to an injury that did not heal and rotted her other foot. I made her a chair with wheels, and she moves around pretty good. She waits to see you."

"So much," I said without thinking. "My Spirit has led me to so much."

Shard stayed quiet, and I did not know if the mention of my Spirit troubled him or if his mind had moved to other thoughts.

"Grey Doe died. Near Seneca," he said. "She found herself beneath a heavy wagon. She could not move fast enough in snow. Her shoulder slowed her. The food rotted in the storehouses and still the agent Rinehart would not let the people eat. So Grey Doe was weak as well as slow. Mr. Parrish tried to help, but Rhinehart told the army not to listen to him."

"Mr. Parrish did write a letter."

"You know of this?" he asked, turned in surprise.

"Before Wren died. He asked that she and Grey Doe and Lukwsh and Wuzzie go as family. That you asked for this. All but Wuzzie made sense."

"You have seen these words?"

I shook my head. "It belongs to Wuzzie's story. Wuzzie set me on this search for Lukwsh and Wren. Helped me find you."

"Wuzzie?"

"Wuzzie is in Salem. In the Oregon Asylum. Until last year, my husband was the doctor who looked after that one."

Shard rode quietly, shook his head. "We are a small family walking around a circle."

"Wuzzie does not speak, is caught in a web. Still is. You knew about...?"

His eyes remained forward helping the horse pick its way in the growing twilight. The roar of the river as we approached it drowned out conversation as we followed the road toward the inn. Pale lamplight flickered in the window, warm and welcoming.

"Did you know about Wuzzie?" I asked again when the night sounds allowed it.

He nodded yes. "How is what I do not wish to think of. Lukwsh knows more."

The horse stumbled in the growing dark, caught itself, and I grabbed him more tightly at his center.

"As for the others," he continued, "except for Stink Bug, who died in the war, they are scattered. There was no need for fighting. If they had given out the food, none of it would have happened." He paused. "Some went to Walker River with Sarah and her school." The word "Sarah" is bitten like an angry man. "In the end, she could do nothing for us. Others made themselves lost in the eastern towns and alleys. Thirty-eight came to Warm Springs first, then another seventy or so. I came with the last, but it has been almost ten years now." He shook his head as if surprised at how the time had passed.

"A few are back at Malheur, took the land allotments and have farms of their own. Some work at white men's ranches on fields they are familiar with. It is where they gathered seeds and hunted ducks. I would be wary there. Too strange to be taken away from all you know for no reason and then brought back to the same place but told by someone else how you must be. Too hard to make sense of all the time you were away."

"It is a strangeness," I agreed.

We reached the hitching rail at the stone wall of the inn. I slid off the horse, took the rod, and Shard stepped down beside me, led the horse to the trough. He stood, reins loose in his hands. I could feel the heat from his shoulder burning like a branding iron into mine. The horse's soft slurp like a whistle played against the cicadas, the distant falls, the smell of river and dust. Shard leaned back, put his arm around my shoulder, pulled me to him.

"We will make sense of it, together, Asiam."

"Can't you stay another day or two?" This from Mother Sherar. "Seems like we just got you and you're gone. Not even a minute to see Ella or Carrie or meet our newest grandbaby, Mabel!"

"Let the girl be, Mother. Can't you see she's on a mission? Time enough for visitin' when she's made her peace."

"Well, what's left to find?" she said to Joseph. "There he is"—she lifted her palm to Shard, as though directing a choir to sing—"standing right before your eyes, the dead resurrected!"

"For both of us," Shard said, smiling.

"Lukwsh," I told her, "who is like a mother to me, too. I would see her again. And what she may tell me about Wuzzie, the one who sent me on this journey. My first journey, too. I would end it with a healing if I can."

"Well, I know you're doing the right thing. I'm just green with wanting more time of yours, myself. This occasional visit to check on your sweet grapes doesn't seem enough. Hope you can make the reservation in one day. Night comes earlier now you know. That hat looks good on you, even if I did pick it out."

"Like Shard's."

"So it is, Stetsons both. Quality. Functional, too. You can water your horse from it, the weave's so tight."

"Like the baskets my mother makes," Shard said. "Or Sunmiet."

"Why, I suppose that's so," Mother Sherar said, fussed at a thread on my jacket.

"Amber's sound," Joseph said. "Not the prettiest buckskin I've seen. Like the real pale ones myself, or a mule. But he's big and surefooted and will get ye where ye need to be."

Joseph Sherar patted the horse I traded him for. He patted the gelding's rump affectionately, checked the cloth bag and bedroll tied behind my saddle. Stepped back, cane beside him. "And I will enjoy that rod," he said, smiling, "though the offer stands: yours to use anytime you come to visit."

"It will not sadden you, I hope, to know I have another bamboo rod."

"Expected as much," he said. "Tonkin?" He lifted one brow.

"No Tonkin cane." I noticed his relief. "It was Thomas Crickett's only

Tonkin rod and his favorite. I believe it would please him to have it in the hands of someone who will appreciate its balance and its rare value."

Shard had already mounted up as I am once again squeezed by Mother Sherar, surprised as always by the strength of her wiry body, the intensity of her care. Spirit arched himself against my skirt, stepped his soft paws on my moccasins, and purred. I scooped him up.

Father Sherar wiped his nose, sniffed as though struggling with a cold. Cat back on the ground, the big man grabbed me in a bear hug, my face buried in his red vest that smelled of leather and of cabbage.

"Let the Spirit bless ye, darlin'," he whispered to me. He walked me around the horse and gave me a lift up with his hand before I answered.

"He does," I said. "He already does."

We rode out the Tygh Valley road, up the twisting ravine. Sagebrush and rocks and dirt hauled by the hands of many marked the road wide enough for the two of us to ride abreast, broad enough for stagecoaches, which I hoped we would not meet.

Most of the morning we spent in quiet comfort, adjusting to the presence of one held so long in my mind. I hoped Shard would not press too hard about the future—beyond my seeing Lukwsh—for I was in a surprising fog about it.

Amber tossed his head up and down, a spirited horse, the clank of his bit and the sound of hooves on the rocks the only breaks in the calm. Once or twice Shard's eyes reached across the space between us, and I could see he shared the wonder that my eyes were looking back at his.

At Muller's store in Tygh Valley we selected fresh apples brought by freight from Washington. Two small children with eyes like waiting owls peered out from behind the counter. I thought they stared at the feather braided into Shard's hair. The clerk hesitated a moment when Shard handed him coins, watched Shard, who did not drop his eyes. But then Shard reached in his pocket to show his papers.

"Not necessary," the clerk said, shook his head, his dark mustache bobbing as he talked. "Not necessary." He nodded toward the two pairs of eyes below him. "Kids act like they've never seen anyone from the reservation before, but they have. Scoot now," he told them, "quit your staring. Ain't polite." They scampered out. "Course, it ain't often they see a prosperous one with a pretty white woman standing at his side. Sometimes see squaws following their white men, but not the other way around."

Shard stiffened at the words, but I was glad this first of many times had come so I could see what I had learned, how keen my edges had been honed.

"A good mind inspects what is different," I told the clerk, adjusting my leather gloves. "Children notice. It is wisdom winning over foolishness that reveals if what is regarded is treasured or said to not belong."

The clerk was thoughtful then, not sure if I had offered him an insult or some acceptance of his words. "You think their starin' is a compliment, ma'am?"

"It is my choice how I take it, and I take it as one," I said and pulled my hat back on my head, adjusted the chin string. "I have waited a long time to stand beside this man," I told him, taking Shard's arm. "I am pleased that someone noticed."

"There will be slaps like that one, but more painful," Shard said as we rode away. "Before, from Grey Doe and Wuzzie and others because your face was not dark enough. Here, it will be because mine is too dark to be with yours. On the reservation, it may be as before. The Sahaptin-speakers and the Wascos are not all happy we are there; they may not be pleased that you are. Time has not changed some things."

"When I first came to Sherar's Bridge, I did not belong, even though I lived then among the people of my first parents. I did not find the peace I looked for with Sunmiet's people nor Peter's, nor even yours. When I left to live in Salem and walked among the mind-injured there, I did not belong. But I found a way. And now again I will find a way." For I do not walk alone, I thought but did not say.

"I would like to find the way with you, Asiam."

I shook my head, but a seed of worry settled in my stomach at how he would react when the time came to tell him of who walks with me on my journey.

At the stage stop at Wapanitia we gathered up some hard biscuits, hot coffee, and more stares, and did not stay long. We rode through hills of scattered juniper and meandering streams, up higher, past waxy leaves of scrub oak, the orange and red of turning stands of aspen, on into low timber.

A mule deer leaped before us, startled. It surged up a rocky outcropping, almost a straight wall of rocks from trail to sky. He clambered up and over, his muscles rolling, his breathing labored into snorts, his big rack cracking against the rocks and tree roots of the impossible place he had chosen to escape to. Smaller rocks of reds and yellows broke behind him, his feet breaking loose flows of dirt that cascaded like water as he crested the top and disappeared.

It had happened so quickly and with such power we both sat a moment, not sure we had witnessed this escape.

"I would not believe fear could push a deer straight up like that," Shard said.

"Perhaps he sought the view that lies on top," I told him.

Shard laughed. "I have a place to take you, to show you a great high view, if that's what you think."

"At Seekseequa?"

"That is a good place, too. But I think of one far from here. Where there are rocks and cliffs that angle like basket weavings, that overlook another world so far and deep you cannot see the end. The sea. I will take you there if you would have it."

"The ocean! Yes, I would have it," I told him, and in my excitement added, "And you."

Shard exhaled as though he had been holding his breath. "I wondered if you would answer when I asked if I could take you home. Wondered what held you back."

"After we see Lukwsh," I said. "And when what becomes of Wuzzie is decided. I didn't mean to hold back. I am here not just to see Lukwsh or discover more of Wuzzie, but to be with you for as long as you will have me."

We bypassed Simnasho, the oldest village on the reservation settled into the dimple of red hills, beyond a red lake. "Sunmiet is not here, and I am not always welcomed by others without an elder at my side," Shard noted. "You do no qualify." He grinned, looked for the placement of the sun. "We will ride beyond a ways yet, but will need to spend the night. See Lukwsh by midday tomorrow. We will not take time at the agency to show you the mill I work at—just let the agent know that I am back."

At the Warm Springs river, we made a camp in the shadow of massive gray and red rocks marked by caves and outcroppings that looked like piles of red mud melted down the sides, overhangs with water marks like those left in mud by the receding lakes. A small fire heated the coffee, warmed our faces. Stars peeked out brightly in the sky, sparkled in the crisp air.

"In winter, stories are told about this place," Shard said as he unrolled the bedrolls, "of Eagle and his brothers and their slave, Skunk—about that cave there. I am reminded of long nights in the wickiups hearing stories. The children snore and expect the same words each time. They know how the story will end and how it will begin again."

"The elders have good memories, never need to write things down," I said to him, wiping my hands in sand to clean them, rinsing my face with water from the river, watching my rippling image. "I still have my memory necklace, tied knots of time, if I ever wish to know. Remember?" I pulled it out to show him. "Lukwsh or Wren must have put it on Flake's neck. It is almost all I keep from my time walking away from you."

He held one of the knots in his fingers, and we stood close. "I do not know the ending, Asiam," he said. "But I am pleased words were written, not just remembered."

"Without Father Parrish's letter, I doubt this search would have led me here," I said as he stepped away. I lay down on the bedroll, and he covered me up over my shoulders, lay next to me on his.

"I would never have found you," he said, brushing hair back from my cheeks. The horses stomped contented at their tethers. The Warm Springs River gurgled satisfaction to Shard's last words before I fell asleep: "It is the best blend of the old and the new. To hold some things in your mind and to write some others down. Both are needed for a strong pot."

A black dot I had seen from quite a distance in the center of a doorway became a waving woman.

We had passed through the agency with its boarding school and buildings, skirted past skinny-tailed dogs, ridden south along the Deschutes River some distance, then turned west to follow a stream lined with willows and tall grasses that opened to a canyon ever widening, then twisting narrow. The air stirred warm and the canyon welcomed. We rode past clusters of wickiups, a canvas tent or two, before seeing willow corrals and several frame houses, cattle grazing beyond a barn. Barking dogs and wide-eyed children announced our arrival. The black dot, in the center of three homes set in a dimple of bunch grass and sage, became the face of Lukwsh.

"You look no older than a child," Lukwsh shouted, her arms open to me from her chair with wheels. Her gray hair, parted in the center, still flowed from a knot tied behind her neck. Her smile was a dark cave of broken teeth. I had seen her since we had crested the ridge and ridden along the creek almost hidden in a deep channel lined with tall, coarse grass that gave Seekseequa Creek its name.

"No older than a board-baby!" she sang again, clothes flowing loose against her thinner chest, over her knees. Brown stockings rose up from new moccasins that fit flat where feet would be. "No older than a child!"

"I am a child," I cried, "your child." I slipped from Amber, letting Shard take the reins. I ran to her, caught a glimpse of a black puppy peering from beneath her chair, felt the wind take my hat, bounce it on my back while I awkwardly tried to hold Lukwsh's shoulders, kiss her face, her forehead, run my hands over the coarse strings of her hair, capture her, make sure she was real. I felt her reach her arms to mine, hold me, look me over, her fingers clinging to my waist. Her hands kneaded me as though to see if she held flesh, and then I knelt at her feet, buried tears in a lap that smelled of lavender.

"I was a lost child," I cried, "who is so sorry."

"Na, na," she crooned, her wide hands gently stroking my head, her body moving gently back and forward. "You were never lost to us. We never forgot who you were. But it is all right, now. It is all good, now. You are a lost child, found."

She held my shoulders, ran her cool fingers to move hair behind my ears and let me feel the depth of healing rise up from my heart as it realized where it was, at last.

It did not seem long before I felt Shard's hands on my shoulders, lifting me as my sobs quieted. His touch startled me, sent streams of feeling through my being—feelings I was less afraid of now, did not hold back. I would have turned to him when I stood, but my legs were full of prickles and would not hold me up.

"Legs have minds of their own," Lukwsh said as I rubbed my calves back into feeling, one hand balanced in Shard's. "These two have served me well, but now they get to ride around," she said, patting her thighs. "Sometimes this one, Arrow, who hides under me, likes to ride. Or the little ones plump themselves like chickens on my legs and even they go numb! I have to sweep them off. Oh, here they come."

I looked up to see the faces of three children staring like curious does. I watched Arrow finally brave the activity, come to sit beside Lukwsh, wearing a yawn of caution.

"I am their *kasa,* as they say here at Warm Springs. Their grandma," Lukwsh said, leaning down to swoop the puppy into her lap. His tongue hung out of the dark face in happy contentment.

"Oh," I said, and for the first time realized I have had thoughts about a future that may have been in error.

Lukwsh is quick to see the question in my face. "All the children call me *kasa.* So many did not live from Fort Harney that we old ones who did spread ourselves around. But there is room for more," she said, her eyes twinkling as she nodded her chin toward Shard.

"Time enough to talk of such things, old woman," Shard told her. "For now, we are hungry and would eat. Have you done your work?"

Lukwsh's laugh, full and hearty, washed me with joy. The puppy jumped as she turned her chair to enter the coolness of her home.

"You men can think of only two things for women to do, and both things fill you up!" she said over her shoulder, waving one hand in the air.

We finished the meal of wind-dried salmon and corn meal, a pine-nut stew, canned peaches, a huckleberry pie, and fried bread. "I do not make it so good as those from here," Lukwsh told me, "but it is my own way and leaves less oil on your fingers when you eat it. Here," she said to the two little ones still hovering at the open door. "Take what is left to Auntie Pauline."

Chubby fingers snatched at the crisp, fawn-colored bread like hungry birds as the children scampered out the door.

"Tell them my family is home!" she shouted after them. "And for them to come later to see." Then to us she laughed. "As if they need an invitation to find out what happens here."

She let the puppy lick at her fingers before he found his bed of cornhusks, turned three times to plop beside the stove.

The house felt pleasantly warm from the fry bread. We had eaten at a round table made of a single log held by a carved leg at the center. Beyond squatted a wood stove surrounded by a ramp that appeared to make the stove sit inside a wooden box, making it easier for Lukwsh to cook from her chair, to reach the warming oven at the top. Beside the woodstove stood a deep sink lined with a reddish metal and bearing a water handle. It too had been built so Lukwsh's chair could slide under it and she could wash dishes or her hands at a height of ease. Even the tables holding her unfinished baskets or the shelves of herbs and spices that supplied the room with pungency were lower. The windows, too. Shard had cared well for her.

Colored rugs were scattered where her wheels would not catch them. A feeling of lavishness spilled across the tidy room.

"He has made it so I can do for myself, Asiam," Lukwsh said, watching me watch. "Until a few weeks ago, I had a good dog to help, too. Yampah could get my shawl for me and bring in sticks for kindling. But we all get old and die, and Yampah did, too." She sighed. "In that room," she nodded with her head to a closed door across from the main one, "is a bed and thunder bucket so I do not have to find my way out in the night. He is a good son, knows how to walk on another's trail even if the person has no feet." She smiled at her own joke. "It is not easy to find a son so willing to see the world in this way."

Shard's face darkened with the praise. He pulled an obsidian knife from a sheath near the stove and sat down on a high-back chair he had probably made, scraped his fingernails with the knife.

"None were of my own flesh, but it has not mattered."

She wheeled her way to sit where she could look out the window at the tall grasses that gave the creek its name.

"It is so pretty here, quiet, as at the Silvies," I said, coming to stand beside her. I am not sure I've really heard her words. "Wren was your child," I said.

"I said she was the sister of Shard and Stink Bug, who came to me in a different way."

Shard held the knife in midair. "You and my father—she was the only child you two had."

Lukwsh shook her head, turned on her wheels, and returned to the table. She scanned it, found crumbs she scraped with the cup of her hand onto her lap. She rolled to the doorway and lifted her skirts to the breeze. The dog raised his eyebrows but did not leave his bed.

"For the meadowlarks and red-winged blackbirds," she said and chirped for them, watched them hop, hop at the dirt and crumbs in front of the door. "I cannot get a hawk to come to me like Grey Doe did. Have to keep working on that one." She kept her back to us as she spoke again. "Wren came as you, Asiam. She was much smaller. Tiny. Barely born."

"But you carried my father's child…" Shard said, wonder in his voice. He had put the knife down, leaned toward her, his arms on his thighs, eyes at her level.

"We kept her in a winnowing basket at first, she was so small," Lukwsh said.

"Grey Doe told us we would have to stay with her when your time came to deliver. Is that not so? We even went with her and auntie. For what, two, three days?"

"My time came. Yes. You went to Grey Doe. But my baby did not live. Then, as if the Creator could answer my prayers of anger with something sweet, Wren came."

She looked far back into her memories. Softness filled the space between the wrinkles of her face. Quiet settled on the room as each remembered Wren in his or her own way.

Lukwsh turned to me. "Wuzzie brought the child. I do not know where or how Wuzzie found this gift or why I was chosen to receive it, but I took it. As with all gifts. And when years later you were brought, I took you too. But when Wuzzie sent you away, I could not find the strength inside to argue. So much had already been given. I hoped only that you lived and did not hold me angry in your thoughts. And so my prayers are answered. You are here." Tears pooled at her eyes. "You do not seem to hold harsh feelings, so my faith finds fruit. You have been led where you need to be."

I bent to her, held her as tightly as I could. "Yes," I whispered. "I am where I'm supposed to be."

Later in the evening, more joined us. Summer Rain and Thunder Caller; Willow Basket and her child; Leah, soon to marry; names of others I did not know touched their hands to mine gently in the Indian way. They ate then walked back carrying their lamps, their lights twinkling, then disappearing like stars at dawn. Their voices and eyes had welcomed me, not sent angry arrows to my heart.

I fought not to scold myself for waiting, for not finding them before.

It was again the three of us.

"There is enough water to dam the creek and make a mill here," Shard said. "It is worth some effort. Beyond the ridge there, people stay in tents. We could harvest timber and build more houses. If we stayed well, there might be more families here."

"Enough people to need a long house," I said.

Shard cast a quick glance to his mother, and some message passed between them.

"Our people had no long house at the lakes," he reminded me. "Our religion was a private one. We have gone to the long house ceremonies here, and some even know the songs if not the words. It is a good religion, this one with drums, and not so hard to share." I thought he would say something more, but he did not. He stood and walked beneath an arc covered with wild rose vines. "Some elders say many years ago, long before the war, we came here to Seekseequa to find roots, but no one here remembers. Still, it has a feel to it, this place, that is like home."

"Maybe the smell of the water and the grasses," I offered.

"Hmm," Lukwsh agreed, inhaling deeply. "It gets chilly."

We heard crickets, some tiny screeches, and coyotes howled. The latter brought barks from Arrow, dark as the bats that swooped toward the creek. They can be heard, the air moved by their wings felt, but their presence not seen.

"I am a tired old woman," Lukwsh said and began to wheel herself back inside. I rose to help her, but she waved me away. "I am fine. This will be my best night of sleep for a long time. You will not wake me when you slip into my bed later. Just push Arrow out of that place." She smiled, her lips rolling up onto ash-stained gums. "In the morning, we'll speak of Wuzzie. And of the plans I have for who would marry my children."

"And your home?" I asked Shard after she had gone to bed. "You have not shown me, or do you stay here, too?"

He moved back into the lamplight cast through Lukwsh's windows. "There." He pointed to thick foliage in the scoop of a ravine. "I make her an iron to hit, so I can hear her if she calls. I wanted one big house for both of us, but she does not permit this. Says I will have my own family one day. So there is a house back there. The barns here, they belong to me. And the cattle. I work out some, for ranchers, use what Sam Johnson taught me at Malheur. That wagon there"—he pointed in the moonlight to a wagon with a stall built on its back—"for hauling a bull," he said, pride in his voice. "There is a winch to pull him forward if he resists. It is the only one like it, and I can take my bull wherever I want without herding him. He leads a good life, that one."

We were both quiet, let the night winds rise and settle like a sigh.

"I waited so long," I said, "imagined how it would be when...if I saw Lukwsh again someday. Then I'd wipe away the thought, not want to dwell on something impossible. And you—sometimes I would think of you and ache with the wanting to feel your arms around me one more time, to know how you and I might be as we grew older. Now here I am."

"You have a hesitation." He gave me time to continue, but I did not. "Because you married once?"

"Not because I married. Thomas Crickett was a good man, and I became who I am in his presence. Because of him, I am here now, I think." I struggled with how to explain, what words to use. "It is because...of how I walked my path, will choose to walk it in the future. Because I do not know if you will understand this, Shard."

"I listen well."

I praised the dark for hiding his face.

"Once, I hiked in the mountains with Thomas Crickett and some friends of his." I moved to sit on a bench on the south side of Lukwsh's house, felt the day's heat at my back, captured in the wood. Shard retrieved a shawl for me and wrapped me in it, our heads together as we talked. "Each walked at his own pace on that hike, some faster than others. There were beautiful things to see along the trail up to Mount Hood. But I seldom looked. I was busy watching my feet, thinking as I walked. I thought about what would happen when I reached the top, if I would be too tired to come back down. I remembered things I should have done before I left. Always a busy mind.

"Suddenly I looked up and found myself alone, no one else on the trail, no sounds except the wind. I thought I missed a fork in the trail and was ashamed I didn't pay attention, thinking of past things or future but never of where I am. I stopped to see if those behind me would catch up. 'Then I will know I am on the right path,' I decided. But they might be following me and have taken the wrong fork as well! So I picked up my pace to catch those in front, and when I spied Thomas Crickett's familiar coat in the distance, I was overwhelmed with relief. Until later, when one of that group told me they had taken a wrong turn, wandered about before finding the main road again.

"And so I think of this. Why do I spend time on my trail wondering about those I follow or those behind me, letting my mind wander into what lies ahead or what has passed? I lose sight of the way, pay no attention to what is happening *now*, end up doing foolish things. It is what got me into trouble those years before—being angry with Vanilla Leaf and you, walking as one with Summer Rain. Later, I let Stink Bug and Wuzzie, or what I thought they would think, keep me looking for something, searching always but never sure when it was found."

It pleased me that Shard let me speak, did not jump in to tell me what I should have done, made no effort to repair things.

"Something kept me from the present. And then I knew." My mouth was dry. "It was because the only one there with me on the trail when I walk alone is me. Someone so unworthy I did not wish to share her time."

Shard kept his face forward, as though his eyes would violate his soul if he looked at me.

"So I went away to the future or the past."

"It is not how I see you," he said, looking at me now. He thumbed the fullness of my cheeks, wiped at my tears.

"It is not how I am, now."

"Then why be sad?"

"Because I do not know if you will understand what made the difference."

He smiled. "Now I see. This is how you wander into the future yet."

His gentleness encouraged, and so I told him in a whisper still laced with awe and wonder. "I did. Until I listened to my Spirit, the One they call the Lord, the One who called my name."

Shard had taken his hand from behind my back. He leaned forward, elbows resting on knees, waiting.

"This Spirit said I do not need to be afraid. He will give me people, things I need, tasks to do, direction. And I will never walk the trail alone as long as I will listen."

"He gives you a future. And a hope."

His choice of words surprised me, words I had heard myself sometime before. "You know this Spirit?"

He smiled again. "Is this why you keep the wall between us? You think I will not understand the Spirit who is above all others?"

"It is why I think I am here with you after all these years."

"Come with me, Asiam."

His voice carried impatience to it but anticipation as well, like a boy sharing his first kill. He pulled me to my feet, lifted the lantern, and we walked the short distance down a rocky walkway toward his house. He pushed open the door hung on iron hinges, set the lamp on the table, and went to light the wall lamps. The room eased into a warm glow to match my cheeks. He had selected fine and familiar things to surround himself with—willow baskets, wainscoted walls, china on plate shelves, a divan draped with a Hudson Bay blanket, doors leading to two other rooms. But it was with pleasure unanticipated and without limit when I saw where he led me first.

"I have made it with my own hands," he said, "from the leg irons taken off us at the big river when we were freed. I made it to remember how we got through, where our strength came from, and who controls all things."

On the wall before me hung twists of iron that formed a cross so delicate and yet so strong that it needed securing to the wall by heavy leather straps.

"And I have learned to read the English words of the book that says which Spirit is the strongest, the One who gives us hope. There is no reason to be afraid, Asiam." His voice was thick with pride and something else. "Mr. Parrish and his wife and even Mr. Johnson, they all lived with kindness and a rare strength, like iron, that could be fired and made stronger. And they gave it away to me and Lukwsh and Wren and others, did not force it on us, but let us see such love. And so we wished it for ourselves. We trust the same Spirit, Asiam."

He pulled then from beneath his shirt collar a tiny chain that sparkled gold against the darkness of his skin, glittered like moonlight on the river. At the end hung the familiar Christian cross. With its presence in his hand, I knew at last my journey ended. I had found where I belonged.

ROSY EVERLASTING

WE PLANNED TO MARRY within the week at a service officiated by the circuit Presbyterian minister and held in the church at Seekseequa Shard showed me in the morning.

"Built it ourselves," he said. "Picked this spot where two ravines crossed. Perfect place. Someday, we'll have our own Presbyterian minister. For now, we all take turns until the circuit rider comes more than once every three or four months."

The building gleamed with Ponderosa pine inside and out, from the small porch to the steeple. A dozen rows of wooden benches lined either side of a narrow interior flooded with natural lighting from four windows on either side. On a back wall, beside the coat hooks, people had carved their names with dates of their arrival. At the front stood a huge wooden cross flanked by twin tables, one of which held two fawn-colored beeswax candles on either side of a Bible.

As we walked across the floor, Shard noticed a squeak, walked back and forth on a board to make the sound again, decided the cause, then bent with his nails to tighten the squeaky pine.

"And there is no arguing about the old beliefs?"

"We work at putting all things into place," he said, as I walked around the cool room, touched the backs of smooth pews. "Ours always was a solitary connection to the Creator when we stayed at the lakes." He removed a nail from between his lips so I could understand him better. "This Presbyterianism, it tells us how to keep the friendship we have with the Creator but how to include our neighbors as well. There were conversions at Fort Simcoe. Some of those who fell on their faces to claim the Christian God there and in The Dalles wore masks, hid their true feelings. They only danced to win favor. I understood this. But some heard their names called and made him their own."

Shard spoke with firm words that filled me with wonder at the worlds our Spirit led us through, revealed himself inside of, then let us follow him to here.

"I wonder if those I rode with in the wagon were this Presbyterian," I said, thinking of a time so long ago.

"Does it matter?" Shard asked as he came to stand beside me. He folded me in his arms. "What matters is their hearts. They wore the cross."

"You remember that?" I said, pulling back to look at him.

"I found it at the base of Dog Mountain. But I didn't want to share it. I thought it would make you want to go." His look dropped with some embarrassment to the floor. "Only when Wuzzie— Lukwsh said you should have it, then, for your journey."

We stood enfolded in each others arms for a time, listening to the call of ravens in the distance, the warble of songbirds from the rosebush outside the window.

"What they had to give, they gave, my parents did. And Lukwsh, too. A sturdiness to keep going, a wish to have our longings filled, and a Spirit who would do it."

"It is what I hoped for all along," Lukwsh said, her eyes glistening as we shared our plans to marry. "I worried when you talked of long houses, afraid that is all you know, that you will not accept our Christian ways, Asiam. We honor old ways and the ways of others. But we reach out to what we feel is true."

"We could wait longer to marry, to give time for others to join us." I thought of the Sherars and Ella, of Sunmiet and Ann, even the headman, Wewa, and his family, who lived at Seekseequa but traveled now, away.

"Take advantage of the circuit rider coming," Lukwsh said, her chin pointed toward the road. "Have a giveaway later, after you come back and can announce your family."

She grinned, and I heard a cackle not unlike that once given by Grey Doe when she spoke of growing families.

The service would be long with Scripture readings and promises made, followed by much singing and as many kinds of foods as we could gather together in a short time.

"It reminds me of a naming long ago. We had so little time," Lukwsh said as we bustled about, fixing fry bread, adding water to dried huckle-berries for a special pie. "And so it is!" she said as though she just discovered it. "You take on a new name today. Maybe two? Do you say you are Asiam or this Alice M. now?"

I had already considered this. "Alice is easier for people to remember and less formal than 'Mrs. Johnson.' But I will never stop being Shell Flower, or even Asiam."

"Too bad you are not marrying in spring," she said. "We could have a flower festival like the one you missed and bury your arms in them. That would make your eyes shine!"

I laughed. "I'll have no trouble finding shining eyes!"

To marry the one who held me in his mind, I wore my traveling clothes. A purple dress with purple jacket, a hundred tiny pleats, my knots of smoked leather tucked beneath my lavender blouse. Mother Sherar's Stetson hat, chin strings dangling to my hands, covered my widow's peak in the front, let wisps of hair fuzz from the back.

Shard handed me a bouquet of pussytoe stems, the silver-gray shiny against my purple skirt. "I like Mrs. Sherar's name for the pussytoes," he said. "It is how our love is: rosy everlasting."

He stood almost sideways to me after handing me the stems, and I set-tled them in front of me, clasped and unclasped my wet fingers around them, adjusted my hat. I checked my moccasins, too, a special beaded pair made by Vanilla Leaf and handed me with a welcome smile that morning. We waited for the signal to come inside.

My future husband chewed on the side of his finger, his other arm crossed over his stomach, and for a moment my mind flew back, twenty years or more, to the morning I first saw him, first woke inside Lukwsh's lodge and wondered if this boy judged me kindly.

"Do butterflies live in your stomach, too?" I whispered.

He dropped his hand, looked sheepish, stood to face me, both hands on his hips, now, elbows out.

"They only make me wonder if what I hoped for will be better than the wish," he said. Then he smiled, his eyes sparkling in the way that I remembered when we rode together to Steen's Mountain. "Seeing you beside me already makes that so."

Singing rose up behind us. He motioned me to take his arm, and we walked up the steps into Seekseequa Church.

God himself had joined us now together, and we vowed to him and to each other. And who would question that? We stood before him, travelers who had walked the trail he set before us. As if we needed living proof that we did not walk alone, the minister read from a Puritan's prayer as though the author had been eavesdropping on our lives:

> *O Supreme Moving Cause,*
> *May I always love thee,*
> *Submit myself to thee,*
> *Trust thee for all things.*
> *Permit me to rejoice*
> *forever in thy love,*
> *And love, to water my soul.*

"You are husband and wife together," announced the minister, Elijah Miller. "And what God has brought together let no man put asunder." His words were followed by much rejoicing and slaps on the back for Shard, hugs and gentle presses of hands to the face for me.

Before we could walk out, we had a final joining meant to keep us close together, safe inside the love of friends and family. It was what I felt, warm and gathered up within the Hudson Bay blanket they wrapped around us; people blended from my past with new ones, laughter bubbling out like friendly springs at Home Creek.

I looked around the gathering at the smiling faces of Lukwsh and others and for a moment thought I saw Wren and Grey Doe standing there, even Stink Bug. I blinked my eyes. The circle felt almost complete.

My first night as Alice Johnson stays a misty dream. Several times I pinched myself at the way the circle came to close, how the charm was broken. We lay together held in a comforter of down, needed that first week of October. The Hudson Bay wedding blanket was folded at the foot of the bed. In the distance I heard geese call to each other, expected a light fog to lift from the creek in the morning. In a few days, we would leave for the agency to make arrangements for Shard to be gone. A few days after that, a trip to Salem, and then on to Shard's promise of the ocean.

For now, the knot of tangled vines described me, as though I had not held a husband in my arms before.

"There is no reason to be fearful, Asiam. Alice," he corrected himself.

A giggle rose up. "You do not know the woman you choose to sleep with, Mr. Johnson?"

"I know," he said and pulled me tighter to him. "I have waited a lifetime for the privilege. Your name has changed, but you are still the one whose hair is like the sunset. The one I do not wish to live without."

His fingers combed through the kinks of my hair, lifted and fanned the thickness from around my neck. He touched the leather necklace of knots. "You will tell me of the memories sometime?"

"If you want to hear them."

"All that has crossed your walk. I want to know all about those years."

"What about your scars?" I asked. "The real ones on your face—this one here?" My fingers outlined a wound the size of a bullet hole near his shoulder, the ripple of a burn scar on his ribs.

"Not tonight."

"I have new memories to add to my string of knots," I said. I sat up to slip the leather over my head and show him where I tied the last one. "This time at Seekseequa, finding you. They are like notes in a song, these knots."

I touched each one, felt the rhythm of their memory. "My husband—former husband—Thomas Crickett liked words and their past. One comes to me now looking at these knots: *charm*. From an old language no longer spoken, but it meant 'song' and sometimes 'a gathering of finches.' Perhaps that is where the song part came from, the birds in their joy giving us a charm. Now it means more, something that attracts but in a strange way, like the antelope hunt. I liked the old meaning, a song and a gathering. It still smells of smoke."

I held the necklace to my nose, inhaled the fascinating song of my past.

"Smoked hides carry the scent a long time. Keep it off," he said, his hands moving over my fingers and the knots as I started to put it back on. "Remember it, those songs and charms, but do not keep the past between us. There is hope in your life now and a strong Spirit. That is all you need."

And so I took it off, tiptoed across the cool floor to hang it on the side of the mirror. My skin formed bumps. In the lamplight, I saw his reflection in the mirror. Wide shoulders, bare, leaned against twists of iron that formed the headboard made by his hands.

"Come here now," he said, his arms open wide to me as I turned, wide in invitation to where I belonged. "Let there be no old songs between us, now or ever."

"So we will be able to leave directly from Salem?" I asked about arrangements Shard had worked out with the agent and the managers at the mill.

He nodded. "At Empire City there is a mill built by A. J. Simpson. It is a long trip south by ship after we reach the ocean, but there are things to learn from how they manage the logs there." We rode north again to The Dalles, this time on a stage we had picked up at Wapinitia, perched on a juniper flat at the edge of the reservation.

Another couple's knees touched ours as they lodged themselves in the small space across from us. The woman scowled at me from beneath the shade of her bonnet, and her lip curled as she looked at my husband. Her tongue clucked in disgust. Her man slept, his mouth open, lower lip bouncing like a flap of old fat, jarred by the stage wheels attacking the rutted road. She had enough trouble, I decided, ignoring that skirmish.

At the Columbia, we boarded the train west to East Portland then south to Salem, and though it was my husband's first time in these large cities, they neither charmed nor cowered him.

"Some time will pass before we come back," Shard said. "We need to make plans before we leave about Wuzzie and what things you want to take with you from your time in Salem."

I felt a seed of irritation that someone else now started to organize my days. The thought reminded me that I walked a different path now, not just two people on the same road but like a span of horses, two working together on a course neither had walked before.

Some thoughts formed that had not yet been said out loud. They had been swirling in my thinking since Shard and Lukwsh spoke of what they remembered about leaving Fort Harney and Wuzzie's difficult time, things that may have molded into her bad dream. As we jostled along on the bumpy road, I thought of what they told me not long before we left.

"Tell me what you remember about Wuzzie, what happened there," I asked Lukwsh and Shard the day after our marriage. We pushed Lukwsh's chair along the path used to gather willows for baskets.

"It is not yet the best time to choose willow," Lukwsh said, "but I like to see which ones to pick when all the leaves are gone." The trail ran bumpy and narrow. Arrow sniffed in the grasses, beneath bare willow branches, pushed against me, and I remembered how much gladness those balls of fur could give. I decided then not to hold back as I had with Thomas's Benny, but risk the pain of losing for a powerful present joy.

"You must go farther back," Lukwsh said with no joy in her voice, "before the war. None of us wanted to go to the reservation at first. Who wants to give themselves away? And Wuzzie objected. And the army came, treated our headmen like deciders. We just wanted their wisdom when we needed, not to have them speak for us." She shrugged her shoulders. "Who can say what might have happened if we had stayed away?"

"Nothing worse," Shard said.

"There! Go over to that one," Lukwsh pointed to a section of sweeping red willow that branched out wide from the bottom into the open sky like arms of praise. Wind had whipped the leaves bare. "See there, those without branches, the young ones. Cut those." Shard pulled his obsidian knife from its sheath at his waist and began to slice. "This place gave us good willow last year. No breaking when we took the bark with our little moons of obsidian. Some pull the branch through a tin can hole now, so who can know if it is a good willow or what?"

"Not traditional enough for you, Mother?" Shard teased as he brought an armful of branches to her.

"Those short ones," she said, "we save those for the cradle board hood. Weave diamond shapes for the first one. It will be a girl," she said to me and cackled, handed me one of her knives.

I wedged a rock beneath one wheel to balance her and stepped into the willows, my hands awkward from being so long away from the knife. But the rhythm returned, and I found several branches without scars that would make good sapwood when peeled, become as thread to the basket weavers.

We sat for a time letting the warm sun gather us along the bank, stripping bark from the willows that were strong but soft, like the cords along Shard's arms that strained as he worked. In the scraping and stacking, the two began to talk about the days before the war. And after.

"The men were asked to do things as white men. We planted and sowed grain and made hay their way. When we got them, we ran mower and hay forks. I learned to fix them, from Mr. Johnson. We built huge barns and put food there and blankets, when they came. At first, it was not so bad. We were paid in rations for work, but Mr. Parrish understood our way to feed the needy, too."

"To do otherwise would violate the blessing that comes with caring for those less favored," Lukwsh said.

"Mr. Parrish ordered up the sawmill. When it came, we felled trees and planed lumber and sold it to the ranchers. They ran cattle where we once had our wickiups."

"We learned how to blend, na?"

"The women worked with Mary Parrish."

"Yes," Lukwsh said, smiling at the memory. "We called her the White Lily. So soft, her skin, and good to us. She taught us sewing. Some girls are women now and teach at the boarding school at Warm Springs. They know how to make dresses of calico but are not allowed to instruct how to tan hides." She shook her head. "They hear the rhythm of their feet at those machines instead of the drums or children being sung to sleep."

"And then the trouble started," Shard said, his words biting to get this story told. "With Rhinehart and the Bannocks not getting supplies. Everything changed. Some of the Nevada Paiutes were at the agency with us and confused things. A few left with Oytes, who raided near Canyon City and wanted to join up with the Umatillas and fight the war. I thought about it, but it would solve nothing. But after that mix-up, even if you did nothing wrong, you had to stay on the reservation. They kept food from us, though beef was stacked in the warehouses. We grumbled but no one listened. Wuzzie rattled the agent workers, and with the raids and rumors, it turned bad."

"I know some of this," I told them, "from the newspaper and Sarah's book. But not Wuzzie's part or what might help her now."

"We were not even a part of the war," Shard said, telling all in order, not letting me rush them. "But when the army took those who did fight, they did not separate us. They herded all Indians into Fort Harney. It was a cold month, lots of snow. There were five or six hundred. Many from different places. Some had fought, but most had stayed away from the fighting. They drove us like cattle into Fort Harney. Named for an army man who killed Sioux." He spit to rid himself of the bad taste. "Like cattle, dividing men from women and children into barracks meant for thirty. Almost one hundred squeezed into such little places."

Shard became silent for a time. My eyes watched my fingers stripping willows.

He stood up, stepped a little apart from us, his wide hands at his hips, eyes across Seekseequa Creek, opening to the past.

"Wuzzie and other leaders, they tried to tell the soldiers once again that we had not fought them, that we did not shoot our rifles at uniforms, had only farmed and learned their ways. Wuzzie's voice was high and scratchy from the days of talking and the worry over the women and the children whom we had not seen. He pulled at his shoulder like he did in disgust, stomped on the unseen spider he threw to the ground. So cold! And the wind drove snow into our faces like tiny obsidian chips. Our eyes dried up. Our breath froze and so did our lips so when we talked we sounded foolish, like feeble-minded men.

"Sarah Winnemucca came to interpret. For the army. And for a night we were hopeful she would say what words they needed to hear. But they did not. And in a morning so cold we no longer felt our feet, she came to tell us all that we would leave this Rattlesnake Creek and march to Yakima, to a fort near that reservation."

"Mr. Parrish came with her, then with White Lily. The women begged her to help," Lukwsh said. "Her face streaked with tears, but she could do nothing." Lukwsh's hands stopped working, her eyes tangled in the past, all energy went into remembering. "Wren became sicker."

"I asked for the letter from Father Parrish, and he said he would write it. I asked Wuzzie to go with them for the healing Wren needed."

"Her skin, so pale and cold. We could not warm her up," Lukwsh said, rubbing her hands together even now to gather warmth. "We asked for Wuzzie to pray for her. Wuzzie leaned over, sang the songs even though she could not hear them. He gave her the army coat some soldiers handed from the supply building, but it failed her. Wren died."

She began to cry, her voice a wail, and I wondered if this remembering had value.

"She cannot tell the stories now. She remembered them all, each small item told many times to make the story real. She cannot make our hearts light up with her gentle touch. No kind hands to winnow and weave tule dogs, set children to laughing." Lukwsh made no effort to wipe the tears that fell down her face and washed her neck with grief. "Wuzzie too was like a motherless cow," she said to Shard.

He nodded agreement.

"Bawling and swinging around, knocking people and things down by hopping and jumping. Maybe because Wren arrived by those hands," Lukwsh continued, looking at her own.

"Maybe Wuzzie understood that everything slipped away," Shard said.

"Wuzzie became foolish in grief, and my heart split open, then filled with ice when I felt Wren's spirit go. The stillness of a clear river bottom came across her face. I had already lost you, Asiam, and Stink Bug, and then Wren."

"I did not fight the soldiers," Shard said, his voice slicing the still air like a new spear. "I could have lost no more if I had! We did what they asked, gave what they wanted so we could save our lives. And we lost those too."

"Wuzzie became wild with chanting." Lukwsh's eyes glistened as she talked. "Singing and tearing at the chests of soldiers who guarded us and were as cold as we were."

"But they had coats," Shard reminded her, "and boots."

"Yes. All the soldiers had coats and boots and ate three meals. We could smell the beef. And we saw smoke coming from the commander's quarters. They had a warm place."

Shard spoke more quickly, as though wanting to get it over with now. "Then we know what Yakima is, a prison away from our root places and grass places and lakes of our past. Wuzzie harped again at the soldiers with this news, threatened them with spells and powers. The soldiers were bothered by this small person cackling like a magpie in their ears, shaking sticks at them, pulling spiders from his chest, warning them of bad dreams and death to their kind. Wuzzie tried to arrange for Wren's body, but they sent him away.

"Then as if it were not bad enough that we must walk five hundred miles in leg irons like mules pushing waist-high snow over mountains, some soldiers came into the barracks late. They entered where Wuzzie stayed along with the stink of men who had not bathed, who oozed fear from our skin."

"It was the night after Wren died." Lukwsh took over the story. "The snow drifted deep outside, a blizzard. We were all like frozen lakes, but still two came to teach Wuzzie a lesson while he slept."

"They sneaked in," Shard said, and I sensed they had spoken this story in their minds a hundred times. "Snow blew through the door behind them. They ripped the thin blanket from Wuzzie. He howled, and they laughed and tore the clothes off him. They hit on his head with their fat fists, like little boys playing. We shouted for them to stop. Some were slow to come out of fitful sleep. The soldiers laughed. Finally our noises were enough to make them stop.

"But what they saw in their lamplight when they held back their fists was not a beaten man. And all of us saw too that Wuzzie was not a beaten man. Not a man at all.

"Those closest cried loudly, wanted to blame our troubles on Wuzzie, now, who pretended to be what he was not. People are always looking for someone else to blame for where they are. No one knew what should happen to one who deceived. Wuzzie became foolish in talking after that. He screamed and jumped about, his body—her body—exposed now for the woman she was. They grabbed at her and laughed, and she kicked and scratched. When they had her pinned tightly with their arms, she lost all strength, curled into a ball. Someone wrapped a blanket around her and carried her to the women's tents, but there was much distress with this plan, too, until Lukwsh said Wuzzie could be with her, as family. They laid the ball of blanket on the floor and left."

"Did Wuzzie speak?"

"She never speaks," Lukwsh said. "I never heard her speak again. In the morning, we put her on a wagon with one or two old ones that I walked beside. Until my foot froze, then I rode too some, until Yakima, and the black and pain must be cut off. Maybe looking after her was good for me. Took me from thinking too much on my own pain. I didn't think of Wren so much. Wuzzie kept me from watching babies be born and die, left in the snow." She lifted her hands as if to say, "Who knows?"

"She did not eat," Lukwsh said. "She wished to die, I think. We lost both Wren and Wuzzie, but one made it to Vancouver, silent as a dead person. And then they took her somewhere else when we got there, for her mind sickness, maybe. I never saw her again."

"She has spoken," I told them. They both looked at me with surprise. "Only a word or two. She offered a gift of tules she made into a dog. Like Wren's. She asked for help."

"She said these things to you?" Lukwsh asked in a voice of wonder.

"She spoke my Indian name, Thocmetone, and walked in from my past."

Dr. Adams greeted my new husband. We met Arlita and shared our stories of Wuzzie while sitting in Dr. Adams's office. Shard had not seen her yet, and I had told him he would not recognize the woman with the long hair, the bushy eyebrows that lay like fuzzy insects meeting above her nose.

"So you think it might be the shame of it, of having pretended to be what she wasn't, that's what resulted in this mutism?" Arlita asked.

"Maybe not being able to save Wren," I added.

"It seems like such a drastic response," Arlita said. "I mean, to remain silent for years because of something you can do nothing more about."

"Such a tragic event as a young woman's death associated with the disclosure could have added to the trauma," Dr. Adams said. "And who knows what happened to her, by the soldiers. We know she created a remarkable inner world to have lived so successfully as a man those years. Not sure how that was accomplished even."

"She stayed alone," Shard said. "Wore clothing of skin and is so small that her size could not be used to judge. She joined from another band, long years ago, almost before anyone noticed or remembers. Suddenly appeared, able to heal wounds, interpret dreams, was accepted for what he had to give. *She* was accepted."

"Suppose so. Could have happened that way. And with the chaos of the internment, the cold, the futility of it all, watching one's personal power slip away. Suppose it would be like going under the spell of another. Could cause someone to crack easily enough. Question now is what to do about it. Do we have her see you, Mr. Johnson, someone else from her past? Or talk about what we know? Or what?"

"A white man without answers," Shard said, "rare." He smiled and Dr. Adams grunted back, but they had a sharing of minds.

"What do you think, Mrs. Crick—ah, Johnson?"

"Alice," I said. "This is what I wish for. To greet her, see if she recognizes Shard, let her see that life went on, talk to her of Lukwsh." I took a deep breath, deliberately did not look at Shard's face. "And one more thing. Ask if she will come back with us when we return."

"Do you think that's wise?" Arlita said.

"When did you choose this fork in the road?" Shard asked, turning to look at me, a new dimension in this match he had not counted on.

"Lukwsh asked it, but I like the plan. She says together, with Wuzzie's legs and Lukwsh's words, they might make a whole person living in that house. And they could. Wuzzie did best when surrounded by tule reeds and the work of her hands—that's when she spoke. Might let her know she has a place to be, is wanted. That seems the strongest healing herb. And for a time, Lukwsh can speak for her."

We all sat quietly in Dr. Adams's office, the clock ticking while he considered.

"At least *I* need to see her again," I said, standing. It was a promise I had made. "She meant it for evil by sending me away, but God turned it for good. I'll tell her that much, at least, then let her make her choice for the rest."

"Are you sure this view is worth this ocean voyage?" I asked my husband. We had left the sandy beach below Yaquina Bay. The train from Salem took us west across flat fields of flax and hops, grasses and grains, through dusky coastal mountains covered with forests so dense the day seemed dark but for the spatter of sunlight filtering through the tree tops. My old feeling of tightness in closed spaces crept across my chest.

At Newport, I saw the ocean like a vast sky over the desert wearing the color of pale tears.

"This is not the sight I want for you," Shard said as I stared.

"But this is beautiful." My words a whisper. "So like the rhythm of the drums, so like water rushing through a falls. And nothing to stand between us and this water."

"Just the docks and ships." Shard laughed. "We will go to a high place to see this ocean, and you will remember then Dog Mountain, the one you tried to climb before you fell."

"I do not need to be reminded of the fall," I said.

We walked planks built out onto the bay and boarded a small boat with six other passengers and bobbed a short distance to a ship heading south.

"We could have climbed one of the hills there." I pointed to the shrub- and tree-covered ridges rising up behind the little town of gray buildings spackled with seagull waste and sand.

"What we will see together for the first time is more amazing than any other. It is said that the rocks offshore are the color of the stems of rosy everlastings and lie at angles as though they've been driven up from underneath. The ridges are flat above them, with open spaces you would never know were there, protected from wind by firs and pines. Then you can walk almost straight out toward the ocean and look a hundred feet below. The shoreline rises so straight up from waves that throw themselves against the rocks that we must be careful when we look over not to get dizzy and lose our balance."

"I am already dizzy. And with a headache. And my stomach would turn itself inside out. I am not sure it is a good plan that we bob on this ocean on a piece of wood."

He laughed. "The captain will not be happy hearing you call his ship a piece of wood. We go to Empire City and then take a buggy to Cape Gregory, above Coos Bay. Then you will see the ocean as it is meant to be."

The sea breezes were strong on board ship, and we stepped below deck.

Shard took the offered blanket from the steward, and we chose a seat where we could still see the thick foliage of the shoreline, watch white clouds amble like chubby children across the sky.

"Do you think she will come with us when we get back?" I asked him.

"I don't know. She did not take much notice in me. She did not remember me."

"Oh, but her eyes flickered in recognition. And when you said 'Lukwsh,' I thought she turned to you with her whole body."

"You've a better sense then," he said. "She sat like a stone to me, just as she did when the soldiers took her out, only not rolled into a ball. She looked like an old woman instead of a hairless man." He tucked the blanket around my legs, put his arm around me. "Why not try to sleep? Let this large lake be your lullaby."

I dozed. And in my sleep I dreamed of a small child climbing, climbing to the top, then soaring from a rimrock ridge. She flew like a swan, graceful, long, thin neck that arced bare without feathers, like the baldness of a man. She flew above a circle of antelope that became a burst of flowers of yellows and reds and purple shooting stars. A baby cried, and the flowers opened wider in a spray of tiny *wada* seeds that filled the air. One small seed drifted above the others, swirled around and dove as clean as the cut of an obsidian knife right toward me, falling faster to my soul. I woke with a start, breathing hard, my mouth dry.

"What's wrong?" Shard asked. He leaned over me.

"Just a dream," I said, collecting myself. "About climbing and seeds and flowers. Foolishness."

"Dreams are mixed up." He sat back and pulled me into his chest.

"And a baby," I told him, looking at my flat stomach for the first time in a different way.

We stood on the cliff overlooking the ocean a day after arriving in Empire City. What Shard had shared was true. The surf pounded on angled rocks and sprayed and surged in a way I could not imagine without seeing. Seagulls squawked and dipped in the currents; massive egrets set their wings and drifted across the sky. And the view swept farther than I had ever seen, into another world, another time. I sat smaller in the presence of so much water and might, and yet fuller.

"How does the ride in the piece of wood feel now? Was it worth it?"

I squeezed my husband. "It is more beautiful than anything I have ever seen." I shivered.

He turned me by the shoulder, then took my hand to lead me along a trail away from the ocean. We entered a dense stand of firs. We bent low, twisted around following a footpath to the clearing we had been promised. Only the distant surf touched the quiet. The sun glittered through the tops of the surrounding timber. He unfolded a blanket we brought with us, sat down, crossed his legs, and motioned me beside him.

"We won't stay long," he said. "The weather changes quickly. I don't wish to compete with a squall."

"I think I know what will make Wuzzie come back with us," I said, burrowing against him like a puppy seeking pets. "It came to me in a dream. First, our baby can never have too many *moo'a*, and—"

"Our baby? This is something you already know?" His voice had bubbles behind it. They worked their way to the surface of his smile.

"I already know. It is not sea sickness I carry with me to this dry ground. And second," I continued, "we will tell her she is needed to be there at a beginning again. To help as she did with her own child, Wren."

He sat silent, considered what I said. A flock of egrets cleared the spiky fir tops, flew over us, and dipped so low I could hear the beat of the wind against their wings.

"Are you so certain of our baby that you are sure of Wuzzie's too?"

"I am sure. Wuzzie gave up what was her own. To Lukwsh. Now Lukwsh gives back, but Wuzzie is needed, too. It's what makes the circle complete."

His hands crossed over my breast, lay protectively over me, his mind deep in thought.

"This may not surprise you then, either, you know so many things," he said after a time, pulling back to sit beside me. His coat pocket gave up a small package which he handed me, then he leaned on one elbow to watch me open it. "It is for you to wear around your neck. A reminder of who controls the circle that is our present, past, and future."

"And that is not me?" I said, smiling.

He laughed.

My fingers clumsily worked at the small clasp until it opened. Shard took out his gift: a tiny gold cross to hang on the gold necklace that was my mother's. He hooked it onto the chain I wore around my neck.

"Like yours," I said.

"There is another."

From the bottom of the box his wide fingers removed a slender ring he slipped onto my finger. It too was gold and not much wider than a willow thread. But a weave not unlike one of Lukwsh's willow baskets made its way around the edge.

"There," he said as I admired the gifts, the sounds of the surf to our backs. "A circle for your finger. From beginning to end, it means you are in my heart, everlasting. Where you belong, where you are loved."

I rested my hand on my stomach. The dappled light through the trees picked up the thin design of the ring. Shard picked up my hand, held it, laced his fingers into mine.

"I think of that time when I climbed and Wuzzie found me," I told him, my voice thick with tears, remembering that someone cared for me, found value in my life.

"It led you here," he said. I burrowed closer to his chest.

"I climbed up high before I fell. And climbed again."

After a time Shard smiled, then spoke out loud my thoughts: "So, now you see what your wishing to climb higher leads to."

"All I need," I told him, resting in the warmth of his presence, the promise of our future. "Enough love to water my soul forever."

AS I AM

Seven Years Later

"HOPE," I WHISPERED. "Come here. Sh-h-h."

"Can't you keep your children quiet, woman?" Shard asked. His voice laughed.

"My children? I was not alone when they happened along. And you must whisper."

But he waved me quiet and moved out of sight, ducking beneath the sagebrush. It was late in the month of May, and Home Creek rushed behind us, gurgling full of snowmelt from Steen's Mountain.

"Shh-h-h, Mama. There they are!" Our oldest child, Waurega, spoke from my right, and she blended scolding with surprise as she pointed.

"All right, I see them," I whispered. "Go tell your papa and Ezra. They are beyond that rise. Or were. Hope and I will walk back and let the *moo'a* know. We will meet you three by the hollow cottonwood beside the creek. Just below that hawk's beak rock, all right?"

She nodded and crept her way in front of me toward her father and brother, her pinafore dragging in the dust, flouncing over her well-worn moccasins. A beaded barrette held her dark hair that reached almost to her waist. I looked toward the rimrock, amazed that I once climbed it in the night.

The world was awash with golds and greens over greasewood and sage. Tiny purple shooting stars and blankets of the smallest yellow flowers covered the desert as far as I could see. We walked, my youngest and I, until Hope put her hands up to be lifted.

"You are such a big girl," I told her. "I hope I can carry you all the way."

"Hope can carry you," she said and giggled, her dark blond sausage curls catching the air as she twisted and turned at my hip. She fingered an old, worn necklace of leather knots draped around her neck. "I see them, Mama! I do!"

"I know, Sweetgum. We'll head that way as soon as we let the *moo'a* know. So they can come with us if they want."

"*Moo'a* Lukwsh can't wheel her way."

"No, but she can ride with us on the horse if she wants."

"You won't make me miss the antelope?"

"No," I said and touched her widow's peak lightly, brushed dust from her face. "We'll just tell them, then we'll head back, see if Wuzzie wants to walk with us."

The two old women sat in the shade of the wagon we had taken for our camping trip to the desert. Blankets made a pillow for their backs as they caught the shade. They stripped bark on willow sections Wuzzie had apparently cut for her and Lukwsh. An older Arrow panted in the shade, tied with a piece of cordage to the wheel of Lukwsh's chair.

Only one day here remained. The next day we would begin the journey back to Warm Springs and the lives we had there: Shard still at the mill and at our growing ranch; me as a mother who spent some time at the Indian clinic, helped with healing, cooked with Lukwsh and Wuzzie at the church. Full lives, with the need to blend always old with new for strength.

Wuzzie stood and shaded her unpatched eye with her hand, recognized us, and shook Lukwsh's shoulder and pointed.

Lukwsh's arm swayed in the air, gentle as sweet rice grass arching into breeze. Arrow stood and barked. Hope waved back wildly from her perch on my hip, urging me, "Wave, Mama. Wave at *Moo'a*," and I do, the joys of my life so like the welcoming waves of *moo'as* on a May morning.

"We've found them," I said, depositing my youngest child at the old women's feet. I stretched from the effort of carrying this squirmy girl.

"You cannot charm them," Lukwsh said looking up at me, eyes shaded. "Not enough of you."

"No, we just want to walk beside them, let the children see. Who knows when such a large herd will gather again?"

"It is a gift that you should find them on just a short trip here," Lukwsh said.

"A *namaka*," I said.

"That word has two meanings," Lukwsh said, reminding me for just a moment of Thomas Crickett. "Did I tell you? It means 'gift' but it also means 'to feed.'" She sat quietly stripping willows with her double-edged obsidian knife, and then she added words to nourish and water my soul, filling me with understanding of the way my life was fed. "To feed someone in the ways they need, their mind and body and their spirit too, that is a gift, na?"

"Perhaps the best of all," I said.

She looked up at me and sighed. "It is like being young again, seeing this place. It does not leave bad dreams for you?"

I smiled and nodded my no.

"Do you want to walk with us, Wuzzie?" I asked.

The woman, spindly as a spider still, shook her head, pointed to Lukwsh with her chin.

"Oh, go if you want," Lukwsh said. "I will sit here fine." But Wuzzie nodded her head firmly, plopped back down, and began stripping bark.

"Oh, come, *Moo'a*." Hope pleaded in her tiny voice and pulled on Lukwsh's fingers. "Mama says we could put you on the horse or try to push the chair."

"That old chair would make them curious, na? You go. I keep the dog here and this talkative woman beside me."

She patted Wuzzie's leg. Wuzzie smiled and motioned us back out to the desert. She used no words, had not these years. But I believed it was of her own choosing, not because she lived within a nightmare, all alone. And I carried hope that when she wished, she would speak to those who loved her, called her their own.

Hope and I made our way the short distance to the rise near a cottonwood, skirted around dried snakeskins shed in the sun. We met up with Ezra, now five, and Waurega, six, and their father.

"Ready?" he said, and the children nodded, seriously eager. "Remember what we practiced?" They nodded their heads.

Waurega stood a minute watching me step behind her father, put my hands on his hips, bend my head to his back.

"Ezra, you do the same to your sister, and Hope, you be the tail to him. Go ahead. Like Mama and Papa. Waurega will follow us, and when we stop, you can stand up slowly and see the pronghorns. You will hear them snort and sniff, but don't talk or move too quickly. Ready?"

They quickly stood behind each other, bent, and like their parents, began to walk as one. Shard led us along the far side of the little rise until he was sure we were across from the herd, still downwind. Then with slow steps, dust barely lifted into the still air, his moccasins turned left, and we crested the little rise.

I twisted, looked back under my arm to see that the children followed, and they did, eyes glued to the ground. As I turned back, I saw the breadth and size of the herd, the fawn stripes of their necks, the deeper brown of their sides. They grazed slowly, their bodies like heat moving across the desert. Meadowlarks charmed us with their songs.

"Look," Shard whispered, did not move quickly or point. "Stand still." When our children came up behind us, we stood and motioned them to do the same.

Their mouths hung open. They were stunned by the size of the herd, by how closely they had walked as one, close to these several hundred antelope. We heard the animals snort, heard what sounded like the crackle of a low fire as they walked through the greasewood, broke sagebrush with their shoulders. The strong scent of sage and juniper drifted to us. A faint breeze brushed our faces, let us know we were downwind.

We stayed a long time watching. Black horns lifted and lowered as they grazed. They pulled at tender bunch grass dotting the desert while these children watched like church mice, quiet, bringing no attention to themselves. Birds chirped, a red-tailed hawk's piercing call carried from the distance.

Who knows how long we stood breathing in this place.

"Turn back now," Shard said quietly. "Still walk as one."

Puffs of dust rose as we made our way back to Home Creek. I felt a grin rising up from somewhere deep inside, a joy that said I had not harmed a person by my walking in this way, did not earn what happened when I walked that way before.

"The tail of my animal is trying to direct the head," Shard said as we moved farther from the herd where it seemed safe to talk. "I can feel it through your fingers."

"Not directing. Just thinking, and my fingers hold on too tight."

"What's the thought, then?" he asked, twisting behind us to see the children.

"I am considering this, husband," I told him as I stood up tall and turned with open arms to the three children, who now came running across the desert, scattering up sand like a desert mist. "That I am pleased I did not let the terrors of my future or the errors of my past keep me from this place."

"Your mind is like a grinding wheel," he said, his kind eyes smiling.

I felt the rush of my children gathering themselves around my legs, my husband's hands at my shoulders as he steadied me in the sand.

"Tell us the story again, Mama," Waurega said breathless. "About the antelope and how you came to this place and found Papa."

"How Papa found Mama," Ezra corrected.

"Yes," my husband said, smiling. "Tell us what you know from those years of tying knots."

"That my life is like a burden basket filled with nourishing seeds," I said. "And best of all," I added, laughing, almost shouting over my shoulder as I embraced each child in turn, "I know my Spirit still walks with me and loves me as I am."

AUTHOR'S NOTE

Love to Water My Soul is the second in a series about frontier people seeking dreams. It is a work of fiction woven with two strands of fact.

The first strand chronicles the Wadaduka people (also know as Wada'Tika), "seed eaters" of southeastern Oregon who lived in harmony with mountains and marshes, deserts and lakes. The people moved in small family clusters across a wide expanse of Great Basin land in northern Nevada and southeastern Oregon, seeking seeds, joining with elk eaters and salmon eaters, sometimes traveling farther south to gather cattails near Stillwater Marsh or trade with Klamath, Modoc, and Umatillas, perhaps gather roots near the Cascades. The legacy of the Wadaduka band as portrayed in this story follows historical accounts of the seasons of their years and the impact of non-Indians on their lives and traditions, including the formation in 1872 of one of the largest Indian reservations in the country, setting aside 1.8 million acres. The promise of its development was never kept.

The Wadaduka stories are centered in the Steens Mountain area, in the high desert near Home Creek, near the marshes at what is now part of the Malheur National Wildlife Refuge and the ancient lakes fed by the Silvies and Malheur Rivers, close to the present towns of Burns, Oregon, and north, near Canyon City and south to the small town of Frenchglen. The portrayal of the way in which contact with non-Indians changed them, the destruction as well as individual kindnesses brought by Indian agents and soldiers, and the war that took the people from their homeland and force-marched them five hundred miles across two mountain ranges in the dead of winter to a prison in Washington Territory is also based on tragic fact. So is the controversial role of Sarah Winnemucca, the sinister acts of Agent Rhinehart, and the valued Agent Parrish and his wife, Mary, and the blacksmith named Johnson and their efforts to retain dignity and worth and to preserve a sense of place for people whose language has no word for good-bye.

The Paiute language used in this book reflects the dialect and spelling of those now living at Warm Springs. Some Paiute words—for which none could be found at Warm Springs—are from the Walker River and Stillwater Marsh areas.

Efforts were made to accurately portray life in the 1800s. Evidence supports the daily routines that consumed both frontier and Wadaduka peoples' lives, the nature of the antelope and rabbit hunts, the place of dogs as duck hunters and friends, the earthquake of December 1872 and tremors that preceded it, the spirituality and the variety of Christian influences, as well as the role of the Ghost Dance religion as early as the 1870s in the Northwest. The newspaper accounts that open several chapters are authentic from the 1800s. The Oregon Insane Asylum did exist and attempted to incorporate "advanced" therapies such as using animals and different kinds of foods first introduced by the Grahamites (Sylvester Graham of Graham cracker fame) to cure the "foolish and feeble-minded." And while there was no Wuzzie in actuality, there is an account of such a person's life choice in a Northwest journal dated 1811. And the lives of Jane and Joseph Sherar, Indian Peter and his wife, Mary, Crickett, and their experiences at Sherar's Bridge first introduced in *A Sweetness to the Soul* are also people of reality.

The return of many of the Wadaduka to the Seekseequa Creek area of the Warm Springs Reservation and their roles as ranchers and blacksmiths and seamstresses and millwrights are also based on historical accounts. The Seekseequa Church, once Presbyterian, still stands. And a descendant of headman and later chief We-ah-wee-wah, Wilson Wewa, serves as the current director of the Culture and Heritage Department at Warm Springs.

History also relates the unfortunate fact that the Malheur Reservation was not retained for the Wadaduka people to return to after their imprisonment. In 1883, while the people still wallowed in slave-like conditions in Washington prisons, building canals by hand, all but a small amount of the rich bottom land of Harney Valley was returned to the public domain since "there weren't any Indians living on the reservation." Title to the current 771 acres, but a tiny portion of the original 1.8 million acre reserve now known as the Burns-Paiute Reservation, was not received until 1972. Most descendants of this Wadaduka band live now near the Oregon town of Burns on the Burns-Paiute Reservation and on the Warm Springs Reservation in Central Oregon where the Paiute tribe is one of three within the Confederated Tribes of Warm Springs. Efforts to increase the Paiute language and retain the ways of the Wadaduka people are underway through the Culture and Heritage Departments and with the support of tribal councils.

The second strand of fact is the story of Asiam. While accounts of captivity of non-Indians by native peoples abound in late nineteenth- and early twentieth-century literature, they are often based on stories of white people held against their will by native peoples. The story portrayed of Alice M, or Asiam, is quite different and is based on truth. I first heard it shortly after meeting my husband of twenty years. My future mother-in-law, Zelma Waurega Kirkpatrick, shared the story of her great-grandmother who was found by natives in the southeast and raised by them and later especially befriended by a young Indian man. However different from them she may have felt, they were her only family.

Because of some tragedy, as an adolescent, she was forced to leave. The young man who befriended her gave her advice on leaving and how to survive. Her hiding in the log while her pursuers sat discussing her is based on fact. She arrived eventually in a small town, received care from a white family, and later married a doctor. At his death, she returned to the small town, and there, like the accomplishment of a distant hope, was found by the young man of her youth who had held her in his mind. They married, and one of their daughters was my husband's great-grandmother.

In *Love to Water My Soul,* these two fibers of fact are woven together as fiction meant to encourage and entertain. Like Shell Flower's string of knots, this is a memory told many times. It is a memory I hope has touched your heart.

e nanooma (Paiute)—my relatives (family)

hitse—friend

hooopu (Paiute)—cradle board

ikauxau (Wasco)—owl

Kahkwa Pelton (Chinoogan)—"Like Pelton," meaning foolish or insane

kapn (Sahaptin)—root digger

kasa (Sahaptin)—maternal grandmother; also a term of affection

kooma yagapu (Paiute)—"weeps for a husband"

lukwsh (Sahaptin)—sweet cous, root, same as tsooga

moo'a (Pauite)—grandmother

nabawici (Stillwater)—marking of a lost child

namaka (Paiute/Stillwater)—gift; in Warm Springs-area Paiute, means "give to eat" or "feed"

nano (Stillwater)—together

Nch'i Wana (Sahaptin)—"The Great River" (Columbia)

onga'a (Paiute)—baby

paa (Paiute)—water

paahoona (Paiute)—river

piawabi (Stillwater)—master mother; term of affection between husband and wife

poohaga'yoo (Paiute)—having spirit power

poozea (Paiute)—stink bug; same as tiish

pooha (Paiute)—spirit power

shaptakai (Sahaptin)—Indian suitcase

siwash (Chinookan jargon)—savage

tibo (Paiute)—white person

Tlhxni (Sahaptin)—Sherar's Bridge

tiish (Sahaptin)—stink bug

Tonowama (Chinoogan jargon)—Harney Lake

tsooga (Paiute)—an edible root

wada—species of gathered seed

Wadaduka (Paiute)—"wada-eaters"; name of the band of northern
    Paiutes. Also seen as Wada'Tika
wehe (Paiute)—knife
xali-xali—wren

Phrases:
    Uhamasu tukapu? (Paiute)—"Have you eaten?" (A sign of greeting)
    Ka suda nosena wunayoo (Paiute)—"Take away my bad dream."
    E tumatza'yoo (Paiute)—"Help me!"

With thanks to Henry Millstein, Pat Miller, and Shirley Tufti and the Paiute Language Class at the Confederated Tribes of Warm Springs; the Culture and Heritage Department of the Confederated Tribes of Warm Springs; and Catherine Fowler and Margaret Wheat's work in books cited previously.

DON'T MISS OUT ON THIS DRAMATIC STORY FOR ALL LOVERS OF HISTORY, ROMANCE, AND FAITH

A Sweetness to the Soul: Dreamcatcher Series, Book 1

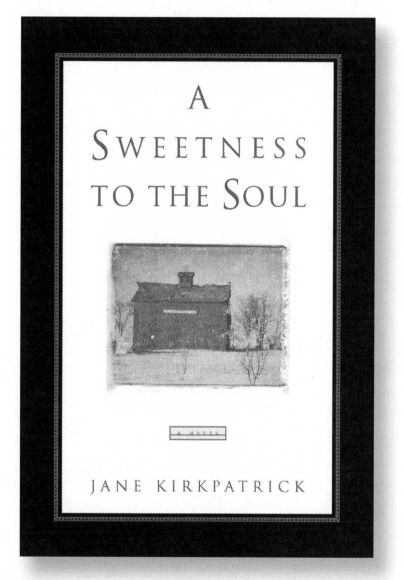

Based on historical characters and events, *A Sweetness to the Soul* recounts the captivating story of young, spirited Oregon pioneer Jane Herbert who at the age of twelve faces a tragedy that begins a life-long search for forgiveness and love. In the years that follow, young Jane finds herself involved in an unusual and touching romance with a dreamer sixteen years her senior, struggles to make peace with an emotionally distant mother, and fights to build a family of her own. Filled with heart-warming insight and glimpses of real-life pain, *A Sweetness to the Soul* paints a brilliant picture of love that conquers all obstacles and offers a powerful testimony to the miracle of God's healing power.

ISBN 0-88070-765-8

A POWERFUL MESSAGE THAT MONEY CAN'T BUY

A Gathering of Finches: Dreamcatcher Series, Book 3

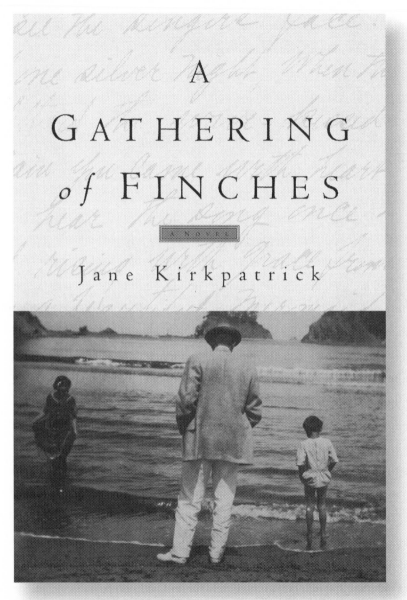

Based on historical characters and events, *A Gathering of Finches* tells the story of a turn-of-the-century Oregon coastal couple and the consequences of their choices, as seen through the eyes of the wife, her sister, and her native American maid. Along the way, the reader will discover that money and possessions can't buy happiness or forgiveness, nor can they permit us to escape the consequences of our choices. The story emphasizes the message that real meaning is found in the relationships we nurture and in living our lives in obedience to God.

ISBN 1-57673-082-4

TEACHER'S FAITH EARNS TRIBE'S LOVE ON THE FLORIDA FRONTIER

Mystic Sweet Communion

Set in turn-of-the-century Florida, this frontier saga traces the life of Ivy Cromartie Stranahan, the first English-speaking teacher in the region, as she struggles to teach school in the Seminole Nation and lead native American families to Christ. Ivy is disliked by tribal leaders in spite of her obvious love for their children, yet she eventually overcomes their resistance and serves as their spokesman in negotiations with the U S government. Already scarred by her mother's tragic death in childbirth, Ivy overcomes her husband's suicide and other devastating disappointments to share her faith with her adopted people and eventually earn their love.

ISBN 1-57673-293-2

www.letstalkfiction.com